C000173668

DUDLEY PUBLIC LIBRARIES

The loan of this book may be renewed if not required by other readers, by contacting the library from which it was borrowed.

CP/494

000003003190

A POTTERIES BOY

"elderly citizens who had stood the test of time..."

A POTTERIES BOY

A story of friendship and adversity in
smoky pre-war Stoke-on-Trent

Written and Illustrated by

J. E. HAYWARD

YOUCAXTON PUBLICATIONS
OXFORD & SHREWSBURY

ISBN 978-1-912419-18-0
Printed and bound in Great Britain.
Published by YouCaxton Publications 2018

YouCaxton Publications
enquiries@youcaxton.co.uk

IN MEMORY OF MY FATHER

WALTER HAYWARD

1919-2013

Contents

List of Illustrations   ix

Preface   xi

Chapters

1.   Walter's Dragon   1

2.   A Favour From The Grunters   12

3.   A Bad Case of The Grunters   19

4.   Bigger And Bigger!   27

5.   A Helpful Lift Home   34

6.   A Gargoyle At The Window   48

7.   A Friend From the Past   56

8.   The Sniper   65

9.   An Old Romance   73

10.   Hands Like Soup Tureens   83

11.   A Chip Or Two   96

12.   An Imminent Arrival   107

13.   Bad Dreams   113

14.   Cocooned   121

15.   Soap And Water Save The Day   133

16.   Dragon's Day Out   144

17.   Two Puppies   152

18.   Beset By Evil Things   162

19.   Peril!   168

20.   A Prince And Princess   179

21.   Loved – And Respected!   190

22.   An Unwelcome Guest   204

23.   A Fellow Reader   209

24.   A Visit From The Wizards   218

25.   A Terrible Case Of The Grunters!   224

26.   The Dragon's Voice   228

27.   Two Swans And A Carton Of Eggs   237

28.	Cupids In The Coving	255
29.	The Spices Of India	261
30.	The Telephone Rings	269
31.	Five, Not Six	275
32.	A Close Call	281
33.	Something Foul	292
34.	A Knock On The Door	305
35.	Transformations	319
36.	Meanwhile…	325
37.	Something Really Rotten	331
38.	A Freak Wind	339
39.	A Christmas Card	359
40.	Walter's Dragon	371
	Epilogue	394
	A Brief Explanation and Glossary	415
	Acknowledgements	420

Illustrations

Frontispiece
"elderly citizens who had stood the test of time..."   ii

"with the roll of drawings under his arm..."   11
"a well-aimed kick..."   18
"Dragon Knights..."   26
"They grew bigger and bigger..."   33
"He had never had such a ride before..."   47
"Old Ma was not to be taken lightly..."   55
"so astonished that the pipe fell out of his mouth..."   64
"there was his kiln, perfect in its bottle-like rotundity..."   72
"You know a lot, but you don't know everything..."   82
"hands the size of soup tureens..."   95
"Edna's life was no fairy tale..."   106
"A box was being prepared for Dragon..."   112
"The soft smog swaddled The Grove ..."   120
"They studied the strange creature carefully..."   132
"approaching the huge vase, Billie held up the knife..."   143
"Dragon loomed out of the smog..."   151
"The Poos became silent, expectant..."   161
"like two children in a fairy tale, beset by evil things..."   167
"'OLD MA: INSIDE!' shouted the headline..."   178
"Prince shoved his head into the tub..."   189
"six men, heads bowed in effort..."   203
"He sniffed cautiously..."   208
"one lamplit evening ..."   217
"Soon the sound of the Humber was heard roaring off..."   223
"The daily paper was now all Old Ma craved..."   227
"He leapt into the hovel ..."   236

"like two heraldic beasts from
    an illuminated manuscript..."   254
"Sometimes there was buttered toast,
    and sometimes pikelets..."   260
"momentarily afraid of the dark..."   268
"a small white inn somewhere in the Black Country..."   274
"The Poos had been busy too..."   280
"an anxious little crowd had gathered..."   291
"Old Ma attacked again and again..."   304
"He suddenly looked much more like
    the eleven-year-old boy he was..."   318
"sending her spinning out over the marl pit..."   324
"All was quiet. All was calm..."   330
"she fainted dead away..."   338
"She seized the sharp spade..."   358
"The clock ticked slowly on..."   370
"clutching each other high above the snowy street..."   393
"I never thought it would end up there..."   414

Bottle Ovens   419

Preface

Walter Hayward, my father, died on the 1st of October, 2013. He had been the kindest of fathers, a lovely man about whom no one ever said a bad word.

As the year after his death went by I kept him close to me by imagining his childhood in the streets of Northwood in Stoke on Trent: the little house where he lived with his three aunties, The Grove School nearby and just a few streets away, Northwood Park, a green oasis in a town of bottle ovens and pot-banks.

Then one night, the beginnings of this story came into my mind, and soon I was busy inventing all Walter's friends and neighbours, his teachers and headmaster, creating for him a close friendly neighbourhood like the one I am sure he grew up in. The Potteries has always been a friendly place and this is reflected in the story - but in this tale there is an element of evil too!

Good and evil, love and hate, friendship and bullying, loss and restoration: all these ideas find expression in this story of transformation in which the realism of daily life is tinged with whimsy and a touch of the supernatural and the warm industrial landscape which Walter and his pals inhabit has sprung partly from real places, partly from pages of old photographs but most of all from my imagination.

In real life, Walter grew up to be a designer and Art Director for Royal Doulton, the great company for which he worked from the age of fourteen until his retirement at the age of sixty-five, except for the war years when he served with the Royal Artillery from 1940-1946. (His army discharge papers from April 1946 state that his military conduct was exemplary.) He was most well-known for his Bunnykins nursery-ware but the bulk of his time was spent designing many of the beautiful dinner services for which the company was world famous. In 1984 he had the honour of being presented to Princess Diana when she visited the factory at Nile Street in Burslem.

Stoke on Trent was a truly amazing place when Walter was a boy. Thousands of bottle ovens peopled the landscape, blackening the skies and the city with their smoke but firing in their bellies china of astonishing beauty, potted and cast, glazed and gilded by generations of workers whose skills created a world-wide demand for the city's exports - and the story is as much a tribute to this unique city as it is to my father's memory.

But my book is not a biography: it is a tale inspired by a loving father and the wonderful city from which he sprang. Yet I hope I have been true to the spirit of this modest, gifted man. I hope so.

Jean E Hayward
February 2018

Chapter One

Walter's Dragon

"I'm the Red Baron! Rat-a-tat-tat! Rat-a-tat-tat!"

Lefty Knype zoomed over the grass, arms spread wide, down to where Walter and Pongy Johnson were sailing an empty sardine tin on the rippling waters of the pond.

"Rat-a-tat-tat. Rat-a-tat-tat!" cried Lefty, circling the perimeter of the pond and taking out Sopwith Pups left and right before landing heavily at Pongy's side.

"Steady mate!" cried Pongy, "You'll have it over!"

The little ship wallowed and took on water.

"She's going under!" said Walter. "Quick Pongy, bail her out!"

Pongy leant forward but his craft was now out of reach, performing a slow spin as the breeze quickened. Gradually the ripples overwhelmed the vessel and it sank slowly, the golden decking glinting through the murky pond-waters until the boys could see it no more.

Pongy leapt up. "Rat-a-tat-tat!" he cried. "Rat-a-tat-tat!"

The three boys flew homewards in formation, sweeping up the formal terraces and over the damp lawns of the park until they were flying low over the cobblestones and past the sooty terraces of Walter's home-town. The city of coal and clay lay spread out before them, thronged with the rotund shapes of the bottle ovens which peopled its landscape, transforming earth and stone into cups and saucers, teapots and jugs, lavatories and washbasins, or gilded and shimmering vases so perfect that their least aspect hid the trials and tribulations of a hundred years.

Although it was only the beginning of September, smoke poured from the long terraces, billowing up from the ranges

1

below where mutton stews were bubbling and kettles were steaming for the evening meal.

"School tomorrow!" said Walter dismally as the three Fokker tri-planes came into land at the top of his street. "Maths, maths and more maths! Awful!"

"Craft and clay first thing though, Walter," said Pongy helpfully.

"Algebra!" his friend replied gloomily, all the afternoon's fun disappearing in a moment. "Algebra *and* the Grunters!"

"Then make us something *big* this term!" said Lefty positively, a boy who never thought small.

"Yes!" cried Pongy, zooming around Walter in a tight figure of eight. "Make us something *enormous* mate!"

Everyone knew how much Walter hated maths and loved modelling. He despaired daily of his maths lessons with The Dumpling but lived for the craft and clay sessions. His small square bedroom was lined with a menagerie of clay and plasticine figures, exact in form and proportion, all conjured from Walter's imagination by the dexterity of his nimble fingers.

"Make me a clay boat!" said Pongy encouragingly.

"It'd sink!" laughed Walter, brightening at the thought of his craft and clay lessons. "It can't be all bad!" he thought.

"Well, watch out for them Grunters!" called Pongy as he and Lefty banked for home. "See you tomorrow mate!"

"See you," said Walter, waving a cheery farewell as his pals sped off, their guns fading into the distance as he entered the alleyway.

Thud! A meaty fist grabbed him and he was mashed up against the sooty wall. Two bloated red faces were shoved into his: he had been caught by the Grunter twins.

"Been having fun, have you Walter?" asked Billie, tightening his grip on Walter's collar so that breathing became difficult.

"Mind your own business," wheezed Walter. "Oww!"

Willie trod heavily on Walter's toes. It was akin to being stepped on by Mr. Jones' milk-horse.

"Fun's over, Walter," said Willie. "New term, new torture!"

"Get off!" Walter wheezed. "Go have a wash. You smell funny! Owww!"

Billie persecuted one foot and Willie the other. The Grunters were massive, like twin elephants, but Walter struggled hard and caught Billie sharply on the shin. Then he heard the click of his garden gate and the speedy approach of Auntie Sally's heels over the cobblestoned entry.

"Clear off!" she cried, flicking her wet tea towel at their bare legs. "Pick on somebody your own size!"

"Get yer tomorrer!" they laughed from a safe distance. "Tomorrer Walter!"

"Inside dear," said Auntie Sally. "Tea and then bed. School tomorrow."

Walter sighed heavily and followed his auntie down the alleyway and in at the wooden gate. Narrow beds of red geraniums lined the little yard where a tidy lawn, no wider than a ruler, stretched greenly from Walter's feet to the open kitchen door. He could smell beef stew with dumplings, and, hidden amongst the rich aromas a higher, sharper note. Rhubarb crumble!

"Come on Walter," said Auntie Minnie, meeting him at the door. "Put it behind you and come and sit down. Have your tea with Louie. She's had a letter from Hetty, you'll like that."

The kitchen of the little house where Walter lived with his three aunties was a cosy, welcoming place. Pushed up against the window was a square table set with colourful earthenware on an embroidered cloth. Books filled the chimney alcoves and china and glass twinkled on the dresser. Summer and winter a fire burned in the grate and morning and evening Sally moved steadily to and fro between the scullery and the kitchen, cooking, baking and tea-making. The round-green topped tin in the larder was rarely without its sponge cake and almond slices or fruit scones lay moist and fresh in their tins on the shelf above. It was a warm and happy home.

Walter ate his tea and listened to the chatter of his aunts but the thought of school hung heavily on him.

"Maths *and* the Grunter's!" he thought again as he went to bed that night. "And it's ages 'till Christmas! Ages and ages!"

But he had "The Wizard" under his arm and that made things much better. A few moments later he lay propped up in his wooden bed reading the comic in the cone of dim light cast from above. Walter was soon lost in Arctic wastes, traversing terrifying crevasses, eking out meagre rations and battling huge polar bears with the help of his Eskimo guide. Then again, he was a secret agent, knowing and tough, trekking the dry deserts of Afghanistan, rallying tribesmen to his cause, sunburned, pith-helmeted, a force to be reckoned with.

Sleepily, he turned the page to a new story and read for a moment or two – then he sat up, full of a sudden energy. A magician had magicked a dragon right out of a hat! The dragon spat smoke and flame: it set the magician's eyebrows on fire and singed his moustache! This was really something! Walter knew it couldn't be true but what he loved was the idea of it: that someone had thought of magicking a *dragon* out of a hat, instead of a rabbit or a hand of cards.

"Make us something big," Lefty had said and it occurred to him, right there, that he could magic up a dragon too, a stupendous dragon made of clay, coiled around a pot so enormous that nothing like it had ever been seen before. He saw it in his mind's eye: a breather of fire, a slayer of Grunters.

"My very own dragon," he thought excitedly. "Cor!"

Walter had a sketch pad under his bed and a good 5b pencil which made bold dark marks on the white paper. He began straight away to draw. The pot, he realised immediately, must be massive enough to hold the huge encircling dragon and strong enough to bear its great weight. A small pot simply would not do.

At this point, Auntie Sally called upstairs.

"Put out your light, Walter. School tomorrow!"

"Yes Auntie," he replied, and carried on drawing.

Ordinarily, he might have quietly finished a page or two of his comic and then settled down to sleep. But Walter was too engrossed and his stubborn streak had surfaced. The tall vase took shape beneath his hand: almost filling the page it swelled from a narrow base, blooming into beautiful fat curves at its fullest point, before skating gracefully inward towards its rim.

Below him, the three aunts, reading or knitting, began to sense an unnatural energy above their heads and twice more they called up "Walter! Put out your light!"

But it wasn't until the little bedroom floor was littered with paper sheets all describing sections and cross sections, vases with handles and vases without, that Auntie Sally, by now thoroughly annoyed, mounted the narrow stairs and flung open the door.

"Walter!" she cried. "Put out your light!"

The light was rapidly extinguished. Walter lay in the dark with his heart pounding at the thought of his very own dragon. He couldn't see it clearly yet but still joy surged up from within, along with an equal measure of impatience. Walter tossed and turned. How long before he could show Potty his magnificent plans? His bruised toes were forgotten and the looming maths lessons were suddenly much less important.

"Nine o' clock!" he thought, turning over impatiently. "Craft and clay!"

But by eleven o' clock Walter lay fast asleep in the little house at the top of the hill, as the kitchen clock ticked softly on and Mr. Bateman's cat kept watch by the gently smoking chimney stacks.

§

Walter's favourite breakfast was bread and dripping.

"Cor!" he usually thought as Auntie Sally placed two thickly covered doorsteps in front of him. "Lovely!"

The next morning, however, Walter tumbled downstairs with his shirt done up wrongly and his jumper on back to front. All he could think about was his dragon, though its features were still obscure.

"But it's going to be massive!" he told himself as he struggled with the bootlaces he had not undone the night before.

"Don't fuss, Auntie!" he cried, seizing a doorstep and cramming it into his mouth untasted. A large piece broke off and stuck to the back- to-front jumper.

"Sit down and eat properly!" Sally admonished him but before she could say another word the back door flew open and slammed shut, leaving the two aunts astonished in the empty kitchen.

Minnie looked at Sally open mouthed.

"Whatever's got into *him*?" she cried.

Sally shook her head. "Rude!" she said crossly. "If he comes home like that he'll have a good hiding before bedtime!"

Walter raced down the hill to school with the roll of drawings under his arm. It was a bright day with a little breeze which set the chimney smoke trailing off in grey lumpy rivers over the rooftops.

"Morning Walter," called Mr. Bateman as the boy rushed past number sixty-six but he received no answer as Walter, blind to the smoky glories of the new day, pelted onwards towards The Grove.

"Strange," thought Mr. Bateman, knocking his pipe out against the wall, "polite boy normally. Wonder if it's them Grunters?"

The Grove stood in Turner Street at the bottom of the hill. Woolly- jumpered children streamed towards it from all directions in two's and three's but none at Walter's pace. The clock on the school tower showed ten to nine as he sped through the tall gates and across the open playground. Ahead of him large blue double doors lay slightly ajar.

"Good!" he thought. "He's there!"

"Potty!" he cried, bursting into the craft and clay room like a small locomotive with a good head of steam. "Potty! I've got an idea!"

Potty straightened up. He had been re-filling the big clay bin for the start of the new term.

"Hello, Walter," he said smiling. "An idea?"

Kindly old Mr. Bateman had not been the only person watching Walter's mad rush to school that morning. Standing in the early morning shadow of a large black bottle oven was Old Ma Grunter, grinding her gums and watching Walter through narrowed eyes. Behind her stood the twins.

"'im!" she hissed. "What's 'e got there? What's that little grub so excited about?"

She dug Willie viciously in the ribs with her elbow.

"Find out," she said. "Find out what's in them papers. Chops tonight."

She left the twins and entered a little alleyway, where the sparrows fell silent and the busy housewives, pinning up their sheets in the smoky air, quickly turned and shut fast their kitchen doors, waiting with thumping hearts until Old

Ma was well past and the sooty sparrows had begun to chirp once more.

§

Potty didn't go straight home that evening. Instead, he hurried over to the telephone box at the end of the street and made a call to his friends at the glaze laboratory in Kidsgrove. Then he made his way through the busy streets to Alf's house.

The pot-banks were spilling out their workers into the late afternoon air and the yards were thronged with cloth-capped men and women in aprons and headscarves, all intent on getting home for their teas and then an hour in the allotment or an evening of putting the children to bed. Out they streamed, past the fat bodies of the bottle ovens and down the glistening streets where yellow lights sprang on and the smoky chimneys redoubled their sooty efforts for the evening meal. Potty threaded his way through the hurrying crowds, his mind full of Walter's great idea.

"And what an idea!" thought Potty.

He had been taken aback by the sheer scale of Walter's imaginings and he knew they needed help. Potty had useful friends all over the city of coal and clay, many, like Alf, with a lifetime's experience behind them, men who could be relied upon and trusted; men with slip in their veins whose fathers and grandfathers, and their fathers and grandfathers before them, had laboured in the heat and the cold of the pot banks and who knew, only too well, the hazards and the pitfalls that lay in wait for those, like Walter, who tried to wrest something wonderful, something magnificent, from the grey and lumpen clay beneath their feet.

"How big, Potty?" asked Alf, his jaw dropping as he sat opposite his friend by the hearth, his cup rattling in its saucer. "*And* a dragon too? What? A *moulded* dragon? Three dimensional? Not just painted?" He shook his head. "*How* big? Wherever will we fire all that?"

Potty laughed. "Not in the little school kiln," he said. "But I believe he'll make it, Alf," he went on seriously, "with the right help of course. He will make it. He's a marvellous modeller!"

"Wants ter be a modeller, does he?" asked Alf kindly, filling his pipe then passing the tobacco pouch over to Potty.

"Oh yes, I believe he does," said Potty, puffing hard. "Big ambition, I believe."

Walter thought of little else. He loved the bottle ovens which peopled the city, the warm round brick edifices like so many industrial vases spouting plumes of smoke instead of flowers. They were a population unto themselves, these bottle ovens, elderly citizens who had stood the test of time, well known to their human neighbours, respected and relied upon, the pillars of their communities.

Built in their thousands, they dominated the city, engulfing it in a smothering blanket of soot and smoke each week as the fires were lit beneath them and the flames roared up their chimney bags, baking the city's wares in their rough saggars. And Walter dreamed of filling these ovens with figures of his own creation: with the lions and tigers which romped through his mind; with the elephants and monkeys in Hetty's letters; with the dogs and cats and horses which he daily saw around him on the grimy, familiar streets of his hometown.

"Well," said Alf finally, as Potty rose to go. "I'll do my very best fer him, mate."

"No one better Alf," said Potty. "Thank you."

"Hard road ahead though," said Alf. "I've never fired a single object that big before, not in all my years at Spode, then Minton! He doesn't do anything by halves, I'll say that fer him!"

He paused.

"And there's another thing," he said. "Nothing that big'll go through a clammins, or the hovel either. Both openings'll have to be enlarged. Another iron frame'll 'ave ter be made. And that won't be cheap!" he exclaimed. "I can't see anybody letting yer do that – let alone paying fer it!"

The two men looked at each other. Potty shook his head.

"We'll just have to deal with problems as we meet them, Alf," he said. "One thing at a time."

Potty shook hands and left, quickening his pace as he hurried home for a belated supper.

"At least we've got Alf," he thought. "None better. Best fireman in his day. Walter's lucky there. But a fireman's no good without a kiln!"

He looked around at the bottle ovens, darker still against the evening sky. All over the city the bottle ovens were busy, full, depended upon for the city's livelihood.

"No room in any of them for Walter's dragon," he thought ruefully. "But he is determined!" He shook his head. "Whatever shall I do?" he thought, "If I try everywhere but just can't find him a kiln?"

"with the roll of drawings under his arm..."

Chapter Two

A Favour From The Grunters

Walter's maths lessons *were* pure misery but Mrs. Dumpleton was a kindly soul who looked for more in her little pupils than an ability to find square roots and common denominators. But Walter struggled daily, hampered not only by a natural disinclination for such feats but now by his magnificent obsession.

Dragons filled his margins and his endpapers and crept day by day into the spaces between sums and the spaces meant for sums, or maps, or essays, or anything really, that he should have been working on but wasn't. By now the whole school, indeed the whole neighbourhood, was aware of his glorious preoccupation and his kindly teachers indulged him since The Grove was a school which strove to foster talent in all its forms, but especially creative talent which was the very lifeblood of the city of coal and clay.

"Drawings, Walter!" Potty had said. "You must draw and draw until you know every inch of your dragon, and then, and only then, can you begin to make it."

So Walter drew, and the walls of the craft and clay room soon filled with his creations: fine elegant renditions of dragons like iguanas, dragons like lizards; frilled dragons, collared dragons, dragons with three claws, dragons with four. Long looping roiling dragons that flowed across the paper like scaly rivers; great winged dragons he envisaged, with leathery bat-like wings which folded up or down like the top of a long shiny car. Still the final form eluded him. His was an epic undertaking and as the first two weeks went past it began to take its toll.

The aunts despaired daily as Walter rushed off to school, more or less breakfast-less, and returned home after hours, wild eyed, possessed, struggling through his meal like one through quicksand, then tossing and turning at night, often sleepless in his quest for the perfect dragon, *his* very own dragon to be brought to life by the cunning of his own small hands.

Every morning Mr. Bateman would call, "Good morning Walter. 'ow's it going?" but he rarely received an answer. Just sometimes, yards further on, Walter would come to and call back, "Still drawing Mr. Bateman! Not ready yet...."

And the Grunter twins were quick to take advantage. Several times they had caught him and stripped him of his pocket money, unspent in his jacket pocket. His toes had more bruises, though Willie had a black eye too.

"He's making a big vase, Gran," Billie had told Old Ma. "He's doing lots of drawings. They're up on the wall."

"Vase!" sneered Old Ma as she made the boy's tea that night, frying pork chops in a blackened pan over the kitchen fire. "What's 'e want with a *vase*?"

"It's a dragon vase, Gran," said Willie, saliva filling his mouth at the sight of the bloody chops hissing and spitting in the greasy pan. "It'll be bigger than anything, they say."

"They say, they say," sneered Old Ma, splashing the fat so that it flared and spat onto Billie's bare legs. "We'll see about that! Sit down!"

The twins exchanged glances and grinned. It was as good as a license to torment, to trouble, to destroy.

"Alright boys?" said Harold Grunter, coming in from his butcher's shop at the front of the house.

"Alright Dad," said the twins and bent their heads greedily to their meal. They never bothered their father with their schemes and he never bothered them.

"Cashing up now, Bertha," he called and he and his wife set about their books while Old Ma sat and smoked at the kitchen table, a baleful, twisted presence who sent a shudder of fearful excitement through her thuggish grandsons.

"We'll have him," they whispered as they mopped up the grease with even greasier chips. "This term'll be a bad one for him."

They looked at each other and smiled, "A really bad one!" they snorted together and laughed.

Old Ma drew in the cigarette smoke and blew it out through bloodless lips.

"It had better be," she said, lighting another cigarette and casting a scornful glance over at her son and daughter in law, busy with their accounts. "It had better be…"

§

The pocket money had been only the start of it. On the second Friday of term Walter stayed late at school as he now did every night. Mr. Slope, the school caretaker, was an unwilling aide, paid a little extra to stay a little later and lock up after Walter had finished.

"Of course, Mr. Pinch," he had said when the Headmaster had asked him for this favour. "Anything for The Grove, you know that, sir."

But secretly he resented being late for his tea every night.

"Bloody kid!" he thought. "Waste of my bloody time!"

So he swept and tutted as Walter worked away at his drawings, oblivious to Mr. Slope's resentment, intent only on the curve of a claw or the shape of a scale.

"Vale at home!" muttered Mr. Slope on Friday as the hands on the clock spun closer and closer to seven o' clock. "Missing it for this puppy!"

He thumped the wet mop around the room harder and harder until, passing close to Walter's bare little legs, he slopped them with cold dirty water.

Walter looked up.

"Oh!" he said. "Alright, Mr. Slope?"

"Oh yes!" said Mr. Slope. "Everything's fine. Vale's at home but everything's fine!"

"Oh dear!" said Walter. "I've nearly done. I can lock that door if you like and I'll come early on Monday to give you the keys."

The unscrupulous Slope didn't need asking twice. He had his brown overall off and his overcoat on before Walter could make another stroke.

"Early then!" Walter heard as the blue doors banged shut behind him.

"I had better get back," he thought. "In a minute."

He bent his head and was once more lost in Dragon Land, climbing steep sided valleys in a misty volcanic era long ago. At his back, the blue doors swung open noiselessly.

"Gotcha!" cried the Grunters, seizing Walter and pulling him struggling from his stool.

"Gerroff!" cried Walter. "Gerroff! Gerroff! Gerroff!"

But there was no one to hear him. Staff and pupils had long since quit the premises and an unnatural silence reined over The Grove, broken only by the thumps and scufflings of Walter and the Grunters as the little ceramicist fought hard against his unequal assailants.

"In here!" grunted Billie, pushing open the heavy lid of the big clay bin. "Shove him in here!"

Together they lifted the boy, a mere mite in their great meaty grips.

Walter caught Willie on the chin with a well-aimed kick.

"You want to put something on those pimples!" he said as the lid slammed shut and the clasp went down.

"Ram this in!" said Billie, shoving a teaspoon into the hasp so that struggle as he might, Walter would never push open the lid. But he lay quietly, knowing that pleas would be useless and anyway he was too proud to beg anything of the Grunter twins.

"Shall we rip up his drawings?" asked Willie and Walter could hear the rustle of paper as the brothers scavenged amongst his work.

"Better not," said Billie at last, reluctantly. "Old Pinch'd give us hell. Come on bruv – let's go tell her!" and they roared off into the night, the big blue doors banging behind them until all was quiet once more.

It was very damp in the clay bin and rather cold. But it wasn't uncomfortable, clay being naturally soft and malleable. Walter lay back and waited.

"They'll soon start looking for me when I don't come home," he reasoned, "and this is the first place they'll look."

He made himself comfortable with a little pillow of clay and amused himself by modelling a four-toed dragon's foot in the dark. He had drawn it so many times he now knew it by heart.

"Easier than you might think," he said to himself, tracing its outline gently with the tip of his finger. And there's plenty of air in here…"

By the time Sally and Minnie found him at seven-thirty, Walter had made an array of dragon's feet as well as a small head and a miniature tail. He lined them up on a shelf before they left, feeling very pleased with himself. He looked at the tiny models sitting amongst the dusty craft implements and smiled.

"Come on dear," said Minnie, pulling him away, "Home…."

Sally was almost speechless with rage at the Grunter's cruelty, but Walter couldn't stop talking as his aunts, taking an arm each, hurried him across the playground and up the hill towards a hot meal and a warm bath.

"Not hard at all," he said excitedly, "surprising how you can feel....came out just as I wanted....think I can start to model it now....much bigger of course....absolutely massive Auntie....start on scale models next week....done me a favour....speeded things up....ought to thank them really..."

Walter went to bed happy, though he still tossed and turned and slept very little, consumed as he was with the prospect of finally making his dragon instead of simply drawing it. He could still feel the clay beneath his fingernails, dry and crumbly now, but the sensation of damp clay remained, the sheer joy of moulding and modelling, of shaping and making, until there was a perfect foot, a perfect tail!

"Can't you sleep dear?" asked Sally at twelve o' clock as she peeped carefully around his door.

"It's all going round and round, Auntie," said Walter. "Do you think they'd let me go to school on Saturday too?"

"a well-aimed kick..."

Chapter Three
A Bad Case of The Grunters

Walter didn't squeal on the Grunters or on Mr. Slope either, come to that. He was a staunch Vale fan too and attended every Saturday match at the Old Recreation Ground, standing in the rain and the smoky fog, cheering on his team to victory, then making his way home with a paper of chips, disappointed but never downcast. So he quite understood Mr. Slope's desire to be there and said nothing.

"Cheated in the second half?" he said to the grumpy caretaker as he handed over the keys at eight o'clock on Monday morning. "Heard that ref needs glasses. Thanks Mr. Slope."

But Pongy Johnson knew all about it.

"My Mum was talking to Thelma on Saturday," he told Lefty on Monday morning. "You know, his Auntie Minnie's friend, the one who can never keep her mouth shut, my mum says. They put 'im in the clay bin Lefty! The clay bin!"

Lefty balled his fists. He was furious.

"Them sausage gobblers!" he cried. "What's up with 'em? Why can't they leave 'im alone?"

Pongy shook his head.

"I don't know, mate. It's always been the same, ever since 'e was little. But it's got to stop. I've got an idea."

Soon a good-sized crowd had gathered around Pongy and Lefty in the playground, whilst Walter worked away inside.

"Remember that story Miss Winsom read us last year?" Pongy asked, looking around. "The one about the Round Table, King Arthur an' all that?"

Some children had a very short memory for such tales

and looked rather blank but others cried, "Yes! Knights of the Round Table Pongy!" "Swords!" "Damsels in distress!"

"What are you thinking Pongy?" asked Lefty, puzzled.

"Walter needs a company of knights," said Pongy grandly - "An' that's us! We can't let them Grunters carry on pinching 'is pocket money an' sticking 'im in bins! We need to protect 'im! Who's with me?"

The roar was unanimous and all over the playground children flocked to Pongy's side. The Grunter twins lounged against a wall and watched from a distance. Nobody ever wanted to play with them.

"Will there be swords, Pongy?" asked Steven Smallbody hopefully.

Pongy shook his head.

"Eyes an' ears," he said, "an' never leave 'im alone, un-protected, like. There's more of us than there is of them – big as they are." He glanced disdainfully across at the Grunters. "They won't bother 'im if we're around."

Everyone liked Walter. No one had a bad word to say about him, ever.

"He made me a dip – a dip – a diplo – a diplodocus – cus!" said little Nancy Dancer, blushing. "I love Walter!"

"Right then!" declared Lefty. "We're Walter's knights!" He looked at Pongy. "Are we knights of the Round Table, same as in the book?"

Pongy looked stumped.

"I don't know," he said. "There isn't really a *table* involved...."

"But there is a dragon," said Herbert Sherburt, the brainiest child in the school. "And a vase. What about the Shining Knights of the Imperial Dragon Vase?" He smirked. "I am clever," he thought.

No one agreed.

"It's a bit long," said Pongy, "Though you're on the right track...."

"Dragon Knights!" cried little Gillian Smallbody, jumping up and down. "We're Dragon Knights, Pongy!"

Everyone shouted approval. Sword fighting broke out on a grand scale and chargers galloped around the jousting grounds. Pongy and Lefty gathered a few trusty knights together and headed for the blue doors.

"Hello Potty," said Pongy. "Can we come in? Thanks. What you got there, Walter? Cor! That's good! Look Lefty, a dragon's foot! Cor!"

But he said not a word in front of Potty nor did he make much of a fuss about it with Walter, who never liked to bother anybody if he could help it. But from then on, he did generally feel much safer and all of his pocket money, now largely protected, he spent on aniseed balls and gobstoppers for his knights at The Grove, until Mr. Pinch had to outlaw the continual sucking and slurping in class. It was impossible to finish an Empire Gobstopper during the dinner-hour, much less in a playtime!

The Headmaster was no fool. He knew the Grunters well and despaired at The Grove's failure to turn them around, to make them into bright and happy children like the rest of his charges.

"Keep an eye on the Grunter boys," he had advised his staff. "Don't let them anywhere near the craft and clay room."

Sabotage, he knew, was a real possibility though he was determined it should not happen. Walter, he was quite sure, was doing something exceptional, but all the children at The Grove were treated with the same respect, regardless of intellect or talent. Though he struggled to show kindness, though he knew that he terrified them daily, Old Pinch had at his heart only the wellbeing of these children whose futures seemed bound to the city of coal and clay, whose lives would be spent in its factories and pot banks, pugging and jollying, moulding and jiggering, casting and fettling, painting and packing, sending out the bottle ovens' bright and beautiful wares all over the world, to grace the shelves of department stores in Paris and New York, Rome and Rio de Janeiro.

"But hardly surprising with a grandmother like that," he thought of the twins, as he passed down the corridor to the craft and clay room. " Very difficult to overcome that sort of indoctrination. Very difficult indeed!"

He pushed open the door. Walter was busy with his small-scale dragon models but he stood to attention when Mr. Pinch entered the room.

"No more gobstoppers, Walter!" the headmaster roared.

Walter jumped. "No sir!" he said. "Crisps, sir?"

"Playtime only!" Mr. Pinch barked, a red flush creeping up his cheeks. "If only I could be a little less of a disciplinarian," he thought. "Necessary with the Grunter twins, but hardly with a boy like this! I'm not at the front now...."

Walter still stood to attention.

"He always goes red after he's shouted," he thought. "I wonder why?"

"Good work, Walter," said Mr. Pinch. "But no more gobstoppers!"

He left Walter playing with the shape of a dragon's wing and went back to his study. A small mirror hung on the wall above his reports' cupboard. It showed a still handsome man in his early fifties but Mr. Pinch turned away in disgust.

"Red in the face again!" he thought. "Pathetic!"

There was hardly a kinder soul in all the city of coal and clay than Captain John Pinch, hero of Mons and Neuve Chapelle and veteran of the Hundred Days Offensive. Cool under fire, stalwart in the defence of his men, Pinch was a soldier who came through the abyss with his humanity intact, determined more than ever to make a difference in the world, though it might only be in a back-street school in an industrial city far from the green wooded hills of his native Kent.

"If only you could lighten up a bit, man!" he berated himself. "You're not sending them over the top!"

He flushed anew at the thought of his constant, uncalled for severity.

"I wonder," he thought, "if they ever realise my bark is worse than my bite?"

He looked out of the window at the children running around the playground. Over by the tower half a dozen boys were playing airplanes, others were involved in games of tag, whilst one or two little groups of girls were at hopscotch, their white little legs leaping nimby in and out of the chalked squares. Another group stood near the blue doors to the craft and clay room, supplemented from time to time by children who left their games and joined their friends guarding the entrance.

"Walter's Knights," he said to himself with a happy smile. "Wonderful children! Wonderful!"

§

Billie and Willie Grunter, not at all grateful for Walter's silence, had gone home in disgust.

"Dragon Knights!" they had sneered. "We'll have him! One time or another!"

But they found it harder and harder to catch Walter on his own and impossible to get anywhere near his dragon vase.

When they came home from school Harold and Bertha were usually in the shop, serving a long queue of housewives who clutched their shopping bags nervously and cast constant glances towards the back. Harold's meat was always good, and well- priced, but they feared the appearance of Old Ma and were prepared at any moment to rush out, empty handed. They knew their husbands would understand. Even the most carnivorous of husbands put the safety of his wife above a pork chop. No one could bear the proximity of Old Ma Grunter.

"She's the very Devil!" they said in the safety of their warm kitchens. "Stay clear of 'er son!"

People not only crossed the street to avoid Old Ma, they disappeared up side streets and into alleyways, into churches and chapels and even other people's back yards. No one could remember a time when she had not been feared.

"She's just plain evil!" they said and no one dared look her in the eye.

Old Ma enjoyed her notoriety. She stalked the streets in her buttoned boots and her mangy fox fur, grinding her gums with delight as shoppers melted away in front of her. But her neighbours were right. Old Ma Grunter *was* evil personified; she was evil through and through and those who were suddenly trapped next to her in a queue at the chip shop, or at the bookies, felt it seep into their bones like a damp and horrible plague, freezing them with terror, so that struggling free they would rush home to their families and the bottle of whiskey in the corner cupboard. A Bad Case of the Grunters, it was called locally, and was treated sympathetically by all the neighbours.

"'e looked into 'er *eyes"*, it might be whispered. "Into 'er *eyes*!"

"Shouldn't 'a' done that…" would be the shaken reply. "Doctor bin called?"

Bertha too feared her mother in law and practised rarely to be alone with her. She clung to the shop and to Harold, who, though strongly disliking his mother, turned a deaf ear to all he heard about her.

"People round here are superstitious," he told himself. "They think they're living in a folk story or something. Stupid!"

So the twins dwelt largely with Old Ma, sandwiched between the butcher's shop and the slaughter house at the back.

"You'll have to be sharper, thickheads!" snapped Old Ma when she heard of the Dragon Knights. She gripped her grandsons' ears painfully. "'im and 'is *vase*! Who does he think 'e is?"

She spat into the fire, narrowly missing the frying pan full of thick greasy sausages.

Billie rubbed his ear.

"We'll get him!" he said. "Won't we Willie? We'll get him!"

"Bound to slip up soon," snorted Willie, eying the sausages greedily. "Can't keep an eye on him forever. We'll get our chance Gran. And when we do, we'll make it count!"

"Dragon Knights..."

Chapter Four

Bigger And Bigger!

Walter now began a feverish period of prototype modelling and coiling.

"Wonderful drawings, son," Potty had said on the Monday morning. "Very precise."

Potty and Walter made their way around the room, carefully studying the sheets which hung on the walls, describing the great vase and its dragon from all angles, inside and out.

Potty peered at Walter's notes, the neat little figures which listed the vase's dimensions. He swallowed hard.

"Even a bottle oven," he said quietly, "would have to be altered to get something of, er, this size through its door, Walter."

"Oh," said Walter.

"Their entrances are quite narrow, you see," said Potty.

"Oh," said Walter.

"And then we would have to get it from here to, er, there," Potty went on thoughtfully. "Enormously heavy, I should think."

"Oh," said Walter.

"Much taller than you are yourself, son," said Potty. "Taller than anyone come to that."

Walter was quiet. So consumed had he been in his quest for the perfect dragon that he had given little thought to the practicalities of building and firing his magnificent vision.

"Well," said Potty eventually, "let me worry about all that."

Walter sighed. It was all a lot more complicated than he had ever imagined and a lot more difficult than magicking a dragon out of a top hat.

"Now," said Potty as he opened the clay bin, "I don't believe you have, er, tackled anything on this scale before, Walter?"

Walter shook his head.

"Just little things, Potty," he said.

"Exactly." Potty sucked in his cheeks. "Practise, Walter, practise!" he said, depositing a large lump of grey clay onto the board in front of him.

Walter's heart began to beat faster.

"You've done a little coiling?" Potty went on. "Familiar with the technique?"

Walter nodded. He itched to begin.

"Right then," said Potty, handing Walter a cutting wire. "Start coiling vases, son, bigger and bigger. Experiment. Thicker coils at the bottom than at the top. You'll be working on the table for a while yet, but eventually you'll have to work on a board on the floor and use ladders."

It suddenly struck Walter how much he had to learn. So, for two weeks Walter spent all his spare time coiling and coiling, rolling the long sausages of clay on the table, cross hatching the top coil and applying slip before adding another one on top. He grew more and more adept and his vases shapelier and shapelier. They grew bigger and bigger too though none yet approached the projected size of his dragon vase.

"You're doing well, son," said Potty on the second Friday of Walter's clay work. "Carry on like this and I can see you building your vase in the second half of term."

"Cor!" said Walter. "Will it be done for Christmas, Potty?"

"A ceramicist can never be sure of such things, Walter," said Potty cautiously. "There is much to consider. We don't have a kiln yet."

Walter's shoulders sank. Their biggest problem, and as yet unsolved.

Potty looked at his disappointed face.

"But you have much to look forward to," he said encouragingly. "Next week, in addition to your vase work, I shall begin to teach you mould making."

Walter leapt up in delight.

"Mould making!" he cried. "Cor Potty!"

"Indeed," said Potty. "It is an essential skill Walter. Your dragon must be made a little larger than you would like, sliced into, er, appropriate pieces and moulds made for each part. Then you can cast the parts and reassemble them to form a hollow dragon which your vase can carry without collapsing. A solid dragon would be much too heavy and, er, quite unprofessional."

Walter was struck dumb with delight. He hadn't expected to learn mould making until he went to art school in the following September. Mould making was a man's job!

§

Walter ran home so fast that night that his six little Dragon Knights could hardly keep up with him.

"Wait for us, Walter!" cried little Nancy Dancer, her stick-like legs streaking after her charge, but Walter was so excited he would have probably outrun even the Grunters on that day.

"Mould making!" he shouted as he burst in the back door. "I'm mould making on Monday!"

"Wonderful dear," said Minnie, "but don't wake Louie, will you?"

"It's alright, dear, I'm awake," Louie called from the front room. "Mould making you say? Well, that is progress!"

Walter ran in to see her. Louie was the oldest of Walter's aunts and the first to hold him when he had arrived, wrapped in a Paisley shawl, at the little house at the top of the sooty street. Already very old when Walter was a baby, Louie rarely left her room, settled amongst her knitting and embroidery like a mouse in its nest of shredded paper. The little room was filled with the work of her busy hands and bright invention: the fire-screen with its glowing wool-work, the cushions and chair-backs worked in silk threads and the framed, wall-hung tapestries of flowery vases and thatched cottages.

Here, as he grew, she had cradled him on her lap and told him stories of the pot-banks where she had worked as a paintress all her life. She described the pounding puggers and the clever mould makers, the jiggers and the jollyers, the saggar makers and their bottom knockers: the young lads in long aprons whose wooden mallets were almost as tall as themselves. Louie filled his head with flower makers, decorators and gilders – the stories went on and on and Walter never grew tired of listening to them.

But Louie had other stories too, which grew out of the letters which arrived regularly from Africa, so that Walter had always been eager for the postman to come bearing a heavily creased envelope with a cargo of strange and exciting stamps. The stamps he had for his album but the stories he had to wait for until Louie had read and digested all the news from the shores of Lake Victoria. Her school-friend, Hetty Hornblower, had married a Methodist minister and her letters were full of the lively African children with their bright faces and eager minds.

With Walter curled in her lap, Louie had told him of their lives in the emerald forest with its elephants, monkeys and giraffes, exciting creatures which soon overran his bedroom in little plasticine forms. As Louie's stories unfolded, his fingers would work away so that by the time the tale was told there were the chief protagonists, all lined up on the flat arm of the chair.

In his grey and smoky childhood, Hetty's letters opened a window onto a world of vivid colour and vibrant sound, onto a far-off place of waterfalls, rivers, and lakes swimming with strange and startling fish. He saw gem-like frogs and jewel-like birds; feathers and furs of every kind burst out of the pages and the colours stained Walter's imagination like deep-set dyes.

Now, as he sat beside Louie, Walter conjured up these colours and heard the flit of the humming bird and the raucous calls of the chimpanzees echoing around the shadowy forest. The myriad shining greens, the heat soaked reds and golds, the azure African blues: these colours would become the beautiful lustres of his marvellous vase, the life force of his great and terrible dragon.

Sally came in with a cup of tea for them both and Walter was startled from his reverie.

"Auntie Sally," he said. "Potty is going to collect my glazes tomorrow. From the new lab in Kidsgrove. He says they're wizards there! He says to ask you if I can go too please? There's a lot to discuss, glaze wise."

Sally smiled.

"And how are you getting there?" she asked, tucking Louie's shawl a little more closely around her. "It's quite a way you know!"

"That's the best part!" said Walter cheerfully. "We're borrowing Mr. Beany's horse and cart. She's called Gwenny! We're going to drop off his deliveries along the way."

"Sounds like an adventure to me," said Louie, smiling. "I'm sure that's alright, isn't it dear?"

"I suppose so," said Sally, with a little frown. "What's Potty like with a horse? Unreliable articles, if you ask me."

"Oh," said Walter happily, "Bit of an expert I think!"

"Oh, is he?" said Sally. "Well, don't come complaining to

31

me if it runs off with you! None of our family has ever had anything to do with horses! Too much sense for that!"

Walter smiled and hugged Louie. Life was getting very exciting.

"I'll tell you all about it when I get back, Auntie!" he said.

"They grew bigger and bigger..."

Chapter Five
A Helpful Lift Home

Mr. Beany ran the great dry-goods store not far from Walter's house at the top of the hill. When Walter and Potty were standing in his stable yard at nine o' clock the next day, he gave them a few words of advice about handling Gwenny.

"She's a bit of a rum 'un, I can't lie to yer," he said, sucking hard on a boiled sweet as they stood surveying the dappled mare. "Yer'll 'ave to be careful with 'er Potty, else she'll 'ave yer all over the shop! Cart should slow 'er down a bit, like, an' yer can always slam its brakes on if yer feel 'ers getting away from yer. Yer'd never know 'ers twenty, that's fer sure!"

He laughed and patted Gwenny on the withers. She turned and snapped at him but the harness cheated her and she stamped her foot instead. Mr. Beany stood back respectfully.

"'er's bin a good 'orse, give or take a bit," he said with a sigh. "Sprout's off with a bad leg. Did I tell yer that?"

Sprout was the delivery boy who had been off work for two weeks now. He had annoyed Gwenny with his constant tuneless whistling and was consequently at his mother's, with a leg swathed in bandages on top of a cold compress.

Walter and Potty looked at the horse with due respect. Walter ventured to stroke her very, very softly on her nose, just to one side of her white, furry nostril. Immediately her head went down and she gave a great warm sigh.

"Bloody 'ell!" cried Mr. Beany. "'er likes you, Walter! Better get off while 'er's in a good mood. Sure you'll manage, Potty?"

"Oh, yes, I'm sure," said Potty a trifle loftily. He had always fancied himself as a horseman but until this moment life had denied him the opportunity of proving it. "Up you get Walter, alongside me. Two ceramicists together, ha-ha!"

Now that real leather reins were in his hands he felt a little nervous. He released the handbrake and shook the reins. Gwenny lifted her head and surged forward.

"Oh, I wouldn't shake the reins like that!" Mr. Beany advised as the cart left the yard. "'er won't like that at all. Just little clucks Potty, an' little polite requests, yer know, like "Walk on Gwenny," or "Wait please Gwenny.""

The horse and cart ploughed ahead into the Saturday morning traffic.

"An don't let 'er near any carrots!" they heard distantly as the equipage rounded the corner and Mr. Beany was lost from view. "Keep 'er away from greengrocers, Potty!" He went inside, shaking his head. "Boody 'ell," he thought. "I 'ope they 'eard me!"

The October morning was still chilly so Potty spread a little red rug over his knees and Walter wrapped himself up in some soft old flour sacks. He had never had such a ride before and he intended to enjoy it. The roads were crowded with other horse drawn vehicles, small open trucks, shiny black cars and fearless cyclists dodging in and out of the traffic.

One by one the crates and packages were dropped off at small corner shops, where mops and brooms, bundles of kindling and crates of pop huddled in the doorways. It seemed a long journey, with all the stopping and starting, but to Walter it was as good as a trip abroad. Gwenny must truly have taken to Walter for she gave Potty very little trouble apart from lunging at cyclists, whom she hated, and veering stubbornly away from man hole covers, which she distrusted. But she pulled them steadily up the cobbled stone bridges over the city's canals, where the murky waters reflected the sooty facades of the pottery factories along their banks.

"Perhaps it's like Venice," Walter thought, "but better because we've got the pot-banks."

All along the way, Walter caught glimpses of the life to which he aspired. Through tunnelled archways into busy courtyards, he saw carts being loaded with straw-stuffed willow crates bearing the pot- banks' finished goods. Tea and coffee-sets he imagined, dinner- services and chamber-pots, finished with transfers and gilding, or painted and sponged, all ready for the horses to draw them to the railway sidings. And there in the distance, as they reached the brow of a hill, were the bright train lines snaking into a halt where patient horses stood heads down as ant-men scurried to and fro, lifting and carrying, humping and shouldering the crates into the stationary wagons.

"There's no-where else like this in the world," thought Walter euphorically, as Gwenny took a snap at a passing slip cart.

Spread out below him, a panorama of marl pits, bottle ovens and dark terraces was pierced here and there by the tower of a sooty church, its windows catching the easterly sun. It was grey, grey, grey and black – "But lovely!" thought Walter, wanting for the first time not only to use clay, but paint also, to put down on paper the shaft of sunlight filtering through the filthy clouds and illuminating the tops of the barges as they glided beneath him, carrying the coal to the kilns, the source at once of the grit and glory of Walter's hometown.

"What will these glazes be like, Potty?" he asked, breaking the companionable silence in which they had been travelling.

"Excellent, I believe," said Potty. "Alf and I discussed it all with them in the Potter's Daughter last week. Sorry you couldn't be present, Walter. The very latest lustres. Designed for use on biscuit so we'll get away with only two firings. Er, steady on Gwenny, steady old girl."

"But will they be bright?" asked Walter anxiously. "They must be bright, Potty!"

"I have every confidence they will," said Potty, gently discouraging Gwenny from savaging a mounted delivery boy whose basket was full of offensively smelling onions. "But our gods can be cruel Walter, you know that. There are no guarantees for the ceramicist. We must be inured to disaster Walter, inured to it!"

"Watch out, Potty!" cried Walter, jolted out of his worries by the sudden spinning of the cart through forty- five degrees.

Gwenny had smelt the green-grocer's a hundred yards before she had seen it but had feigned ignorance until the last moment when, dead level with the colourful arrangement of vegetables outside the window, she performed a rapid left hand turn and plunged headfirst into the carrot display. The cart was sent skidding out behind her, blocking the road in a transverse manner and almost annihilating a pack of cubs exiting the Methodist Hall on the other side of the road.

Potty hauled on the reins but this only incensed Gwenny, who tossed cabbages and potatoes into the air, although none of the carrots were wasted.

The grocer came out of his shop, waving his arms about in a furious manner.

"Get that ruddy 'orse out of my veg!" he bellowed.

But try as he might, Potty could not get Gwenny to budge nor did her bit seem to be any impediment to her either as carrot after carrot disappeared and the grocer became almost incandescent with anger.

"This is going to cost you!" he roared at Potty, who was doing his gentlemanly best with his difficult female companion.

"Come on Gwenny," tried Walter, getting down and tugging on her right hand rein. "Come on, Gwenny dear, come on!"

But Walter was no match for a box full of carrots. The cubs, picking themselves up from the roadway, rushed over and immediately made things worse. Most cubs are small, but these mites, bred as they were on soot and grime, were tiny, spindly creatures, great in spirit but weak in arm and leg. And they had very little horse sense.

"Come on, missus!" they piped in their infant tones, laying their tiny hands against Gwenny's great feathery legs and endeavouring to push her aside.

"Shove over, duck!" they cried, heaving their insignificant bodies, four or five at a time, against her mountainous dappled shoulder.

Deep in the carrot box, Gwenny registered a degree or two of irritation. She lashed her tail and stamped her foot.

"It's working!" the cubs cried, redoubling their puny efforts, throwing their featherweight frames against her great immovable legs and bouncing off into the gutter.

"Take care, boys!" warned an anxious Potty but Gwenny had had enough.

Thunk! As quick as lightening she sent one tiny assailant flying into a tub of potatoes and thwak! another landed head first in the wet fish display next door. The smallest cub of all sailed backwards to land with a little thud in the back of the cart where Walter picked him up and dusted him down.

"Perhaps if you could remove carrot box, sir," said Potty, suddenly inspired. "And Walter, if you could then offer one or two to Gwenny...."

Once the livid shopkeeper had hoisted the box up and out of Gwenny's reach and her attention had been drawn by the available carrots in Walter's hand, horse and cart were safely roaded once more.

"That'll be five ruddy bob!" demanded the grocer and Potty gallantly paid up.

"I'm so sorry, Potty," said Walter, feeling guilty that all this had happened because of him. "I'll pay you back, I promise."

"No need, son," said Potty, master of his destiny once more. "As I was, er, saying, a ceramicist must expect disaster, must learn to live with it, Walter. Off we go, please Gwenny," he added a trifle shakily. "Good girl."

They set off once more, the cubs lining up smartly to see them go. Walter and Potty spoke little and were vigilant for the remainder of the journey but Gwenny had sated her carrot lust and plodded along steadily so that they reached the glaze laboratory before twelve o' clock.

§

As they had approached the greengrocer's, neither Walter nor Potty had noticed the sleek Armstrong Siddeley parked a little further up the road outside a gentleman's outfitters. In the back sat a smartly dressed old man with a very sad face.

"It's just six shirts to collect, please John," he said to his chauffeur who stood politely waiting for instructions before disappearing inside the shop.

The old man looked down at his leather gloved hands.

"Must stop looking at those albums," he said to himself regretfully. "Does y' no good, Jollie. Won't bring them back, any of them."

Tears appeared in his blue eyes and coursed down his cheeks so that he took out a clean white handkerchief and dabbed at his face.

Just then he heard the sound of Mr. Beany's cart skidding across the cobbles followed by the angry shouts of the unfortunate greengrocer. He looked up and saw the devastation that Gwenny was wrecking. As he watched a tiny crease appeared in the corner of his mouth, then his lips twitched into a smile. He felt a strange sensation bubbling in his chest and an urge to let it out at his mouth.

"Why, you're laughing, old boy!" he thought in amazement as tears poured down his pink cheeks and his shoulders began to heave uncontrollably. "Shouldn't laugh at it but Whooo-whooo!"

He gave himself up to merriment, unknown for so long.

"Look, John, look!" he cried to his startled chauffer when he returned with the new shirts done up in a brown paper package. "Marvellous horse! Marvellous!"

As Gwenny passed by him he saluted her, dabbing the tears of laughter away from his face.

"Alright sir?" asked the chauffeur, twisting round in his seat anxiously. "Everything alright?"

"Marvellous!" said the old man. "Home John! Marvellous horse! Marvellous!"

§

"Sixpence to watch your 'orse, sir!"

Potty had no sooner drawn up at the kerbside than a very grubby little girl had sprung out of nowhere and laid her hands gently on Gwenny's reins.

"I love 'orses, I do," she said. "I'll look after 'er proper. For sixpence, like," she added hopefully.

Potty paid up and Walter added another tuppence from his blazer pocket.

"Might as well," he thought, "can't buy any gobstoppers...."

He fetched the nose bag from the back of the cart and the little girl showed him how to fix it to Gwenny's bridle.

"What's your name?" he asked the ragged child.

"Margaret," she chirped as Walter and Potty mounted the steps to the front door of the prestigious glaze laboratory. "Take yer time, er'll be alreet with me!"

"Cor!" thought Walter, "Fancy me coming here!"

"It's very modern Potty," he whispered as they went in through the big glass doors. "I didn't expect it to be like this!"

"Everything here is up to date, Walter," said Potty. "This is the very best place to come."

The glaze wizards were very different from the way Walter had imagined them too. If he had expected old men in pointed hats and flowing robes, then Isabella and Theodora were a bit of a disappointment, though they were very stylish women indeed whose smart suits and modish shoes would not have been out of place on a Milanese catwalk. They ran forward to greet him.

"Potty!" they cried. "Walter! Come in, come in!"

Tea and biscuits were followed by a tour of the laboratories so that soon Walter's head was bursting with technical information. He was given trial pieces to handle so that he could both see and feel the lustrous glazes produced by the people there. He was shown the dry powders sitting in their glass jars, the metal oxides which when transformed by the heat of the bottle oven would turn into vivid rainbows of colour: bright, imperishable glazes which would endure until the end of history, and beyond.

"Potty has told us all about your project, Walter," said Isabella. "We think we have just the thing for you!"

Theodora took down a large jar and handed it to Walter. Inside was a brown, muddy-looking powder but Walter knew that its dullness was deceptive. It could be anything when fired!

"We've been trialling a new range of lustres," she said, "and we think they will be ideal for your vase. They are lustre glazes made to go straight onto biscuit, so your dragon need only be fired twice!"

Walter nodded, this much Potty had said.

"Your dragon vase will be a magnificent showpiece for our new range," said Isabella enthusiastically. "If you are willing to trial them, Walter?"

Walter was silent for a moment. How much of a risk was he taking with these new lustres? On the other hand, where else could he find such material in the quantities required for his huge vase? The school's glazes were dull affairs, dark brown or sludgy-looking greens. They wouldn't do at all!

"Will, er, will they be lovely and bright?" he asked, embarrassed to look a gift horse in the mouth. "Will they come out like this?"

He looked at the beautiful trial pieces that lay around him. It seemed too much to hope for.

Both wizards surveyed him kindly.

"We understand you will be having Alf as your fireman," said Theodora. "We have entered into discussions with him and Alf being Alf and the very best person for the job, we feel as confident as it is possible to be that our glazes will perform well, dear."

"But there are no certainties in this business, Walter," said Isabella. "There is always risk."

Walter nodded. "We must be inured to disaster," he said sagely. "Inured to it!"

The glaze wizards smiled. Theodora lead them to a little storeroom and showed Walter the shelves of black pottery jars that had been set aside for him. One by one she read out the labels and described the final colours of the fired glazes. At Walter's request, she made little notes on the labels of the jars that he chose and Isabella helped Potty to pack them safely inside strong cardboard boxes which they tied securely with thick hairy string and set on a little trolly. Potty pushed it along the bright corridor to the big glass doors. Walter could see Gwenny snoozing, safe in the company of her grubby minder.

"Any luck with the bottle oven yet, Potty?" asked Isabella hopefully. Potty and Walter shook their heads.

"I'm still looking around," Potty said, trying to sound more confident than he felt. "Bill's doing the same, keeping an eye out. If we were lent a disused one, then of course he could repair it. We'll keep looking, won't we, Walter?"

Walter nodded but his spirits suddenly sank. "It's all very well having boxes and boxes of glazes," he thought, "But if we can't find a kiln soon, what will be the point?"

Theodora and Isabella leant forward and shook his hand.

"Nothing is ever straight forward, Walter," said Theodora kindly. "But never give up. Keep going, things will work out, I'm sure of it."

"Yes, never give up," said Isabella, giving him a peck on the cheek. "We will pop over and visit you once you start building it, sometime after half term, Potty says. Don't rush it dear, take your time. If all goes well you will have a vase bigger and better than anything Minton have ever produced – or Spode!"

All this went around and around in Walter's head on the return journey. The nosebag of oats had reinvigorated Gwenny. She set off at a very sprightly pace so that Potty had little time to talk and Walter sat quietly, the conical coal tips on the horizon going unnoticed, and the upright tracery of the winding gear, with its great wheel drawn in fine silhouette against the evening sun, made no impression on him either.

"Will my dragon vase ever be made?" he wondered, serious doubt creeping in for the first time, like cold flood water under a parlour door.

There on the cart was the magic he had dreamt of when he first engendered his dragon: there were the shining scales, the fiery breath; there were all the rich hues of Africa waiting to burst forth from their glass and cardboard containers, if only a bottle oven could be found! But the sleepless nights, the long hours and the endless excitement of creation were finally taking their toll on Walter whose mood spiralled further and further down as Gwenny pulled him steadily closer and closer to home.

He was bought out of himself by a nudge from Potty.

"Look Walter! Look at that grand old man over there! He looks exhausted!"

Walter looked up to see a well-dressed old man sitting on the low wall of a Baptist Chapel at the bottom of a steep hill. Another mile or so and Walter would be home. The elderly gentleman was sitting bent forward with both hands clasped on top of his walking stick. He seemed rather out of breath.

"Oh dear," said Walter. "Shall we offer him a lift, Potty?"

"Get down, son, and help him on board," said Potty, bringing Gwenny to a neat halt.

But the elderly gent was unable to climb up beside Potty, the driver's seat was simply too high.

"If I lower the tail-flap, sir," Walter asked respectfully, "do you think you could sit in the back with me?"

With a bit of gentle manoeuvring the elderly man was soon made comfortable on the empty flour-sacks beside the cardboard boxes. All at once he looked at Walter and burst into helpless giggles. His eyes watered, his nose ran and he had to fish helplessly in his overcoat for his handkerchief.

"Whooo-whooo," he wheezed, before finally subsiding and giving his face a good wipe.

"This is the horse with the carrots, isn't it?" he exclaimed. "Haven't laughed so much for years! Marvellous! Marvellous! She's a one! What's her name?"

"Gwenny," replied Walter, thinking it hadn't seemed so funny at the time. "She's twenty!"

"Wonderful old girl," the man chortled. "Never seen anything so funny. Those cubs...." And off he went again into snuffles of helpless laughter all the way up the hill.

When they reached the top though, he pulled himself together and addressed Potty and Walter very politely.

"The Siddeley broke down again," he informed them. "Walked the last four miles. So grateful for the lift. Getting on a bit now. Sorry to laugh so much but done me the world of good."

For a moment he looked sad again and quite a different person.

"Would you be so kind as to drop me at Prospect House, please? Couple of streets away. First left, on to the end, then left again."

Potty was only too pleased to help, although he had a bit of a battle with Gwenny, who, knowing herself to be practically home, thoroughly resented this last minute detour.

"Aaahm," said Potty, reining Gwenny back timidly as she tried to pull into the middle of the road, the smell of her stable wafting through the intervening streets and calling her home.

"Knows her own mind!" roared the elderly gentleman, stuffing his handkerchief in his mouth and almost choking to death. "Had a horse like that myself once. No end of trouble with her – marvellous! Marvellous!" And off he went again.

But the elderly gentleman was soon dropped off outside a smart villa with large wrought iron gates and a circular driveway. He thanked Potty and Walter profusely and found a lump of sugar in his pocket for Gwenny.

"Never leave home without one," he said by way of explanation. "Much better than a car," he said as he opened his gates, and with a final lift of his hat, turned and went into his house.

"Admirable old gentleman," said Potty and Walter agreed.

Walter arrived home exhausted but elated. The old man had done him good too. His depression had lifted and he couldn't wait for tomorrow to come. But he was so very, very tired and much as he wanted to regale his aunties with the day's adventures, he was soon fast asleep in the arm chair and had to be carried upstairs by Sally and Minnie in a deep, deep sleep. Sally pulled the covers over the sleeping boy.

"About time he had a proper night's sleep," she said. "This vase of his Minnie, it seems like a lot of trouble to me!"

But Minnie shook her head.

"He's got to do it, Sally," she said. "I think it's his destiny."

Minnie went downstairs looking thoughtful. She followed Sally into the kitchen and soon the sisters were deep in conversation.

"Well," said Sally finally, as she put the last pan away, "I think it's a good idea – and about time too! Not speaking for all these years!"

Minnie blushed.

"I have been a bit foolish," she said. "And I'm sure he will help. He was always the soul of generosity."

"You and your pride, Minnie," said Sally, not unkindly. "Well, I hope it goes well for you. Louie will be pleased when she hears. After all these years!"

Gwenny took Potty back to her stable and Potty used Mr. Beany's wheel-barrow to take home the precious boxes of glazes. Tomorrow he would lock them safely in the storeroom.

"I hope he gets to use them after all this," thought Potty despondently. "I've got to find him a kiln somewhere. I just have to!"

"He had never had such a ride before..."

Chapter Six

A Gargoyle At The Window

The next morning the Grunter twins woke up simultaneously, as they always did. Billie Grunter's bottom was suspended only inches above his brother in the bottom bunk and Willie often felt in danger of suffocation.

"Awake bruv?" asked Billie, leaning his great weight over the edge of the top bunk and peering down at Willie.

"Eraaagh, yes," said Willie yawning.

It was Sunday and he was hoping for a morning in bed.

"What are we going to do about him?" asked Billie, and Willie knew straightaway what he meant.

"Can't get near the craft and clay room," he said. "Old Pinch's seen to that. Can't get him coming or going these days, either."

"We did say we'd have him," said Billie, heaving his bulk down onto the linoleum. It was turning chilly and the floor struck cold to his great bare feet. He pulled on his grey socks and then got dressed quickly.

"Too tired to think," said Willie sleepily, reluctant to move out of his warm burrow.

Billie pulled the bedclothes back.

"You'd better get up," he said anxiously. "I can hear her banging about."

Old Ma was not to be taken lightly and he knew that they were disappointing her.

After their bacon and eggs, cooked as usual in the black fat of Old Ma's frying pan, Billie said, "It's got really hard to catch him on his own, Gran. There's always somebody about these days when we want to duff him up!"

She spun, skillet in hand, and shot them a glance so withering that they ducked their heads and studied the kitchen floor.

"You 'opeless little toads!" she spat, waving the greasy skillet in their faces. "Can't yer even teach *that* little maggot a lesson? Vase!" she spat. "'im an' is *vase!*"

She crashed the frying pan back onto the hearth and swept their eggy plates off the table.

"*Twins!*" she sneered, "Yer 'aven't got a brain-cell between yer!"

She stormed off into the scullery, clattering the dishes ferociously while the twins sat, head down, wishing they had said nothing. But tormenting Walter had always been fun and they didn't want to give it up now. Five minutes later she reappeared, a smirk twisting her mouth so that the thin cigarette bobbed loosely in one corner.

"Come here, my darlings," she said, twisting their ears sharply as they leaned in towards the diminutive old woman. "Listen to granny!"

§

Walter had slept for over twelve hours. He had dreamed the most marvellous dreams in which his dragon vase was not only made and fired, but also glazed in the most extraordinary colours. Even Queen Mary had come to see it!

Twelve o'clock found him at the kitchen table, munching doorsteps of bread and dripping and for the first time in weeks noticing what he was eating. It was a crisp, cool day and an easterly wind had blown away much of the weekend's smoke so that sunlight poured in through the little window and sparkled on the rim of his plate.

"This is great!" thought Walter happily. "I've got my glazes and loads of time to build my vase." He saw his great dragon in his mind's eye and chewed contentedly. "Cor!" he thought again. "My very own dragon!"

Suddenly, a large mottled face was pushed up against the window so that the glass flattened and distorted its features. It was frighteningly grotesque and Walter jumped back. The outside door was opened a crack and another beefy mug was pushed inside.

"S'not original, Walter! S'all been done before! That stupid vase of yours! Chinese have been making 'em for years. Hundreds and hundreds of years! Yer just copying, Walter! Yer a *copycat*!"

"Copycat! Copycat!" sang the gargoyl at the window. "S'not even that big Walter. Our Gran's potty's bigger than that!"

Auntie Sally came in from the front room and quickly seized her broom. She rushed out but their mocking calls echoed around the little alley, "Copycat! Copycat! Walter's a copycat!"

Walter sat stunned under this deadliest of insults. The trouble was, Walter knew there was some truth to it. The Chinese had made dragon vases and they were wonderful. He had seen photographs of them in a book in Hanley library and Potty had a magazine with a picture of a Ming dragon pot, though none of them came near the intended size of Walter's dragon. Still, he sat shocked and as the sun went in behind a grey dirty cloud he shivered unhappily.

"What's the matter, Walter?" asked Sally brusquely as she came back into the house. "You're not taking any notice of those fools, are you?"

"They've got a point though, haven't they?" said Walter. "I'm not really doing something original, am I?"

Sally was out of her depth.

"Wait till Minnie gets back," she said. "She's only over at Thelma and Bill's. She'll be here soon."

She left him sitting at the table, the doorsteps unfinished on his plate. He twiddled a crust between his fingers, making it into a sort of doughy putty.

"Is there any real point?" he asked himself. "If it's all been done before?"

Sally came and took away his plate.

"You'll have to do better than that at dinner," she said kindly. "Look, here's Minnie now!"

Sally and Minnie spoke in low voices in the scullery and then Minnie came into the kitchen and crossed to the chimney-piece where she took down a large, heavy book. It was a volume that Walter had always avoided, even on a really boring Sunday evening. It was simply too big and the print was very small; there were no illustrations either, and that always went against a book in Walter's estimation.

Minnie held it up.

"Do you know what this is, Walter?" she asked brightly.

"Boring?" said Walter honestly.

"Shakespeare, Walter!" said Minnie smiling.

"Just as I thought, then," thought Walter. His Auntie Minnie was clever but sometimes he wished she wouldn't try to improve him.

"And what did Shakespeare write?" Minnie went on, placing the book on the table and opening it up in front of her nephew.

"Plays, Auntie?" said Walter, feeling there was no escape but thinking it an odd time for an English lesson.

"Stories Walter! That's what they are – stories!" Minnie said, flipping through the tissue thin pages. "Some of the greatest stories in the world, read for hundreds of years by people all around the world. Everybody knows about William Shakespeare! Want a story about murder? Or jealousy? Or revenge? Shakespeare's your man. Nobody better!"

"Oh," said Walter, determined more than ever never to touch the book.

"And where do you think he got these stories, Walter?" Minnie asked.

"His head, Auntie?" This seemed the only likely answer.

"No!" said Minnie triumphantly. "He pinched them! From other people's books! Hardly an original story in there at all!"

"Cor!" said Walter, the light beginning to dawn.

"And do you know what?" Minnie went on, now well into her stride. "He made them better – so much better than the originals that there is no comparison at all! He took something good and transformed it into something utterly marvellous!"

Walter smiled. The book might not be such a dead loss after all. But he still wouldn't read it.

"So what do you think about the Grunters now, dear?" said Minnie, dusting the Shakespeare and putting it back on the chimneypiece.

"Blockheads!" said Walter, grinning widely.

"Blockheads!" Minnie agreed. "You are working in a great tradition. The tradition of the dragon vase. You're not copying! You are developing the genre into something magnificent, something huge and amazing!"

"But there're lots of problems, Auntie," Walter said philosophically. "I haven't even got a bottle oven yet."

"Well," said Minnie, giving the fire a vigorous thrust with the poker so that flames spurted up and the coals collapsed with a sigh. "Don't take your coat off when you get back from Sunday School this afternoon. We're going straight out."

"Are we?" said Walter in surprise. "Pongy's made a boat. They're taking it up to the pond, Auntie."

After the tedium of Sunday School he was usually left to play with Pongy and Lefty for the rest of the afternoon. It was the best free hour or so before the new week began, and it was a sunny day. Walter looked hopefully out of the window, as if that might change Minnie's mind.

"Never mind that, dear," said Minnie resolutely. "And have your drawings ready to take with you. There's someone I want you to show them to."

§

Very few children enjoyed Sunday School and Walter was not one of them. It was dull, pious, and often very cold. Wintry light streamed in through the plain windows and the radiator rarely worked. It was two hours of tedium with a bit of horse-play at the beginning and end, if he was lucky. But at least the Grunters never attended and with a lump of plasticine in his pocket Walter was able to model in peace if he kept quiet and murmured amen along with his friends. Old Parable was grateful for a quiet class and he knew very well that it wasn't piety that kept Walter's head down.

"That dragon again!" he smiled as he distributed the grimy hymn books and saw a small four-toed foot whipped out of sight into Walter's pocket. "Still, the Devil makes work for idle hands..."

Like the rest of the city, Old Parable had read with interest all about Walter's Dragon in The Sentinel on Friday night.

SHOOLBOY MAKES MASSIVE POT

... the headline had read, tucked away on page six amongst reports on council business and an account of a man who regularly ate seven meat pies for breakfast. Walter had been a little disappointed.

"He came this morning," he had told his aunties as they read the small article on the Friday evening. "He appeared at the blue doors and asked Potty if he could come in and talk to me. He took a photo of the vase I'd been coiling but I told him the real one would be much bigger. I showed him some of my practise dragon moulds too, but they're not in here. No photo either."

All of Walter's friends and neighbours had read the little article with interest and more besides. Across the city of coal and clay many people began to take an interest in the small potter and his huge self-imposed task.

"Shame there's no photo," they had said, and the more curious had rung The Sentinel and complained. "I hope we're going to hear more about this!" they said and Alan Padder, sitting behind his paper strewn desk with its half-empty cups of cold coffee, suddenly began to sniff a real story and wished he'd written a better article.

Walter wished that Old Parable could get through his stories a lot quicker.

"Two hours!" he thought as he made his way home under a clear sky. "All that stuff about hide and seek and knocking on doors! Could have been up the park with Pongy!"

The wind had whirled around the chimneys and bottle ovens, ripping away the remnants of the weekend's smoke so that the late afternoon was even sunnier and Walter was even more reluctant to miss an outing with his friends.

But Minnie was waiting for him when he got home, a wet face-flannel in one hand and a comb in the other.

"Get you drawings, dear," she said, and moments later they were off, Minnie towing him along briskly in a determined and business-like manner.

"Old Ma was not to be taken lightly..."

Chapter Seven
A Friend From the Past

"Where are we going, Auntie?" he queried as they reached the top of the hill and set off in the direction of the park where the streets became a little wider and the houses a little bigger.

But Minnie didn't answer. She had a far-away look in her eyes so that after a few attempts Walter gave up and concentrated on keeping up with his mysterious aunt. Then, rounding a corner, there they were, outside the same iron gates which opened onto the old gentleman's villa.

"I was here yesterday!" Walter said in astonishment. "We gave him a lift!"

Minnie was surprised too.

"Oh!" she said. "Well, he knows we're coming. And a lift you say? That's all to the good!"

With a tilt of her chin Minnie pushed open the gates and together they crunched up the gravel drive to the handsome front door. Walter didn't know anyone who had a front garden, let alone one with laurel bushes which gleamed in the light streaming from the windows and apple trees which waved their branches beyond the garden wall.

"Well," he thought, suddenly feeling hot all over, "I do know *those* apple trees...."

The door was opened by a smart tweeny in black.

"Hello Rosie, dear," said Minnie. "This is Walter. I don't think you've met him?"

"Hello Walter," said the tweeny brightly. Step inside Minnie," she continued. "Mr. Jollie is expecting you."

The square hallway gave onto the parlour and Walter was surprised to see the elderly gentleman pacing up and down in front of the fire in a highly agitated manner. When he saw Minnie he stopped and seemed lost for words.

"Hello, Edward," said Minnie softly, stepping forward and taking him by the hand. "It's so lovely to see you again. It's been such a long time. How are you, my dear?"

All of a sudden Mr. Jollie's shoulders dropped and he blew out a huge sigh of relief.

"Minnie!" he said. "Dear lady. So sorry. So sorry. Hope you have forgiven me!"

And before Walter knew what was happening his Auntie Minnie and the elderly gentleman were hugging and patting each other on the back and crying little tears of joy.

"This is a bit much!" he thought and wished he hadn't come.

The next moment a whirlwind of white curls knocked him off his feet and sent him sprawling onto the hearthrug. He felt cold wet noses and warm wet tongues on his face.

"Jigger-Poo! Jolly-Poo! Naughty dogs! Heel! Heel!"

The curly whirlwind subsided immediately and Walter was able to see that it was comprised of two large white poodles, bright eyed and pink tongued, who now sat like a pair of fabulous bookends on either side of the elderly gentleman.

"Cor!" said Walter. "They're nice!"

The dogs needed no second invitation and Walter was once again submerged in a woolly tide. His face was suddenly cleaner than it had been for weeks.

If Auntie Minnie had broken the ice, the Poos had plunged straight in, and the atmosphere in the lovely room was now relaxed and inviting. Proper introductions took place, cakes and cups of tea appeared, the fire danced and gleamed in the marble hearth and Walter soon started to feel more at ease.

Every so often, as they sat around the fire, Mr. Jollie leant forward and began to say, "I am sorry my...." But Minnie just patted his hand kindly and said, "No need, Edward,"

A POTTERIES BOY

until, having been a school teacher after all, and only able to stand so much interruption, she said firmly, "Now Edward! The past is the past! Let us put it behind us. I've been very foolish and just to be on friendly terms again is a great joy to me. We have been silly! No more now, please!"

Mr. Jollie smiled a happy smile and nodded quietly. The Poos looked from one to the other, then gave Minnie's brogues a good licking and settled down on the rug.

Minnie politely drained her cup of tea and put it down daintily. She looked at Walter and began.

"I had two reasons for coming today, Edward," she said. "The first is happily resolved – no, no, say no more! The second is to do with Walter here."

"Dear boy," broke in Mr. Jollie. "Kind little chap...."

"Yes indeed" said Minnie, "But we have a favour to ask, don't we, Walter?"

Walter was completely in the dark. He had no idea why he was there and he looked at Minnie in bewilderment.

Minnie continued, a little overwrought. "It's a lot to ask of you, Edward....a great deal in fact...."

"Anything, Minnie, anything," said Mr. Jollie encouragingly.

"You say that now, Edward," said Minnie blushing. "I haven't told you what it is yet. Have you been reading The Sentinel lately? Have you heard about the great dragon vase a little boy is making?"

"Heard about it? Nobody's talking about anything else round here!" roared Mr. Jollie. "John says it's taking ages to get served nowadays!" He chuckled, then almost choked on his sponge finger. "Not Walter, is it? It is? *Is it*? Marvellous, Walter! Marvellous!"

His excitement set off the Poos again who began leaping and frolicking, licking shoes and faces, their stiff pom-pom tails in danger of whisking off the cups and saucers and sending them flying. Lightly threatened with the other room, they consented to sit, not lie, as Minnie unfolded Walter's difficulties one by one.

"Needs a kiln! That's it!" cried Mr. Jollie in glee. "A bottle oven and a lot of coal!"

He sat forward excitedly as Walter's eyebrows shot up and his mouth fell open in surprise. So that was why he was there!

"Pleased to help, Minnie," Mr. Jollie went on. "Marvellous! Marvellous! Walter and Gwenny helped me more than you could know….ever since…."

And here his voice trailed off and he looked sadly at the two silver framed photographs on the chimneypiece. Two handsome young men in uniform stood with their rifles, eternally gazing out upon their childhood home.

"Oh, Edward dear, I'm so sorry," said Minnie, touching his arm lightly. "We've always felt for you. So many…."

"Yes Minnie, so many," he said. "But I could never get over it. Jollie and Sons. What was the point? Fashions changed after the war. Hadn't the heart to keep up. Let it all slide…. Shut it down….years ago now…. years and years…."

The Poos whined softly and Jolly Poo, who was closest, rested her head on Mr. Jollie's knee and looked up at him with her gentle dark eyes.

"I know, Edward," said Minnie, "but it's all still there."

"Right!" said Mr. Jollie, stroking Jolly Poo's head and smiling across at Walter who sat like one in a dream, his cream horn half eaten and his tea gone cold. "Number one kiln! Just the job! Do nicely for your second firing too. Needs repairing, goes without saying….Thousand times more cheerful since yesterday…. Those cubs…." And a broad smile lit up his face. "Marvellous horse! Marvellous!"

He started to wheeze and whoo again until the Poos became quite agitated, which calmed him down.

"Quite right!" he said, wiping his eyes and giving each Poo a kindly kiss on the nose. "But feeling a new man since yesterday. Haven't had this on for years," he said a trifle vainly, flicking a spotted silk necktie. "But to business! To business! Got a drawing there, Walter?"

"Stand up and show Mr. Jollie," said Minnie quickly. Walter stood up.

"Now or never," he thought and gave his sheet of paper a sharp outward flick – so that there it was – the dragon vase, big and bold on the imperial sheet, the dragon rearing up across the vase and eyeing Mr. Jollie wickedly.

Mr. Jollie was so astonished that his pipe fell out of his open mouth. It was caught deftly by Jigger Poo who soon spat it out with a cough.

"How big, Walter?" he said, leaning forward to see Walter's pencilled measurements. "How big?"

Walter spread his arms as wide as they would go and then indicated that the vase was actually much bigger than that. Much, much bigger.

Mr. Jollie simply stared and stared until Walter began to feel uneasy.

"Don't you like it, sir?" he said.

"Like it? Like it?" cried Mr. Jollie. "Never seen anything like it. Marvellous! Marvellous! Whoo-whoo," he wheezed, "Knocks anything Doulton are doing into a cocked hat!"

Suddenly he calmed down.

"Bit of a beggar to fire, Walter," he said, relighting his pipe and sucking on it hard. "Something that size. Never get that in a muffle kiln! Or a saggar either! Better tell me all about it...."

And the rest of the evening, one of the best of Walter's life, was spent deep in technical discussions with the profoundly knowledgeable old gentleman. There wasn't much he didn't know about pottery, and soon he had learned all about Walter's team too: Potty and Alfred, and Minnie's friend Thelma and her husband, Bill, a builder of bottle ovens like his father and grandfather before him.

"I had a good chat with Bill this morning," Minnie told Mr. Jollie. "He's retired now of course but very keen to help."

"Just the man!" Mr. Jollie agreed, "Known him off and on for years. Soon sort the old kiln out with him around!"

"He always buys me plasticine at Christmas!" Walter said. He liked Thelma and Bill very much.

He began to like Mr. Jollie very much too. He gazed around the beautiful room with its cosy chairs and bright furnishings. Then he looked at the photographs on the chimneypiece of the two handsome young men who had never come home again. He wondered how Auntie Minnie knew Mr. Jollie and why they had not spoken for so long, but he knew he would never ask her.

"That's her business after all," he thought.

Minnie and Mr. Jollie were busy making arrangements for everyone to meet at Mr. Jollie's yard the next day at four o' clock.

"We'll pick you up from school, dear," said Minnie. "I'm sure Bill and Alf will meet us there, and Potty too. Then we can see what needs doing. How exciting, Walter! A bottle oven at last!"

"Cor!" thought Walter. "My very own bottle kiln!"

"Marvellous!" said Mr. Jollie finally, as they stood in the hallway saying their goodbyes. "How far have you got then, Walter?"

"Potty's teaching me how to make moulds," Walter said, "on a fairly small scale at the moment. Sometime soon I shall build the vase, then after that I shall start to model my dragon full size so we can make the final moulds. Then we can cast the pieces and assemble them on the vase. The problem will be keeping it all damp for weeks so it doesn't dry and crack."

"Rather!" said Mr. Jollie. "Big project. Lots of challenges! But first problem solved. Got your kiln now. Marvellous! Marvellous!"

"Thank you very much, sir," said Walter smiling, "I can't wait for tomorrow! See you, Rosie!"

They left and hurried home through the dark streets, Minnie humming a little tune.

Sally and Louie were looking out for them at the front window whose light spilled out onto the dark pavement. Sally opened the door eagerly and quick glances were exchanged. Minnie nodded happily.

"Oh, I am glad, Minnie," Sally said. "About time too!"

Louie gave her younger sister a hug and squeezed her hand.

"Well done, darling," she said.

The kettle was soon whistling and the family sat down to tea and a discussion of the evening's events.

"Poor Edward, said Sally at one point. "He never could get over it."

Walter knew about the First World War. His own family had lost three cousins, all bright young men with interesting careers ahead of them. He had read some of their letters and their photographs lined his way to bed each night, a sort of sepia guard of honour as he mounted the stairs. Harold first, then Sid, then Pat, serious young men in military caps and worsted uniforms, his unknown uncles lost to time and war.

"I'm glad Mr. Jollie's feeling so much happier," he thought as he climbed the stairs to bed that night. "Good old Gwenny! And a horse! Fancy that!"

Mr. Jollie had told Walter that he was getting rid of the Siddeley and going back to a horse and carriage.

"Against the tide, Walter!" he said, "But a car's no fun at

all! Breaks down, no character! Give me a horse I say! Got my eye on one already," he added and winked conspiratorially at the little boy. "Dragon! Four year old! Hell of a character! Black as soot and the Devil's own son! Sorry Minnie... Have some fun with him...whooo....whooo!"

Walter had been amazed.

"Another Dragon!" he thought as he drifted off to sleep that night. But in his dreams his own dragon insisted on turning into a huge black horse with fiery eyes, which reared and rampaged across his vase, assuming greater and greater proportions until it broke free of the clay and carried Walter off, deeper and deeper into a deep dark tunnel of sleep from which he had to be shaken awake in the morning.

"Wake up, Walter!" Auntie Minnie cried, "Your Dragon Knights are at the door!"

"so astonished that the pipe fell out of his mouth..."

Chapter Eight

The Sniper

On Monday morning, the Grunters were waiting on either side of the school gates but Walter passed through unmolested with Pongy and Lefty and little Nancy Dancer in the vanguard.

"Copy-cat! Copycat!" sneered Billie as they approached.

Little Nancy stopped and looked him up and down.

"He's working in a great tradition," she said scathingly. "He's developing the genre. What would you know about anything! Go an' help your mother make some pies – an' try not to eat 'em all!"

Pongy and Lefty roared and Walter smiled.

He went inside the blue doors to tell Potty the good news and left the twins kicking the brick pillars of the gateway.

"We'll have to do better than this," said Willie angrily. "I'd like to chop him up an' bake him in a pie like that Sweeny Todd fella grandma told us about!"

"Too stringy, bruv," said Billie, "But don't worry, he'll have a bad afternoon. Dumpling's off. We've got The Sniper instead!"

An ugly grin broke over Willie's face. "The Sniper?" he said happily. "Well, that's him sorted then!"

He looked relieved and his shoulders dropped. The previous evening had not been a pleasant one. Old Ma had been in a particularly vicious mood, as she often was on a Sunday. Something about the nine o' clock church bells always put her in a violent temper for the rest of the day so that Harold and Bertha took refuge in the slaughterhouse and the twins kept their heads down, spending the evening busy with their weekend homework.

Last night Old Ma had sat in the kitchen armchair as usual, The Sentinel folded sharply in her lap. She smoked and studied her nephews intently. After a while she spat into her empty teacup, then leaned over towards Billie, who was finishing his maths homework, and Willie, who was copying it. Reaching out her claw-like hand, Old Ma tore a strip off Willie's exercise book so that his long division was divided in half.

"Gran!" he protested, but then fell silent at a dig in the ribs from his brother.

Old Ma twisted the piece of arithmetic into a spiral and lit it at the fire, then applied it to a Player's Navy Cut.

"Get into trouble fer that, will yer?" she asked mildly, smiling at Willie's discomfort. "Then get 'im in trouble!" she spat, springing out of her chair with such force that the twins leapt up and backed towards the door.

"He's dead!" Billie had cried as they stood at the foot of the stairs. "He's dead, I tell you Gran, dead!"

"He's as good as dead anyway," thought Billie as they crossed the playground, past little groups of Dragon Knights who shrugged indifferently and turned their backs on the twins, knowing Walter was safe with Potty. "We won't have to do a thing today. The Sniper'll do it all for us!"

Mondays had always been a very mixed lot for Walter. He had two hours of craft and clay at nine o'clock but then double maths in the afternoon, a vast trackless desert of misery in which he always failed to locate any oasis of hope or understanding. Even the daily kindnesses of Mrs. Dumpling could not assuage his hopeless boredom and his complete despair. But when Walter filed into the room that Monday he knew he was a lost man.

Everyone dreaded the reappearance of The Sniper. Sent in occasionally from the teaching-pool, Roberta Snippet was darkly sleek and reminded Walter of a house beetle in its shiny sinister carapace. Unlike the other staff at The Grove her aim was to embarrass and to humiliate, and to punish rather than to protect. The Sniper chose her targets well. The weak, the unknowing, the easily terrified went down under her fire like summer wheat beneath the scythe; then caned and throbbing, they sat in petrified submission, too miserable to add up four and four let alone pronounce upon a square root. Her own personal cane, made thinner and sharper with prolonged use, lay prominently on her desk.

Walter sat and struggled with a long division of fiendish proportions. For fifteen minutes it had gone on and on, no remainder dividing evenly to bring the torture to an end but instead always providing yet more figures to be further divided until Walter was lost in a mathematical maze with no idea of where he had come from or where he was going to. Furthermore, he had run out of paper. Even the rough blue inside cover of his jotter was full of hopeless higgeldy-piggeldy calculations leading nowhere. Walter broke out into a sweat. His book, he well knew, was filled not just with arithmetic but with dragons splayed brazenly across the pages in half a dozen splendidly different attitudes.

"Whatever was I thinking of?" he asked himself, sweat trickling down between his shoulder blades. He knew the book would have to be handed in soon – and the time came now!

"Walter!" The Sniper's voice rang out in the silent classroom. "Why aren't you working?"

"I've run out of paper Miss. Sorry Miss." Walter knew there was no escape and behind him he heard Willie give a low snicker.

The Sniper stared at Walter.

"Bring it out here. Now!" she said.

Walter trouped out and stood beside The Sniper's desk. Billie and Willie nudged each other in glee, careful to keep their gestures small, below the parapet. They could hardly wait for what would come next. Everyone knew about Walter's maths book, and all his other books, come to that.

The sharp pink finger nails flicked through the evidence of Walter's mathematical crimes, stopping abruptly as a defiantly beautiful dragon displayed itself on a right-hand page, all sinuous curves disporting themselves over the whole lined surface. The class held its breath; the Grunters almost burst.

Slowly The Sniper's head revolved in Walter's direction. She wanted badly to cane him, but knew The Grove took a dim view of corporal punishment. After a short inward struggle, she handed him a piece of chalk.

"One hundred and fifty lines!" she snapped. "I will not draw dragons in my school-book! Vile boy!" she added, resuming her seat and scanning the terrified faces of her little pupils.

Walter took the white stick, and, with his back to the class, began his laborious task at the chalk-face. To fit one hundred and fifty lines into the limited space was a challenge in itself and Walter knew The Sniper was willing him to fail. He began carefully and steadily, his neat writing and steady arm producing line after line of even, legible sentences. The class began to relax and breathe again. The Grunters began to feel disappointed: they had hoped to see him whipped at least. Walter soldiered on as The Sniper's attacks on the class recommenced but as the afternoon drew on his arm began to tire and his attention began to wander. Billie and Willie held their breaths, nudging and waiting until suddenly Willie's arm shot up.

"Miss Snippet! Miss Snippet!" he cried importantly.

Her cold eyes glared at him.

"What is it, boy?" she asked.

"He's written it wrong, Miss! Look what it sez, Miss!"

The Sniper turned and stared, outrage stiffening her body into the likeness of a praying mantis about to devour the head of its tiny mate. There on the blackboard, in Walter's now faltering hand, stood the defiant lines:

"I will draw dragons in my schoolbooks."

To make things worse, the unevenness of his lettering had produced an unintentionally defiant tone, so that it seemed to say:

"I WILL draw dragons in my schoolbooks."

The class froze but the Grunters had never felt happier. The Sniper lifted her thin cane and advanced on the little potter.

"Hold out your hand," she said.

Walter put his hands inside his pockets.

"I won't be able to make anything if she wrecks my hands!" he thought reasonably. "And it wasn't a deliberate mistake!"

The Sniper screeched and launched herself at him, seizing him by his jumper, but before she could strike the classroom door flew open and in strode Mr. Pinch.

"Ah," he said. "Problems? Stand in the corner, Walter. A word, Miss Snippet?"

The door closed behind the two teachers but no one spoke. When The Sniper returned to the maths class a minute later she was minus the cane and her thin cheeks were decidedly pink.

"You will stay there, Walter," she said coldly, "until I have finished my marking after school and Mr. Slope is ready to lock up. The rest of you – pages 21 to 27. Every sum. Pages 28 to 35 - homework! Willie Grunter! Why is your book defaced! Five hundred lines: I will not deface my schoolbooks!"

The faintest ripple of laughter accompanied Willie to the dusty chalkboard. Huge and red-faced, he shot an angry look at Walter standing amongst the broken chairs on the other side of the blackboard. But Walter didn't look back, nor did he take any joy in his enemy's discomfort as Willie rubbed out Walter's lines and began his own. His great day lay in ruins: he would not be there to see his kiln for the first time with all the others. It was a bitter disappointment indeed.

"But Old Pinch!" he thought. "Saving my bacon like that! Cor!"

At three-thirty his friends trouped out, heads low in sympathy. Miss Snippet sniffed with evident enjoyment, her pen scratching away at her paperwork as the hands on the big clock moved slowly on, each second a minute, each minute an hour. Four o' clock passed and then four- thirty.

"They'll all be there now," Walter thought miserably. "Bill and Thelma, Alf and Potty and Mr. Jollie."

He imagined Bill walking around the kiln with Mr. Jollie, pointing out loose brickwork or examining the flues with Alf.

"I've let people down," he thought and began to worry about his other schoolbooks.

His English and History books bore similar designs: indeed, some of his best dragons ever came between the Tudors and the Stuarts. But in this his anxiety was misplaced, since his other teachers quite coveted these unique and vigorous drawings, several of which were secretly removed leaving Walter with puzzling gaps in his subjects, so that, for example, Elizabeth 1st led straight onto James 2nd and Oliver Cromwell came nowhere at all. Miss Snippet was not liked at the Grove and when Pongy Johnson salted her canister of Earl Grey the next day, no serious attempt was made to find the culprit. By the end of the week she was gone, the lovely Miss Nellie Lush replacing her.

Walter and Willie suffered on until the clock showed six o' clock, when Mr. Slope put his head around the door.

"Locking up," he said peremptorily and that was that, freedom!

Willie knocked the chalk dust off his hands and glowered at Walter.

"I'll have you for this!" he said and vanished.

Walter was surprised to see Sally waiting outside the gates with a large bulky shopping bag in her hand.

"Sorry, Auntie," he said.

"Never mind. Don't do it again," she said. "Potty's been to see me and I know all about it and so do the rest of the team. They've made a start, Walter – but you haven't missed much," she added quickly. "And we're all having a kiln party, a bonfire really, right by the bottle oven! There's baked potatoes already in and I've plenty of cheese and butter in here. Come along dear, let's not waste any more time! Minnie's there already."

"there was his kiln, perfect in its bottle-like rotundity..."

Chapter Nine

An Old Romance

Jollie and Sons was only a short walk from the school, the quickest way being to take a short cut through Bill's allotment. The allotments lay on a ridge of land overlooking the pottery and commanding a wide view of that part of town. The land had been bequeathed to the council in 1910 by George Shufflebottom, a bone merchant, and going to the allotments was known locally as "going round the bottoms". Entered on one side by an arched gateway in a high brick wall, the path through the allotments meandered between plots, some neatly cropped, others less so, until Bill's patch, the neatest of all, gave onto Mr. Jollie's yard through a little yellow gate.

It was a dark afternoon, the far horizon blurry with smoke so that the city's chimneys stood up as black smudgy shapes against a general gloom. The sky was louring too, the sooty clouds giving the feel of a far later winter's evening and Walter felt the first nip of cold. He paused as Sally clicked through the little yellow gate ahead of him, and looked down on the scene below. There was his kiln, perfect in its bottle-like rotundity, black against the blacker factory walls, shadows dancing over its smoky brickwork as the flames of the bonfire leapt up, rivalling the dahlias and chrysanthemums on the allotments in their sunset hues. Walter stood transfixed amongst Bill's cabbages.

"Cor!" he thought happily. "Can it really be happening?"

He pushed through the little gate and crossed the space to the crowd of people gathered around the fire. Potty and Minnie came forward to meet him.

"Ah, Walter, said Potty. Glad you could make it. Er, plenty of paper in my cupboard son. Just help yourself."

"Thanks Potty," said Walter. "Sorry, Auntie Minnie."

There was much laughter and the misery of the afternoon was quickly forgotten amongst all the questions Walter wanted to ask. Bill and Mr. Jollie took him over the kiln with the help of two good torches.

"My grandfather built 'er, Walter," Bill told him proudly. "Bit of work 'ere an' there an' she'll be right as rain. Biggest job'll be altering the doorway to get your vase through! That'll take a bit of doing right enough."

"Marvellous!" said Mr. Jollie, disentangling himself from the overexcited Poos. "Nothing we can't handle, Walter. Sit *down* Jolly Poo!"

"Good oven, this," said Alf, coming up behind them with a big tin mug of tea. "Flues need cleaning out, naturally after all this time." He took a big gulp and then bent down again to examine one of the fire-mouths. "She's alright," he said. "We'll have a test firing first though. No good putting your work inside without doing that first - in a few weeks," he added, looking at Walter's excited face. "Potty can knock up something biggish and then we'll fire that first. Never know in this game," he added sagely. "Many a slip twixt cup and lip."

Walter nodded. He ran his hands over the curved inside of the hovel which swept upwards into utter darkness, row upon row of bricks ascending in a perfect concavity until they narrowed into the neck of the bottle sixty feet above his head.

"All made by hand, these bricks," he thought, and he marvelled at the temperatures that they had withstood, firing after firing, year after year, long after the hands that had made them had turned to dust. Mr. Jollie read his mind.

"Marvellous thing, clay!" he chortled. "Bricks, washbasins, crockery – anything you like! Fired a few things in here, Walter!"

Then he looked sad and Walter knew he was thinking of his sons and the future that they had been denied, all the lovely things that they had never lived to see coming out of the kiln, still warm, still touched by the transformative magic of fire. Jigger Poo jumped up and licked Mr. Jollie's face and Jolly Poo whined softly.

"Quite right! Quite right!" said Mr. Jollie. "Come inside the oven Walter. Some of the old saggars still in there."

They stepped through the narrow opening into the kiln itself. Piled neatly around the circumference, the earthenware saggars were thick with cobwebby dirt and dust. A few lay at their feet and Walter looked inside and saw, to his amazement, the glint of pure white china in the torchlight.

"Something's in here!" he cried.

"Ah, yes, never got around to it," said Mr. Jollie, but before sadness overtook him again Walter began handing the things out and exclaiming over them.

"This is lovely!" he said excitedly, passing a fluted moustache cup to his friend. "And this, and this!"

"Made a lot of those before the war," Mr. Jollie said. "But they went out of fashion afterwards. Don't see chaps with such big moustaches these days. Still got mine of course!"

The Poos wagged their tails and investigated the saggars, pawing and scraping as Walter lifted out more and more lovely wares.

"Look – candlesticks!" he cried, "And – oh – china dogs – and look! Poodles! China poodles!"

"Good Lord! Forgotten about them!" said Mr. Jollie eagerly, holding one in each hand. "Very popular line these – sold thousands. Marvellous! Marvellous! Lot went to America, you know," he said proudly. " But plenty left in the factory too. Finished, perfect! Aunts like a pair, d'you think?"

"I'm sure they would, thank you," said Walter, pleased to see Mr. Jollie so happy again. "But what will you do with all this?"

He gestured at the saggars lining the kiln, full of exquisite white china: all beautiful, all perfect, like long lost treasure in an Egyptian tomb.

"Well, presents of course, presents," Mr. Jollie said, rubbing his nose thoughtfully. "But everything can go on Thelma's stall, bit of a thank you for Bill's hard work, eh Walter?"

Thelma had a china and glass-ware stall at the Victoria Market in Hanley. Walter knew she would be delighted. Suddenly they heard her voice calling them over to the bonfire.

"Come on you lot," she cried. "Taters are ready. Come an' get it!"

Black and crisp, the potatoes had been raked from the edges of the fire, then buttered and covered in crumbly Cheshire cheese. Hot tea and cold ginger beer were passed around and the yard became silent as the food went down. The sky was now black and the yard was black too, except where the little party sat amongst the circle of firelight as the old wood spat and crackled, throwing up flames of turquoise and green where patches of ancient paintwork succumbed to the heat and the fire became creative, filling the dark with stupendous colours, here for a moment and then gone in an instant. Walter thought of the colours of his vase and hoped that Alf's fires would transform them and fix them forever.

Rosie had come along too, smart in her little black coat and hat and dainty in all she did. Sitting next to Walter on an old packing case she ate her potato tidily, unlike Walter whose mouth was soon covered in grease.

"Let's explore," she said, picking up a torch and passing Walter a hanky to wipe his mouth. "Mr. Jollie showed me around inside earlier. Come on, before they say it's time to go home."

The shadows deepened as they moved away from the bonfire. Rosie pushed open a blue door into the factory itself. Even after so many years of neglect the sweet heavy smell of the pot-bank was still there.

"Best smell in the world," thought Walter, breathing deeply.

There it all was, the slip room with its tanks and paddles, the workshops with their throwing wheels and workbenches, the mould- room piled high with plaster casts, and ladders, dust-laden, disappearing up into darkness.

"Look! Look!" they said as their torch-beams made little discoveries: a set of brushes on a bench, a forgotten sponge, a half-turned candlestick forgotten on a lathe, dusty now and crumbling, never to be immortalised by the heat of Mr. Jollie's kiln.

"What's that?" asked Rosie, pointing to a large spoked wheel on a wooden mount.

"Cor!" said Walter. "That's old, that is! Out of the Ark! Somebody used to stand and spin that and it had ropes that went to a potter's wheel and they spun it round for the potter. They don't use them now."

"You know a lot, you do," said Rosie quietly, "but you don't know everything."

"No," said Walter in surprise. "What do you mean?"

Rosie looked down.

"Not sure as I should tell you, really," she said.

"Oh?" Walter wasn't sure he wanted to know.

"Well," said Rosie, bursting to tell and determined to go on even without encouragement. "Why do you think Mr. Jollie's helping you so much?

Walter had wondered about this. He could see for himself that his new friend had cheered up a great deal since the incident with Gwenny and the cubs and he knew it meant a lot to Mr. Jollie to be feeling so much better. And he did seem to know Auntie Minnie – but even so....

"He's known your Auntie Minnie a long time," said Rosie quietly.

"I gathered that," said Walter, feeling a little uncomfortable.

"Since they were young," Rosie went on. "Your Auntie Minnie and her friend Esther were great pals with Mr. Jollie and his younger brother Robert. They was always out dancing and socialising. My mum was tweeny with that family before me – an' my nan before her. In the nineties this was. Not much our family doesn't know about the Jollies; they've always been good employers. My mum was really pleased when I was took on."

Walter said nothing. He wasn't sure where this was going, but he was curious, nevertheless.

"Well, anyway," Rosie continued, a little uncertainly - she didn't want to offend her new friend. "Robert Jollie was very sweet on your Auntie Minnie an' she liked him a lot, nan says. He was a clever man too, a botanist. He travelled all over the world collecting plants 'n' flowers for people. Some of his trees are in Biddulph Grange!"

Walter raised his eyebrows and Rosie took this as encouragement.

"But my nan says that Mr. Jollie, our Mr. Jollie, was in love with her too, but never stood a chance against Robert, so he always kept quiet about it. But nan could tell. She felt sorry for him."

Walter's eyebrows had by now disappeared into his fringe. He had never for an instant imagined any of his aunts having a romantic past.

"So what happened?" he heard himself say.

"Robert was due to go on a long expedition to the Pacific Islands," said Rosie. "Polynesia, wherever that is! And he asked your Auntie Minnie to marry him when he got back. She was over the moon, my nan said. Everyone knew about it."

"Cor!" said Walter.

"Yes," said Rosie, "But they was never properly engaged. No ring or anything. My nan didn't like that. She thought he was a bit of a chancer – an' he was!" Rosie's face was flushed and angry. "He never came back! He met a Polynesian lady an' married her instead!"

Walter's mouth had travelled in the opposite direction to his eyebrows and now hung open in disbelief.

"It's all true, Walter, I wouldn't tell you a lie," said Rosie, looking at him kindly, peering into his face in the little pool of light cast by their torches.

Darkness lay all around them, and darkness lay outside too, the damp sooty darkness of a Potteries evening. In the silence of the big empty room they could still hear laughter in the yard outside, though the crackle of the bonfire had subsided. Rosie knew it would be over soon.

"Should I be hearing all this?" Walter thought, but he did want to know the end of the story. "It was a long time ago," he mused, "and it's turned out alright in the end. Thanks to my dragon!"

"Was Auntie Minnie very upset?" he asked.

"She was very dignified, Thelma says, but yes, it did hit her hard. But she's like the rest of your aunties, Walter, very strong. Not the sort to go off into a decline," Rosie said. "The trouble was, Robert never came back an' explained it all to her. An' he never wrote either. That was rotten, that was. An' Mr. Jollie, Edward Jollie, he was so distressed about it he didn't know what to do. He was proper embarrassed by his brother, nan says, an' he really went downhill for a bit. Felt his brother had shamed him, though it wasn't his fault, not at all."

"So why didn't he and Auntie Minnie speak for ages?" asked Walter. He had learnt that much, at least.

"Well," said Rosie, "this is the worstest bit. Minnie went round to our Mr. Jollie a couple of weeks after she'd learnt from Thelma that Robert was married an' all. I suppose she wanted some answers. Anyway, she went round to Prospect House an' they was given cakes an' tea by nan. Very difficult atmosphere, she said."

"I can imagine," said Walter sympathetically.

"Yes. An' then it got a whole lot worse," said Rosie. "Mr. Jollie had apologised on his brother's behalf, though it weren't his fault, and apologised for not coming to see her."

"So what went wrong?" asked Walter, puzzled.

"Well, Mr. Jollie had been in love with Minnie for so long, he couldn't stop himself. He proposed right then and there! Minnie was upset! She felt her feelings hadn't been taken into consideration. She is very proud, your auntie, Walter. Nan says she left in a hurry and Mr. Jollie was left feeling much worse than before!"

Walter couldn't make head or tail of it.

"Didn't she like Mr. Jollie?" he asked.

"Of course she did!" cried Rosie. "But she'd *loved* Robert! Our nan says she must have felt like a cup of tea being passed around when Edward proposed. That's why she got so cross over it. It was bad timing. It wasn't tactful, like. Anyway, that was it. They was both so embarrassed they didn't meet again an' if they was passing on the street they looked the other way. Very sad really, because Minnie was fond of him an' he'd really loved her."

Walter was stunned, though he struggled to understand all the feelings involved which Rosie seemed so at home with.

"So he wants to make it up to Auntie Minnie?" he said at last.

"Of course! He's missed her all these years - decades, Walter! He knew he couldn't ask her again…. Though perhaps if he'd waited long enough…."

"But he married someone," said Walter.

"Yes, and a good job too. He was very happy with Florence," said Rosie, "But she died when the twins were young, and then he lost them in the war as well...."

Rosie's voice trailed off and they stood in silence.

"But he's been talking about nothing but your vase!" said Rosie suddenly. "So don't think it's all because of him and Minnie. He's over the moon to have a big project like this. "Marvellous!" he keeps saying. "Marvellous! Marvellous!" You've made a great friend there, Walter! Come on! Let's join the others!"

"You know a lot, but you don't know everything..."

Chapter Ten

Hands Like Soup Tureens

Walter was up especially early the next day. He had arranged to meet Bill at the bottle oven so that he could see, in daylight, the restoration work that would have to be done. He ran through the allotments and saw Bill leaning a long ladder up against the oven; more long ladders lay on the ground close by, with all Bill's tools and bags of sand and cement.

"Hello Bill," said Walter. "It's a long way up!"

"Oh, dunner worry," said Bill. "It's meat an' drink to me, lad. See that up there?" he pointed to a twiggy branch which was growing out near the neck of the bottle. Walter nodded. "That's what happens when things get left alone," Bill went on. "Nature takes over. But she's alright, by an' large. Oh look, here's Alf."

Alf had come in by the little alleyway.

"Morning Bill, morning Walter," he said, sucking his teeth and looking up at the kiln. Five minutes ago, a bus driver had stopped and wound down his window.

"Not much pressure then, Alf?" he'd said laughing. "I've heard it's as big as my bus!"

There was no spite in it: everyone wished him well and everyone wanted to see the great dragon vase come out of the kiln in one perfect piece but, thought Alf, "The pressure is on!"

He had fired thousands of bottle ovens in his time but he had never felt so anxious, the stakes had never seemed so high as they did now.

Bill looked at his friend.

"Dunner worry, mate," he said. "There'll be at least half a dozen of us working on her. We'll get them flues sorted.

She's a good oven, this one. Off yer go, Walter lad. Don't be late. Yer don't want more lines!"

Had Walter glanced up at the allotments he would have seen Pongy waiting for him on top of the ridge, but, fearing to be late, he hared off through the little alley in the hope of shaving a few seconds off his journey. Running around the corner of a packing yard he crashed straight into the Grunter twins who seized him in an instant and pinned him up against a wall.

"Gotcha! You little twerp!" crowed Billie, shoving his sweaty red face into Walter's.

Walter twisted and squirmed in the grip of their great meaty fists but they had him as in a vice.

"Check his pockets," said Billie. "See what he's got."

Willie plunged into Walter's blazer pockets and came up with a dragon's head, two old bus tickets and a semi-sucked gobstopper covered in blazer felt.

"Is that it?" roared Billie, plastering Walter even more forcefully against the brickwork. "Look in his other pockets, bruv!"

Willie turfed out the pockets of Walter's shorts. There was nothing, not even a clean hanky.

"You useless little maggot," he bellowed, dropping the dragon's head and crushing it underfoot.

Walter struggled harder but the knobbles on his spine were scraping against the brickwork.

"Let's push him in the cut!" said Billie. "Same as last summer!" and he jerked Walter forward by his collar.

"Gerroff!" he shouted. "Gerroff! Gerroff! "Gerroff!"

And suddenly, they did.

"Ooooffff!" said Billie.

"Ooff-ooff!" agreed Willie.

The burly frames of two warehousemen had the twins squashed up against the wall, tighter than apples in a cider press.

84

"On yer way, Walter," said one and off he went, caught up at the end of the street by an anxious Pongy Johnson with Stephen Smallbody and his sister in tow.

"Taste of your own medicine, eh?" said the bigger of the two men as the twins heaved and quivered in their grips. "Let 'em go George," he said. "But," he went on, prodding Willie with a finger like a small iron bar, "George 'ere is a special constable, aren't yer George?"

"I am," said the handsome young man. "You had better not cross my path again!"

"Right!" said the other. "If we see yer after Walter again, yer really for it!" The finger jabbed Willie's chest. "Got it?"

The twins nodded.

"Push off then, yer rotten little apples," he said, wiping his hands on his dusty apron.

The twins were late for school by ten minutes and having no convincing explanation were given an hour's detention at the end of the day, during which they were asked to sweep the playground.

"Have you noticed," said Willie angrily, "That the more we have a go, the worse off we seem to come?"

"We do bruv!" agreed Billie. "But I don't fancy telling her we haven't tried!"

He swept harder to get done more quickly as Mr. Slope carefully inspected the ground that they had covered, tutting here and there at the odd overlooked leaf.

"It's just not the fun it used to be!" he thought as they handed back the brooms at the end of their hour's penance. "Why's she got it in for the little twerp anyway? He's never got anything worth nicking. What's up with her?"

§

That week and the next one saw Walter busy with his coiling and his mould making. Every free minute was spent in the craft and clay room, well wrapped up against the cold. As time went on he began to worry that he would never accomplish his task, and that it would never be done for Christmas. On the Friday before half-term Potty came in with a broad smile on his face.

"Good news, Walter!" he said. "Mr. Pinch is allowing you the full use of this room over the half term, if you would like it, son."

"Cor Potty!" cried Walter. "I can model my full-size vase then! Will you be here?"

"Some of the time, yes," said Potty. "Mr. Slope will be here too and you will have your friends of course. No need to be solitary."

"Oh, that's alright," said Walter happily. "I can model my full-sized dragon when you come back and then we can make all the casts. But how shall I keep my vase damp, Potty? All that time?"

"Pack it inside with wet newspaper," said Potty, "And I'll bring you some large cotton sheets to soak and lay over it. Should be alright if Mr. Slope turns off the radiators."

Potty also told Walter that he would be receiving several deliveries of a better type of clay for his ultimate dragon vase.

"Ground with stone," he said, "to make it stronger. Slip too, of course."

§

The week of half-term was a momentous one for Walter. On the Monday morning he was waiting impatiently for Mr. Slope outside the blue doors at eight-thirty but it wasn't until half-past nine that he spotted Harry Mudd trundling the heavy barrow of clay across the playground, a gaunt hollow-eyed youth with hands the size of soup tureens. He was the thinnest person Walter had ever seen.

"Gorra delivery for Mr. Potterton," Harry said. "About, is 'e?"

"Er, no, I'm afraid not," Walter replied, eyeing the contents of the barrow eagerly. "But that's for me, I think."

"Dunner tell me I've lumped this lot half a mile fer a little kid!" Harry said in disgust, thumping the barrow down just outside the blue doors. He lit a thin cigarette. "Waste of my bloody time!" he said, coughing.

Walter never met belligerence with more of the same.

"I've got some sandwiches inside," he said. "We can share them and I'll show you my work."

Harry quickly pushed the barrow up the step and into the craft and clay room. All around stood Walter's prototypes in different shapes and sizes and alongside them were his many dragon forms: spiky dragons, scaly dragons, dragons with wings and dragons without. It was wonderful but Harry noticed none of it.

"What's in them sandwiches?" he asked.

"Beef and tomato," said Walter, handing the whole lot over. "You're very welcome."

They disappeared in a trice, showing up as large knots in Harry's throat as he worked them down.

"Bit of alright, that," he said, rubbing a grubby soup tureen over his mouth. "Gorrenything else?

Walter found a dusty fruit pastille in his blazer pocket and handed it over. Finally, Harry's gaze came to rest on a tiny dragon's foot lying next to a pot of brushes. It was immaculate in every detail: the ankle joint with its knobbly bones, the tendons stretching tautly to the grasping toes, the vicious curving claws that dug into Harry's palm as he picked it up carefully and held it in one of his great bony hands. Harry touched the minute scales with the gentlest of forefingers.

"You made this, did yer, Walter?" he asked.

Walter nodded.

"An' all the rest?"

Walter nodded again.

"S' brilliant. S'workerart. S'bettern bloody Wedgwood," he said, "all them bloody nymphs an' things."

He lit another cigarette, carefully blowing the smoke away from the little foot.

"Anything yer want, Walter, an' I'll gerrit fer yer. Just lerrus know."

Walter was overwhelmed.

"I've always got sandwiches," he said, "And most of the time I forget to eat them. You're always welcome."

And so a new and lasting friendship was born. Day by day Harry arrived with his barrow loads of clay and hour by hour, the vase rose from its board on the floor as Walter coiled and stuck, cross-hatched and smoothed, his fingers nimble and adept, all his former hard work making them so practised and sure that the gigantic vase bloomed beneath his hands, strong and beautiful. As it grew, Mr. Slope and Potty arranged stepladders and planks around it so that Walter could build the vase upwards and then inwards, Potty often holding onto the little potter as he leaned out from the ladders which Mr. Slope and George steadied and kept firm.

"I couldn't have done it without you all," said Walter towards the end of the week, when he and Mr. Slope were discussing the likelihood of a weekend victory by The Vale as they shrouded the vast vase in its wet sheets. "I'd never have done it without all those ladders and things."

Mr. Slope had undergone something of a transformation, albeit not inside a bottle oven. He had read Alan Padder's first article with a certain amount of contempt but when people began to stop him in the street to ask about the progress of the magnificent vase, Mr. Slope started to draw himself up and impress upon his listeners the importance of his own role in the enterprise.

"He's refining the dragon's tail," he might say loftily, or "Of course temperature and humidity are key, but I don't begrudge the hours I put in. Not at all."

People would shake his hand and go away even more curious than before.

At the end of the half term break, Alan Padder came to see Walter again and Mr. Slope managed to get into the back of the photograph of Walter standing with his mountainous vase.

BIGGEST POT EVER!

,,... The Sentinel shouted on its third page that night. This time the reporter had taken pains to describe Walter's designs in great detail and to provide not only a large clear photograph of his massive vase but also an account of the marvellous dragon he would soon be making too.

All over the city people read with interest and growing excitement. Before long they started to turn up at The Grove, where they would knock politely at the blue doors and ask to see Walter at work. Mr. Slope now felt elevated to the position of Guardian of the Vase.

"Step away from the Vase please," he would growl, should anyone approach too closely. But Walter was always more than happy to talk to people and enjoyed the new friends he made. One day he noticed an exceptionally grubby little girl standing with her equally grubby parents.

It took him a moment to place her and then he said, "Hello, Margaret. Fancy seeing you!"

"We've come to see yer vase," she said, "But really, don't you think it'd be better with an an 'orse on top instead?"

Thus, the Grunter twins found it harder than ever to get at Walter, guarded as he was by the Dragon Knights and, it seemed to them, by almost everybody else in the neighbourhood too. The more they failed the more they hated him, and they saw too a change for the worse in Old Ma, whose antagonism knew no bounds so that Billie and Willie had begun to dread going home at the end of the day, hanging about instead in doorways and alleyways, incurring always scathing looks and shaken heads from those passing by. They itched to get inside the craft and clay room but it was always too closely guarded, even during half term. Mr. Slope had suddenly become very protective, and, worse than that, George Brittain, the special constable, was his nephew.

"Alright boys?" their father would say when they finally showed up.

"Alright Dad," they would answer, giving their mother a sideways smile as she cleaned the counters or swept up the sawdust on the floor.

"You'd better hurry," she would say, barely looking at them. "She had your tea ready ages ago."

§

On the last afternoon of the half term Mr. Pinch went to see Walter in the craft and clay room. He stopped short in astonishment as he walked through the door. There in the middle of the room was the most enormous pot he had ever seen. Smoothly finished, Walter had coiled it strongly so that it held its curves beautifully. Walter was busy up a set of step ladders, stuffing wet newspaper down inside the huge vessel.

"Going well, Walter?" Mr. Pinch asked, finding it hard to keep a note of admiration out of his voice but as determined as ever to appear severe and unapproachable.

Walter climbed down.

"Yes sir," he said. "I have to put these wet cloths over it now so it doesn't dry out."

He remounted the ladder but struggled to open up the cloth and fling it over the vase.

Mr. Pinch found himself saying, "Let me help you," and together they swathed the gigantic pot, whose rim exceeded the height of Mr. Pinch himself.

"It must be seven feet tall!" he exclaimed, stepping back as Walter fussed with the draperies, ensuring every part of the clay was cold and wet.

"And then the dragon on top of that," Walter said, matter of factly.

Mr. Pinch was struck dumb. He thought he had understood Walter's magnificent project but now that it was half made he was taken aback by the sheer size of the thing, its technical accomplishment, its marvellous virtuosity. He studied the drawings on the walls and looked again at the many small model dragons that lay here and there around the room. It suddenly dawned on him that Walter was now in a race against time to model and cast his full-sized dragon, let alone attach it to the vase. Nothing must be allowed to dry, that much he was sure of.

"Ask your Auntie Minnie if she will come to see me on Monday," he said. "There is something I need to ask her."

Walter nodded. "Yes sir," he said.

There was something Walter himself had been wanting to ask his headmaster for a few days now. He had begun to feel troubled at the cost of his dragon vase. All that coal to come from Mr. Jollie and now all this special clay. He looked at the floor and scrubbed his toe over a patch of wet slip.

"Mr. Pinch, sir," he said awkwardly. "All this clay? Tons of it, sir? "Who's paying for it, sir?"

Mr. Pinch blushed. A great wave of red swept up from his boots, encompassing his knees and his belly and pouring out from the top of his collar and into his cheeks and nose. As Walter watched, his Headmaster grew redder and redder until his handsome face seemed to burn with a fiery light in the grey room. Beads of sweat trickled down his forehead, gathered on his brow and crept down his nose onto his moustache.

Walter watched in astonishment. "Cor!" he thought. "I think Old Pinch's bought it for me! I never would've thought that!"

"Er, thank you very much, sir," he began, "I didn't expect...."

"Walter!" roared Mr. Pinch. "Do you think The Grove cannot afford a bit of clay now and again? Do you think the Board of Education, in its Infinite Wisdom, cannot provide a small boy with a means to an end?"

He strode to the door.

"Your thanks duly noted," he added before disappearing from Walter's astonished sight.

Walter rechecked the wet cloths and then went home but Mr. Pinch sat with his head in his hands, his heart pounding, waiting until the crimson tide had ebbed from his face before he could walk home.

"Never show any familiarity" had been his motto in the trenches and he was unable to abandon it now. Personal favours could never be discovered: they hadn't been then and they couldn't be now. Insubordination in war had been unthinkable and so he had maintained his distance - and he did so now. But his letters home from the front, dutiful and loving as they had been, were yet shopping lists which he had begged his sisters to fill, so that they had shopped for chocolate and cigarettes or any little luxury that could be had in war-time England. They had knitted gloves, socks, scarves, mufflers and puttees, anything to alleviate the suffering of his men in the water filled dugouts amongst the terrible mud of the Western Front.

Packed with care and sent to the regiment, these boxes had been forwarded to the trenches until, battered but whole, they had reached Mr. Pinch and his troops. Given anonymously, the lieutenant had smiled as he distributed the gifts to the lice-ridden soldiers, who, always looking the other way, had thanked Captain Pinch in their hearts and respected his secret. Of course they had known! If only Captain Pinch had opened his eyes he would have seen that loyalty and deep admiration, rather than mere discipline, bound his men to him in an unshakable bond, to be broken only by death. He had led by example and taken no special privileges for himself, guarding the meagre rights of his men fiercely and alleviating their conditions as best he could. He had been loved and respected, as much for his kindnesses as for his bravery and self-sacrifice. But four years of war had wound John Pinch tighter than ever and now he looked on with envy at those, who, like Miss Lush, easily and charmingly commanded both respect and love from their small charges whilst he himself felt cut off from the school, the lonely Head that bore the crown.

Mr. Pinch set off through the autumnal streets, past the blackened church with its slender yellow sycamores, up the hill and alongside the park where the leaves had turned to the colours in Mr. Pinch's paintbox. He looked a little happier.

"I'll paint them this weekend," he thought. "Bright autumnal colours against a blue grey sky!"

He hurried into his house facing the park and went straight to his painting materials upstairs. His spare room was his studio, never being used in any other capacity. Mr. Pinch lived alone, and, truth to tell, he was a lonely man.

"hands the size of soup tureens..."

Chapter Eleven
A Chip Or Two

Walter was exhausted. He had slept for twelve hours and had missed an outing to see Tom Mix at the Regent with Pongy and Lefty. It had been "Riders of the Purple Sage", one of Walter's favourites, and he was really disappointed when he woke up. It wasn't just the film he had missed, it was all the fun of throwing popcorn and ice-lolly sticks down onto the unfortunates in the stalls below, often onto the Grunters themselves.

Walter stretched and smiled. Perhaps he could do that next Saturday instead - on his birthday! He lay luxuriating in the warmth of the little bed, rubbing his fingers which still ached from his week's tremendous work. He had done it! His massive vase, which just six weeks ago existed only as black lines on paper, now stood taller than Potty, taller even than Mr.Pinch, and wider in circumference than the linked arms of three grown men. He snuggled down, sure that Sally would soon call him for his dinner. He began to marshal his thoughts, planning his use of time over the weeks ahead. But there was still so much to be done and all the time the worry that the clay might dry, the clay might crack and his magnificent vase would crumble and decay before his beautiful dragon could even alight upon it.

§

Auntie Minnie knocked on Mr. Pinch's door at ten o' clock on Monday morning. When she was seated with a cup of tea in her hand, Mr. Pinch outlined his plans to help Walter accomplish his goal in time.

"So, no more lessons this term," he said finally. "Except when he can do nothing – when it is inside the kiln, for example. All the rest of the time, and evenings too, as now of course, to be spent in the craft and clay room, aided by Mr. Potterton and his, er, associates."

Minnie was quite taken aback. Lessons were sacrosanct!

"Not a wise decision, surely, Mr. Pinch," she asked sharply, tapping her neat little foot on the parquet floor. "He is already behind with his maths."

Fortunately, Minnie had not seen Walter's history or geography books with their odd gaps and dragons instead of maps or she would have been concerned about those subjects too. But Mr. Pinch was quite sure that a boy like Walter would always find his way around the world, should he ever need to do so. He stood up and walked around his desk to Minnie.

"Madam – Minnie," he said, taking her little gloved hand in his. "This is really something quite, er, unusual. I wonder if you have realised...."

And Minnie suddenly wondered if she had. There had been so much to think about, what with her memories of Robert and her renewed friendship with Edward, the finding of the kiln, the gift of the glazes – it had been so much for a person to take in, she thought. "No wonder I've lost sight of the vase itself with everything that has gone on around it," she mused, staring down at the little cup and saucer. "But I bet Louie hasn't. Bless her!"

"Very well, Mr. Pinch," Minnie said, more amenably. "A little homework at the weekends then, but mainly he needs to be out in the fresh air. And please Headmaster, by no means let it all go to his head. A big vase is one thing, a big-headed child is quite another! Goodbye, Mr. Pinch."

Mr. Pinch saw Minnie to the door. He knew Walter's auntie very well and admired her enormously. He watched her cross the playground, very smart and upright in her tight cloche hat and her low-waisted coat.

"What a pity she never married," he thought, picking up the morning's registers. "I must be doing something right," he said to himself. "No absences at all that half term!"

§

"Nice man," thought Minnie, dusting a smear of chalk off her glove. "Pity he never married."

And off she went to see Thelma at the market for more news of the kiln.

The Victoria Market was a cosy warren of colourful stalls which sold almost everything that Sally and Minnie needed for the little house at the top of the hill. Thelma's china and glass stall was right in the middle, and Minnie squeezed herself in through the narrow gap at the side and sat down on one of the two fold-up, fold-down chairs. Thelma was discreetly finishing a pork pie - since Mr. Jollie's gift of the lovely bone china she had been rushed off her feet. Customers were regularly three deep at her stall, so she had to seize her moments for lunch and a cup of tea.

"Morning Minnie," she mumbled, wiping her lips on a cut-work napkin from Daphne's over the way. "How's Walter doing?"

"Well, Thelma , thank you," Minnie replied, pouring herself a cup of tea from her thermos. "He's actually finished the vase now. Over seven feet tall, believe it or not!"

"Cor!" said Thelma. "*Seven feet!*"

"I know!" said Minnie. "It's really all getting a bit beyond me, this vase of his. We thought it was extraordinary at first – all that rushing off, not eating, not sleeping. Worried us to death. Then he seemed to settle down and get on with it a bit more steadily – but now!"

Minnie took a sip of her tea and looked dazedly over the rim of her cup.

"Too be honest," she said quietly, "it's only just dawned on me what's happening. John Pinch has cancelled Walter's classes! I ask you Thelma, who'd have thought it? Our Walter making something so - so – and at his age too! I can hardly believe it!"

"Well it's about time you did catch on, Minnie," laughed Thelma. "People talk of nothing else. It's always, "I'll have a poodle, Thelma, and 'ow's Walter getting on?" The world an' his wife knows about that dragon vase – an' our Bill's part in it too!" Thelma added proudly. "Umpteen times a day I'm 'aving to give updates on that bottle oven: what needs doing to it? When's the test firing? I 'ave to go over it brick by brick with Bill in bed at night so's I can answer all their questions! I should say it is time you caught on, Minnie!"

"Well of course," sniffed Minnie, "I did find the kiln for him but we've been more worried about him keeping body and soul together than anything else!"

Thelma smiled. She unwrapped two almond slices and passed one to her friend.

"Wonderful, though, isn't it Minnie," she said, patting Minnie's hand. "A proper little Potteries' boy he is! Everybody's behind him. Except them Grunters," she added, her face darkening. "'ad that Old Ma in 'ere this morning. Pure poison she is. Dropped one of them little moustache cups – on purpose mind!"

"Oh dear!" laughed Minnie. "And she needs one as well!"

"Minnie!" screamed Thelma. "I've never heard you say anything like that before!"

"Well, it's true enough," said Minnie grimly. "You know how she's been behind those boys all the time, egging them on from one bad deed to another. You know they had Walter the other day again, don't you?"

Thelma nodded. Everyone knew.

"Lucky George and Fred were there," she said.

"Very lucky," agreed Minnie. "I've been and thanked them. I taught George, you know," she added, draining her cup daintily. "He was a lovely boy, really lovely – and he's a splendid young man now."

"'e is an' all," agreed Thelma, getting up as the crowds began to gather again. "A bit of a bobby-dazzler alright! Our Rosie's really struck on 'im, an' I think the feeling's mutual!"

Minnie smiled at the thought of this young romance and sighed softly. She watched as the pennies and shillings changed hands and pin-trays, poodles and candlesticks were picked up, whispered about, then passed over to Thelma to be wrapped up in The Sentinel.

"Mind you," Thelma continued, plumping down again when the crowd had passed, "'is mother was a lovely woman too. Remember 'er, Minnie? Esther Brittain? Beautiful woman, as I remember."

"She was, Thelma, she was," said Minnie quite sadly. "A great friend too, when I was young. And a wonderful mother. She gave George the best start in life a boy could have. Not like"- and here Minnie grimaced and made a twisted gesture - "those twins don't stand a chance, nasty as they are! Their mother's alright in a passive sort of way, but with a grandmother like that, whatever will become of them?"

"That's not your worry, Minnie!" said the ever-practical Thelma. "Let 'em get on with it. You've enough on your plate as it is."

As she spoke, a small female figure appeared in the entrance to the market, hovered uncertainly, then made her way cautiously towards Thelma's stall, stopping often to look at other stalls on the way in an unconvincing, abstracted manner, as if her mind were somewhere else entirely.

"Look Minnie!" whispered Thelma. "See little Edna Robbin over there? This must be the tenth time she's been in 'ere in five days!"

Minnie and Thelma both knew Edna Robbin, the little washer-woman of Snowflake Street. Beautiful and sweet-natured in her youth, Edna had won the hearts of young men for miles around, but had married her childhood sweetheart at sixteen and had born him seven sons by the time she was twenty- five. Her husband she had lost in Hanley Deep Pit, and her sons in the Great War. Not one was left.

Edna had been bereft and penniless, almost the poorest of the poor. Everyone had sought to help her but Edna was proud and struggled with her grief alone, taking charity from no one, but instead passing the years between the copper and the dolly- tub, a red-haired wraith amid the soap and the steam, whose fair skin was made translucent by their actions so that at sixty her face was girlish still, though her hands and arms were reddened and sore.

A passer-by, peering over Edna's wall, might have thought himself in a fairy tale, as the steamy coppers boiled in the blackened yard and the elfin figure moved amongst and around, stirring, rubbing, lifting, scrubbing; now revealed by the flapping white sheets hung up to dry in the smoky air, now hidden from view by those same sheets and the steam and the smoke of the place. But Edna's life was no fairy tale. No luxuries passed her threshold and she had on her walls only the photographs of those she had lost, and those she loved still.

"It's them poodles," whispered Thelma. "She comes twice a day an' asks me if she can 'andle 'em, thanks me, an' puts 'em back an' goes away. I'd give 'er a pair gladly but she's a worker, is Edna. Never asked anyone for owt in 'er life."

"Poor thing," murmured Minnie.

She and her sisters loved the pair Mr. Jollie had given them. They were so bold and life-like, so fine in their making, so real in their expressiveness; the paintress had caught the light in their eyes and the wetness of their noses. Neither Minnie nor Thelma could envisage a house without china: in this town of all towns a home devoid of china was a home devoid of life, or so it seemed to them.

"I'd willingly buy her a pair, Thelma," Minnie said softly.

"No good, Minnie, you'd offend her," said Thelma, shaking her head.

"Haven't you got damaged pair?" asked Minnie hopefully. "Something she could afford?"

Thelma's head went down and Minnie hushed. Edna was now right by the stall.

"Can I help you, Mrs. Robbin?" Thelma asked politely.

"May I see the poodles again, please?" asked Edna shyly.

Thelma reached and handed her a pair, one for each work-roughened hand. They were large figures and Edna clasped them firmly around their middles. She looked at them, rapt, drawing them close, studying them quietly.

At last she asked,"Er, how much are these dogs a pair, please?"

Thelma sweated.

"Well, er, Mrs. Robbin, I've been asking one an' six a pair, but, well, they was give me, as everyone knows an' understands, so I could do 'em a bit less you know, no skin off my nose, like," she said, all in one breath.

A faint flush suffused the delicate skin of Edna's cheeks, tinting them with colour, as the brush of a paintress enlivens the ivory cheeks of a figurine.

"Oh no, thank you Thelma," she said, handing the poodles back hurriedly. "Very kind. No thank you."

"Never mind, duck," said Thelma awkwardly. But then she said, "I don't suppose you'd be interested in taking any of these damaged 'uns off my 'ands, would you? I've a box of 'em under 'ere," and reaching down she pulled a poodle from a cardboard box, giving it a sharp tap against the table leg as she did so.

Minnie, anticipating her, broke into a sudden fit of coughing.

"They're still nice," said Thelma, handing Edna a poodle now sporting a small chip on the inside of its left hind paw. "But people are very fussy – I mean, neither me nor Minnie minds a chip or two, do we Minnie?"

Minnie shook her head quickly.

"And it's a shame for them to just sit there," Thelma went on, turning to Minnie for support.

"There's another one here," said Minnie, and bending forward in another fit of coughing she gave a second poodle a sharp rap against her vacuum flask. "Cracked front leg," she said brightly. "Bit of a shame but not very noticeable if you stand it the other way around. Pity people are so fussy.... lovely thing."

She passed it to Edna. The damage was indeed very slight and to a true lover of beautiful things perhaps of no real importance. Thelma and Minnie held their breaths. Minnie covered her anxiety with more coughing and Thelma began to bustle, needlessly moving her stock around, tutting and puffing, and looking anywhere but at Edna.

Finally, "Er, how much are you asking for this pair, Thelma?" was the almost whispered question they had been hoping for.

Sweat broke out afresh on Thelma's brow and she suddenly felt very damp under her armpits. Rapidly she tried to calculate the weekly rate of laundry minus outgoings....

"What about fourpence?" she stuttered, then as Edna's face clouded and she began to pass the poodles back, "Or, well, sixpence then! That's fair, isn't it, Minnie?" she said desperately.

"Very fair," nodded Minnie, smiling as the hands bearing the poodles retreated close to Edna's breast.

"Then I'll take them, thank you Thelma," said Edna, her face breaking into a beautiful smile. "Thank you very much."

Thelma, turning away to hide her furious blushes, wrapped the poodles well, each one in a protective shell of old Sentinels. Edna tucked them tenderly well down inside her old cloth bag.

"What'll you name them?" asked Minnie kindly. "Our two are Ellen and Doris. Lady dogs of course!"

Edna paused, caught out. Seven poodles she could have named in an instance – but two?

"What are the names of the two I see with Mr. Jollie," she asked Minnie politely. "They *are* lovely dogs."

"They are indeed - and very lively!" laughed Minnie. "Jolly-Poo and Jigger-Poo. Very appropriate of course," she replied.

"Jigger and Jolly," mused Edna. Then brightening she said, "I think Soap and Water would be more appropriate for these two!"

Thelma and Minnie laughed.

"Have you been to see what Minnie's nephew is doing?" Thelma asked.

"I've been following him in the paper," said Edna shyly, "but I haven't liked to go round there, as some do." She stood awkwardly. "I think it's wonderful," she said.

"Do go, Edna," said Minnie. "I don't think you've really met Walter since he was very small. Do go – he'd love to show you, Edna."

Thelma and Minnie watched the retreating figure, carefully shepherding her precious bag through the afternoon throng.

"I've never seen 'er so 'appy," said Thelma, "An 'an all for a couple of china dogs. God bless her."

Minnie packed away her thermos and said goodbye to Thelma, making her way quickly across town to the meat market for the evening meal. As she bought the chops and watched them being wrapped in greaseproof paper, Minnie was not unaware of the ease of her own life and the daily soapy struggle of little Edna Robbin's.

"Edna's life was no fairy tale..."

Chapter Twelve

An Imminent Arrival

Mr. Jollie had not been so vigorous in years. He sprang out of bed in the mornings like a young poodle, eager for the day ahead. Rosie was now having to rise at five-thirty to prepare his breakfast, shine his shoes and have his overcoat brushed and ready in the hallway.

Before visiting Bill at the bottle oven, it was now Mr. Jollie's habit to drive out with Mr. Beany and Gwenny on their early morning rounds, delivering dry goods to the little shops all over town.

"Mind if I drive, Beany?" he would say as the pale faced grocer surrendered his place and handed the reins to the elderly gentleman.

"Must get the hang of it before Dragon arrives, y'know!" Mr. Jollie would cry, as Gwenny, always resistant to his aids, ploughed headlong towards oncoming vehicles, so that the drivers, white visaged and disbelieving, had to wrench their wheels violently, their narrow tyres skidding on the damp cobbles.

"Wretched cars!" he would cry, undaunted, though Mr. Beany went paler still.

"Trot on, Gwenny!" Mr. Jollie would declare, gathering Gwenny's reins and urging her on afresh.

"Out of the habit a bit now! But getting the hang of it though, eh, old girl?" he would cry, pleased with himself as Gwenny yet again launched forward with scant regard for cyclists or pedestrians, scattering schoolchildren before her like leaves in the wind.

Mr. Beany was a phlegmatic man, used to Gwenny's caprices, but his nerves were severely tested by these early morning adventures and he was looking forward to the arrival of Dragon, when Mr. Jollie would have a horse of his own to manage, as best he could. A box was being prepared for Dragon in the store's stable-yard, right next to Gwenny's. Having no stables of his own, Mr. Jollie had entered into a mutually beneficial arrangement with the grocer, a man who had not fully faced up to the prospect of having an eighteen-hand Dragon on his property. Enquiries put to his brother at Endon, regarding Dragon's progress and his fitness for driving in harness, usually elicited a cautious reply.

"He's, er, not, er, unlike Gwenny in his disposition," Patrick Beany would say. "Very forward going. Bit sharp, like."

And Mr. Beany would have to reconcile himself to waiting a little longer to be free from the daily terrors of Mr. Jollie's equestrian arts.

Mr. Jollie had made the journey out to Endon several times to see his great black horse.

"He's marvellous, Walter! Marvellous!" he would tell his little friend as they visited Gwenny in her stable, where Mr. Jollie would pat the white mare, feeding her sugar, whilst Walter stood quietly, softly stroking the velvety muzzle and the wide soft nostrils.

Mr. Jollie always called into The Grove last thing, as Walter was finishing his day's work. Together they would walk up the hill to Mr. Beany's yard, sometimes with a Dragon Knight in attendance, or sometimes just the two of them, deep in conversation about Walter's dragon and the moulds he was making, the fineness of his castings and the technical difficulties of fitting the dragon to the gigantic vase. Mr. Jollie brought Walter all the news from the kiln so that he knew exactly how Bill and Alf were progressing in their renovation and remodelling.

And every day, they would stop and discuss it all with Mr. Bateman at number sixty-six, a mould-maker of many years' experience, an unexpected ally and an invaluable helpmate in the craft and clay room.

"You've come a long way, Walter," he said one Tuesday night, as Walter and Mr. Jollie paused once more to confer with him. "You've made a bit of progress since them days when yer used to fly past me with yer 'ead in the clouds!

It was true. For two weeks now Walter had been bringing his dragon to life, its perfect form so clearly ensconced in his head, that he had hardly needed to refer to his drawings or his many dragon models. Bonfire night had passed him by, Pongy and Lefty eschewing the delights of bangers and Catherine wheels to keep him company as he practised his cold art in the chilly craft and clay room. Pongy had stood on a bench to watch the rockets whizzing up into the dark air, exclaiming as they rose up like inverted comets before breaking into wild bursts of colour - then vanishing in mid-air, leaving the sky blacker and more wintry than before.

"They only last a minute," Pongy had said reflectively. "Less, really. Your dragon's going to last forever, mate. But it is *cold* in 'ere!"

Then, a sudden jittering explosiveness had shattered their calm as the blue doors banged shut and half a dozen jumping jacks skittered noisily around the room, bouncing about harm-lessly amongst Walter's trial pieces which lay here and there under the tables. One had landed next to Lefty, engrossed in the section of tail that Walter was modelling. He had leapt up like a rocket and raced out of the room.

Few people were faster than Lefty Knype and even fewer chose to put themselves at a disadvantage with him. He had come back a few minutes later and settled down again quietly, watching as Walter modelled the dragon's scales minutely, the layers diminishing in size as they approached the curling tip of the tail, where each tiny platelet was no bigger than an England's Glory match-head. Walter had raised his eyebrows.

"Grunters," Lefty had sighed. "They won't be coming back…"

Walter had even forgone a trip to the pictures on his birthday, preferring instead to work on a Saturday too, when Mr. Slope had offered him the opportunity. They had listened to the football on the wireless while the autumn rain poured down outside and Mr. Slope made endless brews to keep them warm. At two o'clock Edna had come by, as she often did now, bearing a chocolate cake with twelve small candles which Mr. Slope had lit for Walter to blow out. Edna had smiled and guessed secretly at what he wished for. She had been to the kiln and told him that all was well: when he was ready the kiln would be ready too. As if by magic Harry Mudd had appeared, delighted to be included in the birthday celebration and then invited, along with Pongy and Lefty, to a slap-up birthday meal at the little house.

Auntie Sally had bustled about, happy to see Walter at the table with his friends, tucking into bangers and mash, followed by a trifle deep in double-cream and an iced Victoria sponge.

"A bit of normality," she had thought, smiling at Louie as she handed her some cake, "but I'm glad that great gawking lad doesn't live here! However does his mother fill him up?"

"So," continued Mr. Bateman, "we're getting there, are we? Nearly done now, I think?"

Walter nodded.

"We are," he said and thought how strange that sounded. "I should have finally attached the last piece of the dragon by the end of the week. Tomorrow and Thursday Potty's helping me with the wings, then I just have the crest to do on Friday. Thanks for all your help Mr. Bateman. Then I've got to get out all the wet paper and let it dry for a week or so. I can work on it a bit more in the leather stage, sharpening up the detail and so on. That's right, isn't it, Mr. Jollie?"

"That's right! Marvellous! Marvellous!" cried Mr. Jollie. "Well, better get on. Gwenny will be waiting!"

When the two friends reached Mr. Beany's yard they found him looking out for them in some excitement.

"Just had our Pat on the phone," he said, rushing over to them. "Dragon's coming over this Friday, early! What do you think of that!"

"Marvellous!" sang Mr. Jollie. "Take him out for a spin right away! Just the thing, eh, Walter?"

Walter smiled and congratulated his friend but he really wasn't too sure. He felt he knew something about dragons by now and he couldn't help wondering if Mr. Jollie had bitten off more than he could chew. Dragons were rarely what you expected them to be.

Mr. Beany went back inside to listen to his favourite show on the wireless.

"I won't be going out with '*im* ever again and that's for sure!" he thought, as he settled down with a bottle of Guinness and a packet of crisps. "He'll be on his own now – an' jolly good luck to 'im!"

"A box was being prepared for Dragon..."

Chapter Thirteen

Bad Dreams

Sometimes, when they felt sure they would not be seen, Billie and Willie hid behind Bill's shed on the allotments and watched Alf and Bill at work on the bottle oven. They saw it re-bricked and re-pointed, and its firemouths and flues cleaned out and made good; but they were astonished to see its openings enlarged, and, eavesdropping, were startled to hear of the size of the dragon vase. It was a torment to them, but try as they might, there seemed to be no opportunity of waylaying the little potter, and even less of getting into the craft and clay room. The Dragon Knights were everywhere.

"Don't know what we'd do without those lads!" Louie had cried one day, after a church outing with Minnie. They had passed Old Ma at the bottom of the street and Louie had been shocked to see the real depth of malice in her eye.

"Don't worry, Auntie!" Walter had reassured her. "Nobody's got a bigger punch than Lefty Knype and someone's around for me at any time of day!"

Walter felt safe, like a child paddling in the shallows of a mighty ocean, who feels only the warm sunlit ripples about his feet, unaware of the vast reserves of energy at his back which are building and building, sending stronger and stronger waves against the shore until suddenly he is toppled and thrashing in a great foaming wave, lucky to be rescued by a swift mother or father, bundled into warm clothing and given a lesson on the nature of waves: their swiftness, their suddenness, their absolute treachery.

He never gave a thought to Old Ma - and yet she was there, like a dark wave building on his horizon, becoming ever more vicious in her intent, more obsessive, more deranged.

Her heart was a poisoned wasteland where nothing good could be found, where no seed of kindness or generosity could take root. It was a blackened soil, deep and dark, untouched by light or love. But resentment flourished there, and malice, fed daily by the twins' failures and Walter's success, so that by the time he was finishing his great vase, casting and attaching the mighty wings of his wonderful dragon, Old Ma's malevolence had reached a fever pitch which nothing but the worst extremes could appease. Although she trod the same streets as those around her, she lived in her own world of malcontent and malignity, in a fiefdom built up year after year by spite and rancour and vindictiveness.

Now, in her eighty-sixth year, as sinewy and strong as an old rooster who has outlived his likeliness for the pot, Old Ma had turned herself into something less than human, something, as her neighbours feared, altogether more demonic. The butcher's shop, so ordinary with its Minton tiles and freshly sawdusted floor, hid, unbeknown to its white-aproned and complacent proprietor, an old woman who was slowly shaping herself into a fragment of the Evil One himself.

The weather, too, turned for the worse, the city of coal and clay becoming shrouded not merely in its grimy blanket of smoke but in a thick and impenetrable smog through which people stumbled with scarves over their mouths, listening carefully for oncoming traffic, blind to all vehicles until the very last minute, the ring of hooves on cobblestones dulled down to a soft muffled clop, the roar of an engine to a cat's purr.

The soft smog swaddled The Grove, islanding it from the outside world. Inside their warm classrooms the children coughed and sniffled but Walter worked on in the bitter cold of the craft and clay room, ordered every so often to spend half-an-hour by the Headmaster's fire.

By Thursday evening the vase was almost complete, wanting only a little detail here and there. Walter and Potty stood and surveyed it, the huge grey pot with its encircling dragon, and neither of them could quite believe that they had come so far. Like a strange cold mirage, the dragon hovered over the room, it gigantic form dwarfing its tiny creator as it looked down upon him.

"We've nearly done it, Potty," said Walter happily, putting on his overcoat.

"You have son," said Potty. "I always knew you would." He paused. "But firing it is another matter Walter. We've spoken about that before."

Walter nodded. Soon it would be taken out of his hands and then all he could do would be to wait and hope.

Pongy and Herbert Sherburt appeared in the doorway.

"Cor!" they both said at once. "The wings! Cor! The wings!"

"Lefty has a bad cold" said Herbert as they accompanied Walter home. He coughed. "And I think I'm coming down with it too," he added.

"Everybody's getting it," snuffled Pongy, blowing his nose into a grubby handkerchief. "There aren't so many of us about for you now, Walter."

"Nobody can see me in this fog anyway," said Walter blithely, "so don't worry about that, Pongy. Stay at home and get better."

Walter was right, the fog did give him cover but it gave cover to his enemies too. Mr. Pinch, looking out of his study window at the blankness outside could see no one coming and going, nor could he see the blue doors which guarded Walter and his dragon. For the first time in weeks the little potter was truly vulnerable. But he had no other thought in his mind than the urge to complete his work and at the end of each day he slept well, exhausted by the long hours and the physical strain of readying his dragon for the fire.

§

The twins, on the other hand, were not sleeping well, nor did they speak to one another, going about instead with their heads sunken into the collars of their blazers like two giant tortoises retreating from the world. They avoided each other's eyes but felt the force of Old Ma's basilisk gaze on them day and night; sleep had become a terror to them and their dreams were a twisting and toiling labyrinth from which they were desperate to escape. Each boy dreamt the same dream and each boy woke nightly shouting out in a hot and breathless fever, so that their mother rushed in to calm them whilst old Ma's imperative voice could be heard from the landing, saying, "It's only them fatty chops, Bertha. Leave 'em alone!"

But Old Ma knew well enough the reason for her grandsons' descent into terror each night. On Tuesday evening, she had screwed up The Sentinel and thrown it onto the fire, watching a photograph of Walter burn with vicious satisfaction. The twins watched sullenly, then started as she drew something from the cushion behind her back. It was a long butcher's knife, worn thin with the cutting of flesh but sharp still, the firelight glinting on its honed edge when she laid it on the table in front of them.

"There's a fog coming," she had said, "even you can't fail this time!"

The twins sat frozen with horror. Neither had expected this. This had not featured in their wildest fantasies. True, Old Ma had shaped them from the cradle, twisting them into mean spirited bullies, into grandsons who had relished her evil reputation and enjoyed the fear in other people's eyes. But neither had expected this. They sat still and said nothing, wanting their father to arrive, for the first time wanting to confide in him, wanting the comfort of their mother's arms – but Harold and Bertha were in the slaughter house making up link after link of black pudding, oblivious to their sons' jeopardy.

Old Ma eyed them with amusement and gave a little laugh.

"This is Squealer," she said softly, running a skinny finger down the length of the blade. "It was me granda's- so quick, so sharp!"

The boys looked at her aghast, Willie stunned into silence and Billie struggling to speak.

"But gran..." he began.

Her flat black eyes bored into him so that he sickened and halted, putting his head down like Willie to avoid her gaze. But Old Ma pushed the knife over to him, twisting his fingers around the shagreen handle and holding them there in a tight, cold grip. Her hand tightened so that Billie was forced to meet her eyes. He shuddered convulsively but her finger nails dug in, compelling his attention.

"Yer nothing to me," she said, "nothing! And if yer don't do this!" and here she lifted Billie's arm and made a stabbing lunge at the empty air in front of him, "then I'll 'ave the pair of yer butchered an' jointed an' sold in the shop before anybody misses yer! An' yer useless mother an' all!" she added smoothly.

Willie burst into convulsive sobs but Old Ma was at his back in a moment, with the knife laid against his throat.

"Yer'll do it," she whispered, "because yer knows me by now. Yer much better off being me friend than me enemy! Friday. Not a day sooner, not a day later." She made the very slightest of cuts on Willie's chin. "Just something on account," she crooned, "in case yer fail...."

Now the knife lay under Willie's mattress, burning through the old flock filling into his back bacon. The dreadful nights and the silent days passed, the thick fog shrouding their misery so that no one noticed the change in the boys who went about with sunken eyes and drooping shoulders. Miss Lush thought that they were quieter than usual but everyone was coming down with the cold and she attributed their lack of spirits to that.

"What's the matter with your chin?" she asked Willie on Wednesday.

"Fell in the fog," he said sullenly, wishing he could tell her the truth but feeling cut off from normal discourse, as if he and Billie were living apart from everyone else in a place of horror, where Bella Lugosi crept about in the shadows and bats flickered around the chimney pots at night.

In a disturbing and unlooked-for reversal of their fortunes the two boys saw fate playing into their hands as more and more of the Dragon Knights succumbed to the cold and even the staff struggled to teach their classes, let alone police the corridors and playground. Mr. Pinch's head ached as if it were likely to split, so he kept to his study, occasionally surveying the smog pressed up against his window, then retreating to his desk once more.

Glumly, the twins saw that there could be no excuse for failure this time. Sickness and the smog had combined to offer them the perfect opportunity and the time was now ripe for the climax of their grandmother's ghastly vendetta - though they quailed at the thought of what they must do. To do it was unthinkable: yet to return home with it undone was now a nightmare in itself.

As daylight seeped into their bedroom on Friday morning both twins buried their heads in their pillows and wept. But they were dressed by eight-thirty and the dreadful knife was taped to Billie's thigh, well hidden beneath his long winter trousers. It seemed to weigh down his leg like a leaden weight, though his heart was heavier still.

"The soft smog swaddled The Grove ..."

Chapter Fourteen

Cocooned

This day of peril became known in north Staffordshire as Poodle Friday, though when Walter awoke he had no inkling of the dangers that lay ahead in the grey obscurity of the smoggy town. He drew back his curtains, and pressed his nose up against the wet glass but he could no longer see the houses on the other side of the narrow street. Buildings which yesterday had appeared merely as faint pencil-shaded silhouettes on a soft grey ground were today invisible, the little house seeming to exist in a cocoon of grubby cotton wool, insulated from all the sights and sounds of the world outside. The smog appeared to have seeped into his bedroom too, rendering it damp and gloomy, so that Walter was glad to hurry down to the kitchen with its hot range and Auntie Sally's hustle and bustle.

Sally looked at Walter eating his bread and dripping quietly, ruminatively. Gone were the great grasping bites, the impatient shoving back of the chair and the bolt down the path to the gate and school beyond. Louie came in and sat beside him.

"Another two weeks or so," he said reflectively, "and I shall be decorating it. It seems unreal, somehow."

"It's very exciting dear," said Louie positively. "And I believe they are test firing the kiln next week with something Potty has coiled up?"

"Yes," said Walter, "Potty's made a big rough vase about half the size of mine. Time to go now," he added, getting up and throwing on his overcoat and scarf. "Mr. Pinch is holding a meeting about firing my dragon. I mustn't be late!"

"Here's your cap," said Sally, "and don't give away all your lunch today!"

Sally let him out of the front door, the back yard and alleyway being too deep in mystery on a morning such as this.

"Mind how you go!" she said, landing a peck on his cheek. "Keep to the wall and mind how you cross the road."

Walter had never known a smog such as this in all his years in the city of coal and clay. When the door shut behind him he felt utterly alone, stranded, as if he were a boy living in a cloud rather than on a familiar street. The smog pressed in upon him so that his scarf soon became wet, damp from his breath within and even damper from the clammy assault of the smog without. He put out his left hand and trailed it along the brick walls of the terrace, counting the doorways until he arrived at Turner Street. Even the school tower was no longer evident. Crossing carefully, he fumbled his way to the railings, and by working along them he found the school gates. The playground stretched ahead, a vast fog-bound continent which lay between him and the blue doors. Then Potty opened them and a weak yellow halo appeared, guiding Walter in to his safe harbour like a friendly beacon beckoning a watchful navigator.

"Hello Potty!" cried Walter. "What a day!"

"Hello son," said Potty. "I was sure you would come but very few children have turned out today. The Headmaster is providing some sustenance and then sending them home before lunchtime. Very unusual," he added.

"Cor!" said Walter. "Can I stay?"

"Oh yes," said Potty, "Mr. Slope will be here and George will be assisting him with the boiler too, later on. So you will have company. But come along, Walter, they are waiting for us in Mr. Pinch's room."

A great fire was blazing away in the Headmaster's study and Bill and Alf were seated on either side of the hearth, each with an adoring Poo pressed up against his legs, eying the toast that they were consuming as if it were more desirable than lamb chops. Mr. Pinch was busy toasting more bread but he came forward and seated Walter on a little stool next to Mr. Jollie.

"Well done, Walter," he said stiffly, handing him a small plate of toast. "I was sure you would come. Indeed," he added, looking around, "Very good of everyone to turn out on a day like this. No public transport anywhere, I believe." He turned and resumed his business with the toasting fork.

"Good show, Walter!" cried Mr. Jollie, patting him on the back. "Only a bit of fog! Marvellous! Marvellous!"

Alf had absent mindedly buttered his toast on top of a pile of reports and the butter had soaked well into some of them. Rosie was busy dabbing at Lefty's with her little handkerchief but she glanced up and smiled.

"We'd never have got here without the Poo's," she said. "They seemed to know where they were going alright."

"True! True!" cried Mr. Jollie as the Poo's wagged their tails furiously and Jigger Poo quickly scooped up an unattended slice, crunching it with evident satisfaction.

"Walter, meet Mr. Bunger," said Mr. Pinch, laying the last few slices on a clean plate ready to be buttered. "Burt, er, Mr. Bunger, is a placer, Walter. He will be looking after your dragon when it gets to the kiln. Setting it in the most advantageous position, you know. Mr. Bunger – Walter!"

Walter leaned forward and shook hands with the huge man sitting across from him. All the damp and cold that had seeped into Walter on the way to school seemed to be burnt away by the fierce heat of the big man's hand.

"Proud ter meet yer, Walter," said Burt Bunger. "Yer've made summat different, that's fer sure! It's a bit out of the ordinary way, like, but we're all 'ere to do our best fer yer!"

He looked around at the rest of the team who all nodded eagerly.

"Yer main problem, Walter, as I see it," Burt went on, "is the lack of a sagger ter fire it in. 'course no sagger could be made fer it, that's obvious. It's way too big an' too awkward - especially with that dragon of yours!"

Walter nodded. Potty had talked to him about this.

"It'll be rather at the mercy of the fires, won't it?" he asked, "Without a saggar?"

"That's right, lad," said Burt. "Kiln'll be full of gases an' smoke an' such like. Without a saggar your vase can be spoilt an' blackened."

"But Burt's got an idea, haven't you, Burt?" said Alf eagerly.

"Of sorts," said Burt, his bald head shining in the glow of the fire. He rubbed his big red beard with his hand and looked thoughtful. "Best I can do is ter make a tall stockade of saggers around it," he said. "Build 'em up, like, so they offer it some protection from the worst of the weather in there. No promises though young 'un." He looked at Walter and shook his head. "Yer breaking new ground 'ere, Walter!"

Walter couldn't help feeling a bit glum. He hadn't foreseen any of these problems! Alf looked at him sympathetically. Of all those present he was the one who empathised most closely with Walter. The fires were his responsibility; it would soon be over to him.

"Too foggy to do owt with the kiln today, Walter," said Bill, finishing his toast and picking up his cup of tea. "An' anyway we've finished 'er now, just a bit of tidying up to do."

"That's right!" said Alf more positively. "She's ready to go! Pity about this fog or we would have taken Potty's test piece over - but we can do that tomorrow, weather permitting, and fire it then. Coal's arrived. By the end of the week we'll know if we can crack on with yours, Walter. 'ow about that?"

"Thank you," said Walter, feeling excited and fearful all at the same time.

He knew that he had to trust in the expertise of these men and wish for a good helping of luck to go with it. A potter always needed some luck, Potty said.

"Thank you all very much," he said. "And thank you for all the coal Mr. Jollie," he added. "And for the bottle oven of course!"

"Marvellous!" said Mr. Jollie. "Marvellous Walter! Best thing for years. For years and years…." he added a little sadly.

Just then the door opened a crack and a small face appeared around its edge.

"er, Mr. Pinch, sir," came the quavering voice of Phillip Slipp, "The baker's come sir. 'er, 'ow many buns are you buying for the school, sir?"

Mr. Pinch's face reddened like the sun on a Japanese flag.

"Goodness gracious, boy!" he roared, conscious at once of the unmerited reproof but unable to soften it. "A bun for each child of course! Dismissed!"

Phillip vanished as Burt and Bill politely maintained straight faces. They had all heard about the unique form of Mr. Pinch's philanthropy. Mr. Jollie looked at the floor though, feeling sympathy for the Headmaster. Walter rose and edged towards the door.

"Yes, yes, off you go, Walter," said Mr. Pinch, miserable at his unwonted outburst. "If only…" he thought. "If only you could unbend just a little, man! There was no need for that!"

"So that's the way it is," mused Mr. Jollie, wiping the toast crumbs from his moustache and taking his walking stick from Rosie with a polite little nod. The Poos jumped to his side, all thoughts of toast forgotten. "Well, well," he thought, "poor Mr. Pinch. I shall have to see what I can do about that!"

Rosie crossed the room and opened the door. Everyone took their leave, Mr. Pinch huffing and puffing his goodbyes, the red gradually seeping out of his handsome face like a beetroot stain leaving a good white shirt in one of Edna Robbin's buckets. Alone in his study once more, he sifted through the pile of greasy reports and wondered what they had made of his outburst.

"You are *ridiculous* Pinch!" he thought unhappily. He looked out of the window but the world was a blank and no answer came from the smoggy air. "But to reveal any affection for them?" he asked himself. "*Surely* not? No! No!"

Yet he did feel affection for them, having deep resevoirs of kindly feeling which lay behind everything he did for the school - but which he feared might swamp him if ever so small a hole were made in his grim reserve. He sat down at his desk and stared glumly at his spattered blotter. "I've always been the same!" he thought. "It's hopeless!"

Mr. Pinch's childhood amongst the wooded hills of the Kentish Weald should have been an idyllic one. Far from the smoke and sweat of Victorian London, he had a playground as wide and green as the African forests which Walter dreamt of. He had trees to climb and streams to dam, lanes in which to blackberry and damp morning meadows in which to hunt the mushroom. But he had little love.

He had a nursery and a nurse and a little later a tutor before he was sent to boarding school. But the daily love of a father and mother was something little John Pinch never knew. Yet Major Pinch saw himself as the best of fathers, teaching his son, by his cold and imperious manner, the art of self-restraint so necessary in a soldier. By the time young John went to Stonehill Manor, his warm and childish heart had been buried beneath layers of constraint and he was unable to befriend the other unhappy children in the freezing dormitory. He was instead silent and insular, like a leveret buried in a wasteland of snow.

§

Mr. Jollie and Rosie stood looking up in wonder at the great vase which filled the middle of the room. They walked all around it, almost on tiptoe, astonished at the huge dragon from which Jolly Poo and Jigger Poo sat at a respectful distance, cocking their heads from side to side as they studied the strange creature carefully. But it offered them no threat and they soon subsided into a warm woolly pile on Potty's cold floor. Rosie looked over at the blue doors.

"Good job they're double," she laughed. "Mr. Pinch'd 'ave to knock a wall down else!"

Only the dragon's crest was lacking. Walter itched to get on with it but politeness constrained him.

"What's this, Walter?" asked Rosie, pointing to a tiny sphere of clay balanced in the vase's rim.

"That's the dragon's pearl, Rosie," Mr. Jollie answered for him. "A dragon is always chasing a pearl, y' know. Represents wisdom – or happiness – eh, Walter?"

Walter nodded. He had been reading about it in a library book that Minnie had bought for him.

"It looks as if it might fall in!" laughed Rosie.

"Well," said Walter seriously and with a wisdom beyond his years, "it seems to me happiness is a bit like that. One minute you think you've got it, then the next you're dissatisfied and bothering about something else again."

Mr. Jollie shook his head. The Poos watched him and sat up.

"Pearl's there to be taken, Walter!" he said, buttoning up his overcoat and taking his scarf from Rosie. "No good being down in the dumps – have to get on with things, y'know!" he continued, rubbing his hands together vigorously. His kindly face broke into a huge smile. "Dragon's already here Walter!

Came last night! Gave Beany a surprise, what! Already had the door off his stable! Marvellous! Marvellous!"

Tears of laughter trickled down the old man's cheeks as he fished for his handkerchief.

"Taking him out shortly," he said when he had recovered. "Fancy a spin, eh, Walter? Sit up beside me and put him through his paces, eh? Marvellous! Marvellous!"

Walter paled and Rosie caught his eye and shook her head.

"Sorry Mr. Jollie," he said. "I'm at school today and I'm just about to finish the head off...." He looked out of the window anxiously. "But the fog?" he said, regarding his friend with obvious concern.

The Poos looked from one to the other and whined softly. Mr. Jollie patted them consolingly.

"Only a bit of mist up by Beany's," he chortled. "Clear up soon enough, don't y' worry! Off we go Rosie old girl! Give us a wave as we pass, eh? Marvellous! Marvellous!"

And off he went into the smoggy morning, with Jolly Poo on one side and Jigger Poo on the other, Rosie stepping closely behind them, very glad for once that she had the house to do up with Tilly and several best shirts to starch.

Walter was left wondering at the reversal in Mr. Jollie's philosophy. He seemed a different person to the one Sally and Minnie had talked about and Walter already knew that Mr. Jollie now intended to re-open his factory, vase or no vase.

"Electrical insulators, Walter!" he had said one day, on the way to see Gwenny. "They're the way forward now! Kilns will all be electric before long, y' know! Think of that, eh, Walter? Marvellous!"

Walter had found it impossible to imagine, having grown up amongst the smoking, belching bottle ovens, with their great comfortable curves and their lovely fat bodies of hand-made blackened brick. He had hoped Mr. Jollie was wrong.

Who could imagine the city without its coal-fired ovens? He had been filled with a sense of unease at Mr. Jollie's words. Suddenly the future, which he had never before questioned, seemed uncertain and strange.

"Electric kilns!" he had wondered, looking around him at the dirty skyline with its forest of well-known, well-loved chimneys spouting thick bouts of sooty foliage. "Cor! I hope not!"

Potty came in from his storeroom, carrying his overcoat and scarf.

"Oh," he said. "I didn't hear them go! I'm afraid my wife is unwell, Walter. This cold, you know. I shall be here to see the test piece off, however. About eight o' clock Walter. See you then."

"I hope she gets well soon, Potty," said Walter. "I'll be here another two hours or so, I think. I've got to put the crest on and then clear out all the wet paper inside. Then I'll go home. See you tomorrow, Potty."

"Goodbye then, son," Potty said, donning his coat and scarf. He pulled his cap well down about his ears. "It's freezing in here," he went on, looking at Walter with concern. "Don't stay any longer than you need to, Walter, and get by the fire sometimes too. I shall be glad to have the heating on again next week."

"Me too, Potty!" said Walter. "It's colder than Vladivostock in here!"

"Let Mr. Slope know when you're finished," said Potty. "He's down in the boiler room with George at the moment. And they'll hold the ladders if you need them."

Alone in the cavernous room, Walter felt as if he were in a world of his own. The smog, piled thickly against the big windows, muffled any comings and goings on the road outside. Even the sounds from the other classrooms were unusually distant, as if a wide empty space lay between him and the rest of the school. Walter felt relaxed, his mind almost as blank as the fog outside. If all went well, if the kiln worked its magic, every part of his magnificent vase would be fused into an harmonious whole, so that, bar sudden shock, earthquake or war, the unity of the form would be preserved for all time.

"Thousands of years, perhaps," he hoped as he shaped the scimitar-like scales of the dragon's crest.

"I won't bother Mr. Slope," he thought, as he climbed the ladders. He leaned over and slowly, gingerly, positioned the crest onto the head of the dragon and pressed it home.

Walter walked around and around the vase for a long time, lost in the contemplation of what he had made. Long ago, it seemed, he had sat up in bed and envisaged a dragon like no other, a breather of fire, a slayer of Grunters! Now, here it was! Round and round he walked, seeing the vase not in its grey drabness but in all the forest hues that he and Louie had planned for it. But time was passing and the room was very cold.

Then at eleven o'clock, the school doors opened and the freed children poured forth into the smoggy day, shouting and exclaiming as they made their way through the all enfolding air, their cries reaching Walter dimly so that he was hardly conscious of their exit. Nobody noticed where the Grunter twins went.

Inside, the cold seeped further and further into Walter's many layers, penetrating his overcoat, his blazer, his two woolly jumpers and flannel shirts, not to mention his three sets of woolly underwear. Finally, he began to cough and shiver. Mr. Slope appeared in the doorway and looked at him in alarm.

"Are you still 'ere?" he said. "I thought you was by the fire by now. It's past eleven you know. You'd better go an' get warm, matey."

Mr. Slope looked at the vase and saw himself in the paper again.

"I'll give The Sentinel a bell, shall I?" he said. "That bloke wanted a picture of it today."

Walter nodded but he suddenly felt quite unwell.

"I might not be here though," he said, "I'm off home after I've got all the wet paper out. It will take me about ten minutes, I think."

"I shall be here all day," said Mr. Slope importantly, "So you can leave it with me when you've done. But I should 'urry up if I were you, chum."

He went off, leaving Walter up a ladder, steadily fishing inside the vase with a long wire hook with which he pulled out the trails of wet paper, so that the vase could dry evenly, inside and out.

And that is how the Grunter twins found him, his back to the blue doors, carefully, so carefully balancing on the ladders, reaching down for the last length of paper which was reluctant to part with the damp clay. Willie and Billie stood in the doorway, well hidden by the blanket of smog, and in Billie's hand was Old Ma's dreadful knife.

"They studied the strange creature carefully..."

Chapter Fifteen

Soap And Water Save The Day

After the meeting, Bill had decided not to waste the day at home and had been out digging up the cabbages on his allotment. One or two other die-hards with a similar philosophy laboured there too, intermittently fortified by the contents of Bill's hip flask. But by eleven o'clock they had all agreed on a surrender, a decision influenced as much by the empty nature of the flask as by the continuing misery of the smoggy day. Bill bundled the large green cabbages into a sack and set out to deliver them to his friends and neighbours. Rounding a corner near The Grove he came up against Edna Robbin, who like Bill was out making deliveries, though her goods were folded neatly in a large shopping trolley which she wheeled cautiously through the blind streets.

"Alright Edna?" he said, taken by surprise. "Bit foggy to be out an' about, duck?"

Edna laughed. "My customers can't wait for their shirts and pants, Bill!" she said. "But this is my last call. Then I shall just pop in and see Walter, as I'm so close."

"You'll 'ave to 'urry then, duck," said Bill kindly. "'e'll be off 'ome soon. 'e's nearly done, you know. 'e won't be 'anging about on a day like this, not if 'e's got any sense! The school's being shut, you know."

"Oh!" said Edna. "I should have thought of that! I'll go now Bill, I'd like to see him finishing it."

Edna had been the keenest of Walter's acolytes from her very first visit, when she had stepped timidly through the blue doors and hovered uncertainly in the doorway, amazed as the little potter worked away on his enormous vase, intent and serious. He had made her welcome straight away and they had become firm friends. From then on, Edna had scrimped and saved, baking little cakes for him when she could afford it and feeling richly rewarded by the fun and laughter she enjoyed with Walter and with Harry Mudd. Potty welcomed the little washerwoman too.

"A very fine lady, Walter," he said one day after she had left them.

"Edna's wizard," Walter had agreed. "She makes top chocolate cake too!

Bill looked at Edna, the smog frizzing her lovely hair under its simple headscarf, her worn coat buttoned tightly around her throat. She had no gloves and her hands were turning blue.

"Well, get home after, as quick as you can," he said. "Have you got room in there for a cabbage?" he went on. Like everyone else he knew that little Edna Robbin carried her china poodles with her wherever she went. "Your Soap an' Water in there, are they duck?" he asked kindly, as Edna moved the contents of her trolley around carefully.

"Thank you, Bill," she said. "That's very kind of you. Yes, in here as usual!"

"Mind 'ow you go then. Ta-ra duck," and Bill went off up the smoggy street as Edna turned towards The Grove.

Nobody laughed at Edna's attachment to her china dogs. They knew that she had been parted from too much in life and understood her desire to have them constantly near her, nestling safely amongst the soft towels and starched shirts of her friends and neighbours. A rich man may feel regretful at leaving his smart car on a city street and Edna felt equally unwilling to leave her beloved poodles at home.

"I've tried leaving them on the chimney-piece," she told people, laughing shyly at her own folly. "And they do sit there quietly! But I always go back for them. I can't help it!"

"Though on a day like this..." she thought doubtfully, as she stepped down into the smog-swathed road.

Soap and Water were all Edna had to call her own, all she had to love in the world – and love them she did, fiercely and passionately. She would have no more children or grandchildren, her poverty precluding even the company of a cat or a dog.

"Whatever would I do if it went hungry?" she would ask. "However could I bear it if it became unwell?"

But with Soap and Water, Edna knew happiness again and her empty house had become a home once more.

She pressed on through the greyness, navigating more by instinct and memory than by sight. Slowly, so slowly, she crossed the wide expanse of playground, fearing to trip and stumble, glad that her poodles were softly cocooned, but telling herself to take one step at a time, just one. She could not see ahead of her, where Willie and Billie, frozen in the doorway, were cloaked by the conspiring smog.

The terrible Grunter twins had not moved, and had hardly breathed, for ten minutes. The knife burned in Billie's hand. He thrust it at Willie, who pushed his brother's arm away fiercely. Nothing was said. Walter continued to fish delicately for the last shred of damp paper, oblivious to the presence of his enemies. Then something strange happened. Tears began to stream down the twins' cheeks, great fat tears as their shoulders heaved and sank rhythmically. Still nothing was said. Billie's head went down and Willie's followed.

They watched as Walter lifted out the stubborn trail of paper with a happy little flourish and descended the ladder. With one last look up at his dragon, and a little pat goodbye, he made his way to the inner door leading to the warmth of Mr. Pinch's study. He paused and gave a great hollow cough, his thin shoulders hunching with the strain. Still the twins stood there, immobile, like huge boulders on a foggy moor. Finally, as the door closed behind Walter, Billie turned to his brother.

"I'm not a ruddy murderer!" he said. "But I'd like to do for her!"

Willie nodded. They had been through hell together. Rotten though they were, Old Ma had overestimated her influence on them. A little light still shone inside, and though they now feared for their own lives, they could not take Walter's.

Now, approaching the huge vase, Billie held up the knife. With a series of swift, devastating strokes, they could wreck what Walter had taken months to make. That at least might save their bacon. Silently, they sized it up, wondering where to strike most damagingly. Yet the more the twins looked at the astonishing dragon, the less they wanted to act. The tiny ray of light deep inside each boy started to brighten and expand until, standing there, side by side, Willie and Billie began to experience something they had never felt before – a sense of beauty, of magnificence. They were, after all, born and bred in the city of coal and clay, and although meat and not clay had been their chief preoccupation, something of the creative, imbued perhaps with the city's smoke, though stunted and squashed by Old Ma's maleficence, now blossomed in their hearts.

Silently, the twins circled the dragon vase, moving around it to the left and looking up all the time. The significance of the pearl was lost on them but the dragon was entrancing. Smog had entered the room through the open doors and they peered through it at the serrated jaw and lolling tongue high above them. They pointed quietly at the gripping claws and the wonderful wings. They gently fingered the overlapping scales and followed the long tail around as it clung to the sides of the vase.

Then a small pang of jealousy stung them, that a boy their age had made this, and Walter at that! Billie lifted the knife again and Willie nodded.

"Go on!" he said.

"Right then!" whispered Billie, leaning over hurriedly and digging the point into the vase at its widest point.

At this moment, Edna, breathing a sigh of relief, pushed her trolley through the blue doors. But instead of finding Walter busy in the act of creation, she saw Billie grotesquely twisting Squealer's blade into the body of the vase. She screamed loudly.

"Oh lummy!" he cried, spinning around so quickly that he tripped over the ladder which clattered on top of him as he fell.

Willie stood like one up to his neck in blood, paralysed by guilt and shame.

Everyone knew the meanness of the Grunters and Edna knew them as well as anyone: her own poor mother had suffered from Old Ma's incessant spite and Edna feared her and blamed her. Now, catching the wretched twins red-handed, in the midst of their clumsy depredations, she lost no time in the defence of Walter's treasure, even at the sacrifice of her own.

She dived into her trolley.

"Take that!" she screamed, flinging Soap at Willie's head. Her aim was good and it floored him.

"And that!" she cried. Water hit Billie on the jaw as he struggled to his feet.

"And that's for mother!" Edna shouted, hurling Bill's cabbage at Willie as he stood up. Bill's cabbages were exceptionally large and firm and Willie went down again, like a skittle under a bowling ball.

"Help! Help!" she screamed. "Grunters! Grunters!"

The inner door was flung open and Mr. Slope and George rushed into the room. George saw the long knife and pushed his uncle back.

"Go for the police, quick!" he cried, rapidly assessing the danger to Edna and himself.

137

He moved forward bravely but the Grunters were quicker than him. They knew their reputation and both wished now that they had never touched Walter's masterpiece. There would be no forgiveness for that! The whole city would be after them!

"Run!" shouted Billie, casting the knife aside.

For two such beefy lads, fed up on fat and offal and sausages, the twins were surprisingly fast. They sprinted to the doors, Willie barging past Edna and sending her sprawling. She clutched empty air in an effort to save herself but went down heavily, her head banging against Potty's utensil cupboard as she did so. George sprang to the doorway but the twins were gone, eaten up by the all-consuming smog.

"Drat it!" he cried, "I've lost them!"

Then he saw Edna, pale and unconscious on the cold floor, and around her the shattered remains of her beloved poodles. Mr. Pinch arrived at great speed and seconds later came two stout policemen with Mr. Slope.

"Lost 'em, sorry lads," said George, indicating the open door and the wall of smog, into which the policemen plunged and instantly disappeared.

Mr. Pinch went for the school's smelling salts. He raised Edna's head tenderly and held them under her nose. She sat up - and seeing the broken faces and limbs of her little dogs burst into loud sobbing.

"Soap and Water!" she sobbed. "Soap and Water!"

Mr. Pinch patted her gently but Edna was inconsolable.

"They were mine!" she wept. "Mine! And now they're gone! Nothing! Nothing! Nothing!"

Edna's distress was so great that Mr. Pinch began to fear for her. He knew well enough that this outpouring of grief was not simply the result of broken china poodles. He knew what Edna had lost, none better.

He cradled her in his arms and rocked her to and fro.

"You're a heroine, Edna, a heroine," he told her as she sobbed, her tears soaking into the thick tweed of his jacket. "Your boys would have been so proud of you," he said tenderly, stroking the damp red hair. "Such brave boys Edna, such lovely lads."

Edna's sobbing faltered and she listened quietly.

"I would have kept them safe if I could," he said. "But such brave souls, Edna, such brave souls!"

Edna's breathing stilled and she lay quietly in Mr. Pinch's arms.

After a few minutes, he said hesitantly, "I will bring you some more poodles Edna. It's the very least I can do. You have saved everything here, you know."

"But they were mine!" she burst out afresh. "And I loved them!"

So Mr. Pinch sat with Edna while she sobbed; it was all he could do.

Ten minutes later Alan Padder put his head around the blue doors and came upon Mr. Pinch and Edna, now quiet and withdrawn, sitting among the poodle shards.

"Oh," he said, surprised and embarrassed. "Shall I call a doctor, Mr. Pinch?"

Mr. Pinch shook his head.

"Perhaps you will assist me?" he said. "Mrs. Robbin would be better in my study, I'm sure."

Edna sat up.

"No," she said quietly. "I'm alright, really I am. I don't want to be a nuisance."

She was helped onto a chair where she sat sadly, cradling the remains of her little companions.

"Mrs. Robbin is a heroine," said Mr. Pinch and in a few words, he told the story of her unselfish bravery.

"Who knows what they would have done," he said finally, in tones of the deepest admiration, "if Mrs. Robbin had not been at hand in our hour of need?"

He walked around the vase and discovered the hole that Billie had made.

"Look at this!" he said, shocked.

Alan Padder photographed the dragon vase, taking careful note of the damage that had been done.

"Can it be repaired?" he asked hopefully.

"I shall consult Mr. Potterton," said Mr. Pinch. "It *may* not be as serious as it looks."

The reporter studied the little washerwoman, so pale and beautiful with the tumbled cascade of her red hair falling about the shabby shoulders of her coat. He looked at the grief-stricken face and the poor worn hands clutching the devastated poodles. He felt pity for her but more than that, he smelt a great story, perhaps the best of his career.

"This vase thing is really shaping up," he thought. And Edna Robbin! There was a story if ever he saw one!

"So you sacrificed the things you loved the most?" he enquired, as Edna wept afresh and Mr. Pinch knelt by her side, dabbing her cheeks with his clean white handkerchief.

And indeed, that night's bold front headline roared:

SOAP AND WATER SAVE THE DAY!

Sitting there distraught in the bitterly cold craft and clay room, Edna felt that her life was over and that she would never recover from such a loss. But fate had much in store for Edna, and all of it was good.

"Where is Walter?" asked Alan Padder suddenly. The shock of Edna's story had driven the whereabouts of the little potter from his mind.

"I'm afraid Walter is ill," said Mr. Pinch, looking anxiously at Edna. "He collapsed and was taken home shortly before these events took place. He may have pneumonia."

"Oh no!" cried Edna. "I must go to him!"

"No, no, Mrs. Robbin," said Mr. Pinch calmly. "He has his aunts. You must rest now. Then I shall walk with you to your home. I am sure Walter will soon be having visitors. Don't distress yourself, my dear."

"A picture, please Mrs. Robbin! Before you go!"

Alan Padder lifted his camera and quickly fitted a new bulb. Before Edna could speak the grey room was lit by a silver flash. Sadness became her, because exhausted as she was, damp and cold and disordered, little Edna Robbin had never looked more beautiful.

§

Walter lay in bed, coughing heavily. But Dr. Deere had been and pronounced it a chesty cold, nothing worse.

"Plenty of hot soup," he said, warming his chilly bottom at the bedroom fire. "Keep him warm. Nice drawings, these Walter. Mind if I...."

"Help yourself," coughed Walter and lying back on his pillows he went instantly to sleep.

When he awoke, the room was dark and a wind was blowing around the chimney pots, so that a little fall of soot dampened the flames in the tiny grate. Minnie's figure rose from the corner of the room and soon the fire was roaring up the chimney once again.

"A cup of tea, dear?" she asked.

"Mr. Jollie didn't go out in the fog, did he?" asked Walter. He coughed again, then said, "He didn't take Dragon out in this, did he Auntie?"

Minnie shook her head.

"I've no idea," she said. "We've been with you all day, dear. But I don't think so, Walter. It would be madness on a day like this. Absolute madness. I'll go down and get your tea."

"It would be madness," thought Walter as he lay under the cosy quilt. But he couldn't stop worrying about his friend. "Surely he didn't go out?" he asked himself repeatedly – but he knew the answer just the same.

"He's bonkers when it comes to horses!" he told Minnie when she reappeared five minutes later. "Absolutely bonkers!"

"approaching the huge vase, Billie held up the knife..."

Chapter Sixteen

Dragon's Day Out

Up at the top of the hill by Mr. Beany's yard the smog was not quite so impenetrable. It was possible to see several yards ahead and even across the road. So, while Walter had been busy with his dragon, Mr. Jollie had been insisting that Mr. Beany harness Dragon to the cart.

"Very grateful for the use of it, Beany," he said. "Ordering a smart little thing next week. Very good of you though. Thank you, Beany."

All Mr. Beany's protests had been in vain.

"Bit of mist, Beany. Bit of mist," Mr. Jollie had insisted. "Marvellous! Bit between my teeth now, don't y'know!"

Dragon, for once, looked as though he did not want to do much of anything at all. He had been lifting his head and smelling the smog all morning, then snorting and retreating to the haynet at the back of his stable. Now, harnessed to the cart, he looked as immovable as a mountain.

Well wrapped up in his overcoat and blanket, Mr. Jollie assumed his driving positon and took up the reins.

"Tiny tap with the whip, sir," advised Mr. Beany cautiously, when the mountain refused to move.

"Oh no, think not, Beany," said Mr. Jollie confidently. "Question of encouragement. Hup Dragon, old boy! Hup! Hup!"

The mountain remained where it was.

Mr. Jollie clicked repeatedly.

"Go on Dragon! Walk on! Click-click! Click-click!"

Mr. Beany mildly proffered the whip again.

"No, no, Beany. No need," said Mr. Jollie, shaking the reins.

"Walk on Dragon. Click-click! Click-click!"

Ten minutes passed and then ten more. Mr. Beany wished he had put on his overcoat too, but politeness kept him at his post. Then Sprout, only half putting it on, limped out from the dry goods store, brandishing a mop.

"'aving trouble, sir?" he shouted, with all the venom of one recently unenamoured of the horse. "'ere, this is what 'e needs!"

Summoning his strength, he gave Dragon a great poke in the backside with the wet mop - and the huge horse shot forward out of the foggy yard like a cannon ball. Dragon raced off down the hill.

"Not so bad after all," he thought, pulling hard on the reins. "Nice to get out!"

The smog soon became a cocoon, so that Dragon surged forward sightlessly and Mr. Jollie could see only his tail, arched and glistening in the gloom.

"Steady, old boy! Steady!" he called, beginning to feel uneasy. "Steady the Buffs! Steady the Buffs!"

But Dragon raced on regardless, never slackening his pace as his hooves slipped on the cobbles and the cart began to slide and swerve alarmingly.

Few people were about and even fewer vehicles. It was the worst smog the city had ever known and most public transport had been cancelled. Dragon's hooves made a muffled thundering sound as he skidded around the corner into Turner Street. The cart swung out widely, forcing Mr. Jollie to grip the front board firmly and wedge his feet against its bottom edge.

"Whoaa, boy! Whoaa!" he cried, but Dragon thundered on.

In their headlong flight from retribution, Billie and Willie were at this point just reaching the gates of The Grove. They heard the approaching cart before they saw it. Then Dragon loomed out of the smog, though the gateposts hid the twins from view.

"Quick!" Billie whispered desperately as it hurtled past. "Jump on!"

And on they leapt simultaneously, landing heavily and instinctively clutching at the wooden sides as Dragon, registering the heavy impact of their bodies, reared and plunged ahead, faster and faster into the darkening coffin of smog.

"Dear me!" cried Mr. Jollie. "Who's that? Who's there?" but no reply came and Mr. Jollie had little time to wonder as Dragon coursed on.

He was able to feel how much faster Dragon became with every yard he covered and every canal bridge he leapt up and down, sending the cart bouncing high into the air then thudding down again onto its groaning axles.

"Have to buy Beany a new cart at this rate," thought the good old man, clinging on for his very life. "Whoaa, Dragon! Whoa!"

Then, unable to see a thing, Mr. Jollie felt the whole cart lift several feet off the ground and perform an alarming mid-air twist. Suddenly, too, it felt lighter and Dragon slowed his pace to a slow gallop as it landed on the far side of the steepest canal bridge in town. The gallop slowed to a canter, the canter to a trot, then the trot to a walk and a standstill.

Mr. Jollie breathed a huge sigh of relief and got down from his seat.

"Marvellous!" he said.

Dragon had come to a standstill outside The Potter's Daughter, an ancient inn with a large stable yard at the rear. Dragon smelt oats. He smelt warm barley and molasses. He smelt hay and security.

Mr. Jollie put his head around the door of the snug.

"Any chance of a stable, dear boy?" he enquired of the diminutive barman, who came forward smiling and wiping his beery hands on his apron before calling for the stable boy to lead the sweating Dragon to his rest.

§

Both Grunters had involuntarily exited the cart in mid-air above the apex of the bridge. Willie had somersaulted to the left and Billie to the right. Neither had had a chance to cry out or save himself before he had spun downwards through the thick smog onto a canal barge below.

Billie had landed heavily on a coal barge travelling southwards, knocking himself unconscious on the unyielding cargo and thus lying quiet and unmoving as the bargees made their way out of the smoggy city, cautiously negotiating the locks and setting their course for Wolverhampton and Birmingham beyond. For many miles Billie slept unaware, his lumpy bed entering his dreams in a strange distorted form so that his unconscious state was disturbed and uneasy, like the terrible nights of the week just past.

Old Ma's ghastly face entered his dreams, her blank eyes searching him out so that he quailed and quivered, whimpering forlornly on the black heap in the middle of the barge. The smog hid his bulk and his whimpers, the bargees being deafened by the steady chunk – chunk of their engine as they navigated their craft between the flat pastures on either side of the smooth dark canal.

When Billie regained full consciousness four hours later, the fog was lifting and he saw a circle of black astonished faces staring down at him. His head still spinning, he moved to roll away and run but was caught and pinioned by strong black arms. He fell back, exhausted and tearful.

"Perhaps I'm in hell," he thought, curling into a ball and sobbing loudly.

The thought that Old Ma would eventually join him made him weep even louder, until the bargemen, standing back, shook their heads and covered him with coal-sacks, before returning to their careful navigation of the increasingly busy waterway.

§

Willie had landed on a north-bound barge, falling squarely onto packing cases, bruising but not breaking his arms and legs. He knew what had happened to him, but not how to deal with it. Fear of the police and of Old Ma kept him quiet and he hid himself away among the crates and the hay, making a deep nest with a heavy blanket of smog for security.

As time wore on, he grew hungry and more and more afraid. The likelihood of capture by George and the constabulary receded but the anonymity of the journey and his blindness in the all-pervading greyness was disturbing and disorienting. Alone, and for the first time without his twin, Willie Grunter had only himself to fall back on. His first instinct was to steal food at night when the barge family were asleep and the vessel was moored by the canal-side, the horse softly tearing at the grass of the towpath, audible but invisible. Stiffly and painfully, he eased himself slowly backwards to the sacks of onions and potatoes piled on the cabin roof. Wishing they were apples, or at least carrots, he bit into them, spitting the potato into the canal but managing a whole onion on the first night and two more during the second.

He could have easily stepped ashore that first night, or on the night that followed but his fear was greater than his hunger. Old Ma's eyes penetrated the fog-enshrouded boat so that his blood froze and the damp chill of the November nights became almost unbearable. Her voice was ever in his head, her menace ever present. Return he could not, and though he longed for the comfort of his brother by his side the overwhelming fear of his grandmother kept him hidden, moving further and further away each day.

He longed to see his mother and father again, absent though they had been for much of his life. Harold had been satisfied that he put good food on the table and that his wife could clothe and shoe them well.

"Want for nowt, those two," he had always told himself when he saw them pass the shop window, giving them a nod as they went on their devious ways each day, happy with outward appearances, questioning nothing.

But Billie and Willie had swaggered through life, squashing and bullying those smaller and weaker, whilst their complacent father and their ineffectual mother tended their business instead of their children.

When Old Pa had died, his wife had come to live at the shop on the unspoken understanding that she would make herself useful. Harold had never loved his mother. Neither did he like her, yet he had entrusted her with the upbringing of his small sons and he had done this heedlessly, with as much forethought as a minnow leaving its babies in the shelter of a crocodile's mouth.

Harold took after his father, like him a man satisfied with the surface of things, busy always with his butchering and his bartering. Young Harold had been constantly at his father's side, working on chops or racks of lamb late into the evening. He was always glad to get away from the kitchen table to run off to school or to the slaughterhouse; he stayed away from his mother who was slyly cruel, given to sudden rages and resentful of all around her.

But he had never understood the depths of his mother's malice or the true extent of her evil. Just sometimes, seeing her huddled with his boys, Harold had felt an uneasy qualm and wondered what they were up to.

"She's got a lot worse, that's for sure," he would think, shaking his head and picking up his pencil again.

It wasn't as if he was ignorant of Old Ma's reputation in the neighbourhood. He knew that people both loathed and feared her but in the same way that he shrugged his shoulders at reports of the twins' bullying, so Harold laughed off A Bad Case of the Grunters when it came to his ears.

"People!" he smirked. "She's not *that* bad!"

Familiarity breeding contempt, Harold saw Old Ma as an unpleasant fixture, something he made use of and tolerated, like a dripping tap or a squeaking door. As long as his business prospered, Harold was a happy man, and since he offered excellent meat at a very reasonable price, it did just that. He kept Old Ma out of the shop and treated his customers well, though he never enjoyed the popularity he sought. In another shop, an extra sausage or two or a steak cut slightly thicker than usual might have elicited a beaming smile. At Grunter's Family Portions such gifts received a quiet thank you, a withdrawn face and a polite exit.

Harold thought he was a good father. Their mother, he knew, had struggled until Old Ma arrived, the old woman's help with breakfasts and teas being a boon to her. So, in his blind complacency, the twins' father had no realisation of their growing iniquity. Like two great apples lying side by side in a neglected store room they had rotted slowly away, each infecting the other until all but the very pips were bad.

But Harold loved them and their struggling and ineffectual mother loved them too. Had they known of Old Ma's reign of terror they would have risen, like lapwings against the scavenging wolf, in a desperate defence of their young. But like Willie, cold and alone in the impenetrable smog, they had been blind, though their eyes would be opened soon!

"Dragon loomed out of the smog..."

Chapter Seventeen

Two Puppies

Around the bottle oven the west wind blew, bringing gales of heavy rain which clattered against Walter's window as he lay in bed, reading happily and thinking of his great vase drying slowly in the craft and clay room whilst Potty's test piece baked in Mr. Jollie's kiln. He knew nothing of the Grunter's attempt on his vase nor of Edna's bravery. No newspapers had been brought into the house and visitors had been sworn to secrecy so that Walter was the only person in the city of coal and clay who knew nothing of Poodle Friday. He had been sleeping deeply, the cold in his chest receding daily so that by Tuesday he was allowed to come downstairs for dinner at twelve o' clock.

A knock on the door bought Thelma and Bill, followed by Burt and then Potty, away from school with special dispensation from Mr. Pinch, who had sent Walter a little light homework. Walter eyed it with distaste.

"What about my dragon, Potty?" he asked soon as they were all sitting around the table. "Is he drying properly?"

"Perfectly, Walter," said Potty blushing a little. He had skilfully mended the hole made by Billie Grunter's knife but felt awkward at concealing the truth from Walter.

"How's Alf?" asked Walter.

"Having a rest now, son," said Potty. "He's seventy- five you know."

"Test piece'll come out on Friday," said Burt, wiping his beard with one of Sally's snowy napkins. " There's no rush. Everything's gone well, Walter. You just get yourself better for the weekend!"

Bill and Thelma nodded.

"Everybody at the market's asking after you, duck," said Thelma. "They sent you a fresh pineapple!" and she nodded at the dresser where the exotic fruit sat waiting for dessert.

Soon they were all tucking into bowls of Sally's hot mutton stew with its tasty dumplings lying half submerged like suety icebergs. As the bowls were scraped clean, talk turned to Mr. Jollie. Walter's eyes opened in horror as he heard of his friend's apocalyptic ride through the smog. Sprout, Bill said, had had a sharp clip round the ear and a day's pay docked. Only Mr. Jollie's support had kept him in his job.

"Youthful spirits, Beany! Youthful Spirits!" he had said and so Sprout still did his rounds, but now on a large black bicycle with a wicker basket front and rear into which he piled his packages.

Sometimes, ploughing up a particularly steep hill with an especially heavy load, Sprout thought there might be an argument for horses, but then again, sailing wildly down the other side, free-wheeling, legs akimbo, he knew there was not. The time was not too far distant when Sprout would have a business of his own, firstly selling and repairing bicycles, and then motor vehicles. Gone would be the friendly horses with their great feathery legs, their canvas nosebags dropping oats onto the city's cobblestones, and their iron shod hooves ringing in the city's streets. Mr. Jollie was indeed swimming against the tide.

He had apparently enjoyed his night at The Potter's Daughter.

"Kept 'em up 'till all hours, I 'eard," laughed Bill, nodding his head at another cup of tea. "'ad 'em all in gales of laughter telling 'em about 'is ride. Bit of a mystery attached to it though," he added mysteriously, looking over the rim of his cup at the ring of faces regarding him. "Some folks are saying the Devil himself hitched a ride with 'im, - an' then got off, in an 'urry, like!"

Sally tut-tutted and shook her head and Minnie gave him a dig with her elbow as she went past with the teapot. Neither of them encouraged talk of the supernatural. But Thelma and Burt found the whole thing very funny and only good manners prevented them from laughing out loud.

"'e's got 'is 'ands full with that one!" said Burt. "Whatever will 'e do with 'im?"

"Yes Potty!" cried Walter, "Whatever will he do with Dragon? He can't keep him, can he?" How hard to part from him, he thought.

"Stop worrying," said Minnie. "I spoke to Edward this morning. Dragon has gone back to Endon for more training. More trouble than he's worth though, if you ask me!" she added, wondering which were more trouble, horses or small ceramicists.

Louie spoke up from her chair by the fire, where she sat wrapped up in shawls, a colourful tea tray on her lap.

"Minnie told me something lovely this morning, dear," she said, looking at Walter and smiling. "Jolly-Poo is having puppies, Walter! Isn't that wonderful?"

The conversation took a very happy turn since they were all dog lovers. Jigger-Poo and Jolly-Poo were great favourites in the locality and the expectation of puppies was something everyone could look forward to.

"Cor!" said Walter, taken aback. "Puppies!"

"Nice of 'im to promise Edna a pair," said Thelma blithely, passing over her cup and saucer. "Least 'e could do I suppose. Much better than Soap and Water anyway!"

She stopped suddenly, horrified, and met Minnie's stony gaze. Everyone froze. The unspeakable topic had been breached and like the smallest of holes in a dam, soon let through the flood.

"Why?" cried Walter. "What's happened to Soap and Water? What's happened to Edna?"

He began to cough again, sputtering up fragments of pineapple so that Sally patted his back gently.

"Time to go back upstairs," she said.

"No!" he cried. He knew they had a secret. "What's up with Edna!" he shouted, jumping up and throwing off his blanket.

"Sit down, son," said Potty, pushing Walter down again. "I'm sorry to have kept it from you but you've been unwell. See how easily you cough. The truth is the Grunter twins got by us somehow, on Friday afternoon. Just after you were brought home. They had a knife..." He shook his head quickly. "It's alright Walter. Edna is safe and so is your dragon. Absolutely safe and sound."

"Edna..." said Walter.

"Edna is coming to tea tomorrow," said Minnie. "Listen to Potty and calm down."

"Edna caught them," said Potty, and told Walter the terrible tale.

He shuddered as he thought of the twins so close, with such a dreadful knife.

"But they didn't use it on me," he thought, and felt strangely calm. "So close apparently, and every chance, but they didn't hurt me!"

Potty told him of the damage done to the vase, and how he had mended it.

"But will it make a difference, Potty?" Walter asked quietly. "When it's fired? Will that be a weak spot?"

"I hope not, son," said Potty, looking steadily at the little ceramicist. "I don't think so. It's been well mended, just damp clay on damp clay. But you know what I always say, Walter."

Walter nodded. He did know. So many difficulties and now this!

"Where are they?" he asked moodily but everybody shrugged.

"They 'aven't been seen since," said Bill. "There's bin plenty of people looking for 'em right enough! But not hide nor hair! Turn up eventually, I expect, like bad pennies!"

"Don't worry about them, son," said Potty. "Everything is locked up safely. Get better and I will see you on Saturday when we take it over. Let's hope for a dry day."

He stood up and began to look for his scarf. The party broke up amid thanks for the lovely food and good wishes for Walter's health. They all kissed Louie goodbye and filed out.

"Their mum an' dad are distraught," Thelma said to Minnie as they stood on the back doorstep. "Been to the police and everything! As if *they* weren't looking for 'em already!" She laughed. "Mind you, police have been asking Harold and Bertha a few questions. They ought ter be asking Old Ma! About time somebody put the feelers on that old bird!"

Thelma went off chuckling but Minnie closed the door with a grim face. Poodle Friday had been no joke to her and she still feared for Walter's safety. She was right to be afraid. Friday would bring him the greatest jeopardy of all.

Potty stayed a little longer, chatting to Louie about the lovely glazes sitting in their jars on his store room shelves. Then he too was gone, his collar turned up against the rainy day, the early afternoon darkening with soot and storm-clouds so that yellow lights twinkled out all along the street and Walter went back upstairs to the sound of wind and rain around the chimney pots. He tried not to think about the damage that had been done to his vase but it was hard not to feel miserable. But The Wizard was at hand and The Wolf of Kabul was excellent company.

"I don't think I'm up to homework, Auntie," he said a little later when Sally bought him a cup of tea.

"You will be tomorrow," she said firmly, "or I shall think you're not up to comics either!"

§

Rosie had given Mr. Jollie a good telling off when he came home on the Saturday morning.

He stood on the doormat, hat in hand, saying, "Quite right, Rosie old girl. Very remiss. More careful next time!"

Then Rosie took his coat and hat and hung them, along with the muffler, on the hall-stand. She began to tell him about Edna's heroism. Mr. Jollie listened open mouthed.

"What?" he cried. "Broke her Soap and Water on them, did she? Brave little thing! Heroine! Marvellous! Marvellous!"

He sent Rosie off to bring Edna back right away. Edna arrived ten minutes later, her hair still damp from the steamy coppers, but wearing her little red hat and well-brushed overcoat. Rosie showed her into the parlour and Mr. Jollie rushed forward.

"Mrs. Robbin!" he cried, "Sit down, dear lady, do!"

Tea and toast were served from a silver tray, then Rosie listened as Mr. Jollie poured out his gratitude so profusely that the little washerwoman sat overwhelmed and shy.

"Saved the whole enterprise!" he declared excitedly, waving his toast about so that Jigger-Poo had every expectation of snatching it cleanly from his hand, being restrained only by his good breeding. "Can't thank you enough dear lady. Marvellous! Heroine! Heroine!"

Then he tactfully and carefully told her how sorry he was about Soap and Water, treating her loss as seriously as he knew how and looking earnestly into her downcast face as she sat modestly in the balloon-backed chair. Edna felt bewildered amongst all the lovely things in Mr. Jollie's room. Then her eyes fell on the two photographs, standing to attention on either side of the ormolu clock. Tears sprang into her eyes. Mr. Jollie was very quick to notice them.

"Same regiment, dear lady, same regiment," he said, and he leaned over and politely patted her roughened hand.

They bowed their heads together so that Rosie, watching from the doorway, wondered whether the visit had been a good idea after all. Mr. Jollie had been so changed of late, it would be awful if he slipped back into his old melancholy, she thought.

Then, as if on cue, Jolly-Poo bounded into the room and Edna was quickly buried in a mound of snowy fur.

"Oooh!" she cried in delight. "Oooh! Oooh! Oooh!"

Jolly-Poo bounced off Edna and onto Mr. Jollie so that he laughed, "Quite right, old thing! Quite right!" he said.

Pushing the dogs into sitting positions he began to feed them corners of buttered toast.

"Love the crusts!" he told Edna happily. "Brings me to my second purpose, dear lady."

He paused and looked a little embarrassed.

"Tricky!" he thought. Woman's business and all that!"

He reached for his pipe and stuffed it carefully with fragrant tobacco. It took a moment to draw and he frowned in concentration. Edna watched him quietly.

"Perhaps he would like some shirts boiled," she thought, "and doesn't like to fix a price...."

"Puppies!" he exploded suddenly. "Puppies, don't y'know, Mrs. Robbin?"

Edna sat back in astonishment. She didn't know what to say.

"Need good homes, y'see!" he went on wildly, waving his pipe-stem at Jolly-Poo, who whined excitedly. Both dogs wagged their pom-poms furiously. They had quite forgotten about the toast.

Edna flushed with surprise and excitement. Jolly-Poo was looking rather rotund. But then she sat back and stilled herself. These were very expensive dogs, she knew. She could not expect anything so fine. Life would not yield her such creatures to care for, to live for, to love....

Mr. Jollie watched her face in dismay. He read her thoughts and knew he must proceed with discretion.

"Proud woman," he thought. "Don't blunder, old chap!"

He puffed silently away as Edna dreamily fondled Jolly-Poo's curls. They were warm, and soft and silky, not cold and hard as Soap and Water had been. Without knowing it, she let out a deep sigh. Mr. Jollie gathered his courage.

"Outstanding bravery!" he sputtered. Edna blushed deeply. "Bottom of my heart, dear lady," he went on hurriedly. "Two puppies, Mrs. Robbin. Two!"

Edna opened her mouth, then closed it again.

"Beg you not to refuse, madam," said Mr. Jollie humbly and he actually went down on one knee as if he were proposing. A huge smile broke onto Edna's face and she nodded her head in acceptance. The Poos went wild, leaping against Edna and Mr. Jollie until he struggled to maintain his balance. Edna laughed. Her life, she knew, would never be the same again. She would work for them, strive for them, struggle for them. She would wash every evening and every weekend. She would not stint. She would slave for them.

Mr. Jollie looked at her anxiously. The hardest part was to come. He cleared his throat but remained at her feet. The Poos became silent, expectant.

"Account at the butchers," Mr. Jollie said earnestly. "Necessary, y'know. Big dogs, y'see. Eat a lot! Don't refuse, Edna," he said. "Please don't refuse!"

And Edna happily realised that she could not. She smiled.

"What good is pride now?" she thought. "Now, when I have been given back my life?"

"Thank you," she said, smiling her beautiful smile. "Thank you very much!"

The Poos exploded in a frenzy of woolly delight, racing round and round the room and barking loudly. Rosie came in and raised her eyebrows.

"A boy and a girl!" cried Mr. Jollie happily. Edna grasped his hand. She could not speak. "More tea Rosie" he cried, "and invite up Cook – and Tilly! We're having a celebration!"

Rosie turned to go, smiling broadly.

"Put a drop or two in it, old girl!" called Mr. Jollie. "And more toast for the Poos, please Rosie! Mustn't forget them! Marvellous! Marvellous!"

Edna thought that at any minute she might wake up, in the silent house with only photographs of the dead for company. But here was Jolly-Poo, warm and loving, pressing her curly head into Edna's lap, and there was Jigger-Poo, loud and boisterous, barking for her attention. She leaned forward and took Mr. Jollie's hand.

"Thank you," she said. "Thank you very much indeed!"

"The Poos became silent, expectant..."

Chapter Eighteen
Beset By Evil Things

Harold and Bertha had not had such a happy weekend. Six minutes after the twins had disappeared into the fog, the two constables had burst into the shop, hot and sweaty in their blue serge and in no mood for any nonsense.

"Shut the shop!" Constable Flatt ordered as Harold and his wife stood shocked, sausages in hand. The queue of customers stumbled back against the Minton tiles.

"Now!" he barked, and the customers, open-mouthed, tripped and stumbled out of the shop, pushing each other onto the foggy street where they turned to see the door slammed shut and the blind wrenched down by the sizeable fist of Constable Penny.

"In the back!" barked Flatt, shoving Harold and Bertha through the archway and into the kitchen.

But Old Ma was standing on the rag rug by the range and she met the policemen with a glare so unnerving it momentarily robbed them of all resolution. Each man felt his heart contract so that he struggled to breathe. Flatt felt himself being sucked down into a dark whirling vortex, but in stumbling he sent a jug spinning from the dresser. As it crashed onto the floor he started and an image of his mother's face came rushing up to meet him, bringing with it a sense of warmth and light. He grabbed Penny and thumped him hard on the chest.

"Arrest them!" he cried, and keeping their eyes averted from Old Ma the constables handcuffed Harold and Bertha, leading them weeping and shaken onto the cobbled yard outside, where little rivulets of blood seeped under the slaughterhouse door.

"Leave 'er till later!" cried Flatt, blowing violently on his whistle. Within seconds the yard was a sea of serge and Harold and Bertha were swept off on a thick sweaty wave which carried them all the way to the police station.

Separated, in dank little interview rooms with no natural light, they felt that the end of their world had come. Then a detective (a man so dour that he was rumoured to curdle milk in the staff canteen) opened the door on Harold and walking swiftly across the room, laid a long sharp knife on the table in front of the unhappy butcher.

"Know this, do you?" Mould asked, planting his hands on either side of the implement and staring hard at his prisoner.

Harold jumped. He did know it. No knife is just any knife. It has its own distinct profile, a personality of blade and handle unique to itself, being worn and polished to an individual sharpness and thinness. Harold looked at it in dismay. He did know that knife.

"Yours, is it Harold?" Mould demanded harshly.

Harold shook his head dumbly. He hadn't seen the knife for years; it had been his great grandfather's.

"Funny that!" said Mould dryly. "Your twins had it less than half an hour ago!"

Harold stared.

"Why?" was all he could say, as his face drained of colour.

"Where are they Harold? Your pair of fat bastards? Where are they hiding?" Mould cried angrily, shoving his face into Harold's.

Harold leapt up.

"Why?" he cried. "Why? What's happened? Bertha!" he shouted. "Bertha! Where are they?"

Detective Mould stood back and looked at Harold. He had been in the game long enough to know guilt when he saw it and to his mind Harold was not a guilty man.

"Sit down Mr. Grunter," he said, and Harold, weeping and shaking his head, sat on the tiny chair and listened as the morning's events were unfolded to him like a horrid dream.

Then his face twisted and a hurricane of anger swept through him, obliterating all his former complacency in one great smash.

"It's her!" he shouted, exploding to his feet so that the furniture went off in all directions. He was a huge man. "It's her! I knew summat was up! It's her, I tell you! Her!"

Six constables rushed in and replanted Harold at the table. A few seconds later Bertha was bought in howling from next door. Harold rose again and husband and wife crashed together, displacing furniture and policemen in equal measure and sobbing loudly in each other's arms.

Even Detective Mould found it difficult to restore order and regain control. Then he listened disbelievingly as Harold described Old Ma's closeness to the twins, her fearful reputation and his own strong dislike of his mother.

"I always thought they were daft," said Harold sadly. "The way folk went on about her. But maybe they were right...."

"She is a nasty old b...." began Bertha before a look from Mould silenced her.

Mould was not a local man. He had come from London only a year before, a hardened officer who had dealt daily with the Eel Pie Gang, and, even worse than them, Pickled Egg Johnny, a man so dangerous he had the whole of Shoreditch and Hackney in his back pocket. He was disinclined to believe in evil grandmothers let alone old women who were in league with the Devil. He had put away plenty of young thugs in the East End and now he wanted the twins themselves, not Old Ma.

"One in each of these rooms," he thought, "and then I shall get to the bottom of this nasty little business."

Mould was not unaware of the saga of Walter's dragon. No one in the city of coal and clay could remain ignorant of it for long and Mould had followed The Sentinel's reports with interest. He had even strolled in to see Walter's progress from time to time and knew of the hostility he faced from the Grunter twins.

"You can do very little against jealousy son," he had said one day. "But bullying is a different matter. Mind your back and come to me if they give you any trouble. Dragon Knights are all very well but that's what I'm here for. Mind if I keep this little foot?"

Walter never thought for a minute of troubling the police. He had no intention of informing on anyone so he just smiled and nodded and said Detective Mould was welcome.

Mould had the four-clawed foot on his desk acting as a paperweight for his charge sheets. He was as keen as anyone to catch Billie and Willie but he blamed Poodle Friday on them, not on their grandmother.

But he had never met Old Ma, had never so much as seen her from across a street. And Mould was a man who prided himself on his logic: he was a firm believer in motive and opportunity. The spoiled and talentless twins, he thought, might easily envy their little classmate and want to destroy what they could not create. He had seen spitefulness accomplish much worse, he thought, thinking of Waterfront Nelly and the terrible vengeance she had wrecked on Spitalfields Poll. Opportunity, he knew, always arose sometime and he suspected that the twins had possessed the knife for weeks.

"You can go!" he suddenly announced, taking the Grunters by surprise. "First sight of those treacherous little sods and I want them round here sharpish. Understood?"

Harold and Bertha nodded dumbly and made a hasty exit. Heads low, they tumbled down the steps to the street, relieved to be breathing the foggy air of freedom - but now neither of them saw their shop as the happy bourne it had used to be. Not wanting to go home, they stood still, looking at each other with frightened faces. Old Ma would be there and they now felt very afraid of her. Detective Mould might be unconvinced, but Harold and Bertha were just beginning to realise what they had been living with day after day, year after year.

"She's wicked, Harold," whimpered Bertha. "As wicked as....as....Bluebeard!"

Harold squeezed her hand and together they made their way home, like two children in a fairy tale, beset by evil things, with no good fairy to help them out of the wood.

"They'll be back, duck," said Harold in bed that night, as he held his weeping wife and tried vainly to comfort her.

He was wrong of course and the next morning found the desperate father and mother once more at the tall outer desk of the Police Station.

"Find them!" begged Bertha. "Find them please! They've never been away before! Not for a night! Never!"

"You're already getting all the 'elp you need!" rasped the unsympathetic Desk Sergeant. "'alf the bloody force's out looking for *them*. What? A *knife*! They'll be found right enough, don't you worry!"

But he was wrong. Billie and Willie were softly disappearing as mile upon mile the barges drew on through the dark canals, bearing the twins further and further away from the city of coal and clay and towards their separate destinies.

"like two children in a fairy tale, beset by evil things..."

Chapter Nineteen
Peril!

The week of Walter's recuperation passed quite happily. On Wednesday Auntie Sally made a beautiful iced lemon cake in honour of Edna's visit. It sat in splendour on the freshly starched table cloth until Edna came through the rain with a present of liquorice bootlaces for Walter at one o'clock. In return, Walter had made a pair of plasticine poodles, one blue and one pink, alive in every detail and nestling amongst tissue paper in an old shoe box, which he had painted to look like a kennel.

"They're lovely, Walter!" Edna exclaimed, parting the tissue paper. "I shall take great care of them. Are they alright to pick up?"

"Oh yes," said Walter. "Just don't throw them at anybody, Edna!"

And Edna actually laughed. There were hugs all round and Edna was thanked again for her bravery. After lunch, they played Ludo and Snakes and Ladders until four o'clock when Edna left with the shoe box tucked carefully under her arm, on her way to visit Jolly-Poo with some lovely beef scraps from a kindly customer.

"And Jigger-Poo too of course," Edna said happily, as she waved them goodbye. "I wouldn't dream of leaving him out!"

Sally and Walter watched her go, giving her a final wave as she turned at the gate and then disappeared into the rainy alleyway.

"Well, Walter, said Sally, wrapping his dressing gown a little more tightly around him, "this vase of yours *has* had an effect on people one way or another! I've never seen Edna so happy! She's a different person! Go on, up the stairs with you!"

On Thursday evening, Pongy Johnson came around and scampered up to visit Walter in his room.

"Cor!" he said. "It's cosy in here, mate!

He took off his coat and stood by the fire, enjoying the fierce heat. Pongy's habitual green jumper always had about it a mixed odour of Brussel sprouts and wet terrier which the heat now intensified. It filled the small room and made Walter smile; Pongy really was the best of friends.

"Your cold better?" he asked.

"Ages ago," said Pongy. "Look what I've got!"

He drew a smuggled Sentinel from under his jumper and Walter leaned forward with interest.

GRUNTERS:GONE!

... read the previous night's headline. Walter read the article quickly as Pongy looked over his shoulder. The paper had made all sorts of conjectures regarding the whereabouts of Billie and Willie, and each one was discussed in whispers, Pongy favouring some and Walter others. But they were all wide of the mark – the Grunter twins, it seemed, had just vanished off the face of the earth.

Pongy was examined closely on the status of the dragon vase.

"Nobody's allowed in there, mate," said Pongy. "Both doors are always locked. Even Old Slope Off can't get in. Only Potty, but he says it's drying really well. It hasn't cracked or anything." He looked around the cosy room. "I wouldn't mind a few days in 'ere," he said, laughing. "But you've got to be better by Saturday! You can't miss it going into the kiln!"

Walter was quite sure that he would be better - but Friday bought such peril that he was lucky to see Saturday at all!

§

By Friday Walter was so much improved that his aunts felt freer to pick up the threads of their normal day to day lives again. Louie, by comparison, had felt increasingly tired and had spent much more time in bed or snuggled in the comfort of her armchair. Walter knew that she was garnering her strength, determined to be on hand to assist him with the glazes when the time came to decorate the dragon vase.

"Glazes are tricky things," she had said. "Too thin and there will be no real colour. Too thick and they may crack or even fall off the vase in firing. I'd like to be able to advise you, my dear."

So, on Friday morning, as Walter slept on, Louie slept too, the little house breathing quietly as outside the city's kilns kept up their perpetual firings, exhaling their clouds of sooty smoke so that the winter sky vanished from sight and a low black pall hugged the rooftops, softly brushing Walter's window and silently entering the cracks and crevices of the building. His dreams took on a sooty flavour and grew darker and darker as he slept more and more deeply after a restless night in which mounting excitement had kept him awake almost until dawn.

Satisfied that her charges were resting safely, Sally planned to resume her work in the blackened church at the bottom of the hill. Set on its apron of green amongst the little terraces, it was the place of worship for all around, Walter's aunties included. Louie had once sung in the choir and Sally was still a great hand with the bees-wax, keeping the pews gleaming softly in the filtered light.

"He's alright, Minnie, if you want to pop out for a minute while I'm gone," she said, pushing a dozen yellow dusters into her cloth bag, along with a big tin of bees-wax. "I could do with some eggs and flour if you don't mind, dear."

"Alright," said Minnie. "I'll do the oven first and then go." She looked in the cupboard for her oven cleaner. "Well, no!" she said in annoyance. "I shall have to go first! We're out of polish!"

She went to the foot of the stairs and listened quietly.

"He's still asleep," she said. She poked her head into Louie's room. "Fast asleep!" she smiled.

Minnie took her basket from the scullery and closed the door softly behind them. No one locked their doors. There was never any need to do so and now that the Grunter twins were gone there seemed to be less need than ever. What a mistake that was!

Minnie went up the hill to Mrs. Lorton's shop and Sally turned the other way, happy at the prospect of a morning in her church and a chat with Flora Shufflebottom, who did the flowers.

"Those windows will have to be done again!" she thought. "And look at the sills! The soot!"

Inside the little house a low fire smouldered in the grate and the clock ticked on the chimneypiece. Louie dreamt of her childhood, of gathering bluebells at Dane Bridge, laughing and splashing in the clear water with her little sisters, happy to be out of the smoky air in the green valleys of The Peaks. Then clouds obscured the summer sky and Louie rolled and groaned as upstairs Walter began to toss and turn, still sunken deep in sleep where his dreams became even darker and now troublesome.

He dreamt he was walking through the familiar landscape of his city, over the cobbles and past the warm fat shapes of the bottle ovens. But the sky became blacker and blacker and the air so thick that he could hardly breathe. In his dream, he thought, "I'm getting worse again. I won't be better for tomorrow!" and he began to sweat, churning the bedclothes in his distress.

He dreamt he was entering a narrow alley, following a black cat which paused and showed him the way. He choked and staggered, holding himself up against the gritty walls which pressed in on him so that the alleyway first narrowed and then towered over him, shutting out the black sky with a tunnel of blackened brick. As he crept along, hoping always to find his own back yard, the tunnel spun slowly - and he was falling, falling, into a well so deep he knew it was bottomless and he would never see home again.

He shouted out loudly but felt a bony hand clamp over his nose and mouth, denying him air. He fought madly against it, freeing his arms from the imprisoning bedclothes and with an immense effort finally ripping the hand away from his face. He surged up, like a whale torpedoing from the deep, gulping for air but coughing, coughing, coughing! Old Ma was crouched over him, rubbing her bruised claw and regarding him viciously. He screamed again in terror, batting her away wildly, almost mad with fright. Her shark-like eyes, dead, flat, began to freeze and sicken him but he fought on, shutting his own eyes and thrashing his head from side to side to deny her another suffocating grip.

And all the time he screamed, screamed from the bottom of his freshly healed lungs so that Minnie, hurrying home with her shopping, finally heard him and rushed headlong down the street and up the stairs to his room.

"Get out! Get out!" she cried, crashing the basket into Old Ma's back, pushing and shoving her out of the room and down the stairs. Minnie darted to her bed, and grabbing her heavy Bible, she beat an unceasing tattoo on Old Ma's head, driving her across the kitchen, never allowing her to turn but pounding her harder and harder until they reached the open door.

Sally was running up the path, armed with a huge brass candlestick.

"Flora saw her!" she cried. "Saw her creep in the gate!"

She waved the candlestick at Old Ma, who gathered her skirts and as nimbly as an alley cat skipped off down the path – straight into the waiting arms of Detective Mould and his men. The redoubtable Flora was not far behind them.

"Just taking him some sweeties, sir," Old Ma simpered, waving a bag of poisonous looking peardrops in his face. "No harm in that, I trust?"

"Blindfold her! Blindfold her!" shouted Constable Flatt, whipping out his handkerchief and lashing it around Old Ma's head, much to the astonishment of his superior.

"Get that off, Constable!" Mould ordered, but he had a mutiny on his hands: Old Ma was cuffed and led away, sightless.

Even inside the station the Duty Officer was reluctant to remove the cloth so Old Ma sat silently in her cell, motionless, blind, but now, thwarted, even more dangerous than ever.

Mould ran back inside with the sisters. Walter was standing in the kitchen in his pyjamas.

"You've been dreaming, Walter!" said Sally quickly.

"No I haven't, Auntie!" cried Walter. "And what's more I'm better and I'm getting on with it!"

The great screams had removed the last trace of fluid from his lungs and he felt strong enough to fight off a whole army of Old Ma's.

"Where is she?" he asked.

"In for questioning, son," said Mould. "What happened here?"

Walter told him and then Minnie told him the rest. He went off, shaking his head.

"Dreams, Bibles…. Whatever next?" he thought as he made his way back to the station. And his men! So fearful, so disobedient! "It wasn't like this in The Met!" he said to himself, thinking affectionately of the Eel Pie Gang, their robberies, their assaults, their utter normality. "Surely she's just a very nasty old woman?" he asked himself, coughing as a thick plume of sooty smoke dived down and enveloped the street. "The rest is all rubbish, surely?"

Despite her unease, Louie had slept through the whole appalling affair. When Thelma and Bill came running up a few minutes later, with most of the neighbourhood behind them, Minnie met them outside the back gate.

"He's alright!" she said. Then, looking at Thelma, she hissed, "And if you ever breathe a word of this to Louie I'll never speak to you again!"

Minnie was so fierce that for a moment Thelma felt offended, but seeing the fear in her friend's eyes she said, "I won't, Minnie! I promise I won't!"

The crowd stood in the narrow alleyway agog with the morning's events. Walter, breakfasted and itching to get back to school, went out to join them.

"She's in the station, Walter," said one of Bill's allotment pals. "I dunner think they'll be letting 'er out either, from what I've 'eard!"

"Dunner worry about 'er any more, Walter," said Bill, coming forward. "The test vase is out - and its good! We took it back first thing. No problems at all. It's fired first class!"

"Cor!" said Walter excitedly, "Thanks Bill!" and he ran off with Lefty Knype close behind him.

But the little crowd was slow to break up. Amazing, they thought, that he had got off so lightly when others had been reduced to A Bad Case of the Grunters after much less contact with Old Ma.

"'e's a little fighter, that's for sure," said Bill, after taking leave of Sally and Minnie. "But 'e's young, I suppose – an' 'e 'as got a stubborn streak!"

He looked at his friends, all good men who had helped to carry Potty's test piece and would be doing the same for Walter's great dragon vase.

"Let's get them allotments dug then!" he said with a deliberate cheerfulness. "We won't have time for digging tomorrow, that's for sure!"

They went off together under the sooty sky, six burly men in flat caps and winter overcoats, each one of them feeling chilled to their very bones at the thought of Old Ma, each very glad indeed that she was incarcerated deep inside the cells of Hanley Police station.

§

"Nice to see you, Potty," said Walter as he came in through the blue doors. "It's a bit better in here now. Cor! That test piece looks good!"

"Walter!" said Potty in surprise. "Does Sally know you're here?"

Walter unwrapped himself in the warm room.

"You don't know, do you?" he said, looking at Potty, and he told him the awful tale, all the time walking around his dragon, touching it here and there and searching for the damage done by Billie Grunter. But Potty had repaired it so well that he could see nothing.

Potty listened in silence, then, as Walter took up a little tool and began to work on the dragon's scales, sharpening them and adding a dragon-like texture, he said, "Not many people get the better of her, son. Don't think about it anymore. She can't hurt you now."

He laid a tiny tissue of wet paper across the dragon's snout which he feared might crack if left alone. Walter went on, silently perfecting the scales, scraping, shaping, smoothing, as the radiators hummed and children played tag in the smoky playground. Finally, he stepped back and put down the little implement.

"That's it," he said.

He swept up around the vase and then looked at Potty.

"Lessons?" he asked doubtfully.

"Lessons son!" said Potty. He looked at Walter's disappointed face and said, "What about the match tonight, Walter? Why not ask Sally if you can come with me and Bob?"

They all went: Potty and his son Bob, Walter, Pongy, Lefty and several of the Dragon Knights too, all jumping up and down, cheering on the Vale at the Old Recreation Ground then grumbling happily about the ref on the way home, their hands warmed with papers of fish and chips as the vinegar ran through The Sentinel and up their coat sleeves.

"No vinegar for me, thanks," Walter always said. "Oooh! Extra chips? Thanks!"

And all along the way they passed the little newsagents with their windows full of Christmas cards and jigsaws, the lighted glass hung with tinsel and coloured baubles.

"Dear me," said Potty. "It gets earlier every year!"

But it wasn't just the glittering windows which drew their attention and made them shiver with excitement: it was the newsagents' boards where the evening's edition lay trapped under a lattice of wires.

OLD MA: INSIDE!

... shouted the headline, and Walter suddenly felt hugely relieved. All the Grunters - gone! And just in time - for tomorrow the great dragon vase would be carried to the kiln! Indeed, there in smaller letters, on each of the boards they passed, The Sentinel declared:

INTO THE KILN!
Dragon Vase: Biscuit Firing Tomorrow!

"What's the weather going to be like Potty?" asked Walter, as they waved goodbye to the rest of the gang.

"Very fair, I believe," said Potty. "Sleep well, son. See you at eight."

"I can't wait!" thought Walter as he brushed his teeth that night, not very thoroughly. "I just can't wait!"

" 'OLD MA: INSIDE!' shouted the headline..."

Chapter Twenty
A Prince And Princess

On the third evening of Willie's journey to the north he was caught in the act of stealing his supper. As he reached for another onion a strong hand shot out and grabbed his wrist.

"Gotcha!" a man's voice thundered and Willie was hauled roughly over the roof of the cabin and dumped hard against the tiller.

"'ere 'e is Mo!" shouted the man, and a white bonneted woman appeared in the cabin doorway, surrounded by three smaller such heads and one of tousled ginger.

"Cor! 'e's a big un, Dad!" cried the ginger-headed boy. "'e can't 'ave been living off onions for long!"

The family burst into good natured laughter and Willie burst into tears.

"Eh lad, don't take on so," said the mother kindly. "We've been waiting to catch thee at it. When did tha get on?"

But Willie snivelled loudly and continued to weep until he was given a huge bowl of potato soup.

He gulped it down and said, "Could I have some more, please?"

More was given, the family watching with raised eyebrows as the level of the soup sank rapidly in the tin bowl.

"'ow long hast tha been on the barge?" asked Mr. Waterhouse at last. "'ow old ar'tha? What ar'tha doing away from 'ome?"

To all of these questions Willie maintained a sullen silence, shrinking inside his damp blazer and staring miserably at the decking.

"'e looks too big for school!" laughed the ginger boy, pointing at Willie's uniform. "P'raps 'e's in disguise!" and all four children laughed noisily at Willie's expense, but he was quite alone and their parents were present so Willie could only scowl and say nothing.

Mr. Waterhouse rose and stepped onto the towpath, saying, "I shall see to our Prince then."

A great bay horse stood quietly grazing a few yards away, munching the withered grasses at the canal's edge. Seeing Mr. Waterhouse collect a tub of feed from the cabin roof, it lifted its head and neighed loudly.

"Coming, lad, coming," said Mr. Waterhouse kindly.

Prince shoved his head into the tub as it was dropped in front of him, then Willie could hear snorting and snuffling noises as the horse grubbed about in his treacly oats. Everyone watched silently as Mr. Waterhouse took out a brush and made gentle sweeps across the horse's back and down each of his bulging sides. The children's faces were dreamy and filled with love for their big brown horse. Willie saw them and felt more alone than ever.

"Well, I've dinner to finish," said Mo. "Flo, Elsie, come on loves – 'elp get me started. Fred, tha can show this young 'un," she gestured at Willie, "a bit about our Princess. If 'e's staying on board 'e'll 'ave to know what's what."

She disappeared into the dark little cabin so that only the smallest bonneted face remained watching Willie, finger in mouth, eyebrows raised.

I'm 'lisabeth," she lisped. "What's thy name?"

"Willie," said the stowaway morosely.

"Come on then, William," said Freddie, "get tha sel' up and take 'old of this."

He thrust the tiller into Willie's hand.

"Boat's moored. We're not going anywhere but tha can still get a feel of it. Right?"

Willie reluctantly stood and took hold of the wooden tiller; smooth to his touch it fitted comfortably into his hand.

"If tha wants to go to the right, tha moves it to the left," said Freddie, putting his hand over Willie's and pushing the tiller fractionally to port.

Willie felt the boat nudge slightly to the right, straining against the heavy ropes which moored it to the bank. He felt a slight thrill and thought of the sea captains in his comic books, ruling the seas in their mighty ships.

"And t' other way to go left," advised Freddie, waving a skinny arm in that direction.

Willie moved the tiller marginally to starboard and again the boat butted slightly in the opposite direction.

"It's easy!" he heard himself say.

Freddie looked at him and smiled.

"Instant expert, thou art!" he cried.

"Where's the engine?" asked Willie sulkily.

"It's 'aving its oats!" laughed Freddie, pointing at Prince. "Has't never been on a barge before?"

Willie shook his head and stuck his hands in his pockets.

"Never mind then," Freddie said warmly. He tapped Willie on the shoulder encouragingly. "Come on, I shall show thee how to moor her."

Freddie carefully untied the mooring ropes, then showed Willie how to wrap them around the bankside cleats. It wasn't difficult but he felt a quiet satisfaction and an unexpected pleasure in this new knowledge. He wanted to know more. The boys walked back down the dark towpath, along the length of the red barge, Freddie pointing out the smart clean paintwork and the shining brass fittings.

"We look after our Princess," he said proudly, and he pointed the smart yellow lettering on the side of the cabin.

NORTHERN PRINCESS it read.

"Is she yours?" asked Willie, feeling an unexpected interest in the boat.

"She will be in time," answered Freddie, bending and polishing a circular window with the cuff of his coat. "She's me Da's. What's thy Da do, William?"

But Willie stood silently, looking down at the damp grass, his face closed and unhappy. Freddie looked at him sympathetically.

"What ar'tha running away from?" he asked at last, but Willie remained tight lipped.

Then Mrs. Waterhouse shouted, "Dinner's ready! Come an' get it!"

And Freddie raced back shouting, "Come on William! Last one on board's a fathead!"

Willie heard himself laugh.

"Was that me?" he thought, feeling puzzled at the little stab of joy the boyish banter bought him.

He sat in the cramped cabin with a tin dish of pork and beans burning through his flannels. Around him the family ate noisily, the father aiming playful punches at Freddie who returned them with gusto.

"'e can't sleep out in all weathers, Fred," Mo said to her husband. "What about that tarpaulin as is folded up in the back there? Cans'tha rig summat up with our Freddie, and I'll find a few blankets?"

That night Willie lay gazing at the stars through a clear country sky, warm and cosy under his blankets and sheltered from the wind by the dirty old tarpaulin. He was no longer hungry and he looked up at the stars with amazement. He had never seen them before. He stayed awake for hours, thrilled and excited, looking up at the shining vault above him, over-awed by the mass of the Milky Way. Willie dimly recalled a class in which Mr. Tellright had tried to impart the wonder of the universe to his smoke-bound little pupils.

"So this is what he meant," Willie mused as he began to

grow sleepy and his eyelids fluttered down. "I wonder if Billie can see them too."

He thought sadly of his brother and of Harold and Bertha, far away by now, sleeping under a smoky blanket in the city of coal and clay. He listened to the strange harsh call of foxes but not knowing what made the sound he shuddered and burrowed down. In its savage intensity, it recalled Old Ma and he sobbed, pulling the blankets over his head. He was not going back! That much he knew!

§

Towards the evening of his first day on the coal barge, Billie's curled up form was prodded by a steel capped toe.

"Gerrup lad," said a deep chesty voice. "Come an' 'ave some supper with us. Life conner be that bad!"

And the man pulled Billie to his feet and pushed him, stumbling over the mountain of coal, towards the glowing cabin. Two thin men, each gathered in half by a thick leather belt, made space for him inside. They were black from head to foot. Heat blasted from an iron stove and the air was thick with tobacco smoke. Billie was handed a steaming mug of tea, made very strong and sugary. As he sipped and snuffled the men watched him indifferently.

A schoolboy by his clothes, they saw, but his size beat any schoolboy they had ever seen! He certainly looked of working age but they were tough unsentimental men, not given to questioning the lives of others.

Curiosity finally getting the better of the youngest though, he leaned forward and asked, "'ow did yer get on the barge, mate? Did yer want a lift somewhere, like?"

Billie shook his head. He had no idea where he was going. Tears trickled down his filthy cheeks, leaving cleaner tracks in their wakes. The man was puzzled. Why would someone hide on a barge if not for a lift?

"What's yer name, then?" he asked.

"Billie," said the twin, too slow to think of an alias but determined to reveal no more.

"'ow old are yer?" the man persisted, though the other two smoked their cigarettes and took little notice.

"Sixteen," lied Billie, knowing he looked it.

The other two roused themselves, putting on thick jackets and very dirty caps.

"Right, Billie," said the man who had brought him back to the cabin. "We're off to the pub," and he waved his hand towards a light shining further off up the towpath, a hundred yards away. "Yer can stop 'ere, if yer like, in the warm. Pass 'im them sarnies, Jim."

The younger man handed Billie a packet of bacon sandwiches. Billie tore it open and ate them ravenously.

"Blimey, Sid, 'e's starving!" said Jim, as the other two looped scarves around their necks.

Finally, the quietest man spoke.

"Yer can stop 'ere lad, or make yer way 'ome, wherever that is. There's nowt ter pinch – only coal. Yer can be 'ere when we get back – or yer can be gone."

And with that the three bargees stepped up out of the cabin and off the boat, soon disappearing into the foggy night.

Billie felt relieved to see them go, though the fog pressed in around the barge and he felt sad and afraid. He huddled close to the stove, wrapping himself in a coarse woollen blanket. He missed Willie dreadfully.

The sandwiches sat queasily in his stomach and his head hurt where he had bashed it against the coal.

He knew he could find his way home if he wanted to: easy enough to walk back up the towpath and ask questions as he went. He couldn't be that far away. But the thought of Old Ma filled him with terror. He shook his head as if to shake her from his mind but her image persisted, blotting out the faces of his father and mother. He began to cry again, softly, snorting into his dirty handkerchief before wiping his nose on his sleeve.

"I didn't do nothing," he sobbed. "I didn't hurt him."

But then he sobbed even louder. He had hurt the dragon vase. There was no getting away from that!

Billie thought of the police searching for him in the fog and of all the explanations he would have to make. His head spun and he felt sick and unwell but as he wept he became aware of noises outside on the towpath. Immediately he quietened and listened, full of fear.

Squeak! Squeak! Squeak! he heard and the sound of something being trundled towards the barge.

"It's 'ere, bruv," said a low voice. "'and me that shovel!"

Then came the sound of crunching coal as someone leapt on board the barge, followed by the clang and scrunch of a shovel dug into the black mountain amidships.

"Cor!" thought Billie. "They're nicking our coal!" And a second later he thought, "And they'll think I'm in on it!"

Without a moment's hesitation, he leapt out and charged over the top of the cabin. In the foggy night he not only looked like all the Grunter he was but surprise added several inches to him in every direction and the shoveller stepped back in alarm.

"That's our coal!" cried Billie, lunging at the man, who, tottering precariously on the avalanching lumps, waved his arms wildly then fell backwards with a great splash in to the black canal.

"Bruv! Bruv!" cried the thief on the bank. "'ere, bruv! 'ere!" and he threw a length of mooring line towards his desperate brother, who struggled towards it through the icy water.

Billie ran up the towpath towards the pub.

"Jim!" he shouted. "They're nicking our coal! Jim! Jim!"

The three men burst out of the pub, pint pots in hand, and met Billie half way.

"They're nicking our coal!" he gasped.

The pint pots were thrown left and right as the men pounded towards their barge. By the time Billie caught up with them, Sid and Tom had the two coal thieves pinned up against a prickly hedge.

"You two! Again!" thundered Tom, glaring angrily at the dripping shoveller. "Ought ter push yer both back in the cut!"

"Ought ter punch yer lights out!" shouted Sid fiercely, shaking his prisoner.

Billie sensed though, that no violence would be done there. He did not feel afraid but curiously proud of himself.

"Good job you was 'ere mate," said Jim, punching him on the arm. "'elp me get the wheels off, will yer?"

He handed Billie a small spanner and between them they upended the two wheelbarrows, removed the squeaky wheels, then tossed them into the canal.

"Won't get far with them now, will yer?" he sneered at the burglars.

"Right!" laughed Sid. "Now, get on!" he ordered, pushing the two crestfallen figures towards the pub.

"Come on lad," he added, beckoning to Billie. "I'll buy yer a pint fer this!"

Billie's mouth dropped open in amazement. He hurried up and joined the bargees in the stuffy bar of the little white inn.

"'ere's them Handy brothers again!" said Tom to the landlord. "Thieving off barges as usual!"

The thieves stood with their heads down, making themselves as small as possible in the crowded room. A great burly man in the corner rose and made his way forward delicately between the small iron tables.

"You," he said, poking the drier thief with a huge forefinger. "You nicked my muvver's favourite brooch, didn't yer?"

The thief trembled and nodded, feeling inside his jacket. He took out a little gold brooch, painted with highland cattle. Gingerly, he handed it over, as if it were a hot coal.

Tears sprang to the big man's eyes.

"My muvver," he said, leering into the shaking man's face, "my muvver would be very, very upset if anything was to go missing again. An' I," he continued, giving the man the tiniest of shakes, "would be very upset too. Savvy?"

The thieves both nodded. Everyone knew Man Mountain Mike. It had been a real mistake to burgle his barge!

"Get lost, yer little toe-rags," he snarled, grabbing each by the collar and flinging them bodily out of the pub.

They disappeared quickly into the fog.

"Who's this, then?" he asked, turning to Billie.

Billie quailed.

"'e's our mystery guest, 'e is!" laughed Sid, clapping Billie on the back. "'e's a bit of alright an' all. 'ave a pint, son," he said, passing Billie a tankard of ale.

As Billie drank the yeasty brew, the bargees related his part in the night's events so that before long he had another three pints lined up on the bar in front of him. He liked the ale, and as time went on he drank them all. Within an hour or so he was fast asleep, snoring with his head on one of the hard little tables as the party continued around him, the subject of much mirth and some surmising.

At eleven o' clock the boatmen drained their pints and looked at each other.

"We can't leave 'im 'ere!" said Jim. "We could do with one of them barrers now!" and he laughed regretfully.

"Arm and a leg each, then," said Tom, raising an eyebrow at Man Mountain Mike.

Billie was lugged back along the towpath and deposited next to the stove where Jim covered him with the dirty blanket.

"Proper mother 'en , you are," said Man Mountain, slapping Jim on the back. "But 'e'll 'ave 'ell of an 'angover tomorrer! There won't be much yer can do about that!"

He was right. When Billie woke the next morning, the fog had lifted and he saw through bleary eyes the horses and cows of north Staffordshire sliding past the barge as it chugged steadily southwards. He tried to sit up but fell back heavily, groaning. The men looked in at him from time to time but he lay like one dead, sick and in pain, wishing he had never been born.

"Prince shoved his head into the tub..."

Chapter Twenty One
Loved – And Respected!

After all the rain of the previous week, Saturday dawned bright and dry with a frosty nip in the air but Walter was up before daybreak and Sally was forced to rise early too, grumbling loudly as she made her way downstairs, stiff limbed and still a little sleepy.

"Goodness me, Walter!" she exclaimed. "Potty won't be at school for another two hours or more!"

But it was no good and she knew it. Walter wolfed down his doorsteps of bread and dripping and was out of the door by ten past six.

He was off to the kiln, and when he got there a little crowd had already assembled in the dark yard. Bill's pals had built a roaring campfire which illuminated the great curve of the bottle oven, shadows leaping and shortening against its bulging sides as the flames danced up and down and the figures moved to and fro. Thelma looked up and saw him coming, paused amongst Bill's cabbages to stare in wonder at the scene.

"'ere 'e is!" called Thelma. "Come on duck! 'ave a bacon sarnie with the rest of us!"

Walter ran through the little gate and onto the yard. Harry Mudd met him, his gigantic hands clutching two bacon sandwiches, one of which he thrust at Walter, though not without a trace of regret. Walter shook his head and Harry relaxed.

"S'great, innit?" he said, grinning from ear to ear. "Thelma's bin feeding me up, 'aven't yer duck?"

Thelma gave him a quick swipe with a clean tea towel.

"Nobody can feed you up!" she said. "Come an' sit down, Walter," she added, but he was already at the doorway of the hovel where he looked into the black interior, cold now but soon to be raised to a massive heat by Alf's hard work.

"Not long now!" the fireman grinned as he and Bill shovelled the glistening coal into wheelbarrows and deposited it closer to the hovel, where Alf could access it more easily once he began feeding his fires.

"Can I help?" asked Walter, keen to do anything to help his dragon.

"Just keep out of the way, Walter!" said Bill, pouring a heavy stream of coal near the boy's feet. "Go an' 'ave another sandwich an' a cup of tea!

"Alf's going to be exhausted," Walter said as he sat next to Harry by the fire.

"Oh, dunner worry, 'e'll be alreet," said Harry. "Tough as old boots 'e is!" He started on a sausage sandwich dripping with brown sauce. He sighed, munching and sipping, in a heaven of his own.

"Yer've come a long way, Walter," he said at last. "All them drawings and protertypes. All them models an' things…." He sighed. "Yer've been a pal to me, Walter. I 'ope it all goes well – I'm sure it will!" he added hastily. "But it's a reet big pot!" he thought to himself. "I've never seen owt like it. Awful if it goes wrong!"

He rose, and slapping Walter on the back, went off to take his turn with the wheelbarrows, giving Alf his time by the fire before his labours began in earnest.

The sky began to lighten as the mounds of coal grew taller and wider. Finally, the job was done and everyone sat around the fire, drinking tea and chatting. Walter was just about to rise and set off for The Grove when Potty appeared, coming through the little alleyway, whistling.

"I've never heard him do that!" thought Walter, surprised. "Hello, Potty," he said.

"Ah, Walter," said Potty smiling. "I thought I might find you here. A great day! A great day indeed! Ready, son?"

And Walter jumped up, his stomach suddenly turning over. Here it was! Time to move the dragon vase!

Together they covered the short distance to the school, through the silent Saturday streets where the gas lamps still shone, gleaming weakly in the approaching daylight. Moment by moment, the buildings around them regained their colours and textures as the watery sun began to show through clouds and a little breeze whisked the last leaves from around the church. The windows of the craft and clay room made bright yellow shapes against the dark school, beckoning them inside.

They were met at the door by Mr. Pinch and Mr. Slope. The Headmaster was struggling so hard to contain his feelings of benevolence towards his small pupil that for a moment Walter thought he was in trouble, but he saw a tray of buns put to one side and smiled. Within minutes they were joined by the allotment team, all good kiln men in their time.

A square platform was brought in from the corridor outside. Potty had had it specially made to carry Walter's enormous vase. Six strong handles were attached – but first the vase must be lifted and manoeuvred on board. The six men surveyed the vase and shook their heads.

"Well," said Potty encouragingly, "it's a lot lighter now that it's dried!"

More heads were shaken, lips were pursed and breath was sucked in noisily. Walter's shoulders sank.

"Might be better if you wasn't 'ere to watch?" suggested Mr. Slope solicitously but Walter shook his head quickly.

"Right then, gentlemen," said Potty, unable to conceal his own nervousness. "If you could, er, take up your places around the vase please."

The six men grouped themselves carefully around the enormous vase and stooped, waiting for Potty's command. Walter hovered. He couldn't help it. He tried not to get under their feet but anxiety got the better of him.

"You will be careful, won't you, Bill?" he said. "Don't hold it here....or here.... or...."

"We won't 'urt it, Walter!" Bill said. "An' we won't knock your dragon off! Just go outside now till we're ready. Go on!"

So he had to go, giving Potty an imploring look as he did so.

The playground was empty and the streets were still quiet, just Mr. Jones' milk cart doing its rounds and a paperboy whistling as he walked jauntily along. He saw Walter and stopped.

"Good luck, mate!" he called, giving the thumbs up before commencing his tune and vanishing around a corner.

An early morning hush reigned over the playground. There was no birdsong, just, strangely enough, the sharp cry of a lone seagull overhead, circling the school on its bright wings. In the houses opposite he saw curtains being drawn back and white faces peering out at him. Everybody knew that this was the day. Soon a trickle of bystanders began to appear and a low hum of conversation replaced the quiet. People waved and he waved back; he shuffled his feet nervously, wishing he were back inside.

Then he heard Mr. Slope open both doors wide, banging them back against the brick wall.

"'ere we go Walter!" he cried. "'ang on to your 'at! He's leaving!"

As Walter turned he saw the six men, heads bowed in effort, carrying his dragon vase out into the open air.

"Cor!" he thought. "It's *huge!*"

He had worked on it so closely for so long that even he had not appreciated its size until now. His heart was pounding as he followed in the team's wake as they crossed the playground and stepped out onto Turner Street. Mr. Pinch came behind with the tray of buns, wishing he had thought to cover them or put them inside a bag.

"You must look like a butler, you fool!" he thought and began to blush furiously. But then, there by the gate was Edna with Mr. Jollie and the Poos.

She handed Jolly-Poo's lead to Mr. Jollie and said, "May I take those off your hands, Headmaster?" and blushed furiously herself.

Alan Padder appeared and ran alongside the procession, his camera flashing intermittently.

"Great day, Walter!" he said. "Lots of interest!"

Potty was immensely relieved that the morning was a fine one. Soft grey clouds were parting overhead and a wintry sunshine was gilding the puddles and the rooftops. Little knots of people had gathered along the way, all waving and wishing Walter good luck; all astonished at the magnificence of the great dragon, so perfect in every detail.

Walter was unprepared though, to find Harold and Bertha standing at one corner, or for their copious good wishes for his success.

"We wish you the very best son, we really do," said Harold, shaking Walter's hand. "Don't we, duck?" he added, looking at Bertha.

Bertha nodded her head vigorously but burst into tears, burying her reddened eyes in a wet handkerchief and leaning hard on Harold. Walter was torn between keeping up with his vase and comforting Bertha.

"They never did me any harm," he said, edging away. "The police can't charge them, I'm sure....They'll be back you know...."

His voice trailed off helplessly. He didn't know that for sure. Nobody did.

"Come along, Walter," said Mr. Pinch, nodding politely at the Grunters.

"Best get off lad," said Harold, putting an arm around his sobbing wife. "You don't want to miss anything on a day like this."

Walter ran of gratefully, catching up with the team as they squeezed through the little alleyway into Mr. Jollie's yard.

"Bit tight in there!" said Bill, his face red and sweating. "Them wings of yours, Walter!"

But they had done well. The vase hadn't budged an inch on its platform and there had been hardly a wobble the whole way. Burt appeared in the widened doorway of the hovel and beckoned them forward.

Mindful of the slippery cobbles, the board and its passenger were eased forward until Burt, backing a step into the hovel, said, "Right lads, this is the worse bit. Lay it there, just outside."

The platform was lowered gently until it rested outside the hovel. Walter looked anxiously at Potty.

"How do they get it in?" he asked.

"Burt knows what he's doing," said Potty, crossing his fingers in his pockets.

Behind him, Edna passed the tray of buns to Thelma and then she crossed her fingers too. Mr. Pinch and Mr. Jollie stood together a little further back and the Poos whined softly, cocking their heads from side to side.

The men looked at Burt who was studying the vase closely.

"Right," he said after a minute or two.

"Right," he repeated, then slowly he gave each man his instructions so that after a short hesitation the vase and its dragon rose in their grip and silently, smoothly, entered first the shallow hovel and then the oven beyond, where it was softly deposited according to Burt's precise commands. Jigger Poo barked loudly and wagged his tail.

The men filed out, full of relief that the dragon was safely stowed.

"Not making another like this, are yer, Walter?" joked one of the team, ruffling the boy's hair as he went past.

They all longed for a pint, but Thelma, ever ready with the teapot, handed each man a mug of hot tea with a beaming smile.

"Thank God that's over then!" she said. "Oh look! Here's Minnie!"

She thrust a mug at Walter but he shook his head. He couldn't manage a thing. He turned and entered the bottle oven, laying his hand on the great sweeping tail. The dragon rose up, grey and vulnerable in the dark interior of the kiln. He looked at its face many feet above him, intent on its pearl of wisdom, seemingly oblivious to its fiery fate.

"Good luck," he said, feeling a lump come into his throat. "See you on Friday!"

"Come on, Walter!" called Bill. "Let's 'ave you outta there! Burt wants to build up his stockade now!"

Walter thought of the heat and the gases and for the first time ever he wondered about going to church to say a little prayer, but the feeling quickly passed.

"Best thing you can do now, Walter, is push off for a bit!" said Bill kindly. "Nothing you can do 'ere. Go an' play for a change, eh Minnie?"

Minnie smiled.

"Come back at tea-time for the bonfire," she said. "Go on dear – have some fun!"

Walter looked doubtful. It was his dragon in there! But Pongy pushed through the little crowd and whispered, "Let's go play knock an' run away!"

A smile broke onto Walter's face. It was his favourite game and he hadn't been naughty for ages. For months now he had drawn, coiled, modelled and moulded. But there really was nothing more he could do. Suddenly, the sun broke strongly through the grey clouds overhead and he shouted, "Come on then, Pongy!"

The two boys sped off over the allotments and ran down the nearest street, banging hard on all the knockers as they went before diving into the alleyway at the bottom. Doors were flung open almost in unison and turbaned heads poked out enquiringly.

"Your door knocked?" they asked, looking around.

Then people began to smile. Could it be?

"About time!" they laughed.

"About time 'e 'ad some fun!"

And with a shake the heads disappeared inside. Walter and Pongy were a little disappointed.

"What about scrumping apples?" proposed Pongy hopefully.

"Too late," said Walter knowledgably. "How about paddling in the pond and coming home with wet feet?"

"Geronimo!" cried Pongy and they raced off to the park - their Africa, their Amazon, their Arctic wilderness.

The winter's day fled past in an orgy of naughtiness so that Walter had a smacked bottom at home-time and Pongy was stopped two weeks' pocket money. But they both felt marvellous and Walter was completely happy. They had been chased by Old Ferret for climbing his acers and angrily berated by the mother of two tiny children who had been soaked to the skin during a re-enactment of the Battle of Jutland. Further afield, they had entered into a bloody affray with two small ruffians from Milton. It had been glorious! Pongy had a black eye and Walter had been punched hard on the chin and had bitten his tongue. Sally was strongly tempted to put him to bed without any supper. She looked at Minnie, who was trying hard not to smile.

"I'm not sure he deserves this bonfire tonight!" she said, but Walter knew she didn't mean it.

They arrived at Mr. Jollie's yard an hour later, bearing bags of potatoes, bacon and sausages, bread and butter and cheese. Bill stood up and burst out laughing.

"I've seen Pongy's shiner!" he said. "Come 'ere an' let's see the damage!"

Walter stuck out his bloody tongue and Bill roared out loud.

"I 'ope the other man looks worse!" he laughed.

"Just so! Just so!" chortled Mr. Jollie. "Whooo! Whooo! Same meself as a boy!" Then, catching Sally's disapproving glare, he added, "Still, discretion the better part of valour, I suppose.... eh, Jigger Poo, eh!"

Walter leaned back against the bottle oven. From a distance, he had seen its thick black smoke coiling above the housetops, just one amongst thousands of smoky prayers sent upwards into the low grey sky every week, to mix and mingle in the fuggy atmosphere, falling sometimes as sooty rain to dirty the housewives' linen or as smuts to besmirch their cleanly sanded doorsteps. But this was his smoke! His! Walter felt the huge heat of the kiln and imagined his dragon breathing this very fire and smoke, a strong and beautiful creature ready to swoop out into the daylight, carrying him far away like Sinbad in the claws of the Giant Roc.

Inside the hovel, the firemouths glowed red and Alf, his back bent to his task, shovelled the rich lumps of anthracite which gleamed with a tarry sheen. He had a long night ahead of him. He was now smoking the vase, building the heat slowly to release the moisture in the clay so that it did not crack and spoil. Then Alf knew he must achieve a massive heat for the transformative magic of the kiln to occur, for it to melt and meld the parts into a whole so that Walter's dragon would live for all eternity, forever chasing its pearl, forever hovering, wings outspread, as it alighted on the magnificent vase.

Alf's face poured sweat and his clothes were sodden despite the cold December evening. Several empty mugs stood witness to his raging thirst and as Walter watched Alf straightened and said, "Fetch us another tea, will yer, Walter?"

"Tea please Thelma!" cried Walter, rushing over to the crackling bonfire, a mug in each hand. He carried them back carefully and Alf blew on them and then gulped them down.

"She's going well, Walter!" he said. "Them flues are drawing great."

"Three days for my biscuit firing," thought Walter, "then plenty of time to cool safely."

"Burt'll be back in come Friday. He's busy till then," said Alf, reading his mind. He threw a few more shovels into a firemouth, then mopped his face. He peered into the spy hole cautiously. "That'll do for a bit, lads," he said, quickly putting on his waistcoat, jumper, jacket and overcoat.

"Here's your cap, Alf," said Walter, handing over the greasy article as the allotment team filed past for a break from their shovelling.

Alf ate a bacon sandwich and then lay down, stretched out on a few old sacks by the roaring fire.

"Wake me up in an hour or so," he said and was out in a moment, falling off the cliff of consciousness into a deep dark chasm of sleep as the firemouths burnt and the dragon baked inside the bottle oven.

The hours until nine o' clock passed slowly and deliciously for Walter. The frosty sky was thick with stars, the Milky Way sweeping across the darker Heavens infinitely far above the smoke which curled up towards it or sometimes dropped down into the yard itself so that they coughed and spluttered and joked. Minnie and Thelma were deep in conversation, Sally taking Thelma's place with the teapot and the butter knife as the potatoes came out of the fire crisp and blackened yet sweet and fluffy on the inside, to be piled with cheese and butter so that they were impossible to eat politely but hot and filling and lovely.

At half past seven Rosie arrived with Jolly-Poo, carrying a soft blanket for her to lie on. She was certainly much rounder these days. Jigger-Poo barked excitedly when he saw her, joining her on the blanket at a safe distance from the fire where he licked and cosseted his expectant wife, fetching her scraps of bacon and sausage until no one's supper was safe from his husbandly scavenging.

"Leave off Jigger-Poo!" cried Thelma, as he made a bid for her sausage roll. "You're worse'n Harry Mudd!"

One by one, their Saturday chores done, Walter's Dragon Knights appeared around the fire, laughing and joking and accepting everything that was offered to them. The yard was a delight, a place of serious enterprise otherwise denied to such children, so they raced and explored, playing tag around the bottle oven until Alf, ready for another great push said, "That's enough! Clear off!"

Edna arrived, bearing tins of chocolate cake and butcher's scraps for Jolly-Poo and her mate. Then at eight o' clock Walter saw Mr. Pinch returning, and Mr. Jollie stroll up to meet him on the allotments where they stood in close conversation amongst the turnips, their heads together, never once looking up at the scene below where the shadows bounded as the children played. For ten minutes they stood, talking quietly, Mr. Pinch occasionally shaking his head, Mr. Jollie nodding his. Then they made their way down through the wintry patch and out by the little yellow gate, stopping just within earshot of Rosie and Walter.

"Every letter, dear fellow," Mr. Jollie was saying, patting Mr.

Pinch on the arm. "Every letter home full of your kindnesses towards them all!"

Mr. Pinch, Walter could see, was red in the face and even perspiring in the frosty air.

"No, no," he stuttered. "Nothing, really nothing...."

"Not true, old chap!" Mr. Jollie insisted. "Loved by every one of them, and more than that – respected!"

He gave the last word such emphasis that Minnie and Thelma raised their heads sharply before dropping once more into their own engrossing conversation.

The two men continued to stand a little way from the fire, just outside its circle of light.

"Mistake to think they didn't know, John," said Mr. Jollie kindly. "Of course they did!"

Mr. Pinch stood dumbfounded. His years in the trenches came back in an instant, the noise, the mud, the filth. His brave company with only their captain to rely on, lice ridden, cold, but uncomplaining. And Edward Jollie's sons among them. Yet terror of indiscipline and its unspeakable consequences had haunted him day and night, keeping him severe and aloof.

"It's the same with the children!" he blurted out suddenly, walking further off when he saw Walter's startled face. "I terrify them!"

Mr. Jollie followed him quickly.

"No need John! No need!" he urged and broke into his now familiar laughter. "Marvellous school! Marvellous children! Won't lose their respect through kindness! Just the opposite old chap! Marvellous! Marvellous!"

Mr. Pinch looked at the ground. His fear of indiscipline was so ingrained that it was difficult to let it go. Then he felt a small warm hand in his own.

"Mr. Pinch, sir," said Pongy Johnson, "come an' 'ave a bacon butty, sir," and he led his Headmaster, unresisting, over to the fire and offered him the luxury of a packing case. "Sit down, if you like, sir," he said graciously. "Walter, pass us that butty, will yer?"

Mr. Jollie sat down next to Walter and talk turned to his plans for the production of china insulators, but all the time he was thinking that he should have said something to Mr. Pinch a long time ago. He felt rueful and a little bit sad.

"Kept too much to myself," he thought. "Selfish! Should have gone to see him, thanked him for the care he took of my boys. Wonderful man, wonderful!"

He smiled as he saw Pongy handing his Headmaster a mug of hot tea and Mr. Pinch taking it politely, with a little nod of thanks and a quick smile at the boy.

"Well," thought Mr. Jollie, "Marvellous! Marvellous! Never too late to mend! Look at me!"

He gazed up at the starry sky, blotted out in part by the smoke which still rose thickly, obscuring the moon and the Milky Way, so that the night seemed darker and the fire brighter by contrast.

"Funny thing, this dragon!" he thought, as Mr. Pinch chatted to Walter about the coming week. "Bought us all together, what! Marvellous! Marvellous! Never would have thought it, but there you are! Marvellous! Simply marvellous!"

At nine o' clock Minnie stood up and brushed off her coat.

"Bedtime!" she said briskly and Walter knew that his magical night was over. He was wise enough to know that such a night would never come again. With his dragon in the kiln it would be lessons as usual until, in a week's time, Bill broke open the clammins and all would be revealed.

"six men, heads bowed in effort..."

Chapter Twenty Two
An Unwelcome Guest

Old Ma was enjoying her time in the cells. She had a room to herself, three meals a day, and, as a suspect rather than a convicted felon, was granted an increasingly large number of privileges. Most of all though, she was enjoying her reign of terror at the police station.

Threatening a solicitor, she had quickly had the blindfold removed and settled down to bide her time. Within hours she had a cosy paraffin heater, an easy chair with a footstool and extra blankets for the bed. When she complained of its hardness another mattress was provided, which she tested with all the sensitivity of a princess.

No one dared look her in the eye and all came and went with their heads down, mumbling compliance and hurrying to get out of the cell. Her favourite prey was young Constable Shrimpe, a youth so deeply afraid of Old Ma that he spent his own wages on treats for her at Mrs. Baker's across the road. A daily Sentinel, Fry's chocolate, sherbert dips and fizzy drinks all found their way into Old Ma's cell. Shrimpe repeatedly begged the Duty Sergeant for a reprieve from the cell rota but the Sergeant gave none. It was every man for himself at Hanley Police Station. No one was a hero.

One morning Shrimpe's mother presented him with a bag of sausages and said, "Try taking the dog in with you, Peter. See how she likes *him*!"

So Shrimpe enlisted the services of Crusher, the station's Alsatian. He was a dog so feared by most officers that he was rarely let out of his compound. Pacing and barking, he raised himself daily to such a pitch of ferocity that he almost slavered for blood.

Shrimpe stood outside the compound and wondered which was worse, the frothing dog or Old Ma. He opened the bag and let the scent of the Co-op Pork and Beef Specials waft into the compound. Crusher quietened and poked his muzzle through the chain link fence. His career had not brought him many sausages: the slightest of wags animated his tail.

"Good boy," quavered Shrimpe, opening the compound and clipping on a leash. He quickly dropped a sausage and Crusher snapped it up. "Good boy," croaked Shrimpe. "Walk on."

As sausage followed sausage, Crusher consented to accompany the trembling Shrimpe into the station - but he stood still at the top of the steps leading down to the cells. He sniffed cautiously, ignoring a proffered sausage, his hackles springing up immediately so that he looked more wolf than dog. He growled. Then a look came into his eye that Shrimpe had never seen there before. It was terror.

Spinning frantically, Crusher tore the leash from Shrimpe's hand and bolted back to his compound where he huddled miserably in the far corner, setting up a constant wailing which neither threats nor sausages could abate. After three days, he was retired from active service and taken home by Mrs. Bustle, the tea-lady, who had always had a soft spot for the big dog.

"Done me a favour there, Constable Shrimpe," she said, cutting him a larger than usual slice of her date loaf. "Smashing pet, he is. Loves a good cuddle, does our Crusher!"

But Old Ma prospered too, growing stronger and nastier every day. Yet Detective Mould was determined that she should remain incarcerated, at least whilst Walter's vase underwent its biscuit firing. He remembered his promise to the boy.

"I'll do what I can," he thought to himself, knowing the difficulty of making a charge of attempted murder stick on such an old woman, weapon-less, armed only with a bag of sweets.

A solicitor, he knew, would soon have her released and his superiors at Stafford would be unlikely to accept the danger that he was now sure she posed. But Mould hadn't served forty years in the Met for nothing. He had a trick or two up his sleeve and he recognised Old Ma's game and played along with it. To ward off a steady stream of enquiries from Stafford, or demands for her release, he produced a whole series of trumped up charges in order to justify her continued detention.

Thus, when she threw her leathery old boot at Shrimpe's retreating back, he charged her with assault and battery. When she poked the lad with her skinny forefinger and demanded yet more liquorice bootlaces he had her down for demanding money with menaces, and when, disliking the thickness of the station's rice pudding, she threw the dish up against the cell door, Mould wrote up a charge of malicious damage.

As the week wore on, Mould's ingenuity began to wear too, but he managed affray, grievous bodily harm and public indecency. By the time Walter's vase was due out of the kiln he had a neat pile of charges levelled against her, all held down by the dragon's-foot paperweight. He became ambitious, determined to keep her out of Walter's way indefinitely – or at least until his vase was not only fired but glazed, shining in its perfection, and stowed somewhere safely away from her spite.

But the whole station was under terrific strain and some days Mould wondered how much longer it could hold out. His initial interview of the old woman had been so unpleasant that he had no wish to repeat it. Feeling much less of a man than he had hitherto thought himself, Mould had gone along with Flatt's entreaties.

"Don't look in 'er eyes, sir! Don't!" his burly officer had pleaded.

Head down, studiously inscribing her statement, Mould had felt an utter fool. Finally, glancing up at his prisoner, he had been met with such utter contempt that his humiliation was complete. His face had reddened and Old Ma's smile became viciously triumphant. Daring to glare at her he had instantly frozen, his stomach sickening, his head spinning. The officer at the door, face averted, rushed forward and slapped his superior on the cheek. Old Ma's exaltation was absolute. With the greatest of efforts Mould had gathered his papers together, and, with as much authority as he could muster, had tucked his pen into his top pocket. But he had kept his eyes on the wall above Old Ma's head.

"You will be detained at His Majesty's pleasure," he had said. "Awaiting further investigations. Take her away!"

Old Ma had smiled with satisfaction.

"Very comfy!" she had cackled on the way out. "Lovely!"

"Get rid of her Sir!" he had been beseeched many times in the days that followed. "We've nothing on her! Let her go!"

But Mould was determined. If he could give Walter some respite, he would, and if he could put up with her then his men would have to do the same. Yet the station was cracking apart and sooner or later the bird would fly!

"He sniffed cautiously…"

Chapter Twenty Three
A Fellow Reader

Edna Robbin's life was in the process of changing dramatically for the better. The story of her heroism, read widely in The Sentinel, had been picked up by the national press too. Her beautiful face gazed out of The Times one morning as it lay on the glossy desk of a soap magnate in Liverpool. Shoving aside his reports, he picked up the paper and read the article attentively. Then he pushed back his chair and sat with his feet up on the desk. His eyes closed, but he wasn't asleep – he was thinking.

A few days later a sleek black car drew up outside Edna's tiny house and a knock echoed through its bare rooms, so that Edna, elbow deep in suds in the damp little scullery, started and thought, "Whoever is that!" No one ever knocked on the front door: all callers came though the wooden gate in the alleyway. Hastily, she dried her arms and patted her bun.

Opening the door, she found a handsome chauffeur and a silver haired gentleman in the smartest overcoat she had ever seen. His shoes were dark pools, his gloves the finest white kid. Edna's neighbours watched in astonishment as he disappeared into the house. Good manners deserted them and they crept underneath Edna's window, straining to hear the conversation inside - but they listened in vain, backs aching as they crouched low beneath the window sill, watched by the amused chauffeur sitting motionless in the powerful car.

Finally, they heard voices approaching the front door and scurried off, gathering in two's and three's further down the street where they hummed and hawed and pretended not to notice as the gentleman shook Edna's hand and respectfully bade her goodbye.

Edna stood watching the car depart with an expression of bewilderment on her face, propping herself up on the door jamb as if she needed its support. Quickly, a little crowd gathered around her.

"What's up, Edna?" asked Mrs. Fellows, squeezing the washerwoman's arm kindly.

"Who's that?" asked Mrs. Flint, craning to see the last of the car as it took the corner majestically.

"What's happening, duck?" queried another neighbour, speaking for the rest of the crowd.

Edna, almost struck dumb, had to be taken inside and made a cup of tea before she could find her voice.

"They want to take pictures of me!" she gasped at last.

Everyone took a step back.

"Whatever for!" they cried.

"Soap!" said Edna. "Soap!"

Then slowly, with much amazement, she told her neighbours that Mr. Bright had asked her to be the face of his latest soap – a very fine soap, he had said, for the very best of complexions.

"To be sold in Woolworths!" gasped Edna, hardly able to swallow the tea she had been given.

"'ow d'yer mean, Edna?" asked her next-door neighbour, a large woman with fourteen children, who had given up worrying about her own complexion long ago, though she envied Edna's.

"They'll put my picture on the packet," said Edna simply. "My picture! Whatever for, do you think?"

She shook her head, bewildered still. The idea was too strange to be believed. But Mrs. Fellows smiled.

"It's that Poodle Friday business, isn't it, Edna?" she said.

Edna nodded and Mrs. Fellows nodded too.

"See, they've got a right good story for publicity, as they call it these days," she said. "And your pretty face to go with it! It's not a bad idea, I'll give 'im that!" She looked around at her neighbours, as if to say, "See! I understand these things!"

"Are they paying you, Edna?" asked Mrs. Flint eagerly.

Edna nodded again. There was still a lump in her throat.

"A lot," she said. "Fifty pounds!"

"Fifty pounds!" they all cried in amazement. "Fifty pounds! Why Edna, you'll be rich!"

Laughing and clapping her on the back, her friends and neighbours were glad that Edna's hard times were over and hardly anyone one begrudged her such good fortune. They had seen her struggles, her bravery, her unaffected kindness and goodwill to all around her.

"When?" she was finally asked. "When are they taking your picture, Edna?"

Edna told them of the arrangements that had been made so that her pictures would shortly be in the shops and on posters and in magazines too.

"And every time they print my picture," said Edna, puzzled and unsure, "they send me one tenth of a farthing, or something like that. Not much, you see," she added humbly.

"Not much, Edna!" cried Mrs. Flint. "Love a duck! You'll have masses of money Edna! Think of all the soap bars, all the magazines and newspapers! Think of all the posters everywhere!"

"Oh dear!" cried Edna, suddenly upset. "Whatever shall I do with it all?"

"Don't worry, duck," said Mrs. Fellows soothingly. "We'll ask Mr. Jollie. He'll give you some good advice, Edna. And you can do a lot of good in the world, with money like that," she added. "You can help a lot of people if you want to, duck!"

Edna sat up and smiled radiantly.

"Oh, I can!" she cried. "I can! I can!"

Events progressed quickly so that before long her face, pure and enchanting amongst its masses of cloudy red hair, graced the packets of Red Robin Soap on sale in Woolworth's. Large enamelled signs appeared in some districts, much admired by passers-by though Edna hurried past them head down on her way to and from the library in Hanley.

Freed from the drudgery of her former life, Edna at last had the leisure to read. Visiting the library twice weekly, she garnered great armfuls of books to consume by her fire, filled with delight that life had heaped such time into her lap, more precious than any jewel.

Her first book, "Keeping Your Poodles Perfect", was discussed in great detail with Edward Jollie, with whom she dined every Wednesday night, waited on by a smiling Rosie as two wet black noses rested hopefully on her knees. Edna happily counted the weeks until the birth of Jolly-Poo's puppies, when she could feel them warm and wriggling in her welcoming arms. The weeks up till that time she filled with little kindnesses and with reading, reading, reading.

Then, one lamplit evening, Edna was hastening home from the library when, rounding a corner, she bumped slap into Mr. Pinch, the books tumbling out of her grasp onto the gritty pavement below. He was quicker than Edna in retrieving them, stooping in a flash and wiping them clean with his immaculate handkerchief. He passed them courteously to the trembling Edna, who blushed furiously. The lamplight shone through her tumbled hair, gilding its threads with copper and gold, casting violet shadows beneath her brows and deepening the sea-green of her eyes. She seemed truly a creature from Fairy Land, spirit-like, quite magical in her otherworldliness. But Edna looked down, flurried and unsure.

"Oh dear, Mr. Pinch," she said nervously. "How clumsy of me. I hope they're not spoilt."

"Not at all Mrs. Robbin," he reassured her kindly. "A very good selection, I see. Mr. Hardy and Mr. Dickens?"

"Well, yes," said Edna, still quivering nervously. "But sometimes I struggle, you know…. Some of the words…."

She trailed off but Mr. Pinch leapt in.

"Quite! A good dictionary is what you need, Mrs. Robbin," he said encouragingly. "Especially with Mr. Hardy! Please do borrow one of mine, if you have the time to pop into The Grove." He paused and looked a little apprehensive, "But more than that – if I may suggest – a little light bookish conversation with a fellow reader? A chat about what we are reading? I should enjoy that a great deal, Mrs. Robbin."

Edna's flush deepened and the books shook in her hands. She thanked Mr. Pinch and promised to visit the school that week. Then she hurried off through the enchanted streets, her heart galloping wildly in her chest, blind to everything around her. For some time now Edna's heart had harboured a secret joy and anguish which she communicated to no one. Much to her surprise and astonishment, Edna Robbin had fallen madly in love!

§

In class once again, the days went by very slowly for Walter and he had enormous trouble concentrating on the likes of Nell Gwyn and her oranges or Mr. Newton and his apple. He might no longer be filling his exercise books with drawings of dragons, or secretly modelling a foot or a wing under the cover of his desk, but his attention was, none the less, faraway from such-fruit based learning, or lessons on fractions or collective nouns.

But he was led to ponder on the collective noun for a group of dragons. What might that be, he wondered?

Raising his hand in the middle of Miss Lush's English lesson, he asked, "Miss, what's the collective noun for dragons, Miss?"

Nellie Lush was surprised. They were in the middle of a tricky punctuation exercise: nouns had been on the agenda yesterday and she had no idea at all of the answer. Undaunted, she immediately set the class to work devising one. Little heads bent excitedly to the task, and the answers were many and varied.

"What do you think, Walter?" she asked kindly.

"A bother of dragons, Miss?" he smiled.

She wrote it down on the blackboard.

"Quite!" she said, and everybody laughed.

"A greed of dragons, Miss?" offered brainy Herbert Sherburt, well versed in dragon lore.

"Very good Herbert!" exclaimed Miss Lush, inscribing it squeakily on the black surface.

"A singe of dragons, Miss!" cried little Mary Gardener.

"Excellent dear!" Miss Lush wrote that down too.

"A splendour of dragons!" offered Lefty Knype, with a sudden flush of inspiration.

The class were impressed: Lefty wasn't known for his prowess in English lessons.

"First class, Lefty!" said Miss Lush warmly. "You'll be getting that gold star soon!" and Lefty glowed with pleasure.

"A wisdom of dragons," Herbert suggested again, a little smugly.

Walter liked them all. Just then the door opened and Mr. Pinch came in. The children sat to attention immediately and none met his eye, though Pongy smiled respectfully.

"Ah," he said. "Miss Lush. Just looking for your register? You have it by you?"

"Of course, Headmaster." Nellie fished and fumbled inside her desk, which was not a tidy one.

Her head disappeared inside as various papers and folders were shoved this way and that, her neatly polished nails growing grimy from the dusty bottom of the drawer. A delicate pink flush appeared amongst the fluffy hair beneath her bun and Mr. Pinch looked away politely.

"Here it is!" she cried but the Headmaster's attention had been drawn to the long and interesting list of suggestions on the blackboard.

"Ah," he said again, turning and smiling at the class for the very first time in his career. "How very creative, children! I particularly like "a crisp of dragons"! Whose idea is that?"

Tiny Gillian Smallbody put up a trembling hand. Mr. Pinch's sudden transformation was quite unnerving, like the fairy tale cat who is beheaded before turning into a prince.

"It's mine, Mr. Pinch, sir," she quavered.

Mr. Pinch beamed at her.

"It's *very* good, dear," he said and Gillian smiled, feeling as if the sun had shone on her, filling her with a deep and benign warmth. Mr. Pinch felt wonderful.

"Indeed," he said brightly, "they are all *excellent*. Good work Miss Lush. Very good work!"

Miss Lush fluttered with delight.

"My dictionary, Headmaster, fails to supply us with the standard answer," she said, flipping through her battered copy, much loved and well used.

" In myth they are solitary creatures, not given to appearing in numbers," Mr. Pinch said. "In European tradition they are fearsome beings, much given to devouring young ladies - so perhaps we could speak of a *terror* of dragons. He took up the chalk. "Yet in Wales they have always been seen as benevolent, protective of the country and its leaders.

"He smiled at Walter. "In which case we could speak of a *bodyguard* of dragons!"

"Cor! Sir!" chorused the class in deep admiration. "Cor sir! That's clever, that is, sir!"

"I like *that*!" thought Walter and Miss Lush led the class in a polite round of applause for Mr. Pinch's erudition. Mr. Pinch beamed and felt not the least put out.

"Your suggestions are far better!" he said humbly. "Ingenuity and accuracy all in one! Excellent!"

He looked around at the rows of happy faces.

"Thank you, my dear," he said, tucking the register under his arm. "Carry on children. Great things await you!"

"Well," thought Walter, writing down all the class's suggestions as well as those made by Mr. Pinch. "Well! Mr. Jollie's talk has certainly made a difference there! Who'd have thought it!"

Walter was right. Mr. Pinch had taken his new friend's words to heart and had started the school week determined to be openly benevolent and to hide his affectionate nature no more.

"What a fool you've been, John!" he thought happily as he walked back down the corridor, the children's jolly little faces crowding his mind.

But Mr. Pinch's life was already in a state of transformation: ever since he had held Edna Robbin in his arms on Poodle Friday he had been unable to forget the little washerwoman. Her face floated before him always, a vision of elfin loveliness.

"So beautiful!" he thought. "So brave! So selfless!"

Mr. Pinch was in love!

"one lamplit evening …"

Chapter Twenty Four
A Visit From The Wizards

Louie was feeling stronger and stronger. She was well rested and was now impatient to discuss the glazing of the dragon vase. On Thursday evening Isabella and Theodora came to tea with Potty, and afterwards they all sat around by the fire with the cardboard boxes between them on the hearthrug.

"We wish you so much luck for tomorrow," said Isabella, looking at Walter kindly. "We are sure all will be well but Potty will call us if there are problems and we will be right over."

"Right over!" nodded Theodora, taking a jar out of the box and passing it to Louie, who sat in a state of great excitement, like a child before a laden Christmas Tree.

"A deep, deep midnight blue, Walter," she said, looking into the jar as though it were a starry vault.

Walter took it from her. The powder was disappointingly dull but he knew that the magic of the kiln would be transformative. Isabella and Theodora carefully explained its properties to him and Louie nodded happily, eagerly interrupting now and then, at other times quiet, remembering the lovely things she had painted long ago, and remembering too the hope and dread attendant upon the opening of a bottle oven.

Before long the hearthrug was strewn with the big black jars, each with its rainbow component of colour – this for the dragon's wings, this for his magnificent tail, these and these for the forest hues, for the azure skies, for the golden sheen of scale and claw. To the two glaze wizards they were simply wonderful colours, won from the elements by trial and error, by the steady application of science and industry to mysterious metal oxides, whose arcane properties they had uncovered and won forever for the city of coal and clay. But to Walter and Louie they were miraculous things, containing within them the roar of the waterfall, the exotic calling of jewel-like birds.

"You're allowed time off again from tomorrow!" said Potty as the jars were put back in their box and Theodora and Isabella rose to go.

The glaze wizards laughed, a lovely tinkly sound above the crackling of the fire.

"I expect he's very disappointed about that!" cried Isabella and Louie laughed too, thinking what a great gift life had brought her, now, in the deep midwinter of her life.

"I shall come down to the school," she said. "I'm much stronger now and I should like to be there before you begin on it, dear. Sally and Minnie will take me, won't you girls?"

"Oh, but we will collect you!" said Isabella quickly. "Theodora drives very well you know! I'm afraid I really can't get the hang of it at all!"

"On Friday afternoon, then," said Potty smiling. "The room is very warm now and I will make sure there are no draughts."

Sally nodded. This all sounded very safe and satisfactory.

Walter hugged Louie.

"I can't wait for you to see it, Auntie!" he said. "I just can't wait!"

Sally turned and went into the kitchen. A moment later she came back with a large red and gold cake tin in her hands.

"A little thank you," she said modestly, offering the tin to the glaze wizards. "A Christmas cake. Keep it closed until then and it should be nice and moist."

"Oooh!" cooed Isabella. "A cake, Theo! Thank you very much Sally!"

Theodora lifted the tight lid and gasped.

"It's beautiful!" she cried. "Sally! You're an artist!"

"Oh, she is," said Louie, grasping her sister's hand warmly. "But she hides her light under a bushel!"

Walter looked into the tin and then looked at Sally in amazement. On a pure and snowy surface a green dragon had been worked, sitting next to a big brown bottle oven. It had a great red tongue and huge black claws. HAPPY CHRISTMAS the cake said, and the dragon seemed to wink.

"Cor!" said Walter. "Cor Auntie!" and everyone agreed with him.

"It's really wonderful dear," said Louie. "A real gift."

"You should have been an artist, Sally," said Theodora, replacing the lid carefully as they made their way to the door.

"In another life, perhaps," laughed Sally, winding Isabella's scarf a little more closely to keep out the cold.

Isabella looked at her quietly.

"Nothing beats family," she said softly, kissing Sally's cheek. "Thank you so much, dear."

Soon the sound of their Humber was heard roaring off down the hill and Potty put on his scarf and cap.

"I'll be there at eight," he said. "I think we can expect a few spectators."

He pointed to the freshly delivered Sentinel lying by Louie's chair.

"THE OVEN OPENS TOMORROW!"
Eight a.m.

... it roared in its early edition.

"I hope you sleep well, son," Potty said. "And no matter what, ceramicists are inured to disaster Walter, inured to it."

"Right, Potty!" said Walter, but he knew he wouldn't sleep a wink, and as for being inured – far from it! He felt like a snail without a shell: sensitive, vulnerable, in danger of being crushed.

As Potty left, wheeling the boxes carefully in Mr. Beany's barrow, Minnie came in through the gate and along the path. She had been out to tea at Mr. Jollie's with Thelma and Bill.

"Did you know it's Rosie's sixteenth birthday two weeks tomorrow, Walter?" she said, as she helped Sally to wash up the tea things. "Mr. Jollie is giving a party for her, at six. I shall have to get a present for you, dear."

"Cor! No!" he said. "It'll just be girls won't it? I don't have to go, do I Auntie?"

"Of course you're going, Walter," said Minnie. "Mr. Jollie will be expecting you – they all will."

She washed a glass thoughtfully, holding it up to the light.

"He's very fond of Rosie," she said. "And he always was the soul of generosity. I expect it will be a lovely evening." She sighed. "How marvellous to be so young," she said.

And she washed the same tumbler over again until Sally took it out of her hands and dried it.

"What a shame!" thought Walter suddenly. "She should have married him!"

"Put that away now," ordered Sally a minute later, seeing Walter with the paper spread out on the hearthrug, the pages open at the football fixtures. "Time for bed. Come on dear," she said to Louie, helping her to rise from the fireside and escorting her under the little archway to the front room.

Walter rose reluctantly and made his way upstairs, pausing as usual to look at the photographs of his cousins, lost long ago on the Western Front.

"I shan't sleep a wink," he thought, but he was wrong: as soon as his head hit the pillow he went off into a deep untroubled sleep.

Sally tidied around quietly, enjoying the tranquillity of the nightly ritual as the room was restored to order: the cushions smoothed, the table cloth changed, the cutlery and plates set for the morning. Her sister sat silently watching the flames rise and sink from the last coal of the evening.

Finally, she sighed and said, "I have it on very good authority that George Brittain will propose to Rosie at the party, Sally."

Sally turned and smiled, cup in hand. She too knew that young love would blossom in the wintry night. Her friend Flora Shufflebottom was George's Godmother.

"There's nobody else for our George," Flora had always said. "Only Rosie. Ever since he was this high – only ever Rosie. When she's sixteen, he'll ask her!"

"Oh, yes, dear," Sally said, looking tenderly at her sister. "I don't think she'll refuse him, do you?"

She left Minnie still sitting silently and went off into the scullery to finish the last of her chores, quiet and calm, happy with the choices that she had made in her life.

By the fire, Minnie sighed. "A summer wedding," she thought dreamily. "Roses and lupins, or lilac and apple blossom, silk and champagne. How lovely...."

She poked the fire lightly so that the flames sprang up and shadows danced on the dresser across the room. Still she sat as the clock ticked on the chimneypiece and the red coals shifted and tumbled in the grate. But instead of the black windowpanes, cold and wet, she saw a bright summer of long ago and Robert Jollie's laughing face as he sped past her on his penny-farthing, faster and faster down the leafy lane, leaving her and her beating heart behind in the dust and silence of the summer afternoon.

"Goodnight darling," she called softly to Sally, as tidying the newspaper, she made her way to bed.

"Soon the sound of the Humber was heard roaring off..."

Chapter Twenty Five

A Terrible Case Of The Grunters!

The air inside Old Ma's cell had grown close and black; it seemed to throb deep inside the head of anyone who entered, though fewer and fewer were now willing to risk even the shortest of duties with Old Ma. P.C. Shrimpe was at home, refusing to leave his bed, guarded by a mother who scoffed bitterly at the Sergeant when he called.

"Do your own dirty work!" she told him, brandishing a wet floor mop in his direction. "You've sent him down there long enough! Do it yourself or find another mug to do it for you! He's stopping at home!"

So Old Ma's food was shoved into her cell on a metal tray and the door slammed shut behind it but so long as it was accompanied by an Evening Sentinel, she didn't mind. Had Mould known of this daily acquisition he would have stopped it immediately but the paper was smuggled in, the Desk Sergeant turning a blind eye.

"Small price for a bit of peace and quiet," he thought, looking the other way as the tray went past.

The daily paper was now all Old Ma craved. She had lost her sweet tooth and with it her interest in anything other than Walter and his dragon vase. She followed its progress closely, grinding her gums as she read.

"Let 'im fire it!" she thought. "Let 'im glaze it! Then I'll have 'im and his dragon together! Zum!"

Old Ma's malice consumed her, like a November bonfire consumes fuel- soaked wood. She shrank into herself, her energy becoming so concentrated, so condensed and dark, that Mould, sitting two floors above, felt it sucking at his feet and squeezing the walls inwards as if the building were about to implode and entomb them all.

"I'm sure that crack wasn't there yesterday," he thought, straightening up a portrait of King George and running his hand over a fracture in the plasterwork. He looked up. "And I'd be wise to get my desk shifted from under that ruddy light fitting too!"

But he held on, putting himself and his men at risk, determined to detain her until she would be detained no more.

He no longer suffered interference from Stafford. The Chief Constable had arrived one morning, throwing open Mould's door unannounced. Caught unawares, Mould had leapt to his feet in a salute.

"Take me to this woman, Mould!" the Chief had barked. "Think of your pension, man!"

Mould had no option but to lead him down the two flights of stairs, where the Sergeant unlocked the cell and quickly sheltered behind the door. What followed was the worst Bad Case of the Grunters anyone had ever seen. The unfortunate Chief Constable was stretchered out of the station unconscious, white, and with a barely discernible pulse. At The Royal Infirmary, the doctors struggled to understand his condition and floundered, unable to treat his symptoms too, though cold baths were tried, then electric shocks, before his limp and unresponsive body was flooded with enemas, all to no avail.

For days he lay comatose, close to death, until his youngest granddaughter laid her face on his and wept. Like a thaw setting in to the bleakest of winters, life gradually returned to the Chief, though he never returned to Stafford, preferring instead his garden and the company of his grandchildren, and Stafford, for its part, left Mould and his prisoner well alone.

So Mould endured, marking off the days on his calendar and wishing with all his heart that he had stayed in the Met.

"Come North!" a friend from the force had said. "Nothing ever happens up here. Serve out your last few years in peace!"

Mould grimaced at the irony: Deptford Dan, the slyest of lawyers and his slippery clients the Eel Pie Gang, forever wriggling off on a technicality; Pickled Egg Johnny and his sawn-off shooter, dangerous and deviant; Fancy Percy Pratt, the cutpurse and ladies' man, forever in and out of Wandsworth – how simple life had been, and how rewarding!

"The daily paper was now all Old Ma craved..."

Chapter Twenty Six
The Dragon's Voice

Friday morning broke bright and cold and Bill wrapped up well before leaving for the kiln. The streets were lamplit still and full of people hurrying to work on the pot-banks. Laden carts passed him on their way to the railway sidings, the thick feathery feet of the horses clop-clopping over the cobblestones. Lighted windows shone in little yards where packers worked up to their necks in yellow straw, settling the china into cosy crates for transportation by yet more patient horses waiting quietly in corners, heads down, resting peacefully before the hard work of the day ahead.

Outside the corner newsagents, Mr. Tattle was inserting the morning's headlines into the contraption outside his shop.

"IT'S DRAGON DAY TODAY!"

The Times thundered.

Mr. Tattle glanced up and said, "'ow do, Bill. Off ter open 'er up?"

Bill nodded, keen to get on.

"Good luck then, mate," said Mr. Tattle, "an' all the best to Walter!" he added, wiping the soot off his windowsills before going back inside to his waiting paperboys.

Lefty Knype stuck his head out.

"Got school!" he moaned. "Tell 'im good luck, Bill!"

Bill smiled and nodded many times as he covered the short distance to the door in the wall. If it were up to good wishes alone, the dragon vase would be perfect. He made his way carefully over the allotments, seeking not to stumble in the darkness. He could see no darker cloud against the city's sky: there was no smoke now. The kiln would be cool and

Burt could enter safely. He clicked open the little yellow gate and crossed the yard, swinging his tool bag off his shoulder. A small dark shape leapt up to meet him.

"Why, Walter!" cried Bill in surprise. "'ow long 'ave you been 'ere?"

"Ages!" said Walter. "I woke up really early and couldn't get back to sleep so I've just been sitting here with my back to the oven. It's still a bit warm."

"Well, make yerself useful an' get a fire going then," said Bill, and he began right away to knock out the bricks filling up the clammins, removing them carefully one by one and tossing them into a jumbled heap outside.

But Walter's fingers fumbled with the firelighters and sticks. It was cold and he was nervous. What would they find when the bricks fell down?

"'ere, let me 'elp," came Burt's voice over his shoulder, and between them they soon had a fire crackling and the kettle steaming away. Mr. Jollie arrived just in time for a cup of tea but he had left the Poos at home.

"Serious business, eh Walter?" he said, watching Bill at work with the hammer.

Bang! Bang! Bang! heard Walter, then Bill said, "That's it! She's open!"

Walter rushed over but Burt's big hand held him back.

"Steady on, mate!" he cautioned. "One false move an' we've 'ad our chips! Them saggars'll do a lot of damage if we knock 'em over!"

Bill's allotment team arrived and a chain was organised, Burt carefully removing each saggar which was then passed along to be stored away for the second firing. Potty came hurrying onto the scene, his coat flapping, his buttons undone.

As the stockade was removed Walter stood in the cold, straining to see inside the dark kiln. Mr Jollie and Potty stood beside him and Alf appeared, muffled up to his ears, to take his place at their side. First Walter caught sight of his dragon's head, then its flickering tongue and then the pearl, shining softly in the dim light.

"At least the head's still on!" he thought, torn between jubilance and anxiety, his stomach twisting as each saggar came down.

Though Potty was as nervous as his little pupil he was trying hard to retain a schoolmasterly manner. He crossed his fingers in his pockets and craned his neck to see inside but Burt's huge body blocked the view: there was nothing to do but wait.

Alan Padder arrived with his notebook and camera. He smiled at the anxious boy.

"Another big day for you, Walter," he said. "My editor wants lots of photos. How about one of you inside the kiln with it and another when they bring it out?"

Walter nodded wordlessly but wondered how he would cope if his lovely dragon was broken, perched uselessly on a cracked shell of a vase, its tail in a hundred pieces, its beautiful wings lying shattered on the floor.

"Cry-baby ceramicist!" he thought, picturing the headline gloomily. "That *would* be awful!"

Alan nudged Walter and said, "Look!"

It was full day now, and turning, Walter let out a gasp. Rows and rows of people stood silently on the allotments above the yard. Even at a distance Walter could see that they were being careful not to tread on the cabbages but Bill still shook his head.

"Compacting the soil!" he said, "Ruddy nuisance!"

But he said no more, and passing the last saggar down the chain he looked at Burt with raised eyebrows. Inside the kiln, Burt walked carefully around the great vase, inspecting it inch by inch.

"Yer can come in now, Walter," he said softly. "Mind 'ow yer step in 'ere though. Potty, you too."

Walter didn't need telling twice. He leapt into the hovel and looked inside. There, pale and beautiful against the sooty brick of the kiln, was his monumental vase and there, wings outspread in defiance of any harm, was his wonderful dragon, whole and undiminished. Gingerly, Walter stepped around the vase, taken aback by its smooth perfection, its soft dove-like whiteness. He reached out and counted the toes of his dragon and ran a finger over the immaculate scales.

Flash! Went Alan Padder's camera.

Flash! Flash! Flash!

Potty came in and studied it carefully.

"Let's get it out, Burt," he said.

Alf and Bill fetched the platform from Mr. Jollie's workshop and Walter left the kiln reluctantly. It was dark in there and he was afraid to bring his dragon out, into the light.

The platform was laid outside the hovel and the team entered in. Walter heard Burt's instructions: "One – two – three -lift!" Then the men, stepping backwards, came out with the huge vase in their grip, slowly, slowly, feeling their way until it was lowered guardedly onto the board.

"Marvellous!" cried Mr. Jollie, seizing Walter's hand. "Marvellous Walter! Marvellous!"

A ripple went up from the allotments: the crowd had held its breath then exhaled in a great sigh as the vase found the safety of its platform.

But Potty had his back to Walter, bent over the vase.

"What's the matter?" said Walter in a quavering voice.

Mr. Jollie's smile vanished and his shoulders sagged.

231

Another ripple went around, like the softest of tides against the softest of sands.

Potty turned to the boy.

"Come here," he said.

He pointed to an apple sized star-crack, just above the widest part of the vase. Walter swallowed hard.

"Potty," he said.

"That's where it was damaged son," said Potty. "I'm sorry Walter, I thought I'd fixed it for you."

"Not your fault, Potty!" cried Walter, anger swelling inside him at the Grunter twins. Then he thought of the camera and stood up squarely. He put his hand on his dragon and smiled.

Flash! Flash! Flash!

"Everything alright, Walter?" asked the reporter, coming forward with his notebook.

Potty showed him the damage. There was no point in denying it. Alan shook his head.

"The little wretches!" he said angrily.

A great sigh went up from the allotments, like an oak wood speaking on a windy day. The crowd surged an inch or two closer but Bill headed them off.

"Mind them cabbages, please!" he said. "It's just a little surface crack, nothing ter get excited about!"

"It's really not too bad," said Potty brightly, looking up. "I feel sure it doesn't go all the way through. A surface crack can be filled with glaze, you know, Walter."

He said nothing about being inured to disaster and Walter was grateful for that. And it did seem to be the slightest of surface flaws: such a thing could have occurred anyway during the firing, Grunter twins or no Grunter twins. But Walter knew that the second firing would test his dragon vase severely, seeking out any weaknesses in its construction, and he shuddered even as he smiled.

"The only issue is the integrity of the piece," said Potty. "And this is sound, I'm sure of it."

"Have to test it, Walter," said Mr. Jollie quietly. "Can't tell by looking!"

"Knock it! Knock it, Potty!" came the whisper from the crowd, like the west wind gathering strength in the oak wood, "Knock it, Potty! Knock it!"

"Go on Potty," said Walter, crossing his fingers tightly.

He knew only too well what a knock on the dragon vase would prove. If it responded flatly, with a dull and dreary note, then the vase was cracked all the way through and would break asunder in a second firing. But if it spoke true, like a great gong or a sounding bell, then the vase was whole and the damage negligible.

The crowd drew in its breath as Potty made a fist and lifted his arm. Bill and the team stood around, tense and grim. Potty hesitated, his arm above his head, full of dread. Then he bought his arm down sharply, his fist knocking the vase just above the dragon's foot and immediately a deep bell-like note rang out through the little yard and wafted through the morning air to the breathless crowd standing amongst the cabbage leaves. He knocked again and the second note picked up the reverberations of the first, echoing around the listening yard, beautiful, joyous, uplifting. A ripple of laughter ran out to meet the note of the vase, which was now fading, fading, into the brightening day so that Walter, beaming from ear to ear, knocked again to hear the deep true voice of the thing that he had made.

"What shall I write?" asked Alan. "Seems alright to me!"

"It's more than alright!" cried Potty ecstatically, as Bill and Burt slapped him on the back and Alf lifted Walter shoulder high. "It's more than alright Mr. Padder! It's a triumph!"

"Marvellous!" cried Mr. Jollie, waving his arms at the crowd. "Thought so! Absolutely *Marvellous!*"

The crowd shouted into the frosty air, beating their cold hands together as the great dragon vase was lifted and the team made their way through the narrow entry, Walter still riding high on Alf's shoulders as they passed out into the cheering streets, the factory windows crammed with grinning faces as the dragon strode homewards to The Grove.

Rounding the last corner, Walter's mouth fell open in astonishment. The whole school was lined up in the playground and Mr. Pinch rushed forward to shake his hand. Alf deposited him in front of the Headmaster as the team sedately entered the blue doors and settled the dragon vase once more on the dusty floor of the craft and clay room.

"I'll just nip and telephone the laboratory," said Potty excitedly. "They'll be waiting to hear, Walter! And I expect they'll be over later, son."

"Well done, Walter! Well done!" said Mr. Pinch warmly, almost bursting with a fatherly pride in his small pupil. "I have ordered a half-day holiday for the whole school!"

An enormous cheer went up at his words and some of the infants, keener in their interpretation of Mr. Pinch's offer than he had perhaps intended, started to rush home immediately - though they were headed off by Mr. Slope and his broom before they reached the gates.

Walter looked about him at the Dragon Knights, all so happy on his behalf, and at Mr. Jollie and Alf, deep in conversation together.

"It's only half done, sir," he said. "And everybody's helped me. Auntie Louie is coming this afternoon to start the decoration with me. I've still a long way to go, Mr. Pinch!"

But The Sentinel that night had no reservations.

WALTER : SUCCESS!

... it roared and the full-sized photograph on the front page caught the exact moment when Walter's pals caught him up and carried him aloft through the waiting doors of the craft and clay room.

"He leapt into the hovel ..."

Chapter Twenty Seven
Two Swans And A Carton Of Eggs

By the time the barge reached Manchester Willie felt like an old hand. He could open and shut the lock gates, and knew how to position the boat safely inside the deep dark channel of water. He could now steer confidently on the busy waterways, squeezing past the many laden barges and negotiating the narrow bridges with hardly a bump to a day's work.

Willie was filled with the excitement and wonder of it all, forcing any thoughts of his family and of Old Ma to the back of his mind, focusing instead on the new people and places he saw as the boat pushed steadily onwards through the still water. Often, he walked alongside Prince, happy to cover miles on foot, speaking softly to the great horse at his side and finding that he loved the open countryside with its distant horizons, its grazing cattle and barking dogs.

He loved, too, the cheeriness of the bargees and their jolly lunches and suppers in the pokey cabin of The Northern Princess, or an occasional cup of tea on a mate's boat, where, sitting squashed up between Freddie and his father, Willie felt warm and cosy and safe.

He had no thoughts of going home though his sleep was troubled with longing and his makeshift pillow was often damp with tears. Mr. and Mrs. Waterhouse watched his progress kindly and saw the great hulking boy changing in front of their eyes. He was the first to jump off at a lock, eager to lean his weight against the heavy gates or to wind up the stiff paddles, watching with satisfaction as the dark water poured in or out, feeling himself growing fitter and stronger every day.

Always ready to brush Prince at the end of a long day, preferring to wait for his own meal so long as the gentle giant had his, Willie was changing from the selfish sullen boy who had somersaulted on board the barge less than two weeks ago. Now he had a ready laugh when Freddie poked fun at him or when he tripped or stumbled about his work.

"Nearly had a bath there, Mrs. Waterhouse!" he joked one evening as he missed his footing and went sprawling on the mossy towpath. "Might have had to borrow one of your dresses, Elizabeth!"

Mr. and Mrs. Waterhouse bided their time. They knew what Willie did not: their journey went no further than Rochdale, after which, laden with cotton goods, they turned around The Northern Princess and made a slow and steady return to the city of coal and clay. Willie was existing in a kind of dream world, day by day visiting more and more strange places which opened his eyes and awoke his curiosity, long dormant. He saw how, in the north, the canals were faced by great gaunt buildings, four or five storeys high, their grimy walls lined with row upon row of long windows which stared blankly down at him as he passed underneath with Prince or looked up from the tiller, curious to know what went on in such vast places. Even the biggest pot-bank, he now realised, was built on an altogether different scale to these great northern edifices.

One day, steering carefully past a line of moored barges, he said to Freddie, "What are they for, Freddie, these big places everywhere?"

"Cotton mills," said Freddie proudly. "They get cotton from America an' such places an' then they make them into shirts an' such like. We deliver workmen's overalls and the like on our way back."

Willie was stunned. He had imagined the journey going on and on into a distant unknown future. He was shocked and said nothing in reply but Freddie was quick to notice his friend's discomfort.

"Tha doesn't 'ave to go back if tha doesn't want to, tha knows," he said kindly. "But we must. Why doesn't tha talk it over with mother an' father?"

But Willie shook his head. Nothing could bring him to talk about Old Ma and the terrible injunction she had put upon him. He thought of the dragon vase, so perfect before the knife had dug into it, and of his part in the contemptible deed.

"Go on!" he had said to Billie and now he hung his head in shame, remembering the boy he had used to be.

Slowly, he started to retreat into himself again, his face closed as he manned the locks or walked, mute, alongside the compliant horse. Fred and Mo exchanged glances, but there was little privacy on the barge. Few whispered conversations were possible, so they watched him and smiled encouragingly, worrying secretly about what they would be taking him back to.

"Suppose 'e runs off?" worried Mrs. Waterhouse one evening, when Willie had gone for a solitary stroll along the towpath after supper.

"We've done our best," her husband replied, patting her arm gently. "But I'll call into town tomorrow morning to see if there's anything in the papers about a missing boy. And there's Peter coming up from Stoke behind us – 'e'll be here tomorrow. 'e might 'ave a Sentinel or two, tha knowst."

The next day Fred was up and off the barge before Willie was awake, but he was back in time for breakfast. He shook his head at Mo, who jerked her head backwards, towards a blue and white barge moored close the stern of The Northern Princess.

"I'll see 'im in a bit," said Mr. Waterhouse. "'ere William, budge over an' let the dog see the rabbit!"

He took a steaming mug of tea from his wife and helped himself to a pile of sausage sandwiches.

"Grand!" he said, smiling at Willie. "Going to walk with our Prince today?" he asked, nodding at the brown horse snuffling excitedly in its tub of oats.

Willie nodded back, but, "Please," was all he said.

"Be in Rochdale in no time," Mr. Waterhouse went on, licking the ketchup from his fingers. "Our country up there, tha knowst. Freddie'll go off with thee, an' tha can explore a bit! Get upon moors with 'im Freddie, e's bound to like that!"

Arriving at Rochdale was always something of a holiday for the Waterhouses. They made time to visit friends and family, and if the weather was fine, to fly kites on the open barren moors high above the town. Flying a kite was almost Freddie's favourite thing in the whole world.

"Except our Prince an' Princess!" he had said to Willie. "Nothing beats them!"

Mr. Waterhouse slapped Willie on the back and made his way out of the cabin, his big boots somehow avoiding the little white legs of his children.

"Come on William, let's groom Prince," urged Freddie, at a loss with his new friend's deepening gloom.

They brushed and combed the big horse, lifting his massive feet to pick out the compacted mud and grit underneath. But all was done silently and Freddie could see that Willie was close to tears.

"Tha can stay with us, tha knowst," he said, giving Prince's behind a final swipe of the brush so that it shone like a great glossy chestnut. "Mother an' Father love 'aving thee: tha's been a real 'elp tha knows't, with all the work tha's done!"

But he saw tears trickling down Willie's cheeks and he was afraid to say any more.

"Whatever can it be?" he wondered as he and Willie harnessed Prince to the barge, but Willie remained silent, lost in his own unhappy world.

He remembered his unkindness, his bullying, his meanness to everyone around him, all so different from Freddie's sunny ways - a boy forever kind and full of fun; at odds too, with the open generosity of this working family on their cramped barge, who had taken in a miserable stranger and made him one of their own. Utterly downcast, he dreaded a return to the city of coal and clay and the inevitable discovery of his inglorious past.

"But I've changed!" he thought sadly. "I'm not like that now!"

"Right lads!" called Mr. Waterhouse, jumping off the blue and white barge. "We're leaving in a minute! See you on the way down, Peter. Thanks!"

Willie started off with Prince, taking up the slack on the long tow line, so that after a minute or two The Northern Princess swept slowly off her mooring and the day began.

The morning was a misty one but Willie wasn't cold as he walked alongside Prince. The trees all around were grey and insubstantial, hazy at first then airily beautiful as he drew nearer to them, their branches hung with a film of glittering vapour which caught the early sun, the finer twigs sparkling and diamonding as the boy went past, catching his attention in spite of the gloomy cloud which hovered over him.

As the morning progressed the mist lifted and the sun broke through in earnest. Willie realised that it was the most beautiful day he had ever seen. Along the banks, the pollarded willows glowed amber and red in the direct light, so that the canal sides seemed ablaze, and the deep and lovely blue of the canal itself was in parts on fire with their radiance. The sky arched overhead, cloudless and infinite, and although it was December and not May, blackbirds and thrushes sang in the hawthorn, opening up their throats in the warming air, trilling and shrilling till all the country around was alive with birdsong and Willie stopped in his tracks to listen.

Turning, he watched the barge floating up behind him, still some distance away at the end of its long rope. Fred and Mo had their heads together - then Mo's head flew back and she gave a little cry. But Willie wasn't curious. The beauty of the morning overwhelmed him still and he walked on in silence, speaking quietly to Prince who plodded, as patiently as ever, at his side.

But even though the sun still shone and the birds still sang, darker thoughts began to intrude. Billie wasn't there to share this with him; his mother and father were far away.

"Yet I can't go home!" he thought wretchedly. "Not to *her*!"

But to be on his own without his friends! He shook his head and tears spilled down his cheeks. What was the glory of such a morning, he thought miserably, without his brother by his side?

Prince, sensing the weakness of his partner, stumbled and snorted in unease. Willie put out a hand and patted him.

"Alright, mate," he managed to say.

Then a sudden clattering whoosh filled the air and horse and boy stood still in startled astonishment as two swans swooped overhead and landed noisily on the sunlit canal at their side. In the yellow morning light they glowed against the cobalt water, ruffling and settling their wings against their backs, dazzling, spellbinding, like two heraldic beasts from an illuminated manuscript: unearthly, magical, unreal.

Willie felt a stab of joy deep inside, painful and over-powering. The sudden splendour of the scene broke open his wretched heart and in poured the light and loveliness of the morning, of the swans, of the singing birds, of the whole wintry world. The breeze ruffled his hair and blew gently in Prince's mane. In the depth of winter he smelt no flowers, no blossoms, but the ploughed soil came to him, rich and earthy, and he saw, as if blind before, the tiny leaf buds on the

December boughs, wrapped safely in their papery packaging, in preparation for the approaching spring. A dunnock piped from beneath a hedge, and then another and another. Close by a robin perched and sang, its call echoed by rival robins all up and down the sunny towpath. It was sublime.

Willie wiped his eyes and urged Prince on. He knew that he could no longer live in darkness, closed from his friends, his life poisoned by his dreadful secret. He wanted to be part of the world, not merely to exist alongside it, troubled and unhappy as he had been.

Mr. and Mrs. Waterhouse must be told: he must face up to his past and to the boy that he had been.

"I shall have to tell them!" he thought, burying his face in the thick rough hair of his companion's mane. "About the knife, about Walter – everything!"

Somehow, someway, he knew that must make a better life for himself, no matter how hard or humiliating that might be.

"I've been a toad," he said to the great horse, which touched his open hand hopefully. "And now I've got to turn myself into a prince – like you!"

§

The morning after he had blighted the ambitions of the Handy brothers, Billie lay like a stone in the greasy little bunk on which his new friends had laid him the night before. Never had he encountered such headaches, such nausea. He hoped he might die. Jim tried constantly to ply him with coffee but he turned away, groaning.

At midday Tom came inside the cabin to look at the miserable boy.

"You'd be better after a good fry up," he declared – but Billie's stomach heaved, and shoving the two men aside, he bolted out and was violently sick over the side. All three men roared with laughter.

"You'll feel better now, lad," said Tom, and he did.

As the day wore on, Billie felt able to watch the men at their work. Their's was a stopping and starting sort of journey, delivering sacks of coal to the pubs and small households along the canal. The day grew bright and fair and by mid-afternoon Billie had risen and taken his share of the coal shovelling, filling the barrows and sacks which customers brought to the barge, growing steadily dirtier and dirtier as he did so. All the men had grimy faces, the coal lining their eyes and ingraining itself in their pores. In the evening, they filled a large tin jug and ewer with water from the canal and sluiced it over their hands and faces; then Jim threw Billie a grey rag of a towel and invited him to do the same.

"We go ter the other side of Birmingham, like," said Jim in answer to Billie's enquiry as they sat that evening in the cosy cabin. "We 'ave a lot of regular customers, like, an' this is the easiest way fer 'em ter get it."

"You stopping with us, lad?" asked Tom, looking closely into Billie's face.

The boy nodded but said nothing and Tom shrugged his shoulders and passed him a baked potato.

"Nobody worrying about you?" Sid finally asked, but when Billie shook his head they didn't press him any further.

"Alright enough with us," Tom thought, "an' we'll be back in Stoke in a few weeks. Then we'll see."

He lit a roll-up, and leaning back, blew out a series of smoke rings which drifted up and out of the cabin door, grey and ghostly against the evening sky.

Time went by, and though the men heard Billie's stifled sobs each night as they settled to sleep, they were full of admiration for the way he applied himself during the day. He shovelled and carted, shovelled and bagged, earning little tips for shouldering sacks to the hidden cottages of elderly men and women too frail to undertake the job themselves. The money, just pennies or halfpennies, he took straight to Tom, who simply said, "Keep it, lad."

Billie felt himself growing stronger and leaner and though nothing could persuade him to touch another pint of beer, he loved the companionable evenings in the canal-side pubs where the three men met up with their friends travelling before and behind, or the other way, back up the canal to the city of coal and clay.

He became a firm friend of Man Mountain Mike, whose barge was never far away and who had a beautiful Norton on board, wrapped in tarpaulin against the ever-present damp. It was Man Mountain's pride and joy: late afternoons found him forever fiddling with its engine or polishing its chrome as he sat, huge and off balance, on a tiny three-legged stool.

Billie soon became fascinated. He found that engines excited him and he wanted to know more. He asked Man Mountain to show him the engine of his barge too and soon understood its workings. When Tom's engine faltered and failed one day, spluttering and coughing to a standstill, he said, "Sounds like a blocked fuel pipe to me!"

The men laughed and clapped him on the back but, "He's probably right," said Sid – and so it proved.

Billie and Sid stripped the fuel pipe and took out the tank too, finding its inside thickly sedimented with the detritus of years on the canal. Billie cleaned it thoroughly and rinsed the filter carefully, working it over gently with an old toothbrush of Jim's. Together he and Sid reassembled the fuel supply and the engine burst into life.

"Well," said Tom, "yer worth yer keep, you are, Bill."

Billie had never felt so proud.

"I'm going to do this!" he said to himself. "I'm not a butcher – I'm a mechanic!"

But the thought of the shop, the tiles glowing in the yellow light of a winter's afternoon, filled him with sadness and he longed to be standing there, next to his father and mother and his lost brother Willie.

"But I can't go home!" he thought bitterly. "I can't go home while *she's* still there!"

He dreaded reaching the far side of Birmingham because what would he do then, when his friends turned around and made their way back?

"Perhaps I can get a job," he thought, but he knew he would be unlikely to meet with the same unquestioning camaraderie that he was enjoying on the canal. He would be alone.

Then one night, sitting in a small white inn somewhere in the Black Country, he heard two bargees talking about the Handy brothers and what little wretches they were, given to sneaking and thieving, incorrigible in their dishonesty. Billie's heart thumped as he listened, the sweat breaking out on his forehead and his ears reddening.

"I'm going out for some air," he said. "Excuse me, Jim," and he squeezed out between the tightly packed tables, out into the damp evening air where a slight fog hung over the blackened buildings and lights gleamed in the terraces up the hill.

"I'm as bad as those two!" he thought miserably. "Worse!"

He climbed the steps which wound up from the canal-side and leaned on a wall, looking back down the length of the dark canal.

"They'd hate me if they knew!" he thought, tears springing to his eyes as he turned away from passers-by, hiding his face from the lamplight.

He found a quiet corner in the curve of a wall and sat on a wet oil drum, burying his face in his hands.

"I was horrible!" he thought. "We both were. What was wrong with him making a vase? Nothing! Nothing at all!"

He thought of Squealer digging into the clay and went cold.

"I wish to God I'd never done that!" he thought, rubbing his head as if to rub away his crime. "But I'd never do it now! I'd do anything to make it up to him, anything!"

He thought of his life on the barge, of how he loved the hard work and the camaraderie. He even smiled as he dwelt on all he had learnt from Man Mountain and the others. He thought, too, of the customers he had carted for along the canal, remembering the way he had barrowed coal for an old man whose back was so bent over that he could never see the sky and whose daily struggle had touched a chord in Billie's heart. He had pushed the heavy barrow up a steep lane to an isolated cottage amongst the trees, where the old man lived alone except for the chickens which clucked and pecked around their feet.

He had tried to give Billie a sixpence for his efforts but the boy had shaken his head.

"It's too much," he had said, "and it was nothing to me."

The old man went inside and came out with a carton of eggs which he pushed into Billie's blackened hands.

"You're a good lad," he said. "I wish I'd had a son like you."

And Billie had cried all the way back to the barge, wondering why, when it was so easy to be kind, he had been such a bully all his life.

He wiped his dirty face with an even dirtier hand but his mind had become quieter and he rose to go.

"I'm a different person now," he thought. "That boy has gone. I'm not rotten anymore! And if I can make it up to him, I will!"

But still, as he went back along the towpath he dreaded the discovery of his past, knowing in his heart that sooner or later he must tell all, no matter what the cost. As he climbed on board the barge and sat with the others in the warm and stuffy cabin, he did not know that his time was at hand and soon all would be revealed.

At ten o' clock a knock sounded on the cabin roof and Man Mountain heaved himself into the cabin, a sheaf of newspapers shoved roughly inside his donkey jacket. He looked straight at Billie, who stood up in alarm, as white as biscuit ware beneath his coating of coal dust, his hands and face suddenly clammy and cold.

"It's alright, Bill," said Man Mountain kindly, pushing the overgrown boy back down onto the bunk.

"'ere, 'ave a read yerself!" he said, thrusting a paper at Billie.

"OLD MA! INSIDE!"

cried The Sentinel Man Mountain had acquired from a passing barge along with several other editions of the paper, which told, as in instalments, the dreadful tale of Poodle Friday, the disappearance of the Grunter twins and the arrest and continuing detention of Old Ma.

Billie read the newspaper in astonishment. She had tried to suffocate Walter in his bed! She was inside!

Tom read the papers too, Sid and Jim crowding close on each side. A terrible silence filled the little cabin, and Billie was tempted to bolt for the door but Man Mountain filled the space, his friendly face creased with concern so that Billie felt even more abject, even more despicable.

Finally, Tom put the paper down and stared hard at Billie.

"A knife?" he said coldly. "A *knife*!"

Billie burst out sobbing, a torrent of grief and shame pouring out of him so that he could barely speak.

"I didn't hurt him!" he howled. "I didn't! I didn't hurt him!"

Tom looked at him in disgust.

"Says 'ere you was a bully – you and that brother of yours! A *constant* bully, it says 'ere. Always 'ad it in fer 'im, it says. 'is friends always 'ad ter look out fer 'im, all the ruddy time!" Tom shook his head in disbelief. "I can 'ardly believe it," he said icily. "You nasty little sod!"

"I was!" Billie cried. "I was horrible. I was! I was!" and he howled so terribly that Jim moved over and put his arm around him and Man Mountain groaned and buried his face in his hands.

"Stole 'is pocket money, shut 'im up in *a clay bin!*" Tom went on remorselessly until Sid broke in quietly.

"Alright, Tom," he said. "It's not that straightforward. Percy Johnson 'as family near that shop an' 'e says the grandmother is the very devil! *Nobody* stands up to 'er! She's *really* evil, he says!"

Billie's sobs became hysterical.

"She is!" he cried. "She cut our Willie's chin! She's...."

He could no longer speak and collapsed shuddering in Jim's arms.

"No wonder you wouldn't say who you were!" snapped Tom, his eyes glinting angrily, though in truth he had never heard of the Grunters and of Old Ma.

But Sid and Jim had heard tales of her, stories whispered in horror up and down the canal, like ghost stories around a Christmas fire, enough to make them shiver but happily remote, not a part of their real world. Jim thought back over everything he had heard and shuddered.

"It was all true, then," he thought and squeezed Billie's arm. "Did she ask you to do something terrible?" he asked.

Billie nodded, wiping his nose on his filthy sleeve.

"But we didn't. We wouldn't have done *that*!" he sobbed convulsively.

"What about 'is vase?" Tom asked harshly. "Yer knifed *that*, didn't yer!"

"I did! I did!" wailed Billie, looking round at them despairingly. "And I'm sorry! I'm sorry. I'm not like that anymore. I'm not!"

His distress was so genuine that even Tom's anger began to abate. And the four men could hardly disagree: Billie was a different boy to the one they had read about in the newspaper. He had proved himself a good and honest friend: a really hard worker who never shirked the dirtiest and heaviest of chores.

"I'm different now," he said, wiping his eyes and calming down. "I like engines and boats and motorbikes. I like helping you – I do!"

Tom said nothing but Sid passed him a mug of tea and Man Mountain said, "Yer a mate, Bill, an' nothing's going ter 'appen ter yer. In a week or so we'll all go back together an' sort it all out."

"Yes," said Jim and Sid together, "You're not on yer own lad. We'll all go back with yer!"

"An' tomorrer I'll take yer out on the bike!" Man Mountain said.

Billie's face lit up.

"Really?" he said, the thought of the Norton giving him, if only for a moment, a flush of excited joy.

All of a sudden Jim gasped. His eye had been caught by something they had all missed. He pushed one of The Sentinels at Tom with a look of disbelief.

"It says 'ere that 'e's eleven!" he cried. "'e's only a kid, Tom! A kid!"

Tom read and sat back, staring at Billie.

"Eleven!" he said quietly. "Eleven!" He shook his head and his face seemed to soften a little. "But you were still old enough to know better," he said and Billie's head sunk onto his chest.

"I was," he said. "I know that Tom. I was."

More tea was made and hot cups passed around. Sid fried up a package of back bacon and made thick sandwiches dripping with spicy brown sauce. They were eaten in silence but it was companionable and Billie ate along with the rest.

Finally, Man Mountain said, "Come on Bill, 'elp me get the tarpaulin on," and Billie got up to help his friend and protector, patted warmly on the back by Jim and Sid as he left the cabin.

"Well, this is a rum do," said Tom sourly, when Billie was out of earshot. "I'm going next door for a word with Percy."

He stepped off the barge and, treading softly, made for the lighted windows of a barge moored a little way behind. Tom was an honest man, hardworking and self-reliant and the tales of Billie's misdeeds had shocked him to the core. Outwardly severe, he had grown fond of Billie, pleased to see the boy growing in strength and confidence every day.

"Surely 'e can't be that rotten?" he thought, as he knocked on Percy's cabin roof before entering and listening, narrow eyed, to Percy's grim stories of Old Ma and the oversized twins she had twisted to her use.

Tom scowled as Percy told tale after tale, amazed that in all his comings and goings to and from the city of coal and clay he had heard nothing about her before.

"People are afraid, Tom," said Percy. "Most folks keep their mouths shut. Them lads 'ave been pretty bad, there's no doubt about that – but they 'ad no chance with a grandmother like that! An' their mother's useless!" he added as Tom opened his mouth. "An' their father's always been too busy for 'em. She's 'ad 'em all ter 'erself – an' this's the result!"

He sighed heavily and reached up for two bottles of beer sitting side by side in his tiny cupboard of provisions. The two men sat back and drank the brew silently, listening to the hooting of owls hunting along the towpath. Tom saw the pale shape of a barn owl drifting past, as weightless as the cigarette paper he held in his hand. Then another shape drifted down from a nearby elm and a shrill cry was heard – a little death in the chill December night.

"What are you going to do?" asked Percy, draining his bottle and stowing it under his bunk. "'e seems to 'ave turned himself around, from what you've said. You'd never know who 'e was from these reports – no wonder nobody's recognised 'im!"

Tom nodded and was silent.

"I like the boy," he said at last. "My old man was hard, very hard." He was silent again, remembering the beatings he had taken until he had left home at fourteen to work on the cut. "But he taught me right from wrong, though I couldn't respect 'im fer the way 'e did it." He passed his empty bottle to Percy and stood up to go. "With our 'elp he can put it behind him, perhaps."

"Will yer 'elp 'im with the police?" asked Percy. "They probably understand things a bit better themselves now, I should think - but 'e'll still needs someone to speak up for 'im. An' the other one, wherever 'e is," he added.

"We'll go an' see these parents of 'is first," said Tom. "Then we can go ter the police. 'e'll 'ave ter go back ter school, I suppose!" He still looked stunned. "Eleven!" he said as he stepped off Percy's barge, "Eleven!"

Billie slept better that night than he had done for a very long time. Old Ma was inside! Locked up! The police had got her! He snuggled luxuriously under his grimy blankets, mercifully unaware of Detective Mould's deadly struggle with his grandmother; unaware ,too, of the cracks which were appearing all over the station, growing bigger each day as the black forcefield sucked and sucked at Mould's feet, fracturing the plaster and cracking the bricks so that the building groaned like a dying beast and his men began to mutiny, desperate to be rid of Old Ma and willing to bust open the rule book to do so - even at the cost of their well paid jobs - and their comfortable pensions too!

"like two heraldic beasts from an illuminated manuscript..."

Chapter Twenty Eight
Cupids In The Coving

Walter spent the next two weeks engrossed in decorating the dragon vase, visited often by Louie and sometimes by Isabella and Theodora when their other duties would allow. Mr. Slope checked the radiators assiduously, so that the craft and clay room was warm and cosy though the weather outside was often frosty, and Mr. Pinch kept up a steady supply of tea and biscuits, sometimes supplemented by Edna's wonderful chocolate cakes.

"To keep up your strength, dear lady," he would say to Louie as she sat by Walter, proffering her bourbons and custard creams at regular intervals throughout the day.

Harry Mudd soon caught on and arrived at intervals to finish off the plates.

"If yer sure Louie?" he would say, through a fine spray of crumbs. "Are yer 'aving that digestive, Walter. No? Thanks!"

Walter was too busy to eat biscuits. As the days went by the great vase was transformed from its dove-like whiteness to a drab multi-coloured thing which Harry looked at with alarm.

"What'll them colours be like then, Walter?" he asked nervously at the end of the first week as the vase was finished though the dragon had yet to be painted.

"Lovely!" said Walter happily, and he went on to tell his friend of the hummingbird hues that he and Louie had chosen for the vase and the sunset colours in which the dragon would be robed next week.

"'ard to imagine, mate," said Harry with some concern. "'ave ter see it ter believe it, like. S'orrible at the moment, mate!"

And he gazed wistfully at an empty plate, unconvinced that Walter was not ruining his life's work.

It was indeed difficult to imagine how the flat opaque glazes would be transformed by the magic of the kiln. But Louie's skill had guided Walter's brush, advising him on the thickness or the thinness of the glaze, on short strokes, on long strokes, on great sweeping swirling strokes so that hour by hour the bare clay had disappeared beneath Walter's unwavering hand. It was a huge undertaking, Harry and Potty often holding the ladders as he leaned out several feet above his friends, intent on claw or scale, smoothing his brush over the outspread wings or delicately touching in an eye or a nostril, lost in his world of colour.

Everyone came to see Walter's progress, once again shepherded closely by an anxious Mr. Slope, who maintained a strict five feet of space between Walter's visitors and the dragon vase. He had not been unaffected by the boy's magnificent venture: his sleep was nightly disturbed by visions of destruction, of the vase toppling over and smashing on the concrete floor.

"You were shouting out again last night, Ernest," his wife said peevishly, at the end of the first week of decoration, as she fried his bacon and eggs. "I don't know what's wrong with you these days, dear."

"Don't you, indeed?" replied Mr. Slope testily. "You'd be shouting out yourself if you 'ad the dreams I've been 'aving lately. I dreamt it 'ad grown arms an' legs again like Humpty Dumpty! It ran out into the ruddy playground and climbed up the railings and wouldn't come down, no matter 'ow 'ard I shouted at it. Everbody was laughing at me an' then it stood up an' started balancing on one leg, showing off!"

Mr. Slope mopped his brow and ran his fingers over his shiny pate.

"Just a dream!" said his wife unsympathetically, resentful of her disturbed sleep. "You shouldn't let it get to you so much!" and she deliberately over-fried his eggs, which he liked nice and runny.

"And then it tried running along the top of the railings an' fell off!" recalled the appalled Mr. Slope. "An' I couldn't put it all back together again! Oh, my eggs are hard."

"I shall be glad when it's done!" said his wife, banging the frying pan down into the sink. "And then perhaps we can both get a good night's rest!"

But Walter was sleeping well and his nights were free from unhappy visions. The two weeks were full of contentment, though after the first week Louie stayed at home, thrilled with what she had done, but now easily exhausted and often in bed all day. Her weakness was the only cloud on Walter's horizon and after he had finished for the evening he rushed home to sit by her bed, telling her all about his advances and of the people who had called in to see him during the day.

"Mr. Jollie in again, dear?" asked Louie softly on the Monday of the second week. "Have you heard how *his* Dragon is coming along, Walter?"

"Every day, like clockwork," smiled Walter, smoothing his auntie's pillow gently. "I'm not sure about Dragon though, Auntie. I think they're struggling with him a bit. Perhaps he just needs more time. Mr. Jollie is very excited about the vase though - and about the puppies! And then there's Rosie's party this Friday too."

"Ah," said Minnie quietly. "I don't think you will be seeing much of Rosie in the future, dear."

"No," said Walter frowning. "All that soppy stuff. It's a girl's party really. Still, the Poos will be there and I can play with them." He paused, looking puzzled. "What I can't understand," he said, looking at Louie, "is why Edna always goes to see Mr. Pinch after she's come to see me. She's in there ages as well. Funny, really!"

Louie's eyes opened wide and she suddenly looked much less tired but she said nothing.

"Goodnight dear," she said, snuggling down under her warm winter eiderdown. "Sleep well."

"Edna and John Pinch?" she thought. "Oh, I do hope so, I really do!"

§

Edna always felt a little embarrassed when she went to see Walter, turning pink as she said goodbye to him before opening the door onto the corridor. If she encountered Mr. Slope, she blushed even harder, especially when he gave her an oily smile and insisted on escorting her, with very great politeness, the few feet to the Headmaster's study.

But once inside, Edna was filled with happiness. A cosy fire was always burning with two comfortable chairs pulled up close. Sometimes there was buttered toast and sometimes pikelets. Mr. Pinch would rush forward gallantly, taking Edna's still shabby coat as if it were the richest fur and ushering her to the fireside before pouring out her tea.

Neither of them spoke of their feelings for each other but the room was full of untold desires. Cupids hovered in the coving and golden arrows darted hither and thither, piercing the tender hearts of the Headmaster and his little washerwoman.

Mr. Pinch read Edna those sonnets of Shakespeare which speak of undying love, of love that defeats the ages and remains unchanged by fortune and by time. And Edna would sit trembling, shaken by the lovely verse which expressed so vividly all she felt but could not say. Palely beautiful, she listened as a hamadryad might to a nightingale singing in the topmost branches of its tree. The smoke curled outside the windows but Edna and Mr. Pinch were transported, swept up by the poetry to celestial skies, where, suffering the agonies of the martyrs they felt too the ecstasies of the angels. Such great bliss, in such a little room!

"Sometimes there was buttered toast, and sometimes pikelets..."

Chapter Twenty Nine
The Spices Of India

Another heap of blackly shining coal had been delivered to Mr. Jollie's yard and Bill and Alf had made all ready for the second firing of the dragon vase. The bottle kiln stood waiting and Walter, washing out his brushes on Thursday afternoon, knew that he was almost ready too. His decoration was nearly finished, only the dragon's mouth remained to be painted, but Walter was tired and determined not to rush things.

"I'll do that tomorrow morning," he thought. "I haven't got this far to hurry and make a mess of it!"

Isabella and Theodora had come at half-past three, clapping their hands when they saw what their small friend had achieved.

"That looks like a very fine piece to me!" cried Isabella, walking carefully around the vase and ignoring Mr. Slope's efforts to corral her behind a little table. "Well done, Walter! Very well done!"

"Quite brilliant!" said Theodora, glaring at Mr. Slope as she stepped up close to the vase. "Wonderful brushwork, dear. Wonderful!"

They chatted knowledgably with Potty and left after half an hour, full of excitement and hope, stepping daintily across the playground to the large Humber parked by the kerb, where Harry Mudd stood staring blankly at them as they climbed inside.

"Cor! Walter!" he cried, running into the craft and clay room, all arms and legs and hands. "You're a lucky man! They're *gorgeous*! Gorranything ter eat?"

After another half an hour Harry had left too, stuffing Walter's uneaten sandwiches into his mouth and casting a last worried look at the huge vase.

"I 'ope yer right about them colours," he spluttered through a mouthful of cheese and beetroot. "I really do! See yer tomorrer, mate."

Edna had also come that afternoon, at four o' clock, mysteriously disappearing to visit Mr. Pinch as usual after admiring her little friend's work, pink cheeked and happy, bearing a little book of Donne's poetry under her arm.

"I wonder what it's all about?" he thought half an hour later as he opened the door onto the corridor - but then he stopped short in surprise.

There was Mr. Slope bending down with his ear glued to the Headmaster's door! Walter was about to retreat, shocked, when Mr. Slope saw him, and reddening furiously, beckoned him forward. Walter went reluctantly.

"I'm in the wrong, chum, I know," Mr. Slope admitted, having the decency to look ashamed. "But he's proposing Walter! He's proposing to Edna!"

Walter turned to rush away, but just then the door burst open and out came Mr. Pinch, his handsome face beaming. If he realised his caretaker's indiscretion he was far too elated to worry about it.

"Ah. Mr. Slope," he said. "Walter too. How timely, dear boy. Come in, come in."

In they both went, Mr. Slope at the double and Walter trailing behind like a wet hem. Potty was called in, and one or two other teachers who had lingered at the school, marking or preparing their lessons for the next day.

The study was more than usually cosy. The fire flickered and glinted on a bottle of champagne and roses bloomed softly close by, a huge armful of roses wrapped in pink tissue paper and tied with a great blue bow. Mr. Pinch took Edna's hand and bought her forward, smiling shyly. There was a moment's awkward silence as Mr. Pinch gazed at Edna and she studied the Headmaster's carpet, worn thin by the traffic of many small boots.

"Headmaster?" queried Mr. Slope, hoping to nudge him along.

Walter dug his hands into his pockets and joined Edna in a contemplation of the threadbare Axminster.

Mr. Pinch cleared his throat and looked at the expectant little group.

"I am delighted to tell you," he said, as Edna broke into a happy smile, "delighted to announce that Mrs. Robbin has consented to be my wife. We shall be married at Christmas!"

The champagne was uncorked and the foaming wine was caught in school tumblers, a little chipped and dusty, but nobody minded that.

"Er, not for Walter," said Mr. Pinch hurriedly as Mr. Slope handed the boy a brimming glass, but it was too late. The remainder was taken from him and exchanged for ginger beer, which Walter thought was much nicer anyway.

"Congratulations, sir. Congratulations, Edna," Walter said dutifully, longing for some sort of escape. "Cor! That's nice Edna!" he added as Edna shyly showed him a ring in which rich garnets glowed, full of the spices of India from whence they came.

"My paternal grandmother's," explained Mr. Pinch. "Military family. North West Frontier."

"It's lovely Edna," said Walter. "Shall I tell my aunties?"

"I wonder," he thought as he went home, a little later and a little less foot-sure than usual, "I wonder if they would have met if it hadn't been for Poodle Friday?"

As he climbed the hill, his head swirled with everything that had happened since he had begun making his dragon vase. And best of all was Edna, no longer alone, but now comfortably off and marrying his Headmaster!

"But she won't change," he thought, as he rounded the corner into the entry. "She'll always be Edna and people will always love her."

Then, as he lifted the latch on the tall wooden gate, he thought of the Grunter twins and hesitated, just inside the yard. He looked up at the night sky where the stars were veiled with the smoke of winter fires, though the moon was swimming behind the chimney pots.

"Wherever can they be?" he thought sadly.

He had told no one, but he carried a secret guilt.

"They would never have gone away," he reasoned, "if it wasn't for my dragon vase. They are bad, really bad, but their mum and dad love them. Wherever can they be?"

Then, the memory of Old Ma's hands over his mouth and his desperate struggle to breathe came back in a flash. He shuddered, going cold all over, the hairs on his neck standing up and his teeth chattering. Slamming the gate, he ran up the path to the little house, momentarily afraid of the dark and wanting light and warmth instead. But he had good news to deliver!

"Guess what?" he cried, opening the door and rushing inside. "You'll never guess what's happened today! Not in a million years!"

"Has Mr. Pinch proposed to Edna?" said Minnie, throwing aside her knitting and jumping up from the fireside. "Thought so!" she cried triumphantly and she sat Walter down at the table, a little deflated that she had guessed so easily.

"Uncanny, really," he thought, as he ate his cottage pie, and Minnie and Sally conversed about hats, running in and out of Louie's room for snippets of advice and information. "How did she guess that? I'm the one who's there all the time and I didn't know!"

When all the exclamations had died down, the sisters toasted Edna and Mr. Pinch in small glasses of sweet sherry.

"To two of the nicest people you could ever hope to meet!" said Minnie, raising her glass.

"To a Christmas wedding!" chimed Sally, and the three ladies sipped their sherry, picturing Edna amidst the falling snow, with her red hair and her redder roses, arm in arm with John Pinch as she stepped over the snow- covered green to the sooty little church at the bottom of the hill.

Walter ate his apple sponge-top as Minnie fussed around and Sally said goodnight to Louie.

When the old lady was settled, her pillows propped up comfortably and the covers snuggly covering her thin chest, Louie put her arm on Sally's and said, "They'll never capture it, you know. The wedding photographs. Just black and white, which will fade anyway. Nothing will capture Edna as she will be on that day. You must try to remember it, dear, because a cherished memory is better than a photograph sometimes, I think."

She sighed, holding Sally's hand quietly.

"I see the past so clearly now, so brightly, as if time has polished my memories, not dimmed them. I've had such a happy life dear - I've been so fortunate."

"No more talking now, Louie," said Sally, patting her sister's frail hand, uneasy at her words.

"No," said Louie, "but just the same, Sally, just to say how much I love you and Minnie and how wonderful you are. And what a blessing Walter has been, when we never thought to have a child of our own!"

Sally smoothed the sheet and sat by the bedside, watching as Louie's breaths grew deeper and her eyelids fluttered into sleep. She sat on in the colourful little room, so full of her sister's handiwork – the crinoline ladies forever watering their embroidered gardens, the rich fruits blooming perennially on the china vases.

"How different our lives would have been," she thought sleepily, "without our little boy."

Her mind travelled back to the carefree days of her youth: the works outings to Llangollen and Dovedale; the church harvest suppers and Christmas Nativities; the warmth and strength of the sooty community bound together by its magical industry of fire and flame.

Minnie poked her head around the door, then left quietly, smiling to see Sally nodding off in the comfy chair.

"Up to bed now Walter," she said, tidying the hearth where the ashes had fallen forward, and putting away The Sentinel with its big front page headline:

SATURDAY: SECOND FIRING!

"Nearly ready?" asked Minnie as she saw Walter glance at the headline, smiling happily to himself.

"Nearly ready, Auntie!" he said. "Just a quiet morning tomorrow, finishing the head off, then lessons again in the afternoon."

"And then the party at six," said Minnie. "Don't go forgetting that, young man! I'll have everything ironed for you and I'll shop for the present tomorrow, so you'll have something to take. Don't pull your face like that, dear. I'm sure you'll enjoy it!"

"Right," said Walter glumly. "The party. I don't suppose it'll be much fun though, will it? Just *music* and girls wanting to *dance*? Hopeless really!"

How wrong he was!

Out in the dark December night, Fate was twisting her skeins together just as the wind twisted the smoke around the chimney pots whilst Walter slept, unaware of the twins' imminent return or that their dreadful grandmother's escape was close at hand.

Old Ma had seen the Evening Sentinel.

"Second firing!" she sneered. "We'll see about that!"

Under her pillow lay the Duty Sergeant's keys, surrendered without a fight, indeed willingly given over without the slightest hesitation. Tomorrow morning Old Ma would be out!

"momentarily afraid of the dark..."

Chapter Thirty
The Telephone Rings

For two weeks now the twins had been returning to the city of coal and clay, each on his barge, each ignorant of the other's whereabouts and welfare.

Billie, deeply conscious of Tom's disappointment in him, strove daily to make his master proud of him, and Tom, for his part, pitied the boy and gave him scope to prove himself, trusting him with large sums of money to pay the coal-yards or asking him to write up the grimy ledger and tally the day's takings. Billie didn't let him down.

Out on the speeding Norton Billie experienced an exhilaration he had never dreamt of before.

"Faster! Faster!" he would urge, clinging like a limpet to the huge man in front, leaning with him into the curves, feeling his eyes sting as they burnt along the country roads past the bare trees and the red ploughed fields. He was fearless, loving the harmony of man and machine, determined more than ever to become an engineer, a man people would look up to and respect.

One day, in Bridgnorth, he saw a rail of small dark postcards showing the lopsided castle ruins and the church beyond. Man Mountain saw him looking and quickly put his hand in his pocket.

"Buy one!" he said. "Send it 'ome Bill. Let 'em know yer coming!"

Billie bought a stamp to go with it, writing the card on the barge that night.

"Dear Mum and Dad," it said. "I'm alright. I'll be home soon."

Three days later it popped through the letter box of the shop and lay on the tiled floor amongst the sawdust.

"What's this?" thought Harold – and then, "Bertha! Bertha! Bertha!"

But they hugged the news to themselves, afraid of what people might do or say, and, even more than that, determined that Old Ma should not get to hear of the boy's return.

§

Like his brother, Willie too had had to face the terrible disappointment of the people he had come to love. When he told them his story, haltingly and amidst many tears, he couldn't bring himself to look at Freddie who sat, head down, in stunned disbelief. Then Mr. Whitehouse had produced Peter's Sentinel and read aloud the dreadful story of Poodle Friday whilst Willie stood heartbroken and miserable in the cabin doorway.

"I'm sorry about Edna!" he sobbed. "We didn't hurt Walter, honest we didn't. And Billie only nicked the vase!"

There was silence.

Then Freddie said, "But it says tha brother damaged it, Willie. It says the knife was *twisted* into the clay." Freddie looked at Willie imploringly. He couldn't bear it to be true.

But Willie knew he must tell the whole truth or be forever in the dark. He looked at Freddie and wept.

"I told him to!" he wailed. "I said "Go on!" I did! I did!"

Then Freddie wept too and his little sisters set up such a forlorn howling that Mrs. Waterhouse opened the special treats cupboard and took out five sugar mice.

"I'm sorry!" Willie cried desperately. "It was rotten! We were rotten. We were! We were!" he sank down on the cabin step and buried his face in his hands, overcome with shame and remorse. His shoulders heaved. He had never felt so alone in his life.

"We were scared of her," he said at last, looking up at the strained faces regarding him. "She said she'd kill us! I can't go home!"

He wept even louder, wanting his mother and father. He was, after all, only eleven years old.

Mrs. Waterhouse eased herself forward and pulled him down onto the bunk next to her.

"We've heard all about tha granny now," she said, wiping his face with the tip of her pinafore. "There's been a lot of talk about her up and down the canal these last few days. She's inside now, tha knowst!"

Willie sat up in astonishment and his knees began to shake. "Why?" he said. "How?"

"She tried to suffocate that Walter in 'is bed!" cried Mr. Waterhouse. "She's proper evil that one! Tha's best off out of it William. Tha's better off with us!"

"I thought you'd hate me," said Willie quietly. "I was nothing like you thought I was."

"We think tha's changed, William," said Mrs. Waterhouse. "Tha's been a right good lad with us!"

"I have changed!" cried Willie, floods of tears bursting from him again. "I love it here! I love boats! And horses! But I want my mum!" and he howled and howled.

Finally, Freddie leant over and said kindly, as always, "Give over mate! Tha'll sink the boat!" and everyone laughed, even Willie. "Eleven!" Freddie went on, admiringly. "Whatever were they feeding thee down there? Want my sugar mouse?""

Willie smiled shyly and met Freddie's eye.

"It must have been the oatcakes," he said.

Mr. Waterhouse folded up the paper and slipped it into the bin.

"We'll go back 'ome with thee William," he said. "Till then let's see what tha's made of. With a bit of 'elp tha can grow up into a decent man like tha dad."

"Or better!" he thought, wondering how on earth parents living in the same small house as their two children could have neglected them to such terrible effect.

The next day Freddie took Willie up onto the moors above Rochdale to fly his kite. Willie stood and surveyed the bleak hills swept by the strong northern winds.

"It's another world," he thought. "I can be anybody up here."

He thought of all the new places waiting to be discovered and of travelling to them, just him and a horse and a barge.

"When I'm a man," he thought joyously, "I'll go everywhere, all over England! I'm a bargee, not a butcher!"

The kite leapt and swooped in his hands as Freddie shouted encouragement.

"More string, William, more string!" he urged, or "Reel her in, reel her in!" as the kite rushed down out of the sky like a thing alive, like a tiger of the air.

On the way back, through the steep streets which led to the canal, the boys passed first one red telephone box, and then another.

Willie slowed his pace and looked back.

"What's up?" asked Freddie, his mind on the fish and chips which awaited him on the barge.

"I was wondering if I could, you know, telephone them at home?" said Willie with some embarrassment.

Freddie pushed his friend into the nearest box as quick as a flash and had the receiver lifted and the twopence ready before Willie could think what to say.

It was late in the afternoon and Harold was in the shop, making little piles of silver beside the open till. But trade was not so good these days and his takings were disappointing. He shrugged his shoulders as he slammed shut the till: it didn't seem to matter anymore.

"Damned fool!" he said to himself as he slipped the coins into his cash bag. "You've squandered your boys' lives as a slave to this till. And look where it's got them!"

Then the telephone rang and he went into the little hallway beyond the shop.

"Dad! It's me! Willie!" came the distant voice at the other end. "I'm alright! I'm coming home!"

There were so many tears on both sides that little else could be said until the pips sounded maddingly again and Harold was left clutching a cold receiver, with joy in his heart. Both his boys! Coming home!

"Bertha!" he shouted. "Bertha! Bertha! Bertha!"

"a small white inn somewhere in the Black Country..."
(illustrates Chapter 27)

Chapter Thirty One
Five, Not Six

The day that became known in North Staffordshire as Dragon Friday began with a disappointing drizzle. Mr. Jollie commiserated with Rosie as she drew back the curtains.

"Hope it improves for you, dear girl!" he said. "Better by six o' clock perhaps!"

The preparations for the party had consumed most of the past week and Mr. Jollie had been a busy man. The Poos had been busy too, and, sensing the approaching birth of their puppies, had filled Prospect House with great excitement, neither Mr. Jollie nor Rosie being able to keep up with their antics. Several times a day, Jolly-Poo had dragged off cushions and throws to make a new nest in a new nook so that Rosie despaired of her housework and her employer was forever tripping over heaps of soft furnishings abandoned by the fretful poodle, whose restlessness only increased as the week went on.

"Can't be long now, Rosie," said Mr. Jollie early on Friday morning, surveying the wreck of his beautiful sofa, much of which had been transported to the bathroom by a panting, breathless Jolly-Poo.

At times Jigger-Poo kept up an almost constant barking, relieved only by very long walks in practically any weather. By Friday, he and Mr. Jollie had covered half the city while his furry wife, rotund and happy, basked in the constant affection of Rosie and the cook. Out and about, Jigger-Poo pulling strongly on the leash, Mr. Jollie had visited the city's music shops, coming home stealthily with heavy stacks of glossy recordings under his arm – all the latest songs for Rosie and her friends to dance to on the great wind-up gramophone.

Mr. Jollie was completely happy. On Wednesday, he had rung the florist from the privacy of his study, speaking in whispers with his hand curled around the little mouthpiece.

"Pink," he whispered, "and cream. A dozen large bunches or so....ribbons....y'know the sort of thing."

"Very expensive, sir," the florist had warned, "at this time of year."

"Special Occasion," Mr. Jollie had confided, his voice sinking lower and lower. "Only sixteen once, Mr. Spruce.... only once y'know!"

"Ask John to come in, Rosie, please," he said at eight o'clock on Friday morning, "and then stay in the kitchen till home time, that's a good girl. Leave by the back door today. No peeping, y'know!"

Mr. Jollie and John worked together, moving the drawing room furniture back against the walls.

"Push that over there," said Mr. Jollie, and the two men bent their backs so that soon there was a wide clear space for the dancing.

A knock on the side door, answered swiftly by John, heralded the arrival of the florist and his assistant bearing huge armfuls of roses and lilies, with spools of ribbons trailing from boxes and sturdy clippers tucked into their belts. Within an hour or so the drawing room was transformed into a ballroom befitting a fairy tale and the conservatory bloomed like a midsummer's day.

Delicious smells wafted through from the kitchen where Jolly-Poo lay like an expectant queen, constantly proffered this and that while Jigger-Poo barked and barked, until Mr. Jollie picked up his lead and said, "Righty ho, old boy! Quick visit to Walter, then pop up to see Beany! Find out how Dragon's coming along with that brother of his!" and he set off through the damp with Jolly-Poo barking all the way to The Grove.

§

Out at Endon, Dragon was beginning to tire of the quiet life. He had a long grassy field where he could gallop from one end to the other, easily beating the other horses who joined in joyfully, manes and tails flying, hooves kicking up the soft pasture beneath.

He had been tacked up and trained, ridden and long-reined, lunged, schooled, harnessed, hacked and jumped. At everything he excelled – but only when it suited him. At other times he was impossible, a great black forcefield which withstood all Pat Beany's horsemanship; a creature of volcanic eye and crocodile jaw, a horse one could only stand back from and humbly cajole with a bucket or a full bunch of carrots.

He was fond of his buckets, and, on difficult days, treats were Pat Beany's only way of enticing Dragon back to his field. Once inside, the gate would be slammed shut on him with great relief, the huge horse whipping around in annoyance at the enforced detention, snapping angrily at the proffered carrots and then thundering away, tail high in the air, instantly dismissive of the two-legged inferiors who sought to master him.

Pat Beany had quickly dropped off the soaked sugar beet.

"There'd be no 'olding 'im with that!" he had said to Big Ben, a stable boy of such diminutive proportions that he could hardly be seen behind a barrow-full of hay but who was possessed of a stout heart and the courage of a lion tamer.

Like a Grand National jockey, he had leapt high hedges on Dragon and raced him across the open moorland as if stretching for the finishing post at Aintree. But even he shook his head, as, at the end of four weeks, Dragon still raced round and round the field, refusing to be caught when Big Ben called him, coming forward to the headcollar only when he was ready for a diversion, for a bit more fun outside his narrow field. And sometimes he ran head on at Pat and his boy as if to trample them underfoot, veering off at the last possible moment, leaving them gasping, with an empty headcollar and despairing hearts.

Then on Friday morning, as Rosie drew back Mr. Jollie's curtains and Walter woke up to the last day of work on his wonderful vase, Big Ben went to the field and found only five horses grazing, instead of six.

"Mr. Beany!" he shouted. "Mr. Beany, Sir! 'e's gone! 'e's not in 'is field!"

Rushing across the yard, Mr. Beany stood on the brow of the hill and looked down. There below him, the field stretched greenly from end to end, the soft Staffordshire rain falling steadily on the five remaining horses who looked up, as if to say, "Yes! He's gone! Went some time ago! Sorry!"

"'e's jumped it!" cursed Pat Beany, at a loss to know which direction the great horse had taken.

Leaping into his wagon, he scorched off to search the lanes nearby whilst Big Ben set off on foot, skipping over fences and gates, desperate for a sight of the horse he had failed to conquer.

"'e's never going to respect *me*," he thought. "'e needs somebody else – somebody 'e can look up to," and on he ploughed, through the rain, though the horse was nowhere in sight.

Some miles away, Dragon knew exactly where he was heading. The city, he thought, was the place to be! He remembered his wild ride through the smog with Mr. Jollie and his pulse raced at the thought. Nothing since had rivalled that! He yearned for adventure and excitement. A field was all very well, it had its virtues, but Dragon needed the open road and new horizons!

Dark as an imminent thundercloud, he raced along the grassy verges, terrifying those who stood in his way, arms outstretched as if to catch him – as if they could catch this whirlwind which swept them aside like winter leaves, with lashing hooves and darkly streaming tail. Everyone fell back before him and the way ahead was always open for him to rush on and on, past the fields of somnambulant cows, past the country villas, closer and closer to the city of coal and clay.

On he galloped, through Stockton Brook and over the long straight track of Baddely Green. He thundered through the little crossroads at Milton, scattering a vegetable barrow with a whisk of his tail, galloping on out of the busy village along the muddy road to Carmountside. There he swung right, up the gently sloping lane to Northwood.

"Nearly there," he thought, "but lunch first."

In a flash, he was over a hedge and in amongst the sooty grass still growing on the rich clay soil, even in December. Well hidden, but far from tired, he relaxed and ate his fill.

"The Poos had been busy too..."

Chapter Thirty Two
A Close Call

Still the drizzle came down, augmented now with the soft sooty plumes quietly ascending from the city's bottle ovens. As the morning wore on, the city of coal and clay became enshrouded with a pall so dense that the December day was darkened to the resemblance of a mid-winter evening, though the lamps were not lit and the town lacked the jolly feeling which usually accompanied the end of a working day, when the streets were laced with yellow lights and rest and recreation lay ahead.

In the little house, Louie lay in bed, the smell of the sooty air stealing inside her room, but she rested dreamily, her mind full of the beautiful colours of the dragon vase. As she thought over the work that she and Walter had done together, she was filled with happiness, content that she had done all she could to help her little nephew.

Minnie popped her head around the door.

"Louie," she said softly, "I'm just off to the shops, dear. I've left Rosie's present a bit late, what with one thing and another. Any suggestions, any ideas?"

Louie smiled.

"Oh perfume!" she said. "Always. How I loved perfume at that age. I thought I was so sophisticated," and as she spoke her eyelids closed in sleep.

Minnie shut the front door behind her and set off, wiping a smudge from her face as she went, the air being thick with damp sooty flakes which fell over everything, like black snow. Behind her, the little house was silent, peaceful, the dark drizzle making no sound as it besmirched the windows and doors, stealthily tarnishing the walls as it clung and melted and blackly felting the freshly sanded step.

In the kitchen, Sally sat near the fire polishing her copper and brass as she kept an eye on the ox-tail bubbling gently in a pot on the stove. She didn't hear the front door open slowly. Unlocked, it was Louie's portal to the world outside, secured for the first time when Old Ma's reign of terror began but now trustingly unlatched so that friends and neighbours could greet Louie daily, knocking softly and peeping around the door to see if their friend were awake or asleep.

But it was no friend who now entered the room. Old Ma stood breathing heavily, her face flushed, her nostrils dilated as she pressed the door shut. It had taken just ten minutes to cover the distance between the Police Station and Louie's room. Behind her was a trail of stunned and petrified people, all of them helpless or unwilling to stop her, whether it was the Duty Sergeant who bent down to tie his shoe-lace as she walked past the front desk, or the poor bus conductor who stepped backwards off his vehicle as she skipped on board, falling heavily onto the cobbled road and narrowly missing the great hooves of the brewery's horses as they pulled together up the hill.

She knew that Mould would soon be on her tail.

"Let him try!" she sneered, casting her shark-like eyes around the room. "Let any of 'em try and take *me* again!"

No one, she knew, would risk themselves against her. No one could save Walter, or his dragon vase – or Louie! She crept to the bedside, noiseless and dark, a small clot of contagion, there, in that gentle home.

"Always you!" she hissed, standing close to Louie's pillow. "Always you and your nice little friends! Always you and your painting and your poetry! You and your snotty little sisters! You! You! I always *hated* you!"

Louie awoke, trembling. Her eyes widened and she let out a little cry of fear. Then, folding her hands calmly on the bedspread in front of her, she lay back and closed her eyes.

"It's no good, Betty," she said. "You can't touch me now. I'm full of a happiness you can't destroy, do what you may."

Old Ma choked, grasping her throat and spitting out the phlegm.

"I'll 'ave you," she said softly. "And then I'll 'ave your Walter!"

"No, Betty, you won't," said Louie, opening her eyes and looking into Old Ma's twisted face. "I've been ready for days. Nothing you can do can change that." She smoothed the bedspread as if to demonstrate the perfect peace she felt within. "And Walter has withstood you once, my dear. He will do it again."

Old Ma gasped with anger and seized Louie's arm. Red marks sprang up where the frail flesh was viciously caught and pressed.

"You!" she cried. "You! Always so serene! You! I've *always* hated you!"

She twisted the arm so that Louie gave a small cry, but that was all. She lay smiling, her eyes distant, her heart full of love. She thought of her sisters – what good and kind friends they had been to her all her life. Then the faces of other friends, and of neighbours, filled her mind, the memory of their love and affection pouring into her heart so that she felt it might burst. Love filled the little room like a heady perfume, and Old Ma staggered back, undone.

"And Walter," said Louie aloud, her voice a mere whisper. "And Walter most of all, our little boy!"

The air was full of the sound of beating wings, soft feathery flutterings which hovered around the bed, fanning Louie's peaceful face but stifling Old Ma so that she panted for breath.

She withdrew to the door and opened it, inhaling the murky air noisily. Sally heard the click and came into the room, bearing a cup of tea.

"You!" she screamed in disbelief, launching the crockery across the room so that the rim of the saucer caught Old Ma on the knuckle. "Get out! *Get out!*"

Old Ma hesitated, rubbing her skinny bones. Sally snatched up the poker and threw that but it bounced harmlessly off the door. Old Ma retreated to the doorstep but Sally threw the hearth tidy after her, the brass shovel with the sailing ship handle rattling onto the floor at Old Ma's feet.

"I'll 'ave his *vase*!" sneered the old woman, poking her grisly head around the door and glaring at Louie. "I'll 'ave *that!*"

"No Betty," said Louie in a whisper. "You won't. If only you knew," and she turned to smile at Sally, who pressed her palm against her sister's chest. "If only you knew…."

"You!" shrieked Old Ma, her anger turning in on her so hard that she almost fell, clutching the doorway to save herself. "Always *you!*"

Then she was gone, disappearing like smoke up a chimney so that when Mould arrived a few moments later she was nowhere to be seen.

Louie lay still, her breaths slight and shallow. Sally wrung her hands and sent Constable Flatt for Dr. Deere. He was there in a flash, parking his liquorice black car by the kerb and springing out, bag in hand. By now an anxious little crowd had gathered outside the house and he pushed his way through the umbrellas impatiently.

"For goodness sake, women!" he cried. "Let a man through, will you!"

They parted respectfully but the gap filled up as soon as he had passed, their heads pressed against the door.

"What's 'e saying?"

"I can't 'ear! Shut up Doris!"

"Is she alright?"

"She's pretty bad. Sally looked dreadful!"

A sorrowful silence settled on them and all ears were bent on the scene unfolding inside. At the bottom of the hill, Minnie and Thelma appeared, heads together in conversation as always. Then Minnie looked up and saw the car and the attentive crowd.

"Louie!" she cried, flinging her bag at Thelma and racing up the steep street. Slim and athletic, Minnie was at the door in seconds, leaving Thelma to plod along in her wake. She disappeared inside the house and the door was shut.

"It's Louie, Thelma," said Flora Shufflebottom. "She's really bad I think. I've never seen Sally look like that before...." Her voice trailed off and tears stood in her eyes.

Thelma bowed her head and tears began to flow down her cheeks.

Then, "Where's Walter?" she cried. "Where's Walter?"

"He's at The Grove," said Phyllis Smallbody. "Finishing it off, they say."

"Oh God!" cried Thelma, knowing she could never cover the distance quickly enough. "Who can go?"

Just then, two tall boys appeared at the top of the street and stopped in surprise when they saw the agitated crowd. One of them was extremely dirty. They ran down.

"What's up?" asked the dirty young man.

"It's Louie," said Lilly Wadpugg, looking at the boys curiously but unable to place them. "She's really bad. We need Walter, quick!"

"We'll go!" cried the two handsome boys and they ran off as one, their long legs covering the distance so effectively that in seconds they had rounded the corner and were lost to sight.

"Who was that?" asked Thelma, bewildered.

"I don't know," said Lilly, then her face clouded over and her mouth fell open. "Oh no! Thelma!" she stuttered, grabbing Thelma's forearm and holding it tightly. "It's them, Thelma! I think it's them *Grunter twins*!"

§

Walter had been working with Potty when Mr. Jollie came in at ten o' clock. He had been glazing the dragon's mouth and was balanced precariously on a ladder, brushing the back of its throat a deep peony pink, when he heard Jolly-Poo barking excitedly as he came across the playground.

"Ah," said Potty, holding the ladder tightly, "visitors Walter. Perhaps Mr. Jollie will take the other side of this ladder with me. Oh, er, do be careful, son!"

Mr. Jollie lent a hand while Jigger-Poo watched Walter in admiration, his head first on one side and then another.

"Mr. Slope is, ah, unwell," Potty told Mr. Jollie. "Lumbago, you know."

Mr. Slope was lying in bed, as stiff as a board, enjoying tea and toast and listening to Jelly Roll Morton on his wireless-set.

"Well, it's almost finished," he thought to himself, wiping his fingers on the top sheet and picking up a greasy Who Dunnit. "Be in the kiln tomorrow. Not my problem anymore. Might get a nice few weeks out of this back if I'm lucky...."

Walter made an especially tricky manoeuvre, which caused the ladder to tilt so alarmingly that Potty and Mr. Jollie had to use all their strength to keep it upright, then he put the brush between his teeth and climbed down.

"That's it!" he said. "Thank you. Thanks, Mr. Jollie."

"Marvellous!" said Mr. Jollie. "Absolutely marvellous! Historic, Walter! Absolutely historic!"

"Well done, son," said Potty. "Nobody could have done better. Tidy up, then it will be lunchtime and then lessons again. I'm off to the kiln now. Would you like to accompany me, Mr. Jollie?"

"Was going to see Beany," said Mr. Jollie, rubbing his chin thoughtfully. "But never mind. Better to check all is in order for tomorrow. But see you at six, Walter! Don't forget!"

And the two men went off with the barking poodle, leaving Walter alone with his monumental vase.

He washed his brush and emptied the water into the big white sink, then fetched the broom from Potty's store room and began to sweep absentmindedly, his mind still full of his work. The school was quiet, the distant classrooms under a heavy late morning hush.

"There's nothing more I can do," he thought, poking the brush under a little table. "It'll be in Alf's hands tomorrow!"

He thought of the star crack, filled now with a lustrous glaze, and of the glazes themselves, never before trialled on such a large scale, but he swept on, wiggling out little bits of clay from obscure corners, determined to leave everything pristine for Potty when he returned.

Suddenly, the blue doors burst open and in shot two tall boys, strong and fit but flushed with running hard.

"Walter!" they cried, and Walter, turning, caught unawares with the broom in his hand, at first didn't know who they were.

Then he ran at them, beating them with the long brush and growling like a tigress.

"No!" he roared. "Not again! Leave it alone! Go away!"

But the boys warded off his strokes good naturedly, taking the brush from him and laying it gently aside.

"It's alright, mate," said Billie, "We're not here to hurt you - and we are sorry Walter, really sorry! – but go home Walter! Go home! Louie's ill – I think she's dying Walter! Go home!"

And Walter, almost blind with panic, fled without a moment's hesitation, leaving his dragon vase, sublime in its perfection, alone with the terrible Grunter twins.

Walter had never run so hard in his life. Even when racing on the right wing, desperate to retrieve the honour of his school, Walter's heart had never pumped so fast; never had the blood beaten through his arteries with the force it did now as yard by yard he closed the gap between the school and his Auntie Louie.

Finally, pushing through the crowd he rapped on the door, too breathless to call out to those inside. Thelma knocked too.

"It's Walter," she called softly. "Let him in, Minnie."

The door opened and he fell inside. The doctor sat quietly by Louie's bed, her hand in his, his finger on her pulse. He looked up and nodded at Walter.

"Come here, Walter," he said softly and Sally, tears pouring down her face, led Walter to the bed, her arms around his shoulders, her face bent close to his.

Minnie stood silently beside the doctor, but Walter had eyes only for Louie, the gentlest and sweetest of his aunts, whom he loved more than anyone in the world.

She was so white that Walter's own heart gave a little kick of shock. Tears sprang to his eyes but he bit his lip. Nothing, he thought, must distress this woman, whose soul hovered on the threshold of life, like a young girl standing in an open doorway, looking back into the room but lit from behind by the glow of a summer garden, glorious in its golden light. One step, and she would be over the threshold, lost to those watching and waiting in the little room, leaving forever behind the smoky city, its chill winters and its warm hearts.

Walter looked at the doctor timidly.

"Take her hand," he said.

Tentatively, Walter reached for Louie's hand, clasping it in both of his but finding it so limp and cold that tears coursed down his cheeks and he fought even harder not to make a sound.

In the garden the sun shone and the birds carolled louder and louder. The girl still stood in the doorway, but turned now as if to listen to their melodies, as if to turn away from life in the city of coal and clay.

Then Walter, squeezing the little hand, burst out, "Don't go Auntie! Please don't go!"

He laid his head on her pillow, pressing his hot flushed face against her pale one, wetting her cheek with his streaming tears. Dr. Deere gave a little nod of surprise. He adjusted his grip on Louie's wrist and gasped.

"It's getting stronger!" he said. "Stronger and stronger!"

Sally and Minnie could bear it no longer and wept in each other's arms. They were heard outside by the damp little crowd waiting dejectedly in the rain.

"She's gone!" moaned Thelma, covering her face in her hands.

Tears ran down the sad, kindly faces of Louie's friends and neighbours: they had all loved her, every one.

But inside, Walter felt his hand being given a returning squeeze and he sat up in delight.

"Auntie!" he cried.

The very faintest of smiles lit Louie's pale face, as if a spark, struggling to become a flame, glowed deep inside. As they watched, a little sea-shell pink tinged the white skin and colour seeped back into the smiling mouth.

"Auntie!" cried Walter. "Auntie!"

More and more colour appeared, flooding back rosily until Dr. Deere put down Louie's hand and looked up at Sally and Minnie.

"Remarkable," he said, tucking the hand inside the coverlet. "Beef tea and chicken soup – and plenty of it!"

Louie opened her eyes.

"I could fancy a bit of that!" she said.

Walter leapt up and hugged his aunties. Then he threw the door open wide upon the startled crowd.

"She's alright!" he shouted. "She's alright! Oh Thelma! She's alright!"

"an anxious little crowd had gathered..."

Chapter Thirty Three
Something Foul

Billie and Willie looked around them. There, unmissably, in the centre of the craft and clay room, was the huge dragon vase towering above them, accusatory, fearsome, threatening. They shivered, but walked around it carefully.

"It's been mended!" said Billie happily and the two boys beamed at each other.

"And painted," said Willie, peering closer. " It's a bit dull, like. Seems a shame."

"No, dopey!" laughed Billie. "It'll all change once it's fired. Be all colours then, I should think."

The two boys stood silently, looking at the thing that Walter had created.

"Freddie'd love that dragon!" said Willie. "And the rest of them! I shall have to ask Walter."

"My lot'd like it too," said Billie.

The twins had met on the towpath, their barges converging from opposite directions at the same time. As Willie jumped off the Northern Princess, mooring line in hand, he saw a tall grimy boy staring at him from a barge a few yards downstream.

"What's he staring at?" he wondered and he wiped his face with his sleeve just in case Mo's breakfast of fried eggs was sticking to his cheeks. Willie glanced over again and saw the boy still studying him, hands in pockets, awkward and embarrassed.

"What's up with him?" thought Willie, moving over to untack Prince. He spoke gently to his good friend, offering him a lump of sugar, patting and fussing him affectionately.

He undid straps and buckles, lifting off the thick padded collar along with the surcingle and all its trappings. Still the other boy stared. Then, something in his manner caught Willie's attention and he stared back. His mouth fell open.

"Billie!" he cried. "Billie!"

And the two brothers rushed headlong into each other's arms, crying and laughing and thumping each other on the back.

"You're completely filthy, bruv!" said Willie.

"You stink of horse!" replied Billie and both boys laughed out loud.

"We've changed!" said Billie.

"We have," his brother agreed.

"She's inside, you know," said Willie quietly.

"I wouldn't be here if she wasn't," said Billie. "I've had enough of all *that*!"

Willie was silent, his face downcast.

"We were vile," he said, after a moment or two.

Billie nodded sadly.

"We were," he said. "We've got a lot of making up to do round here. Are your lot helping you?"

"They are," said Willie. "They're really great! They're going to see Mum and Dad and the police and Mr. Pinch."

"And Walter and his aunties," said Billie earnestly. "It's them I want to see the most."

"And Edna," said Willie, his face flushing. "I knocked her over, you know."

"Oh, bruv," said Billie, and both boys sighed deeply.

Soon, both parties came together with much shaking of hands and slapping of backs.

"Squeeze in out of the rain," said Mo and everyone clambered on board the Northern Princess and crammed into the tiny cabin, the small children sitting on the knees of their grimy new friends, studying their black faces in amazement.

"My mummy makes me 'ave a wash," said Elizabeth as she peered at Jim closely.

"I think Bill's mummy'll be making 'im 'ave one too!" laughed Jim and everyone joined in as Mo bought out her grandmother's big brown teapot, a vessel so large that Jim joked he could float it down to the Potter's Daughter with enough coal inside to keep their fires going for a week.

Everyone's spirits were high and there were so many stories to be told that it was late morning before Tom's team stood up and shook hands with Mr. and Mrs. Waterhouse.

"Lovely tea Mo, thanks duck," said Sid warmly, handing her back a blackly imprinted cup. "An' lovely ter meet yer all!" he said, taking some humbugs out of his pockets and handing them to the children who inspected them carefully. Finding them not to be made of soot, they unwrapped them quickly and popped them into their mouths.

"What are you going to do now?" asked Tom, looking at Billie.

"We want to see Walter first," the boy replied, glancing at Willie for confirmation. "To say sorry for everything we've done." He looked glum. He knew that wasn't going to be easy.

"That's right," said Willie. "We want to say sorry first, for everything we did. Then Mum and Dad right after."

"Alright lads," said Tom, "but us lot are off there right away. Dunner keep your Mum an' Dad waiting long! They must be desperate ter see you both!"

Now, standing in the empty craft and clay room, the twins wished they had been able to apologise properly to the little potter.

"He's just left his vase!" said Willie as the doors banged shut behind Walter. "With us!"

"I hope his Auntie's not going to die," said Billie. "But we'd better look after this. Where's Old Slope Off?"

The twins looked inside the storeroom and peeked into the corridor but no caretaker could be found. Neither boy dared to approach Mr. Pinch or venture further into the school. They could hear the distant humming of classrooms but knew they had broken a trust and would be seen as dangerous interlopers, or worse, if they ventured further.

"We can't stay in here," said Billie. "Let's go outside and shut the big doors and guard 'em, like. We can't lock 'em but we can stay till Slope Off gets back from where ever he is. Gone for some fags, perhaps."

"Mum and Dad'll be waiting," said Willie anxiously.

"I know, but I don't feel right leaving it like this, do you?" said Billie. For the last five minutes, he had begun to feel uneasy in a way which he couldn't explain to his twin. His stomach felt queasy, as if he were standing on top of a high cliff, looking down at the jagged rocks below. "I mean, with no Slope or Potty or anything?" he added, looking around blankly.

"No, bruv. Come on then, let's shut them," said Willie, and they heaved the doors to, then slouched against them, their heads down against the grey drizzle driven on by a strengthening wind.

"Hope he hurries up!" said Billie but the minutes passed and the boys became increasingly damp in the soft dirty rain.

Then, out of nowhere, an axe thudded heavily into the door jamb just inches from Willie's head, crunching into the woodwork and sending splinters flying.

"*Guarding* it, are yer?" screeched a voice they both knew. "Out of me way! *I'm* 'aving it!"

"Old Ma!" cried Billie. "Willie! She's out!"

Both boys barred the doors as their fiendish grandmother struggled to gain admittance. But she was lithe and sinuous, with a ferocious strength that astonished the twins as she prised their fingers off the door knob so that they needed all their combined weight to push her off and to keep her away.

Defeated, she drew back and glared at them. Willie felt himself sicken and stumble but Billie grabbed him.

"Don't fear her, bruv!" he cried. "She's evil but we're not! Not anymore! She can do her worst but she's not twisting us again!"

Willie struggled upright and took in a long pull of the smoky air. He felt steadier - but then he saw Old Ma reach inside her skirts and draw out a long thin blade. It was Squealer! Retrieved quietly from the Evidence Store by the craven Shrimpe, it had lain undetected under Old Ma's mattress for weeks and now glinted savagely in her hand. Drawing back her arm, the old woman took aim.

"I shan't miss a second time!" she sneered - but as she spoke a huge form appeared in the gateway and flew across the playground at a speed which belied its massive bulk.

"Dad!" cried Willie as Harold leapt forward and lunged, seizing his mother and lifting her in a great swoop over his head.

Grabbing her skinny ankles in one huge fist, he swung Old Ma around like a prize conker before sweeping her down in a swift arc to smash out her brains on the playground below.

"No Dad! No!" cried Billie, throwing himself forward and intercepting his grandmother, who, merely a little shaken, scrabbled and clawed at her grandson's cheeks, leaving the bright blood running down onto his grubby shirt collar.

"She's not worth it, Dad!" he cried, pushing her away. "She's not worth it!"

Harold let go of the old woman's ankles. He seemed dazed, unable to focus on what was in front of him. Willie plastered himself against the doors.

"She's after the dragon, Dad!" he shouted. "She's not getting him Dad, is she? Is she?"

Harold shook his head. He had come to find his twins. He hadn't expected this. He looked at his dreadful mother, who, knife in hand, had backed off a little but was crouched, ready to spring upon his children.

In the distance, they heard the sounds of police whistles and men calling, "Not 'ere Sarge! She's not 'ere!"

Then came a new sound, a sound most unexpected. Through the grey rain, sweeping now in heavy curtains across the yard, came the clanging, ringing, thundering sound of hooves as Dragon burst upon the scene, storming through the iron gates like a nightmare, like the night-time itself all rolled up into one terrible form, huge, dark, and threatening.

He tore into the middle of the playground and halted abruptly, snorting, pawing the ground and lashing his tail.

"This is more like it!" he thought. "This isn't just grass and a bit of galloping! Something's up! Something's going on!" and he raised his head and sniffed the air, rolling back his upper lip to taste once more the city of coal and clay.

But a strange look came into his eyes: he snorted hard and shook his head violently. Something smelt foul, really foul! He snorted again, even harder, as if to dispel the stench from his nostrils – then he turned and glared at Old Ma. She spun on her nobbly little heels and glared back.

The horse and the old woman locked eyes in a motionless conflict. Old Ma had met her match. Dragon's eyes glowed red: they seemed to spark in their sockets as if the fur around them might, at any moment, catch fire and smoulder and burn. He snorted again and lashed his tail.

Suddenly, Old Ma rushed at him, wielding Squealer viciously, making wide sweeping strokes which Dragon spun at and avoided, rearing, thrashing, kicking out.

The Grunters watched in horror as Old Ma attacked again and again, lunging, thrusting, darting in and out as the great horse stood its ground, never backing off but wheeling, leaping, rising above the knife and then twisting below it. And Old

Ma never seemed to tire. A strong wind blew up, whipping her skirts around and tossing Dragon's main and tail so that he seemed to be part of the wind itself, a torrent of darker air which whirled around Old Ma like a tornado.

"No!" screamed Willie again and again. "Leave him, Grandma! Leave him alone!"

But Old Ma hardly heard him, intent as she was on triumph and on slaughter. Then, for a second, she drew back and Willie saw from her face that this was it, she had seen her way to a kill.

In a trice, she shrank into herself, and then shot forward, squid-like, under Dragon's belly, the knife flashing upwards to disembowel him. But Willie was quicker, throwing himself on top of Squealer as it arced upwards, his arm taking the blow so that his blood leapt out as Dragon spun around to safety and the knife clattered on to the ground. Willie kicked it away and Harold seized it quickly.

"You'll do no more damage with this," he said quietly, coming into himself again and flinging the knife up onto the roof of the school, where it rested harmlessly on the slates. "Billie, quick, tie up Willie's arm!"

He dived at Old Ma, but before he could seize her himself, Dragon had struck, leaping forward and biting hard into her fox fur collar, lifting her shrieking off the ground, then shaking her to and fro terribly, like a terrier with a rat. With a twist of his neck, he threw her high up into the sky where she tumbled head over heels on the wet wind, like a ragged crow tossed helplessly about in the streaming air.

He caught her by the collar once more and set off at a gallop, out of the playground and off down Turner Street, flashing past the blue files of policemen who were streaming towards the commotion at The Grove.

"Stop 'im! Stop 'im!" they shouted – but no one dared.

Into the rainy afternoon he galloped, a huge vanishing thunderstorm, leaving behind him bluer skies where the strong west wind was blowing the city's smoke eastwards, sending billowing black tides streaming off into Derbyshire and Nottinghamshire beyond.

In his teeth, he bore a shrieking bird which flapped and draggled, powerless to free itself though Dragon was sickened by the smell. He wanted rid of her – but not yet! On his travels he had seen just the place: Dragon knew exactly where he was taking Old Ma – and she wouldn't like it one little bit!

"Cor Dad! He's saved him, he's saved the vase!" cried Willie, straining to catch the last of the great horse as he disappeared around the corner and the police poured onto the yard instead, followed closely by Mrs. Grunter and the canal folk. Detective Mould drew up in a car and raced across the yard.

"Bruv! Bruv! Keep still bruv!" wailed Billie. "And my hands are all dirty, Dad! I can't stop the blood! I can't stop the blood, Dad!"

"Hospital!" barked Mould. "Get in the car!" and the Grunters piled inside, Billie holding his brother's arm above his head as the siren shrieked and the big car sped through the streets and Willie Grunter's blood ran down his arm, and his brother's arm too, and Mould vowed that he'd do something, anything, to put that old woman away for good.

"If the horse doesn't finish her off first!" he thought hopefully.

Mr. Pinch ran out of The Grove in astonishment as the car tore away. He had been struggling with the boiler in Mr. Slope's absence and had missed all of the drama until Phillip Slipp tracked him down and said, "Please sir, that Old Ma

Grunter's been fighting a dragon in the playground but she's half killed that Willie Grunter instead, sir, and Miss Lush asked me to say that the radiator's still cold, sir, sorry sir."

Mr. Waterhouse came forward, in a smart white neckcloth, followed by Tom's grimy team, who had done their best with a jug of canal water and a scrap of towel.

"Good morning, gentlemen," said the perplexed Headmaster. "What has happened here?"

There was an awkward silence. No one was quite sure what had happened, though Tom's toe skirted a little puddle of blood. And none of these men were used to dealing with headmasters, especially one as imposing as John Pinch. Then a lively red headed boy detached himself from the group and spoke up.

"I'm Willie Grunter's friend," he said nervously. "'e's been staying with us on our barge and helping us with our Prince and everything. We all like Willie, sir. And Billie was with Tom," and he turned to the coal man who nodded and took off his cap. "We've come to tell thee 'ow good they've been, sir, and 'ow they aren't bad anymore."

He burst into tears.

"And now 'e's 'urt!" he cried. "An' the police 'ave got 'im!"

"Dear, dear," said Mr. Pinch, proffering his white handkerchief to the boy. "I think we had all better go inside, though the heating is off as the boiler is down. Caretaker away, I'm afraid."

"Sid'll take a look at that for you, sir, if you like," offered Tom politely. "Not much he doesn't know about that sort of thing."

In a little while the school was warm once more and a phone call was made to Detective Mould, after which Mr. Pinch understood all that had happened at The Grove. Willie would need a dozen stitches but was hale and hearty, the policeman said, and would be released into the care of his family.

"But he's worried about the horse, apparently," Mr. Pinch said, putting down the phone. "Excuse me," he said. "There is something I must deal with urgently first, if you would be so good as to wait a moment."

He left his study quickly and went straight to the craft and clay room. Finding it empty he half ran to Miss Lush's classroom.

"Excuse me Miss Lush," he said, putting his head around the door. "No Walter? No? Then I must borrow Pongy and Lefty as a matter of urgency. Quickly boys!" he said as the astonished children stood up uncertainly. "Run over to Mr. Potterton at the yard! You know what has occurred? Yes? Tell him what has happened and ask Bill and his team to come here immediately. The vase must be moved now. Right now!"

"Cor sir!" said Potty, deeply impressed at Mr. Pinch's command of the situation. "Be there in a tick, sir! Come on Lefty!"

Walter's friends rushed off but the whole class piled to the front and cried, "But we're the Dragon Knights too, sir! It's up to us to defend 'is dragon as well, sir!"

"Two of you are quite sufficient," smiled Mr. Pinch. "But your loyalty is admirable, children, and you will be allowed to accompany the vase on its journey to the kiln at lunchtime. Thank you, Miss Lush. Please have them ready in half an hour."

"Please sir!" said Phillip Slipp. "Walter's gone 'ome, sir. I saw 'im run off like mad, sir! All the way up the 'ill!"

"Thank you, Phillip," said Mr. Pinch and he closed the door and returned to his study where he settled down to listen to Freddie who was waiting eagerly to begin his tale.

"'e's mad about 'orses, sir," said Freddie. "Our Prince loves 'im, an' our little Elizabeth does too!"

Story followed story and Mr. Pinch sat amazed as he listened to the tales of the Grunter twins' travels. Such willing hard work, such good humour, such interest in things!

"They have changed," he thought joyously, as he waved goodbye to the twins' protectors. "And Willie has risked his own life to save the horse. If only that old woman can be kept away! If only she has gone for good!"

Miss Lush appeared at his back, looking anxious. By now the whole school was awash with the fight between Old Ma and the dragon.

"We don't know why Walter went home, Headmaster," she said. "He should still be in school and ready to attend this afternoon's classes, I believe. One can't help worrying, Headmaster."

No one had informed The Grove. Events at the little house were still too raw and the family had withdrawn into itself. Walter and Sally sat by Louie's bedside, watching as she slept peacefully or drank the soup that Minnie appeared with, sitting on the bed as her sister was propped up, then spooning it gently into the elderly lady's mouth.

"Lovely, dear," Louie would say before sinking back into a deep healing sleep.

But Walter wasn't sleepy. He was angry, bitterly angry, all thoughts of his marvellous vase forgotten. To sneak in here and attack his Auntie! His blood boiled like never before. Never had he known such rage. When a knock came on the door at twelve-thirty he almost jumped out of his skin.

"It's not her, is it, Auntie?" he cried.

But it was only Mr. Pinch, instantly offering his apologies for disturbing such a troubled house. He refused to go in but beckoned Walter to come out and stand on the pavement with him. In a few well-chosen sentences, he related the morning's events and the Grunter twins' heroic part in it. Walter was stunned with disbelief. Willie and Billie – his guardian angels! It was impossible! His anger began to subside just a little but the thought of Old Ma and her attack on Dragon made it erupt so violently that he felt sick and unwell.

Yet Mr. Pinch knew that he must say more.

"I hesitate to tell you, dear boy," he said, "But we must now move your dragon vase today. Bill will brick it up instantly and Alf will start the firing when that is done. We must keep it out of harm's way. We do not know where she is or what she will do. Potty and Bill's team are moving it as we speak and will stay there all night - or until she is caught. Don't worry about your dragon, Walter, we will look after him! She is just one elderly lady, after all!"

"But she is evil, *truly* evil!" he thought as he strode back to school. Like Detective Mould, Mr. Pinch was a rational man who had no time for superstition. After the war, he no longer believed in God either but in the power of good deeds and positive thought and he had supressed any staffroom gossip of Old Ma being in league with the Devil. "All rubbish, surely!" he thought as he sat down at his desk - but a little chill ran down his spine and he shivered despite the warm clanking of the radiator.

"Old Ma attacked again and again..."

Chapter Thirty Four
A Knock On The Door

"Looks as if it's clearing up. Marvellous!" said Mr. Jollie at one o' clock, peering out of the conservatory at the December sky. "Needs to dry up a bit before you string up the lanterns though, John. But marvellous! Marvellous!"

Lanterns already glowed in the lovely conservatory, lighting the roses and casting entrancing shadows amongst the foliage. All was now ready for Rosie's party and Mr. Jollie looked around him with satisfaction. It was perfect. He could have done no more.

The whole morning had been one great rush of preparation, though after leaving the yard he had found time to visit Gwenny and enquire about Dragon.

"Can't get y'brother on the telephone this morning, Beany," he said, when he found the grocer up to his arms in a tub of pearl barley.

"No, I couldn't either," Mr. Beany said. "Usually somebody there this time of day. Still, I'll give him a ring later and let you know what 'e says. Been doing quite a bit of harness work this week, I think. Big day for you, I understand," he went on, changing the subject and smiling at Mr. Jollie. "Anything else I can supply you with, Mr. Jollie? Got some nice fruit jellies in yesterday. Pineapple! No? Well I 'ope it all goes off very nicely for 'er, sir! Sixteen eh? Those were the days eh, sir?" and he winked at Mr. Jollie and began to bustle about, putting up the day's orders for Sprout to deliver on his bicycle.

Jigger-Poo left the store reluctantly. He had discovered a barrel of beefy dog biscuits but had failed to communicate his interest to Mr. Jollie, who, consulting his pocket watch, felt that the day was getting away from him whilst so much remained to be done at home.

He put all thoughts of Dragon out of his mind and returned to Prospect House. Then for the rest of the day the household was so busy that nothing reached it of the events at The Grove. But at half-past five, the Evening Sentinel flopped onto the mat and John, shaken, rushed upstairs to Mr. Jollie who was half in and half out of the bath.

"Really, Jolly-Poo!" he was saying. "Puppies! Marvellous! But what about downstairs, old girl? Nice nest under a table, what!"

The bathroom floor was an unnegotiable mountain of cushions, pillows, throws and overcoats, a Himalaya of soft furnishings, with Jolly-Poo, like a woolly panting Buddah, sprawled on its summit. As John entered, politely looking the other way, Mr. Jollie spotted his towel amongst the foothills and tugged it out.

"Woof!" barked Jigger-Poo. "Woof! Woof! Woof!"

"Quite!" said Mr. Jollie, towelling himself vigorously. "Glad when those puppies are here! Eh, what!"

But John's face was pale and his hand shook as he passed the paper over to his employer.

So much had happened in such a short time, that the editors of The Sentinel, arguing in a stuffy little cubby-hole above the great inky presses, had been unable to decide upon one stand-alone headline to cover the day's events.

Cecil Sharpe tapped the Chief's desk with his pencil.

"Battle of the Grove," he said. "Sums it all up. In a nutshell!"

"No, No!" cried Larry Hackitt. "What about the 'orse? What about 'im? Dragon Saves the Day!" he said. "Much better!"

"You're both wrong," mused the Chief, taking a thick black pencil from behind his ear and inscribing a bold caption in the empty space at the top of the evening's proof.

"Old Ma! Out!" it said. "Everybody wants to know about *her*," he said. "Mould'll have some explaining to do!"

"And the twins? What about them?" cried Cecil sharply. "Heroes – apparently! This time!" he smirked.

"But the 'orse! The 'orse!" clamoured Larry with missionary zeal. "'e's run off with 'er and nobody knows where she is! Or 'e is!" he added, jabbing his inky finger at the paper and smudging the chief's headline. "Mould's got every available man out looking for 'em – an' 'alf the public 'ave joined in as well!" He leaned back against yesterday's news. "That beats everything, that does!"

The Chief's little secretary poked her head around the door.

"Don't forget the vase!" she said pertly. "They'll have started the firing by now. Bought forward a day and done as a matter of urgency. The vase's the thing if you ask me!"

The newspaper-men scratched their heads and Sandra went away to make more tea.

"She's not wrong," said the chief. "None of this would have happened without that!"

Tea was brought in and the arguments continued unabated. Finally, at half- past three the chief gave in.

"Right!" he said, sitting up. "We'll print the lot!" and he rapidly pencilled in half a dozen headlines all over the front page. "Get that down to Black 'Arry," he said, thrusting the sheet at Cecil. "And tell him to be sharp about it! I've got a paper to get out!"

Mr. Jollie stared at the headlines aghast as the paper dampened and tore in his incredulous grip.

"Dragon!" he cried. "John! Dragon! He's gone!"

John had not seen Mr. Jollie so upset for a long time; he loved the old man and dreaded a return of the old unhappiness.

"He'll be found, Mr. Jollie, sir, don't you worry" he said, wrapping him in as many dry articles of clothing as could be retrieved from the resistant Poos. "I'll dress you, sir, then Rosie will be here shortly – and everyone else too!"

He escorted Mr. Jollie along the landing to his bedroom.

"He's a great big horse, sir, he won't come to any harm."

"And I don't suppose anyone's much bothered about her!" he thought. "I hope that's the last we ever hear of *her*!"

But Mr. Jollie moped and dithered. Why hadn't Pat Beany called him, he wanted to know? When did he go missing? What was being done to find him?

Pat Beany was at fault, but he had never lost a horse before and was determined to recapture him and never let on. So he drove further and further afield, ignorant of Dragon's adventures, scouring the Peak District in his lorry whilst Big Ben, having commandeered a friendly baker's van, swept through the countryside to the west of Bagnall as housewives waited in vain for their daily bread or their iced fancies.

"I'd better get out there!" cried Mr. Jollie, kicking off the patent shoes which John was cramming onto his feet. "I've got to get out and look for him, John!"

"It's ten to six!" panted John, seizing Mr. Jollie's feet and forcing the shoes on again. "They'll all be here soon! He'll be grazing somewhere, sir. That's what horses do when they run off! They just find somewhere to graze – and that's it!"

He pulled an evening coat off its hanger and thrust Mr. Jollie's arms inside.

"Poor Rosie," he thought. "It's not going to be much of a party unless he can pull himself together a bit."

But he knew just how much Dragon meant. He wasn't just a horse to the old man – he was his child. Then at six o' clock precisely, the doorbell rang.

"Better answer it, sir?" prompted John kindly, taking his employer's arm and assisting him down the stairs.

He propelled the old man along the hallway to the front door. Mr. Jollie fought hard with himself and tried to straighten his shoulders.

"Come on, Jollie, old boy!" he muttered to himself. "Don't let the little girl down. Steady the Buffs!"

He forced a smile and opened the door – then fell back in surprise against an equally startled John. There on the gravel, silhouetted against the dark winter sky, was a tall handsome boy holding quietly onto the rope of a great black horse.

"Dragon!" cried Mr. Jollie, rushing down the steps and burying his face in the horse's mane.

Dragon snorted.

"How embarrassing!" he thought.

"He just turned up, Mr. Jollie, sir," said Willie, beaming from ear to ear. "At the shop. We were all having tea, all of us, like, and then there was this great banging on the shop door. Dad thought it was a mob!"

Mr. Jollie looked hard at the boy.

"Gracious!" he said. "It's you!"

One of the twins! One of the boys who had tried to wreck Walter's vase! But now his benefactor! The boy who had selflessly fought for Dragon and saved his life!

He seized Willie's hand and pumped it up and down so hard that it hurt.

"Hero!" he cried. "Hero, dear boy! John – more bandages!"

The next moment the driveway was full of people as Rosie and her guests crowded around the great horse in the yellow light streaming out of the doorway. Rosie looked up in wonder at Dragon who lowered his head and sniffed her perfumed hair.

"Goodness!" said Thelma nervously. "You're favoured! Come on, safer inside, I say! Let's get in!"

Mr. Jollie shook hands with everybody and waved them past.

"Rosie! Marvellous! Happy Birthday!" he sang happily. "Make yourself at home. Be there in a jiffy. Marvellous! Marvellous!"

The guests trouped past in two's and three's, only Walter's family were wanting. Soon music drifted out into the dark December evening as John strung Chinese lanterns amongst the trees, so that the drive blossomed with golden moons and this little corner of the city of coal and clay became a place of utter enchantment.

"Dad rang Mr. Beany and he says to take him there, sir?" asked Willie respectfully. "Next to Gwenny? And I'll keep him company all night. I know horses now, sir, I really do!"

"And he came right to you, did he? Did he?" asked Mr. Jollie in wonder as he patted the soft fur of Dragon's muzzle. "Well, job for you here boy! In safe hands with you, and no mistake!"

Willie felt ecstatic. If a huge black bearded pirate had suddenly appeared in a cloud of smoke, swashbuckling and sworded, to lay a great chest of pirate treasure at the schoolboy's feet, with a hearty, "Take it mate – it's all yours!" Willie could not have been more delighted. A job with Dragon! Joy filled him from top to toe, so that he struggled to speak.

"I'll never let him down," he said at last, his eyes shining as he looked at Mr. Jollie. "He'll have all my time – school of course," he added miserably. "Got to go back there. But evenings, weekends, holidays. Every spare moment Mr. Jollie, I promise!"

Mr. Jollie laughed.

"What about a barge, eh, Willie? A barge for Dragon?" He patted the black horse. "What do you think of that, old boy?"

Dragon snorted and thought about it.

"The open towpath instead of the open road," he mused. "It might work," he thought, resting his huge head on Willie's shoulder. "I might go anywhere with him!"

"And Billie?" enquired Mr. Jollie politely. "How's your brother, dear boy?"

"Oh, he's still in the bath!" laughed Willie. "Mum says he won't be clean for a fortnight! He was proper filthy!"

Mr. Jollie thought it better not to mention Old Ma though he did wonder about her disappearance and Dragon's part in it.

"Grandmother, after all," he thought as he waved goodbye to the horse and boy. "Turn up again perhaps. Bad penny. Never been any good, that one. Trouble right from the start!"

He shook his head and turned towards the light, where young people whirled past the windows and the heady scent of roses and lilies spilled out into the dark.

Willie too, said nothing, though he was secretly made wretched at the idea that Dragon might have killed the old woman, wicked as she was. It was a dark shadow that accompanied him on the short journey to Mr. Beany's yard, Dragon sitting nicely behind his shoulder the whole way, calm in his hands, remembering the bravery with which Willie had fought for him.

"At last!" he thought. "Someone I can look up to! Someone who knows what he's doing!"

He snuggled up close and Willie knew he would die for the great horse. He had never thought to love anyone as much as he loved Dragon.

Gwenny greeted her old stable mate with whinnies of delight. Mr. Beany stuck his head round the door at the sound.

"Oh, it's you," he said, not opening the door any further. "You know where to put 'im, next to our Gwenny. Bed's made up an' hay an' what not. Feed's in there an' all. Oh, an' Walter's here too, in with our Gwenny." He paused and looked at Willie curiously. "Expect you've got a lot to say to '*im*," he said, and shut the door.

Willie stood rooted to the spot. He felt more fear now at facing Walter than when he had sprung to Dragon's defence against the knife. Then Dragon snorted and Walter's head popped up above Gwenny's stable door. The two boys beheld each other guardedly.

"I knew you were coming," said Walter. "Mr. Beany told me."

Willie swallowed hard.

"How's your Auntie, Walter?" he asked anxiously, feeling that by Old Ma's actions he had been thrown back into the role of villain. He felt ashamed of his blood, ashamed of his whole family. "Is she going to get better?" he asked humbly, grateful for the company of the great horse whose warm breath seeped down under his scarf and warmed not just his neck but his heart too.

"No thanks to your Grandma," said Walter tersely, looking away. He was still full of anger. Minnie had sent him away to calm down.

"Go and see Gwenny," she had said, pushing him out along the back yard. "Louie just needs to sleep, dear. Come home when you feel a bit better."

Willie still stood there, tongue tied and awkward. Dragon nudged him hopefully. He could smell barley and oats and hay.

"Your pot's safe," said Willie quietly.

"Yes," said Walter, looking at him again. "Mr. Pinch told me you saved it. Thank you." He was silent a minute and then said, "Does it hurt much, your arm?"

"Not too bad," said Willie bravely. In fact, it hurt a good deal and was still throbbing from Mr. Jollie's over enthusiastic handshake.

Walter turned back to Gwenny and began to brush her again, making long soft stokes over the mare's back so that she snorted softly with pleasure as she munched her hay.

"You'd better put him in," he said over his shoulder, and Willie moved forward and slid aside the bolt. Soon Dragon was munching too, his face half buried in the deep bucket as Willie stood by him, running his fingers through the tangled mane.

"There's some brushes over there," said Walter, indicating a little brown cupboard with a broken-down door. "Mr. Beany lets me use them."

Willie found the brushes and started to groom Dragon, though his stomach was churning with anxiety. He wished that Billie was there too.

"I've got to talk to him!" he thought, the blood pounding in his head and his ears burning painfully. "Even if he hates me forever I've got to tell him I'm sorry!"

Then he plucked up his courage and said, "We were vile to you Walter, we know that."

"You won't get an argument from me there!" said Walter, not looking up.

"And we're sorry, we really are!" cried Willie. "We're not like that anymore! We've changed. We're different people now!"

Walter wasn't one to bear grudges but neither could he forget such an attack on one he loved.

"And what about her?" he demanded, straightening up and staring at Willie. "Will she be coming back?"

"I don't know! I don't know!" cried Willie in distress.

He suddenly looked much more like the eleven- year- old boy he was than the ogre of Walter's imagination. Willie ran his hand over the horse eating so peacefully beside him.

"I can't bear to think he's killed her!" he blurted out, his face full of tortured emotion. "She might deserve it for what she's done but I don't want it to be him! I don't want to think he's done something like that!" and he burst into tears, sobbing violently on the partition wall.

Walter put down his brushes and moved over to comfort him.

"I'm sure he hasn't done anything bad," he said reassuringly. "He hasn't got it in him. He's not a mean horse."

He reached over and stroked Dragon's muzzle as he pulled at his hay.

"He's just his own horse, he is! I'm not sure he's ever going to pull a carriage for Mr. Jollie! It'd be like harnessing a hurricane!"

Willie laughed and his face brightened.

"Thanks Walter," he said. "I'm going to be looking after him now – before and after school, like. He's going to live here, with Gwenny. He can meet Prince and Freddie – Freddie's my friend and Prince is his horse, well his Dad's, anyhow."

"Where were you?" asked Walter. "All that time? Where did you go?"

The atmosphere grew warmer and Willie told his tale of life on the canals as Walter listened in amazement.

"It's what I'm going to do," Willie told him earnestly. "I shall be trying out barge work with Dragon for Mr. Jollie. Perhaps he'll take to it, something new every day, like."

"Perhaps," thought Walter, eying the great black horse and wondering whether he would ever be as biddable as the gentle Prince sounded.

At seven o' clock he gave Gwenny a final pat and stowed his brushes away in the little brown cupboard.

"I feel a bit better now," he said. "I've got to get off and get changed. Minnie says I'm to take Rosie her present."

"It's a nice party," said Willie encouragingly. "Music and lanterns and everything."

"My Aunties have been saying that George Brittain's going to ask Rosie to marry him," said Walter warily.

"Oh!" said Willie, "Soppy stuff then, mate! Still, you needn't stay long and you've got the poodles. Nice dogs, them. Where's the straw kept?" he added, looking around.

Walter took him outside and showed him the big golden bales stacked in the adjacent loft. Willie climbed up and pushed down four of the solid bundles, which he laid side by side outside Dragon's stable door.

"Nice double bed!" he laughed, jumping on top and pulling a dusty old horse blanket over himself. Then he sat up again. "Will you shake hands with me Walter?" he said, his heart thumping.

Walter shook his hand.

"Are you sleeping here all night?" he asked in amazement. "On your own?"

"Every night 'till I know she's gone for good," said Willie determinedly. "I'm not letting her anywhere near *him* again!"

"Detective Mould's got men all round our house," said Walter sadly.

"They're everywhere," said Willie. "The streets are full of coppers. But they're no match for *her*, are they?"

Walter was quiet. He thought how lucky he was to have grown up in the little house and not the butcher's shop.

"It must have been dreadful," he said, "having a grand-mother like that."

Willie sat head down, his shoulders slumped.

"When we were very little she used to give us toffees out of a tin on the fireplace," he said. "That was nice. Then it was a toffee if we did what she said."

His face darkened and he was silent for a while as Walter stood like a statue close by.

"Then it was threats as well as promises," Willie went on. "But I'm not making excuses." He looked up at Walter, red-faced. "We did get to like it. We liked being bullies, Walter. Before she went too far!"

He groaned and hid his face in his hands.

Walter shuddered.

"Cor!" he thought. "How awful!"

"Well," he said. "That's in the past now Willie, isn't it? We're mates now, right?"

"Are we?" cried Willie, leaping up. "Are we really? I thought you hated me!"

"I don't hate you, Willie," said Walter. "I thought I did – but I don't. We're friends now, I hope."

Willie hugged him wildly.

"Alright!" squeaked Walter. "I can't breathe, mate!"

Willie stood back and beamed at his little friend.

"You'll never have better mates than me and our Billie," he promised solemnly. "Not ever, for the rest of your life!"

Time was to prove Willie right, for another, greater test stood close at hand, out there in the dark, under the starry sky.

"Can I come and see Prince?" asked Walter.

"Tomorrow!" cried Willie, flushing with happiness. "Come and see them before they go north again."

Walter left and Willie snuggled down under his blanket, remembering the nights he had spent on top of the barge, safe under the tarpaulin and full of Mo's hot supper. He looked up at the stars, strangely clear on this windy Friday night when the city's smoke was blown away as soon as it was made. Thousands of chimneys were pouring out their black clouds - but they raced away across the dark sky, so that the heavens glittered over the city of coal and clay and the rising moon shone like a yellow lamp, like the Chinese lanterns which danced and bobbed in Mr. Jollie's garden, partnered by their lively reflections dancing and bobbing in the lighted windows.

Washed and brushed, Walter made his way there, clutching the bottle of perfume wrapped in tissue and adorned with a silver bow. Willie was right, the police were everywhere, on almost every corner, peering into yards, examining coal sheds and outhouses, leaving not a stone unturned.

"They won't find her *there*, I'm sure!" thought Walter as two burly officers pulled a tarpaulin off a brewery wagon. "But I wonder where she is! Whatever *did* Dragon do with her? Has she really gone for good?"

"He suddenly looked much more like the eleven-year-old boy he was..."

Chapter Thirty Five
Transformations

In a far-flung corner of the city lay a marl pit so deep, so vertiginous as almost to defy imagination. Deeper and deeper it had been dug over the centuries, ton after ton of marl it had yielded, seemingly inexhaustible in its supply of the thick sticky clay. Long frail ladders clung to its sides, each descending vertically, each ending in mid-air, leaving yet another to be scaled below it, and another and another below that.

It was a huge pit, an enormous gaping mouth on the edge of the city, vast in extent yet even greater in depth, a place of terror where not even the bravest urchins strayed, where no games of "I dare you" were played, where no one went, not even the birds and the mice.

To this place, Dragon had brought Old Ma.

Galloping through the city's streets, easily outstripping his pursuers, Dragon had arrived unnoticed at the very brink, shuddering to a halt on the crumbling precipice as the wind tore into his mane and set his tail streaming off behind him like a trail of black smoke. Stepping back from the very edge of the abyss, he lifted his head and shook Old Ma thoroughly again, then tossed her up with a swift crook of his neck, sending her spinning up and out over the marl pit where she hovered on the wind like a ragged bird of prey before spiralling down and down towards its marly depths. Down and down she floated, sinewy and insubstantial: more creature than human, less creature and more *thing*: ghastly, grisly and foul smelling. Dragon snorted and wheeled away. He had no understanding of marl pits, though he had seen a few rubbish tips in his time.

"Right place for *that*!" he thought, proud to have disposed of such a dangerous and objectionable item. "Stinking the place out!"

So down she plopped, wetly into the clay bed which enfolded her quietly, closely, completely. The marl bubbled and was still, its surface as smooth as if it had never been disturbed, the vast pit empty, devoid of life, without movement or sound.

Dragon thundered off in search of a green field, finding one just a little further away; not lush, perhaps, but he jumped its sooty hedge and nibbled the meagre sward, searching out dandelion leaves and the wintry remains of cow parsley along its overgrown perimeters. But it was December, and no matter how much of the pasture he consumed his belly never felt full.

"A hot mash!" he thought wistfully. "Perhaps boiled barley with black treacle!"

But how was he to come by it? Then a face came into his mind. A heroic face: the face of the boy who had fought for him against the knife!

"Of course!" he thought. "I'll go and find him!"

And off he went at the gallop, a blacker shape against the darkening day, clanging and clattering through the little streets until he had found the place where Willie Grunter lived.

But in the depths of the marl pit, something stirred. One torn claw poked above the surface - and then another. Two skinny arms heaved up, spider-like, then finally something resembling a head broke the surface with a roaring, rasping breath. Old Ma was still alive!

The marl pit gave her up with a sucking wheezing gulp, as if it were a portal of Hell disgorging some iniquity in to the world, closing behind her so quickly that she tussled for her foot, now cloven quite in two. The attack on her grandsons had snapped Old Ma's last tenuous bond with humanity, and she now crawled bat-like across the pit bottom towards the stick-thin ladders.

Old Ma's nose had become a beak, savage and sharp, her mouth a mere black slit. Indeed, her whole body had meta-morphosed into something strange and unnatural, something unwieldy and unreal. Like a ghastly inversion of the grub which emerges from its pupae as a fabulous butterfly, Old Ma was expelled from her muddy cocoon as a true incarnation of the Evil One himself, cloven footed and clawed, with sharp little horns poking through her black straw bonnet. Long seen as the very Devil Himself, Old Ma was now truly revealed as one and the same, one twisted fragment of the Evil of the World, one vicious chip off the Original Block.

Plastered in the thick marl, her rags weighed down by its clayey grip, Old Ma struggled up the frail ladders to wreak havoc in the city above. No one saw her rise, step by step, rung by rickety rung, until, gasping, she sprawled on the lip of the pit, clutching at grass not marl. As Dragon munched his hay and Willie kept watch, she crept and slithered along the lanes and back alleyways, a portion of the earth the very bricks were made of, but evil, utterly evil, intent only on destruction, murder and mayhem, a black stain of depravity seeping deeper and deeper into the very heart of the city of coal and clay.

§

Potty stood in the warmth of the bottle oven and took a tot of whiskey from Bill's flask. He felt that he needed it: the day's events had completely unnerved him.

Pongy had rushed upon the men shouting, "She's out! She's out! Old Ma's out!" then gabbled out the whole terrible tale whilst Potty and the team stood aghast, their mouths hanging open in disbelief.

"*Them* twins?" Burt had asked incredulously. "Them Grunter boys? Saved the day?" he scratched his head in puzzlement. "I thought pigs'd fly sooner'n they'd do anyone a good turn!" he said.

"But they did!" Lefty had cried. "They were really brave too. Willie's arm's really cut up they say! Fifty stitches at least!"

Now Potty thought back over the hurried transfer of the precious vase and he shuddered.

"To have come so far and nearly to have lost everything!" he thought, though he smiled at the remembrance of the Dragon Knights trouping alongside in neat crocodiles, shepherded by their teachers and watched over by Mould's men, who had gazed in amazement at Walter's dragon.

He accepted another nip from the flask, enjoying the warmth of the whisky as it went down. The strong wind was also a chilly one and Potty moved even closer to the warm door of the hovel where Alf and were the others were busy with their shovels, piling the rich coal into the firemouths, replenishing the smoke that billowed out and blew away eastwards.

All afternoon, Alf had been building the bottle oven to a massive heat. Peering into the spy hole he saw the flames roaring against Burt's saggars. Inside this stockade, hidden from Alf's inquisitive eye, the glazes were beginning to transform, changing their dull and muddy coats into shining suits of vibrant forest greens and azure blues. Sunset golds were appearing and goldfish yellows; with the blue of summer skies were deep deep midnights spangled with silver stars; and the pearl was beginning to glow with an opalescent sheen, reflecting the dragon's peony pink tongue.

A little while ago Alf had drawn out a Buller's Ring and nodded in satisfaction. The bottle oven was properly hot now - and must be kept that way. No diminution of the temperature could occur if the glazes were to succeed. He had seen enough failures in his time: he knew of firemen who had ruined whole ovens full of ware which had come out grey and spoiled, cracked and crazed, good only for the sherdruck. Then, there was the poor fireman with his reputation ruined and his livelihood lost. But it had never happened to Alf - and he didn't intend to fail now.

He drew back and wiped his burning brow.

"We'll 'ave a rest in a bit," he said, gulping down a cold mug of tea. "She'll be reaching maximum heat in the next hour or so. You needn't all stay – there's plenty of coppers about and I doubt if *she's* anywhere around from what Pongy's said."

It was hard to stray anywhere without bumping into one of Mould's men, it was true, but the men shook their heads worriedly.

"I'll stay here," said Potty, as the kiln men loaded their shovels again. "But Bill, why don't you and Burt pop over to the party for a while? You can update Walter if he's there. Rosie will be pleased to see you, no doubt."

The two men set off through the narrow streets, their shadows stretching out as they passed the gas lights flickering overhead. Above them too, the night sky was thickly woven with fiery stars twinkling in the unreachable firmament.

"Not seen anything like that for a long time, Burt," said Bill, throwing back his head to look up as they paused at the bottom of Mr. Jollie's drive. "Reminds me of when I was in France. Some nights, when there was no shelling and the air was clear, I used to lie on me back an' just look up, away from it all, the whole ruddy mess!"

Burt nodded. He had done the same.

"Used to think they was over me wife an' kids," he said, "same as they was over me. Well, he's got a great night for it Bill – let's go an' see if 'e's 'ere!"

"sending her spinning out over the marl pit..."

Chapter Thirty Six
Meanwhile...

The front door was slightly ajar and they went inside. Refusing to go further than the hallway in their working clothes, they sat and enjoyed pork pies and pints of bitter whilst Walter listened eagerly to all they had to say, sitting cross-legged on the black and white floor with his back against the old grandfather clock. He had hardly had a thought of his vase all afternoon but now he was agog with excitement.

"I shall have to go over there in a bit," he said anxiously as the clock struck nine, its mellifluous notes chiming above the dance music on the gramophone. "I'll just stay a bit longer to be polite."

The party was not really his idea of a good time. He wasn't much interested in dancing – in fact he was very much hoping that Rosie's friends, full of excitement and ginger beer, would leave him well alone. There was Rosie, beautiful in her pink velvet, but she had eyes only for George and had ceased to be anywhere near as much fun as she used to be. There was his good friend Mr. Jollie, but he was buzzing to and fro, happy with his punch ladle and his decanters. There were the Poos, best of all, but they were preoccupied and restless, dragging cushions and coats under tables and chairs, never settling long in one spot and causing more and more hilarity as the evening progressed.

Walter got up and bought out some birthday cake for Bill and Burt.

"I'll go in a bit," he was about to say when there was a loud knocking on the door and a red face appeared around the edge, surmounted by a mop of black windswept hair.

"Mr. Jollie about, lad?" the man asked nervously.

Walter called to Mr. Jollie, who was trying to convince Jigger-Poo to leave Thelma's best coat on its peg in the cloakroom. After a short tug of war the poodle rushed off to commit easier crimes and Mr. Jollie slammed the cloakroom door shut with relief.

"Oh!" he said, looking up and spotting his red-faced visitor. "Wondered when I'd hear from you! Better come in!" he added, opening the door wide.

"Don't like to intrude," said the man, clearly nervous to be inside such a grand house. "Just come to offer my apologies, Mr. Jollie. Won't happen again!"

"It won't Pat, it won't!" said Mr. Jollie firmly. "Dragon's staying at y'brother's from now on! Should've let me know, y'know," he said, fixing the horseman with his blue eyes so that the man's face went from red to puce.

"Looked everywhere for 'im," Pat Beany said earnestly. "Been up as far as Macclesfield, I 'ave! Big Ben's only just got back from Uttoxeter way. Tell you what Mr. Jollie," he said, sensing a softening in the old man's aspect, "I'll send Big Ben over a couple of days a week to 'elp that new lad of yours. Teach 'im to ride and such like. No charge," he added sweetly. "Do what we can to 'elp."

Mr. Jollie never bore a grudge.

"Better join the party," he said. "Walter, show our guest around will you? Marvellous! Marvellous!" he added, graciously palming off Pat Beany so that before Walter knew it he was in the thick of the party again without any hope of an imminent reprieve.

§

In his bath above the shop Billie Grunter was growing more pink and wrinkled by the minute. He had been in there for three hours, Bertha Grunter rushing in to drain off the worst of the black water and to replenish it with hot water from the geyser every half an hour or so.

"We'll all go and see Willie in a bit," said his harassed mother. "You'll have to have another bath tomorrow, Bill. It's all in your pores. I don't think you'll ever be clean again!"

§

In the little house, Louie slept deeply, dreaming of her childhood holidays in Llandudno, hearing the seagulls sweeping across the wide bay, feeling the wet sand between her toes, safe and happy with her mother and father, long, long ago.

Sally and Minnie sat close by, talking in low voices and listening to the soft even breathing of the sister so nearly lost to them.

§

Willie and Big Ben sat on the straw bales, immediately happy in each other's company. They were eating fish and chips and talking about horses. What else?

§

Mr. Slope lay in bed reading the Evening Sentinel.

"Missed out on all the excitement, dear?" sneered his wife as she whisked away his tray. "Shame you won't be in the paper this time, Ernest. Willie Grunter! Just fancy that! A hero! Saved the day and here's you, Guardian of the Vase, flat on your back doing nothing. Hardly seems right, does it?"

The door snapped shut behind her and Ernest Slope sighed. He picked up the paper and then put it down again. He sighed once more and stretched cautiously. Then he pulled his trousers over his pyjamas and bundled on a jumper under his dressing gown.

"Don't wait up!" he shouted as he opened the front door. "I've got responsibilities, I 'ave. Responsibilities!"

§

Alf and the team were still shovelling, feeding the hungry oven as the sweat ran down their faces and in between their shoulder blades. The kiln roared with a fiery life, demanding, urgent, compelling. Potty made up a brew on the bonfire, tickling its embers into flames and feeding it from the pile of old wood stacked close by. Then he handed the steaming mugs around, and the hot men slurped them down gratefully, wishing they held cold beer instead.

"Critical now, Potty," said Alf, drawing out a Bullers Ring and then backing away immediately from the terrific heat. "Got to sustain this now. Next two hours or so – absolutely critical!"

§

Over the city of coal and clay the winds began to drop. In the park the trees ceased their strenuous waving and the bushes ceased their whispering. The ripples lessened on the pond and then vanished into nothingness. The waters were still. But over the rooftops the smoke began once more to hover and then to build into great thick black blankets, piling up above the streets like soft dark quilts on the bed of an invalid, one on top of another, more and more and more.

The feeble street lamps cast lonely pools of light, glinting occasionally on the brass buttons of the policemen stationed on street corners and in alleyways.

All was quiet. All was calm. But Old Ma? What about her? Where was *she*?

"All was quiet. All was calm..."

Chapter Thirty Seven
Something Really Rotten

By half-past nine, George had managed to manoeuvre Rosie into the conservatory. The past hour and a half had been tricky, what with the presentations and the cutting of the birthday cake but now everyone was dancing or talking in the big room, standing around in happy little groups as they sipped their punch and nibbled their cake. Over by the marble fireplace Edna stood with Mr. Pinch, the Indian garnets glowing richly on her hand as she told Thelma of their wedding plans.

"Just a very small ceremony at the Holy Trinity," she said quietly, smiling up at her handsome fiancé who nodded his head. "But then a really *big* reception at The Grove! Everyone welcome – all the children and their teachers! *All* our friends – everyone!"

"And on Christmas Eve!" said Thelma excitedly. "Only one week to go, Edna - and I still haven't got a hat!"

George smiled as he guided Rosie gently amongst the flowers.

"And with any luck *we'll* be there in the summer!" he thought, picturing Rosie in a wedding dress, walking towards him down an aisle decked out with roses and lilies, like those that bloomed softly around them as the lanterns multiplied in the tall dark windows.

Rosie's mother sat discreetly to one side where she could just see the top of Rosie's shining hair and the side of George's flushed face, eager and apprehensive all at the same time. But she had no doubts about George. He had loved her daughter since they were infants at The Grove, whilst Rosie had looked up to and admired the tall boy two years older than herself, feeling heartbroken on the day that he had left her behind for the world of work, with only lessons to look forward to instead of the sight of his curly head chasing around the playground every morning and afternoon.

"Why wait?" thought the mother, and Rosie, pink-cheeked and hopeful, her heart thumping as George took her hand, felt just the same.

George gave a quick look around. They were alone.

"Rosie," he began – but a door was flung open and the cook burst in, waving a wooden spoon and shouting, "Rosie! Rosie! It's starting! Jolly-Poo! Come quick!" and Rosie, laughing, abandoned poor George and ran off to attend on the heavily panting poodle, who, ensconced under the kitchen table amongst a plethora of cook's clean table linen, was busy producing first one small white puppy and then another.

Edna rushed in, closely followed by Walter. Things were certainly picking up! The dragon vase was temporarily forgotten again in his anxiety for the labouring Jolly-Poo.

"Cor!" he said after fifteen minutes had gone by. "Six! Six puppies, Mr. Jollie!"

"Marvellous! Marvellous!" cried the old man, wiping his eyes as he wept with delight. "Clever girl! Oh, yes, Jigger-Poo!" he said as the dog leapt up and put his paws on Mr. Jollie's chest. "Clever boy too! Marvellous! Marvellous!"

Edna stooped to see under the table. Her eyes were moist and she was breathless with delight. Two would be hers, to love and to cherish, but she dared not touch the little damp bundles of fur – so precious were they, so tiny and so vulnerable.

"I think there's another, Mr. Jollie," said Rosie thoughtfully, pressing her hand gently on Jolly-Poo's heaving tummy. "Come on Jolly-Poo," she said gently and she stroked the dog's tired face tenderly.

"Oh dear," fretted Walter, seeing the poodle's exhaustion. "Come on, Jolly-Poo! Come on!"

Edna bit her lip hard. Jigger-Poo became anxious and fussy, nosing the six puppies repeatedly as if assuring himself that they were all still there.

"Where's George?" asked Rosie, looking up with concern. "He knows dogs. Where is he?"

George appeared in the doorway and knelt down quickly beside her.

"She's just tired," he said reassuringly. "That's all. Let's give her a bit more time. Let's all just be quiet for a bit."

So the little group sat silently while the gramophone played across the hallway, its notes wafting in and out with the sound of light conversation as the kitchen door was opened from time to time, one curious guest after another poking his head around, then leaving with shushing noises, tiptoeing back to the drawing room and the enquiring faces of the other guests.

Mr. Jollie calmly stroked Jigger-Poo whilst Rosie soothed the mother. She caught George's eye and smiled mischievously; he blushed furiously and could not return her glance. He had been preparing his proposal all day and was now completely flummoxed.

Then Jolly-Poo began to heave and strain.

"Oh, do help her George!" cried Rosie in alarm. Edna gave a little cry and then stilled herself, though her face was as white as paper.

"Vet?" asked Mr. Jollie sharply but George was unconcerned.

"She'll do it," he said. "Just give her a little longer."

Tension mounted in the kitchen as the cook hovered over all, like a heavy domestic angel with a holy wooden spoon.

Suddenly, Jolly-Poo gave a yelp and a great shuddering heave. A little black head appeared, followed quickly by a damp black body.

"Oh!" cried Walter in delight. "A black one! A black one, Mr. Jollie!"

"Marvellous!" cried the old man, "Absolutely marvellous!"

Edna and Rosie burst into tears but Jolly-Poo busied herself straight away, cleaning up the puppy so that it could join the others, all noisily suckling on her upturned tummy.

"Well!" said the cook, straightening up. "If that don't beat all! Seven! We shall 'ave our 'ands full, that's for sure! Not very hygienic though, if you ask me! And I've plenty to get through as it is...." And she went off into the scullery, grumbling quietly to herself, the clatter of plates and dishes and the loud hiss of the hot water geyser announcing her return to work.

The puppies continued to suckle, little snuffling noises leaking from their tiny noses as they pressed into their mother's warm fur. Jigger-Poo lay down beside them and licked his woolly wife on her face.

Mr. Jollie beamed.

"Marvellous!" he said, surveying them proudly. "Leave them to it now. Marvellous!"

One after the other they trouped back to the drawing room where the other guests greeted them eagerly, anxious to hear the news.

"And there's a black one!" said Walter, again and again. "A little *black* one!"

"Here's to the Poo's!" called Bill from the hallway, raising his pint of bitter. Everyone raised their glasses to toast the happy event. Mr. Pinch squeezed Edna's hand: she was almost dizzy with delight.

George squared his shoulders and steered Rosie once more into the conservatory, where the warm air was full of the scent of roses, heady and romantic. A song of endless love played on the gramophone, its sweet notes spiralling slowly out of the machine to drift languidly around the house, so that the cook, labouring amidst her steam and suds, heard it faintly and stood spellbound as the dish water grew cold in its soapy bowl. Once more Rosie stood, eyes down, modest and hopeful, as George took her small hand in his great one.

"Rosie," he said, his voice deep and warm, and Rosie looked up and screamed. She screamed and screamed and screamed! Then she fainted dead away, caught in George's strong arms before she hit the Minton tiles.

Everyone turned – and more screams split the air. Walter, though he later denied it, screamed louder than anyone.

"What is it? What is it?" he cried, clutching at Mr. Jollie, who, like everyone else, was frozen with shock at the sight of Old Ma with her beak pressed up against the window pane and her scarecrow claws dribbling yellow marl down the black glass.

She pounded the window wildly and pointed at Walter.

"I'll 'ave you!" they heard her muffled cry. "An' then I'll 'ave *it* as well!"

"Good Lord!" said Mr. Pinch, forgetting himself. "It's old Mrs. Grunter!"

He stepped forward towards the conservatory window.

"Madam!" he cried sternly. "Absent yourself! Do!"

He felt a little giddy but John Pinch was made of stern stuff. Thelma looked for Bill but the Headmaster was closer. She grasped his suit sleeve and peered over his shoulder, whilst Edna peeped around the other one.

"It's not *really* 'er, is it?" asked Thelma tremulously. "What's them things sticking out of 'er bonnet? They're not 'orns, are they?" She screamed loudly. "They *are* 'orns!" she shrieked, rushing backwards towards Bill and collapsing heavily in front of him. "They *are*! They *are*!"

Old Ma rattled her claws against the glass in enjoyment. This was even better than P.C. Shrimpe! The dark slit of a mouth widened into a dreadful leer. Then she mimed rocking something gently in her arms, patting it gently and then licking her lips.

Walter's eyes grew rounder and rounder.

"The puppies!" he cried. "She knows about the puppies!"

Old Ma cackled, and then spun quickly, disappearing as terrifyingly as she had appeared. Walter ran to the door but Edna was even quicker.

Bursting into the kitchen they saw the back door-knob turn slowly as an ooze of yellow clay seeped across the sill. Jigger-Poo leapt up and barked loudly. Cook emerged from the scullery, red faced and steamy. She looked hot and bothered.

"Whatever's the matter?" she demanded, seeing the little crowd of people standing transfixed and Jigger-Poo barking frantically at the door. She felt a cold draught and smelt something really rotten.

"Surely not the fish?" she thought, then turning let out a great cry.

Seizing her marble rolling pin she surged across the kitchen, her corsets creaking like Trentham Gardens in a gale.

"I don't think so!" she cried imperiously as Old Ma hesitated on the threshold. "I don't know *what* you are, but you're too dirty for in 'ere!" She prodded Old Ma with the rolling pin. "Be off with you!" she thundered. "And get a good bath yer filthy old devil! 'ere," she said, thrusting a large piece of birthday cake into Old Ma's surprised grip, "'ave that and be off!"

She slammed shut the door and shook her head.

"Beggars!" she exclaimed, rerolling her sleeves and collecting more dishes. "Coming round decent people's 'omes as filthy as that!"

The cook stamped off to the scullery again, well please with her small act of charity. Edna looked at Walter and shook her head. Jigger-Poo sniffed along the edge of the door then returned to the bed under the table. Everyone looked stunned.

"I'll just sit with them, John," said Edna shakily, kneeling down by the puppies and settling herself somewhat uncomfortably on the floor.

"I'll keep you company, my dear," said Mr. Pinch, drawing up two rush seated chairs. "So long as Mr. Jollie doesn't mind?"

"Not at all, old chap," said Mr. Jollie. Like everyone else, he had had a bad fright. "Glad you were here! Funny business that! Very funny!" He shook his head. "Bottle of ten-year-old somewhere," he went on. "Just the thing. Marvellous!"

He moved towards the hall door and Mr. Pinch looked around the room.

"Where's Walter?" he asked in alarm – but Walter was nowhere to be seen and the back door was standing open. They hurried outside and saw the garden gate swinging gently to and fro. Walter had gone and the night was now very dark indeed.

"she fainted dead away..."

Chapter Thirty Eight
A Freak Wind

"She's not having my dragon!" thought Walter, as he ran off in the direction of the yard.

Behind him he could hear Bill and Burt crying, "Wait! Wait!" but he was too anxious to wait and ran on through the dark streets, unafraid now of Old Ma, wanting only to know that his dragon was safe and that Potty and Alf were safe too.

Rounding a sharp corner under a Pretty Robin Soap sign, he ran headlong into Billie Grunter. "Ooof!" they both said, Walter falling down backwards, to be heaved up by the sturdy twin who was now pink and shining from his long bath.

"What's up, Walter?" asked Billie in surprise, brushing him down.

Walter looked closely at Billie. He could see no malice, just an open friendly manner and genuine concern. Mr. and Mrs. Grunter were there too, a greasy package of sausage sandwiches pressed close to Bertha's bosom.

"What's up, son?" asked Mr. Grunter kindly.

Bill and Burt arrived, breathless.

"You might 'ave waited, Walter," complained Bill. "We 'aven't got your young legs an' yer shouldn't be out on yer own. Not now!"

"Why?" asked Billie, going pale. "She's not....?"

"She is!" cried Walter. "She's worse than ever and she was going for the puppies!"

He shook himself free of Burt's restraining hand.

"And she's after my dragon – again!"

Then he dodged around the side of Billie and hared off towards the yard so fast that Bill knew he could not catch up, though Billie ran off quickly in pursuit.

"I'll follow Billie," said Mr. Grunter firmly. "You take those sandwiches to our Willie. Meet at the stable later!"

The three men set off one way and Bertha another.

"Him and his horses!" she moaned unhappily. "No sooner got him home than he's off again! All night, he says, all night!"

Her face was grim as her sturdy shoes thumped the cobble-stones. The twins had come back to her more like men than children, she thought sadly, but they were so much nicer, so much more open and cheerful! She rubbed at the greasy stain developing on the front of her coat.

"Whatever are we going to do about his mother?" she thought, a cold shiver travelling down her spine as if she had been sluiced with a jug of iced water. "Nobody can stop *her*! She's indestructible!"

Willie was right, the streets were full of Mould's men and Walter passed more and more of them as he neared the yard.

"What's up Walter?" they called in alarm as he raced past them. Soon he had a long line of blue uniforms chasing after him so that by the time he reached the door in the wall he had twenty policemen in tow, all breathing heavily and sweating in their heavy serge.

The doorway to the allotments was guarded by the mighty Punch, the biggest sergeant in North Staffordshire. Feared by the law-abiding and by wrongdoers alike, he had nonetheless spent an uncomfortable evening dreading the reappearance of Old Ma. The sight of Walter's anxious face did not reassure him.

"What's up?" he shouted as Walter flashed past him into the allotments.

"She's back!" came the distant reply as Walter flew over the little paths towards the yellow gate.

Punch groaned and drew his truncheon.

"Though much good it'll do against '*er*!" he thought gloomily.

All Mould's men felt the same, though most were prepared to do their duty.

Mr. Jollie's yard had three entrances. One was here, through Bill's allotments and the little yellow gate which Walter now clicked open, stopping short at the sight which greeted him. Another was through the factory itself, permanently locked and used by no one. The third lay through the little alleyway used by Walter as a short cut to school and through which his dragon vase had narrowly entered the yard. Mould's men guarded both ends.

But there was another way, impassable to all but the rats, unknown and unnoticed even by Walter and his pals. The bottle oven had been built close up against one wing of the factory, its great curves seeming to meet the factory wall indivisibly – but that was not quite the case.

Built over eighty years ago, by Bill's grandfather, the slenderest of gaps existed, a space so small and dark that not even a malnourished two year old could have scraped through. But Old Ma had. Through a crevice which even the well-fed rats found a little too snug, Old Ma's bird-like carcass had slipped with ease, her rags encasing little that could be called flesh, her long claws gripping the sooty brick as she eased herself through, all bone and sinew, flat yet tough, like a stringy rooster which no amount of boiling can render succulent.

And there she now stood, in front of the bottle oven, defying the circle of policemen which fringed the yard, untroubled by the river of dark blue figures which poured over the allotments and welled at Walter's back.

Potty detached himself from the crowd in the yard and ran forward to meet Walter.

"She's got Alf penned up in the hovel!" he gasped, his face full of horror. "She's got him backed right up against the clammins! She knows what she's doing Walter! He can't get any more coal to keep up the heat. She's starving the fires, son – and he's dying of thirst in there!"

He paused and a look of complete terror came into his eyes.

"She – she hasn't got any *feet*," he whispered, his voice hollow with dread. "She's got…. She's got *hooves,* Walter!"

Walter had never seen his teacher in such a state. Potty was always so calm, so authoritative. Walter was taken aback. He looked over at Old Ma and swallowed hard.

"He'd just got it up to maximum!" gasped Potty. "It needs to stay there – but now!"

Walter could see the thick cloud of smoke rising from the bottle oven. Alf had done his work well but Potty shook his head and looked at Walter with an anguished face.

"And Alf!" he said desperately. "I – I can't get past her, Walter. I just go sick and giddy!" He did look ill.

Billie had arrived on the scene too and he looked at his teacher with concern, and then said respectfully, "She's my Grandma, sir. Or at least she was. It's my job to go down there."

Potty looked closely at the boy. He had never seen such a change in a person.

"No, no, Billie," he said kindly, trying to pull himself together. "That's not expected of you. No, not at all!"

But Billie would not be held back, nor Walter neither.

"It's my dragon!" he said, feeling hot all over. "This is all my doing – all this!"

"No!" cried Billie, seizing him and looking fiercely into his face. "It's not, Walter! It's all *her* – her and her nastiness and her jealousy!"

He turned and looked at Burt and Bill, and at his father, ashen faced and heaving for breath behind them.

"We've all been afraid of her – for too long!" he said. "That's how she does it. She makes you sick with fear!"

He pushed past Potty and evaded the grasp of Constable Flatt. Walter nipped past too, small and agile, too quick for the clumsy policeman. Burt and Bill surged through after them and Harold stumbled across the yard almost blind with grief and rage. A huge man, he could hardly breath at all after his race through the streets and was almost on the point of collapse. Potty held him up, bean-pole-like, as he staggered and sagged, weighed down not just by his bulk and his heavy lungs but by a guilty conscience too.

Walter could see Alf pressed up against the clammins, wretched and perspiring, desperate for water, his face both flushed and gaunt.

"We need more coal, Walter," he croaked but Old Ma darted at him and he shrank back, the bricks of the clammins searing through his sweat soaked shirt.

Close by lay the mound of glistening coal with its great lumps of tarry anthracite. Bill's spade, newly sharpened for winter digging, stood propped up against the hovel.

Billie staggered too when he saw Old Ma. She had lost her boots in the marl and two sharp little hooves poked out of the ragged ends of her muddy woollen stockings.

"What are *you* staring at!" she screeched, waving her skinny arms threateningly so that the marl-clotted shawl flapped like bedraggled wings.

"Leave him alone, Grandma!" cried Billie angrily. "What's *happened* to you? Leave him alone. Let him out! Let him out *now*!"

Old Ma's answer was a huge block of anthracite which she heaved at Billie's head. He ducked, and the missile landed with a heavy thud on Flatt's foot, inadequately protected by his regulation boot. Another lump followed, and another and another as the little group dodged and swayed.

No one thought to throw anything back. Mad and evil though she was, demon that she had become, they were good people and no violence was offered in return.

Looking around, Walter saw more and more people flooding onto the allotments. Everyone had come out to help him to protect his dragon vase. It was the pride of the city and it was time for them to make a stand.

He had never seen so many people in one place before – except at The Vale, "And there's usually a lot less than this!" he thought.

They had pushed past Mould's men and now filled the length of the little entry too and all corners of the yard. Even the little Dragon Knights were there, circling at Walter's back, having evaded parents and police alike to come his aid.

Stephen Smallbody stared at Old Ma in disbelief and nudged Pongy in the ribs.

"Said we should've 'ad swords," he said. "Eyes an' ears not much good 'ere, mate!"

Then a chant started up, softly at first, growing steadily stronger, until it filled the yard with a great echoing roar. Harry Mudd had started it, standing by the yellow gate with a paper of chips in his big knobbly hands.

"Old Ma! Old Ma!" it went. "Who's afraid of little Old Ma!"

"NOBODY!" resounded the crowd. "NOBODY! NOBODY! **NOBODY!**"

There was strength in numbers. The crowd, the police, Potty and Walter, Billie and Harold, Bill and his team – all felt infused with strength and courage.

But Old Ma surveyed them and cackled. She seized the sharp spade and darted inside the hovel at Alf, who disappeared around the side of the baking oven. The crowd gasped and fell back. Old Ma beat the spade against the clammins so that it rang out and sparks flew off the heavy metal.

George and Rosie pushed their way through, accompanied by her mother and Thelma, who had been liberally fortified by Mr. Jollie's ten-year-old.

"Who's afraid of little Old Ma?" trilled Rosie and the crowd shouted "NOBODY!"

Walter's heart was pounding but he stepped forward and Billie followed.

"Don't!" Walter shouted, his face contorted with anger. "Leave Alf *alone*!"

Old Ma turned to face him and behind her Alf crept forward cautiously, looking hotter than ever.

She stepped onto the yard again, her rags scaly and caked with the baked yellow marl. A little starlight fell through the black smoke and glinted on the edge of Bill's shovel as she began to creep forward towards the two boys, her black eyes fastened on Walter's face.

Billie lunged for Walter's arm to pull him back but Old Ma was too quick for him. Before anyone could prevent her, she had seized the little potter with reptilian swiftness and in a flash she had him pinned up against the hovel, the sharp blade of Bill's spade pressed into his thin white neck.

Everyone went silent. No one dared to move.

"*You!*" she cried. "You and your nice little aunties! You and your precious *vase!*"

The blade bit deeper into his neck but Walter shut his eyes and refused to look at her. He thought of Minnie, so clever and bright, of Sally so busy and attentive, of Louie, so gentle and loving.

He opened his eyes and stared at Old Ma.

"*You!*" he said coldly. "Nobody has *ever* loved *you!*"

The spade bit deeper still. A thin line of blood appeared, trickling down his neck. Billie made a move but Harold held him back.

"No son," he whispered. "Not now."

Walter continued, his voice low but audible.

"No one has ever loved you," he said, as Old Ma's face contorted, terrible in its fury, inhuman, grotesque. "But they would have done once. If you had let them."

Old Ma screamed, a sound so full of pain that the very bricks seemed to shudder.

"Someone loved me, *once* !" she howled, so forlornly that the crowd was stunned by a sudden unexpected pity.

She turned and faced them, a weird mis-shapen creature filled once more with a rush of human emotion.

"I had a man who loved me!" she wailed. "And they killed him! They killed him *dead*!"

Everyone gasped. It couldn't have been Harold's father. He had died at fifty, overweight, with a weak heart. And there had been no love lost there.

"Who?" cried Walter in an unlooked-for anguish. "*Who* loved you, Old Ma?"

But Old Ma's fury had reached its pitch and her last chance was lost.

"*You*!" she shrieked. "As if I'd ever tell *you*!"

As Mr. Jollie's chimney bellowed out a thunderous cloud of smoke, she drew up the spade and swung back her wiry arm, her claws gripping the wooden shaft, her bony shoulders possessed of an unnatural strength.

Billie leapt forward, shoving her hard in the back so that she tottered momentarily and Walter dodged aside. But the crowd looked up and shouted out in astonishment. Above their heads the smoke was turning from black to livid green as a great fiery dragon swam up and out of the chimney, growing

346

larger and larger until it blotted out the dark sky so that all that could be seen was its scaly underside and its vast wings spread umbrella-like over the crowded yard. It circled once and then began its descent, down and down , its long tail lashing, its great red mouth gaping wide.

Old Ma looked up and withered on the spot.

She opened her slit-like mouth and screamed.

Crouching, she tried to bolt across the yard to squeeze back into the crevice by which she had entered the yard. But the crowd surged forward and blocked her path. The Dragon Knights were in the vanguard, careering forward and facing her down.

"Who's afraid of little Old Ma?" sang Nancy Dancer boldly.

"NOBODY! NOBODY! **NOBODY!**" chanted the Dragon Knights as Old Ma spat and dithered.

Then she ran at the children with the spade held high. But a figure in a dressing gown burst through the Dragon Knights waving a broom.

"Step *away* from the children, Madam!" thundered Mr. Slope, fencing at the shovel with his brush as the crowd roared him on. His back was still so stiff that he could barely look up and Old Ma had little power over him, fading as she was minute by minute.

"Cor!" cried the Dragon Knights. "Cor!" cried Walter and Billie. "Old Slope Off's a hero! You're a Dragon Knight, Mr. Slope!"

The dragon sank lower and lower.

Old Ma scurried forwards and then back, darting and jabbing at the children with her spade but Mr. Slope thrust and parried with his broom so that they evaded her blows, never shrinking back, and she seemed to dwindle and fold with each defeated stroke.

Craning up, she saw that the great green dragon was almost upon her, sinking silently through the last few feet of air. Old

Ma squawked and flattened herself against the cobbles but a long scaly leg came down, and a four-clawed foot hooked onto her ratty bodice so that she was plucked shrieking and spitting from the ground, the spade falling from her grasp and clattering onto the cobbled yard. Up and up she went, as the dragon beat its overarching wings, a tiny black flake of a thing which grew more and more insubstantial as the dragon rose higher and higher above the pale upturned faces of the people below.

Potty ran forward and Alf fell into his arms.

Walter was dumbstruck. He had watched frozen with incredulity as the dragon had appeared and circled and unhurriedly descended. He simply could not believe what he was seeing. Nor could anyone else.

Lefty ran over to him and shook him gently, his mouth agape.

"That's *your* dragon, mate!" he said.

"It is!" cried Walter at last. "It is *my* dragon! It *is*! It *is*!"

"Cor!" said Lefty. "I said make something *big* but…." And he trailed off, lost for words like everyone else.

Walter watched and watched as the dragon rose higher: no one knew his dragon better than him! There were the feet he had modelled so carefully, there the long tail he had wrapped around the vase. These were the very wings he had worked on for weeks, dissatisfied with one design after another until finally, there they had been on the table top, dragon-like in their scaly perfection! He started and stepped back. That was his thumb print! There on the neck! Magnified a thousand times! There were the whorls and ridges gleaming under the green smoke, like the engine-turned enamelling on his Auntie Minnie's powder compact.

And that mouth! That huge open mouth with the pink tongue lashing out between the terrible teeth! Walter stared and stared and the crowd stared with him. No one spoke. No one could find a word.

Billie still stood at his side, his arm around the little boy's shoulder. Alf was given a great draught of water and wrapped up warmly in his overcoat and scarf.

The crowd craned its neck as the green dragon circled high high above the bottle oven, the chimney still spouting plumes of smoke, though it was tinged now with azure blues and sunset yellows, all the colours of Walter's vase. Silver spangles flew out of the chimney, erupting into the coloured air like a Standard firework, so that the crowd gasped - and then fell silent as the dragon reared up and spread out its wings, hanging motionless in the coloured sky. From its foot hung a black wispy shred.

Then, as the silver sparks fell glittering to the ground, the dragon drew in its wings and somersaulted down, plunging headfirst into the tall neck of the bottle oven and disappearing into it in a long trail of sparkling smoke. And Old Ma went with it, down down into the fiery depths of Mr. Jollie's kiln.

"Oh!" cried the crowd. "Oh! Oh! Oh!"

Then a deep silence reigned as the coloured air cleared and the sky grew black once more.

"She's gone!" said Harold at last, slumping heavily against the hovel. "Mother! Gone for good!"

Tears coursed down his cheeks but he said nothing more. Billie stood open mouthed, still too amazed to speak. Walter looked uneasily at him.

"I'm sorry, Billie," he said. "She was your grandmother, after all."

Billie shook his head. He was trembling all over.

"Not for a long time," he stuttered. "I don't know what she was in the end. But she wasn't my friend, I know that."

Tears came into his eyes and Rosie stepped forward to give him a hug.

"Come on, Billie," she said tenderly. "Let's get you home – come on, Mr. Grunter, dear. George?" she looked over her shoulder. "Can you get Willie and Mrs. Grunter? They're at Mr. Beany's yard I think. Dragon will be fine now."

George gave Rosie a quick kiss on the top of her head.

"What a woman!" he thought.

He had finally won her hand, determinedly, somewhere inbetween Walter's disappearance and Thelma's resuscitation.

"Of course," he said dutifully, and off he went, pushing through the crowd of people still standing in dazed disbelief, still silent, all eyes still on the tall chimney, like children at the end of a firework display who continue to look at the dark sky, hoping for more and yet more colourful explosions, more rockets and Catherine wheels, more and yet more chrysanthemum bursts of dazzling stars and smoke.

Walter took Billie's cold hand and shook it warmly but Billie burst into tears.

"We were vile to you!" he sobbed as Harold put a huge arm around his son's shoulders. "We did everything we could to make your life a misery!"

He sobbed and sobbed, though Walter said again and again, "That's all done with now, Billie. We're mates now!"

But suddenly, there was Mr. Pinch, wiping Billie's face with his own clean handkerchief.

"Now Billie," he said kindly but firmly. "Enough of this. Stop it young man. You've more than proved yourself here. No one thinks badly of you or your brother anymore. You're fine young men now – and your father and mother are proud of you!"

"Are you, Dad? Are you?" cried Billie, looking up at his father through the folds of the sodden handkerchief.

"We are son! We are!" cried Harold, pressing Billie to him, like a great grizzly bear tenderly enfolding its cub. "And we love you more than anything!"

Billie's sobs subsided and he looked at Walter hopefully. "Are we really mates?" he asked.

Walter grinned.

"Best mates!" he said as Pongy and Lefty slapped Billie on the back and cried, "Yes Billie! Best mates. You're in our gang now!"

At last Billie went off happily with his father, back through the crowded streets where no one looked askance, where everyone nodded sympathetically, back to a happy family life filled with love and affection. Harold had made more than enough money. He would soon close his shop and his boys would have all of his time, and all of Bertha's too.

When just a few years later, Mr. Chamberlain came home, paper in hand, Harold shook his head as he listened to his voice on the BBC.

"That'll never hold water," he thought, looking out at the twins tinkering with Billie's bike in the new sunny garden.

His sons would soon enlist and he wouldn't stand in their way. He knew that evil could not be appeased, and that complacency was an evil in itself. Of all the fathers listening to the wireless on that sunny day, Harold knew that better than any of them.

Slowly the crowd began to drift away from Mr. Jollie's yard, still in a state of shocked disbelief. When they did begin to speak to one another, in low, confidential tones, they found that they could hardly articulate what they had seen, and, more than that, they could not believe it either.

As they made their various ways home, the dragon became less and less real in their minds, soon seeming only a vast cloud of strangely coloured smoke into which Old Ma had been swept up. Perhaps, they wondered, by a maverick current of air.

"Very odd," they admitted, "but we do get some funny winds round 'ere. All them chimneys, like."

By the time doors were opened at home and eager questions asked by those waiting for news of the evening's events, a comparatively flat tale was told.

"Light as a feather, she was," they said. "Could 'ave bin carried off by a mere breeze. Well, she's gone fer good, any-how. Feel a bit sorry for the Grunters though. Terrible thing to 'appen."

Even the dread of Old Ma had dulled down to a strong dislike, as if the old woman had been simply a difficult neighbour, troublesome perhaps, and best avoided.

In the yard itself, even Potty and the rest of the team had begun to doubt the evidence of their own eyes.

"Strange things, er, glazes," murmured Potty, as he picked up a shovel and helped Burt to feed the firemouths again. "Must have a word with Isabella and Theodora. Unexpected by-product, perhaps."

Walter bit his lip. He knew very well what he had seen and nothing would make him doubt it. But he was worried. If all the colours had come out in the form of sparks and smoke – what would be left inside?

"Do you think it's alright, Potty?" he asked, peering with his permission through the spy hole and into the oven where the chimney bags roared and the dragon roasted in his fiery den.

"I should think so, son," said Potty encouragingly. "She only held Alf up for a quarter of an hour or so, though it seemed a lot longer at the time. And he had got it good and hot!"

"Thanks, Alf!" said Walter, turning to the fireman who sat on the heap of coal beside the hovel. "Perhaps you'd better go home and rest?"

Alf drained the huge mug of police-issue tea he had been given.

"Not bloody likely, son!" he said. "Job to do here! Feeling better now." And he got up and took the shovel off Potty.

Detective Mould appeared, gloomy and disappointed.

"Of all the nights to catch those ruddy Handy brothers!" he thought. "As if they couldn't have kept at it a bit longer!"

He had missed all of the excitement and now couldn't get a straight word out of his men.

"What happened here, Walter?" he asked, surveying the peaceful yard where Bill and Alf laboured and Potty and Burt conferred.

Walter didn't know what to say. Could he tell this hardened London detective that his dragon had come to life and rescued him from certain death? The man would think he was mad.

Then Alan Padder arrived. His wife had just given birth to their second child, a lovely little girl, and he was torn between joy and disappointment. The biggest story for years – and he had missed it! He took out his notebook and licked his pencil. Mould and the reporter looked at the silent boy.

"Well?" they said.

Walter sucked in his cheeks. He didn't like to lie but he didn't want to make a fool of himself either.

"It was very very smoky," he said slowly. "It was hard to see. One minute Old Ma was there - going for me and my mates with a spade – and the next she was gone! Up there...." He gestured vaguely.

"Up there, son!" said Mould sharply. "Where up there?"

Alan Padder's pencil hovered over the paper.

"She was swept up," said Walter, "like a feather or a bit of old paper. And then she fell down inside the chimney. She's gone, Detective Mould. Gone for good."

Mould stared at him. Another vague piece of nonsense and from Walter of all people! He had hoped for better.

"There's more to this than meets the eye," he thought. "But I'm not losing any sleep over it. If she's gone, she's gone - and that's a load off my mind!"

Then he was struck by the thought of all the paperwork he must fill in to account for the old woman's death.

"Nothing more you can say, Walter?" he asked hopefully, but Walter shook his head.

"My dragon is safe, I think," he said, smiling at the policeman in a winsome way. "Thanks for everything you've done for me, sir. Thank you very much indeed."

"I passed Pongy and Lefty on the way over," said Alan Padder slyly. "Going on ten to the dozen about a green smoke dragon, they were. Nobody else had much to say," he added, "but they made up for the rest. Huge scaly thing, they said. Had Old Ma in its claws and then dropped her down the chimney?"

Mould glared at him.

"Are you insane?" he asked tersely.

"Well?" insisted Alan, ignoring him and eying Walter closely.

"It might have looked like that," said Walter carefully. "From a certain angle."

He was surprised by his own cunning and also by an overwhelming urge to keep the whole thing secret, to guard his dragon as it had guarded him.

"Potty," he called artlessly. "Do you think the smoke cloud looked like a dragon?"

"Aah," said Potty, blushing. "Perhaps, a little. Funny thing, smoke. Like clouds: we make things out of it. Aah, yes, a little, now I come to think of it."

And that was all they got. Mould went back to struggle with his forms and the strange accidental death of old Mrs.

Grunter whilst Alan Padder retreated with an almost empty notebook to the offices of The Sentinel.

"Is this it?" demanded the Chief in disgust a little later as he read Alan's meagre report. "Freak winds and green smoke dragons. Have you lost your mind?"

"I can only tell it like it is, boss," said Alan resentfully. "Two kids full of it and several star witnesses keeping it buttoned. And Mould couldn't get anything out of *them* either!"

He snatched up his jacket and went out, slamming the door shut behind him. He had a wife and two children to see to!

The Chief sat in his inky cubbyhole and puzzled the whole thing over. He had a night and a day to come up with a good story before Saturday's edition. People would be expecting a good one – but on the other hand The Vale were at home to Stoke in a local non-league derby. He might lead with that. Suddenly weary, the issue of Old Ma Grunter, her malice, her cunning, her sheer vindictiveness, began to seem a lot less important.

"I'll sleep on it," he thought, switching off the light and going downstairs past the silent presses.

When the newspaper flopped through the letter box at six o' clock the next day, Walter raced into Louie's room to pick it up. His auntie was sitting up in bed, crocheting a scarf for Minnie's Christmas present.

"What does it say, dear?" she asked.

Walter had told his aunties everything, right down to the very last detail, and they had tried very hard to believe every word, though Sally had tut-tutted and shaken her head at times.

Walter took the paper over and showed Louie the front page. Walter and Pongy and Billie had been to the match so it was no news to him.

VALE TRIUMPHANT!

... it roared in huge black letters. Then in smaller letters:

Three nil against Stoke!

Louie laughed.

"Look inside," she suggested.

Walter sat and leafed slowly through the paper, his fin-ger-tips blackening as he turned the pages. Then, there at the bottom of page five was a small picture of Old Ma as she had been, many many years ago. Walter stared in surprise. It must have been taken when she was a girl, not much older than Rosie was now. Photography must just have been invented, he thought, looking at the still face in the fuzzy picture, serious, intent – but certainly not evil.

"Look Auntie," he said, passing the paper to Louie. "She looks, well, she looks quite pretty!"

"She was dear," said Louie sadly. "On the outside at least. And she had nice clothes, much better than anyone else's at school. They were always well off, that family." She sighed, resting the paper on the bedspread and leaning back on her pillows. She was quiet for a little while. "But always so jealous," she said sorrowfully. "So covetous, so envious. So resentful of *everything*. It was hard to speak to her – about anything! She never made any friends, you know."

The room was quiet as Louie and Walter sat thinking of the young girl Louie had known so long ago.

"And then when she lost Clovis, she was lost too," said Louie, gazing up at the window where the black evening pressed close up against the panes. "Nobody made any difference to her after that. She should never have married Harold's father."

"Who was *Clovis?*" asked Walter quickly. In his mind, he saw Old Ma's anguished face and he heard her plaintive cry. "Who was *he?*"

"He was hanged dear," said Louie softly. "He murdered his wife, you know. Don't dwell on it dear. It isn't nice to think of and Sally wouldn't want you to know."

Walter was staggered. He had never expected to feel sorry for Old Ma. He studied the picture sadly. She had been human, once.

Then Louie listened as he read out the short article.

"GRUNTER FAMILY MOURNS SAD LOSS"

It said in small black capitals, followed by:

"Freak Winds Send Old Lady To Her Death."

"Cor!" exclaimed Walter. "That's a bit of an understatement, that is!"

Louie opened her eyes and wagged her finger at him mischievously.

"Well," she said. "They can only go on what people tell them can't they, Walter?" and she settled down for another lovely nap, warm and cosy in her little front room, safe and secure at last.

"She seized the sharp spade..."

Chapter Thirty Nine
A Christmas Card

On the following Tuesday, as the great dragon vase cooled steadily in Mr. Jollie's kiln, The Grove broke up for Christmas. The children had been asked to bring board games for the afternoon so Walter chose snakes and ladders and set off down the hill with it under his arm. When he entered the playground, he was set upon by a swarm of tiny girls from the infant classes, all agog with the half-remembered story that the Dragon Knights had told them.

They clustered around Walter with inquisitive little faces, pushing and shoving to get closer to him.

"Did your dragon really save you, Walter?" they cried, their eyes round, their hands clutching his blazer sleeves.

"Did it come to life? Really? Really?" they demanded, jostling and elbowing each other out of the way.

"Pongy says it was *huge*! Was it, Walter? Was it really?" they screamed, quite beside themselves with excitement.

Walter felt uneasy. He couldn't lie to these mites, nor could he make a liar of Pongy – or the rest of the Dragon Knights come to that. He owed them a lot, and more than that, he liked them a lot too. But neither did he want to admit the truth of his magical vase. It was something he felt strongly, deep inside. The dragon was his and he must guard it. Who knew what would happen if the truth got out?

"Well," he said, looking closely at the little children. "It was absolutely *massive*. Bigger than that half of the school," and he gestured towards one wing of The Grove, which was a solid red brick building, very large and impressive.

The children followed his gaze and their mouths fell open.

"It came out of the chimney *glowing*," he went on, "with a *big* red mouth and *sharp* white teeth….AAARGH!" and he sprang grimacing at tiny Emily Diddler so that she jumped and squealed with delight.

"It didn't!" she cried. "It *didn't*!"

"It did," said Walter, "and its claws were *huge* and terrible!"

He made his hands into claws and chased the tots who screamed and screamed and screamed.

"They weren't!" they cried, gathering around him deliriously. "They *weren't*!"

"They were," said Walter, "and its tail lashed the air…. like a *whirlwind*!" he cried with sudden inspiration, whipping his satchel off his shoulder and whirling it round and round.

"Never!" shouted the little girls. "No! No! *No*!"

"You're making it up, Walter!" they cried.

"I'm not," he said truthfully.

"You are! You *are*!" they cried.

By the time Mr. Pinch came out to ring the nine o' clock bell, the infants were more concerned with the coming afternoon – and rightly so! Besides board games instead of lessons, there were rumours of jelly and mince pies, and, most exciting of all – that there would be presents for everyone. And indeed, at three o' clock, a red-robed figure visited each class room in turn and the gifts tumbled out of his sack.

"Happy Christmas children!" came Mr. Pinch's voice from behind his cotton-wool beard. "Thank you for all your hard work! Open them now or leave them for Christmas Day – the choice is yours!"

Very few children waited until Christmas Day.

"Cor! This looks good!" they cried, tearing off Edna's neat paper and opening books and boxes in a flurry of excitement. "Thank you, Mr. Pinch, sir!"

Walter's dragon had faded, as it had done for their parents.

Being children, and so closer to the realm of fairy, it had just taken them a little longer, that was all.

Walter thanked Mr. Pinch as he took his present. He knew his Headmaster would not be there with him when the kiln was opened on Christmas Eve. He would be marrying Edna Robbin in the little church at the bottom of the hill, watched by Minnie and Thelma in their new hats.

"Nice for them," thought Walter, "but I'm glad I'm getting out of it!"

At three thirty the school closed and the children raced out into the cold air. No lessons for two weeks and very little homework! A large group gathered around Pongy and Walter by the blue doors.

"What about the Dragon Knights, Pongy?" asked Steven Smallbody. "Are we still knights then, now….?" He looked a little embarrassed but Billie smiled. He and Willie had plenty of friends now.

"Once a Dragon Knight, always a Dragon Knight, eh, Walter?" said Pongy, running his hands over his shiny new boat with delight.

"Of course!" said Walter. "We'll never be disbanded. All for one and one for all!"

"I think that's a different book, Walter," said Herbert Sherburt but nobody took any notice of him.

"Hurrah!" they cried and off they ran, full of fizz, so that by Wednesday morning their mothers were all looking forward to the start of the new term.

Walter said goodbye to Potty and walked home thoughtfully. After everything, after all his perils, the bottle oven would be the final arbiter of his fate. He wondered whether his dragon would really still be there, or whether it had gone up in a puff of smoke, like Old Ma. And that star crack, filled with glaze and forgotten about for days: what of that? What of the glazes,

361

the vivid African colours, glimpsed so tantalisingly in those clouds of smoke? *Had* Old Ma ruined them or would they come through the immense heat as shining and bright as the glaze wizards had all but promised they would?

Walter fully intended to save Mr. Pinch's gift for Christmas morning but as he lay in his wooden bed that night, the red package repeatedly drew his eye, until at last he put down The Wizard and picked up the present instead. He slid his finger under the wrapping and the sticky-tape came apart. The red paper fell off and Walter held a fat blue book in his hands.

"I'm back where I started!" he thought, as he read the gold embossed title.

"MYSTERY THE MAGICIAN," it said above a colourful picture of a strange man pulling an elephant out of a top hat! Walter settled down and read the book from cover to cover, a little surreptitiously because it was one o' clock before he put the book down. It was a very good tale, indeed it was quite gripping, but Walter felt filled with a sleepy peacefulness as he laid the book aside. An elephant out of a top hat…. but he had no plans for any more gigantic vases. One had been enough!

"I might make some elephants when I get to art school," he thought, as sleep began to wash over him. "I'll make all sorts of things there. But nothing will ever beat my dragon!"

The bells of Holy Trinity sounded their little peal as his eyes closed and he drifted off to dream about his very own dragon, who flew with him up above the city of coal and clay so that he looked down on the silently smoking bottle ovens, threaded like beads on the black canals. But as they swooped in to land on the roof of the little house, Walter's dragon caught his tail on a chimneypot and tumbled to the ground where he was smashed in two. Walter woke with a start. It was only a dream! He sighed with relief. But his dragon *had* been real: he *had* defeated Old Ma and saved his life! Walter knew he hadn't dreamt that.

"If only he's still there!" he prayed as sleep overtook him once more.

§

Walter woke full of impatience on Wednesday morning. Two more days before the kiln would be opened. Forty-eight hours! It was almost more than he could bear.

"You will have to keep busy, dear" said Minnie, and she took him Christmas shopping in Hanley where the sooty town square was full of Christmas trees, their sharp resin cutting through the smoky air.

But Walter already had his tree, delivered by Gwenny and Mr. Beany the night before. It stood in the kitchen, filling the small room with fragrance. Walter had decorated its branches, taking down the old milk tin from the cupboard in the corner and carefully lifting out the colourful glass baubles.

"Cousin Harold bought that one," Louie had said as Walter clipped a robin onto a low bough. "It was always his favourite too."

Walter and Minnie had lunch with Thelma, sitting bunched up behind her stall. Thelma never even mentioned the green smoke dragon, full instead of the Christmas wedding and the summer one to follow that.

Walter roamed off, and spent his pocket money at the sweet stalls where the shiny wrappers were piled high and the sweet cloying scent of the confectionary filled his nostrils. Everyone wished him well.

"Big day on Friday, Walter?" they said as they slipped his fudge into a stripy bag.

"Best of luck, son," they said encouragingly as they added an extra gobstopper or two before flipping over the bag and twisting its corners tight.

"How funny!" thought Walter, his cheeks bulging. "How funny that nobody seems to remember it! It's as if it never happened!"

And nobody mentioned Old Ma either. It was as if she had never existed.

§

On Thursday afternoon, Walter met Willie at Mr. Beany's and they groomed the horses together. Dragon had become very attached to Gwenny though she still reserved the better part of her affection for Walter.

"Did you know Prince is taking Edna to the church?" Willie asked, shortly after they had arrived. "And Pat Beany is bringing in a carriage, a proper old one, all done up like?"

"Cor!" said Walter. "That'll be nice! Christmas Eve and all". He gave Gwenny a good brisk brush on her tummy. "Good job it's not Dragon though!" he added, and they both laughed.

Willie didn't ask about the green smoke dragon so Walter didn't talk about it either, though his mind was still full of it all. Instead Willie talked and talked about his Dragon and Mr. Jollie's plans for them both.

At three o' clock Billie joined them and the three boys went to tea at Prospect House. Rosie opened the door.

"Come and see the puppies," she said straight away.

Jolly-Poo was now in a cosy basket by the drawing room fire, having declined every other venue that Mr. Jollie had offered her. The seven puppies were warm and happy by her side.

"Woof!" barked Jigger-Poo proudly. "Woof! Woof! Woof!"

"Clever boy," said Walter, kneeling and fussing the lovely dog. "Mustn't forget you, must we?"

Mr. Jollie appeared and the twins shook hands politely.

"Nice to see you, Billie," said Mr. Jollie kindly. "How are your Ma and Pa, dear boy?"

"Oh, very well," said Billie. "Dad's selling up, Mr. Jollie. We're moving to Birch Tree Lane, the house with all the apple trees at the back."

Walter remembered those trees and his cheeks went pink. They all knelt around Jolly-Poo's basket and he picked up the little black puppy. It was so warm and woolly. He held it against his face with a dreamy expression.

"It's better than any amount of plasticine," he thought.

Mr. Jollie glanced over at Rosie and nodded. She rose and stepped over to the glossy bureau, taking out a smart white envelope. With a little bob, she handed it to her employer.

"Christmas card for you, Walter," he said, putting it into the boy's hand.

"Oh," said Walter. "I haven't done any. Sorry."

He tore open the stiff paper. To his surprise, instead of a papery card sprinkled with glitter, there was a photograph of the little black puppy! His eyes went round with astonishment.

"Happy Christmas Walter," it read. "I'm all yours!"

"Oh!" he cried. "Oh! Oh! Oh!"

Rosie laughed.

"You should see your face!" she said.

"Cor Walter!" cried the twins, deeply impressed.

"Very welcome, dear boy. Marvellous!" said Mr. Jollie, his face flushed. "Know you'll look after him. None better! Aunties on side - but have to help Sally a bit more. Only fair y' know!"

Walter was ecstatic. He cuddled the puppy close to his heart.

"Thank you," he said, again and again. "Thanks Mr. Jollie. Thank you!"

"What will you call him?" asked the twins, grinning from ear to ear.

"Blackie, of course!" said Walter.

Rosie laughed.

"I thought you were supposed to have an imagination!" she cried. "What about Shadow – or – or...."

"Oh no," said Walter. "He's Blackie, of course he is."

"Eight weeks," said Mr. Jollie, giving Jolly-Poo a kiss on the nose. "Eight weeks here, then you can take him home. But come every day, get to know him. Marvellous! Marvellous!"

Walter held Blackie gently as the tiny dog licked his chin. He thought of his great dragon, quite cool now, waiting silently for the morning to come and for Bill to break open the clammins with his big lump hammer – letting in the light, letting out the truth.

"I think I can bear it," he thought. "If it all goes wrong." He touched Blackie's little wet nose with his own. "At least I think I can."

When Walter got home that night, full of excitement about his new puppy, The Sentinel was waiting on the kitchen table.

"THIS IS IT!
THE OVEN OPENS!"
Tomorrow 9a.m.

... it declared in huge black letters.

Sally put his tea down in front of him. It was cottage pie and apple sponge top – two of his favourites.

"Eat up, Walter," said Sally. "I know what you'll be like tomorrow morning. Up with the birds and out without any breakfast again!"

But Walter had difficulty swallowing. One more night – and then it would all be over! Success or failure: by nine-thirty he would know.

Minnie came in. She had been Christmas shopping and her bags were heavy with fruit and vegetables.

"Everybody's stopped me," she said, taking off her coat. "If good wishes were enough you'd be well away, my dear. Everyone on the bus had a Sentinel and everybody was talking about it. I should think half the city'll be there tomorrow!

Walter plodded on with his meal, chewing hard and swallowing harder. Finally, his plate was clean and he helped Sally to wash up. But what to do with the rest of the evening?

Two hours stretched before him until bedtime, a vast Sahara of endless anticipation and worry. Outside it was dark and cold. Gwenny would be sleeping and Pongy and Lefty not allowed out. He didn't even have any homework! Walter switched on the wireless but that was disappointing too: an endless political programme about trouble in Europe. He switched it off and gazed into the fire. The clock ticked slowly on as the Christmas tree glinted in the firelight. The smell of resin all but overpowered the little room.

"Perhaps I should polish my shoes for the reception," he thought but it seemed too big an effort.

He pulled out his dusty jigsaws from under the dresser. Five hundred pieces to make a picture of Horse Guards Parade. A thousand to see the King at Windsor Castle. He sighed and shoved them back.

"That's no good either," he thought.

Sally stood in the scullery doorway and looked at him.

"What about making something, dear?" she asked sympathetically. "Where's your plasticine?"

"Upstairs, Auntie," he replied and sat on, staring into the flames and tapping his fingers on the flat wooden arm of the chair.

But slowly he began to relax, the resinous scent and the dancing flames gradually inducing an almost trance-like state. In the scullery, Sally and Minnie were busy with their

Christmas preparations, the rich smell of mince pies and oranges wafting through to mingle with the scent of the pine tree and the tarry smell of the sticky black coal.

Edna's face swam into his mind, elfin and lovely, like a fairy queen from a picture book.

"Would she be marrying Mr. Pinch?" he thought, "if she hadn't saved my dragon vase?"

He thought of their wedding in the morning.

"They'd never have had Prince," he mused, "if Willie hadn't gone off on that barge."

More and more speculations crowded his sleepy mind.

"Willie'd never have been on the barge if they hadn't jumped on the back of Dragon's cart. And Mr. Jollie'd never have bought him if he hadn't met me and Gwenny…."

His head began to nod.

"Mr. Jollie hasn't half changed," he thought sleepily. "And Mr. Pinch! Dressing up as Santa! Cor!"

His head nodded further, then the next moment he was dreaming. A huge unopened present sat at the foot of his bed but, try as he might, he couldn't wake himself up to unwrap it. All night, it seemed, he struggled to swim to the surface, desperate to tear off the paper to see what was inside.

Outside the little house, the waning moon shone down and stars sparkled frostily in the clear black sky. The house sparrows fluffed out their feathers as the temperature dropped and Dragon snorted in his stable. All over the city of coal and clay the sooty pot banks enjoyed a seasonal snooze as Walter slept soundly, their chimneys smokeless, their bellies cold.

Above one chimney in particular the stars shone more brightly than the rest, seeming to wink first blue, then pink, then green. Colder grew the night, then colder still, until at three o'clock a soft sifting of snow fell on the window ledges all over town, dusting the pavements at first with icing sugar, and then with thick soft flakes which clung and deepened, so that at five o' clock Mr. Jones struggled with his horse and cart amongst the virgin streets, slipping and sliding in the powdery whiteness as they delivered milk for morning tea and double cream for trifles on Christmas Day.

Yet Walter slept on, though a sense of the new and muffled world outside his window entered his dreams in a quietly troubling way. When he awoke, it would be Christmas Eve.

"The clock ticked slowly on..."

Chapter Forty
Walter's Dragon

Snow was piled deeply around Mr. Jollie's bottle oven.
"WOOF!" said Jigger-Poo "Woof! Woof! Woof!".

"Quite so!" said Mr. Jollie, looking around his snowy yard.
"Problem Jigger-Poo. Problem!"

He had on his stout walking boots so the snow had posed
no problem to him or to Jigger-Poo who had jumped in and
out of the drifts on their way to the yard. But Mr. Jollie shook
his head sadly.

"He will be disappointed," he thought, taking Bill's spade
and digging away at the snow until he had cleared a little path
across the yard to the hovel and made a clear space in front
of it. But the cobbles underneath were icy and treacherous.
This was no day to be moving a dragon vase!

"Ah!" said Bill, coming up behind the old man. "Beat me
to it, Mr. Jollie! Well, this changes things a bit!"

The two men stood silently surveying the waiting oven.
Then Burt arrived, his red beard sparkling with his frosty
breath.

"Of all days!" he said, and joined the other two in silent
contemplation.

"Better not decide anything till he arrives," said Bill eventually, laying down his big hammer on a mound of snow. "It's
going nowhere now. Ruddy shame, that's what I call it!"

§

Mr. Waterhouse plonked down Prince's feed in front of
him and brushed the snow off his heavy rug.

"Well lad," he said, "we shall 'ave to do things a bit different to what we planned. But we'll still get 'er there, that we will!"

He turned to Freddie.

"Fetch me the pincers, son," he said.

He bent and lifted all four feet in turn, working away with the pincers so that in a little while all Prince's shoes lay in a cold heap on the towpath.

"He can go anywhere now, Dad, can't he?" asked Freddie hopefully. "He won't slip, will he?"

"Should 'ave a real good grip if we go slow an' steady," said his father. "An' check 'is feet from time to time. 'an that carriage's got right big wheels. Should crunch along nicely," he laughed. "At least it's only a couple of streets," he added. "But Mr. Pinch'll 'ave to wear 'is wellies to get there!" he said, smiling broadly at the thought.

Tom appeared, the coal barge being moored only a short way down the towpath.

"Morning," he said. "Nice ter see yer again, Fred. Alright, Freddie?"

"Ar'tha 'elping with wedding too?" asked Freddie, offering Tom the steaming mug of tea that Mo had passed up to him.

"Do what we can," said Tom. "Shift a bit of snow 'ere an' there. Get 'em both ter the church an' then ter the reception. Right big party, that right Freddie?"

"Everyone's invited," said Freddie, who had hardly been inside a school, let alone to a big wedding reception inside such a place. "Willie an 'Billie will be there, an' Walter too after he's seen to 'is vase!"

"Not sure that'll be 'appening today, son," said Mr. Waterhouse, rinsing out Prince's bucket in the freezing canal. "Easier to move Edna about today than a great big piece of china."

Tom nodded.

"That's right," he said. "I dunner think they'll risk that today. Not if they want it ter stay in one piece!"

Willie and Billie ran down the snowy slope to the towpath.

"Still on?" asked Willie anxiously.

"Oh yes!" said Freddie excitedly. "Still on, Willie!"

§

Arthur Shortlegg stood in his silk pyjamas, looking down on the snow covered Rolls Royce outside his window. His stubby fingers rolled a cigar thoughtfully as he pondered the day ahead.

"Best laid plans...." he thought, making his way to the bathroom. Although uninvited, he had planned to attend the opening of the kiln and make a speech honouring all those who had been involved in the production of the monumental dragon vase.

He saw himself, magnificent in his Mayoral finery, pictured with the now famous vase, his face on the front page of The Sentinel, and probably, he thought, as he slipped off his pyjamas and turned on the hot tap, on the front covers of some of the nationals as well.

"The Times, perhaps," he thought, reaching for the lavender soap. "Big story this, big as it gets round 'ere!"

Half an hour later he emerged, shining and scented, and padded into the bedroom.

"Mable," he said to the recumbent form under the pink quilt. "Get yer backside out of bed, old girl. We've got a job to do today!"

"It's Christmas Eve," came the sleepy reply. "Mayors dunner work Christmas."

"This one does," said Arthur, prodding Mable in the rear. "'an 'urry up! "We're late as it is!"

Mable turned over and pushed back the bedclothes. She gave Arthur a hard look.

"You're up to something," she said.

"Just 'urry up," he shouted from halfway down the stairs.

In his office he opened a grubby black book and picked up the telephone.

"Time to call in some favours," he thought. "Aah!"

§

Minnie had to shake Walter awake.

"Christmas Eve!" she said. "And your biggest day yet!" but she sounded anxious and Walter sat straight up.

"Why is it so light?" he said.

Leaping out of bed he pulled apart the curtains and gasped.

"Oh!" he cried. "Oh no!"

Sally appeared at the top of the stairs.

"I know," she said quickly. "But they can still *open* the kiln dear – you can still *see* it!"

Walter could see Potty making his way up the street, his long legs making short work of the deep snow. He threw on his clothes quickly and rushed downstairs.

"Wash your face!" cried Sally. "There'll be photos! Wash your face!"

She caught him and gave him a quick scrub with a wet flannel, flattening his hair with a practised sweep of her comb. Walter opened the back door and Potty stepped in, banging the snow off his boots first.

"Now Walter," he said calmly. "This is a little set back only. A mere matter of weather."

"But we can't move it!" wailed Walter. "It's not safe to take it to The Grove!"

"Maybe not," agreed Potty, "but we can open it up, examine it in situ, as it were, and then ask Bill to brick up the clammins again, temporarily. You're not really losing anything, son, just a change of plan."

"No," said Walter a bit dismally. "But I did want to take it back to school today. Mr. Pinch said it would be on display at the wedding reception, on the stage, and everybody could look at it. There's going to be loads of people there," he added mournfully. "And my dragon will still be stuck in the kiln."

Just then there was a sharp knock at the front door.

"Callers!" cried Louie.

"Front door!" exclaimed Minnie. "Whoever can that be! I shall never be ready for the church. And I shall have to wear my long boots! I bet Thelma's fed up!"

She hurried through Louie's room and opened the door, then stepped back in surprise.

"Good morning, Minnie!" said Athur Shortlegg, sweeping off his Mayoral hat in a gesture of extravagant courtesy. It was slightly too large and sat awkwardly over one eye when it was replaced. Beside him Mable gave Minnie a friendly nod.

Both were gowned, their rich red robes glowing against the snowy street, Arthur's dragging a little and wet around the hem. Across their chests, Mable's ample, Arthur's lacking a little in Mayoral breadth, their gold chains sparkled brightly in the morning air.

The sky was a cloudless azure blue and as far as Minnie could see the snow was glittering brilliantly, on rooftops, on pavements and on the whole length of the street itself, buried under four inches of treacherous white.

"Good morning, Arthur!" she said, looking at the sleek black car parked outside, its wheels wrapped up in sturdy chains like embattled rubber warriors. "Snow hasn't stopped you, I see. What…"

"Go through anything, them will, Minnie," Arthur said, "Especially on a day like this. Walter!" he cried as the boy appeared behind his Auntie. "A very big day for this city, my boy! A proud day. A very proud day indeed," and he gave a further flourish of his lopsided hat.

"And a great day to be its Mayor!" he thought, shaking Walter's hand and then elbowing Mable forward to do the same.

Under her red gown Mable was still wearing her nightdress and she was very cold. She had hoped to stay in bed until lunchtime and then attend a reception at the golf club. But Mable was nobody's fool. If Arthur was turning out on a morning like this then there must be something in it for him.

"I bet he's after that vase," she thought suddenly, stepping back hard onto Arthur's big toe. "He wants it for himself, the little wretch! And then he'll sell it on the quiet!" she thought, looking at Walter sympathetically.

Just then Pongy and Lefty came into view, sliding down the steep street, red faced and excited.

"You'll never guess what we've just seen!" they cried.

A strange noise was heard, from the top of the hill, out of sight.

"Cor!" said Walter, stepping out into the snow. "Sounds like drums!"

Arthur Slope drew himself up and adjusted his hat.

Walter," he said grandly. "As your Mayor, I have arranged transport for your magnificent vase. I can't allow a little weather to spoil my…er, your plans!"

"Sounds like bells too!" cried Walter as Sally bundled him into his coat and scarf.

"Your vase can be safely transported anywhere!" said Arthur with a grand flourish of his arm. "The Town Hall perhaps, my boy!" he added, looking slyly at Walter.

"So that's it!" thought Mable. "And then the next thing is he'll be knocking down my dining room wall and bringing the ruddy thing home! He can't keep his fingers off anything that man. Just like the rest of his ruddy family!"

The drums and bells grew louder, filling the clear air, joined by the sound of trumpets as a strange procession came into view at the top of the hill. On tall stilts, skilfully manoeuvred through the deep snow, came two clowns, red nosed and white faced. Baggy trousered, frilled and wigged, they bore between them a great yellow banner.

"POPOV'S RUSSIAN CIRCUS"

... it declared in huge red letters which slowly billowed in and out as the banner waved and dipped past the snowy rooftops.

Minnie pulled on her coat and boots and joined the crowd which was gathering in the street.

"I shall never be ready for this wedding!" she thought. "I haven't even done my hair!"

Closer stalked the towering clowns and behind them appeared a great grey elephant, tasseled and canopied in red and yellow silk .She plodded steadily through the powdery snow which barely reached her gigantic ankles.

"Cor" cried Walter. "Cor! Cor! Cor!"

Sally stood in the doorway and Louie knelt on her bed and peered through the net curtains.

"Look Walter," she cried. "It's a sleigh!"

A huge scarlet sleigh trailed smoothly behind the elephant, unhindered by the lumpy snow. It was long and wide and very capacious.

"Cor!" cried Pongy, seizing Walter's arm and rushing over to the sleigh. "I bet it's for your dragon vase, mate! They're putting it in 'ere!"

"Pleased, Walter?" asked Arthur grandly. "Safe enough in there, don't you think?"

Behind the sleigh came drummers and trumpeters, splitting the air with bangs and shrieks. The sun danced and dazzled on the brass instruments. Boom- boom! went the big bass drum. Rat-a-tat-tat answered the snare drums as the sun glinted on the gold braid of the drummers and glistened on their silks and velvets.

Surreally bright against the newly white world, the circus seemed to have burst forth from the pages of a picture book, like a wonderful pop-up coming suddenly to life.

The elephant and sleigh came to a quiet standstill outside the little house. Behind them a great red and yellow lorry ground to a crunching halt, its chained wheels munching the snow into submission. Inside it were pile of sturdy circus mats, safe and slip-proof, ready to be unloaded at Mr. Jollie's yard by the white toothed Strong Man who now flexed his muscles and beamed at the astonished crowd.

"Boxing Day!" he cried. "See Popov's Circus! Boxing Day!" and he thrust colourful leaflets into the hands of the excited children.

"Can we give you a lift down to the church, Minnie?" asked Mable, as Walter and his friends climbed into the sleigh for the snowy journey to Mr. Jollie's yard.

"Oh, no thank you, Mable," said Minnie, retreating inside the open door. "I'm not ready and it's still a bit early. The service isn't until eleven. But thank you. And thank you for helping Walter. Most unexpected," she added, looking at Mable closely.

"Dunner worry, Minnie," said Mable. "I'll keep an eye on our Arthur. We both know what he's like."

Minnie did know. She had known Arthur Shortlegg all his life. He was a scrounger through and through. She shut the door feeling a little troubled. "At least Potty'll be there," she thought. "And Mr. Jollie. They'll keep an eye on things."

By nine-thirty the whole procession had reached the little alleyway where the boys leapt out and rushed ahead into the yard. The journey had been a circus in itself, the streets thronged with people who had come out hoping to see the dragon vase and who had seen an elephant instead. The elephant waited quietly at the end of the entry, swishing its trunk from side to side.

"They'll never get *that* up *there!*" cried Lilly Waddpugg, surveying the elephant's massive girth and the relatively narrow circumference of the alley. "Look at the size of its bum!"

But the elephant only rested, lifting a foot occasionally as if to complain of the cold and sometimes filling its trunk with snow which it sprayed on the waiting crowd so that they shrieked with delight.

The yellow lorry pulled up and out came the circus mats one by one, so slickly handled that in a trice the yard and its entry were rendered safe.

"Boxing Day!" boomed the Strong Man as he flung the mats down, his huge teeth rivalling the snow in their whiteness. "See Popov's Circus! Boxing Day!"

On the yard Mr. Jollie shook hands all round.

"Marvellous!" he said to the Mayor, who was looking around himself, as pleased as Punch. "Marvellous idea, Mr. Mayor! Marvellous!"

He looked at Walter, standing intently by his side. Mr. Jollie well understood the mixed feelings with which a kiln is unbricked. Potty rested a hand on the boy's shoulder.

"Ready, Walter?" he asked kindly. "Ready?"

But Walter rushed over to the hovel and jumped inside, pressing his face against the now cool clammins. What would they find inside? Would his dragon emerge from the flames phoenix-like, a thing of beauty for ever - or was it lying, even now, broken and devastated, ruined, ugly, gone for ever? He caught Alan Padder's eye, watchful, waiting.

Then he thought of little Blackie and smiled.

"Ready!" he cried, hopping out of the hovel. "Do your worst, Bill!"

A shout went up from the allotments as Bill's hammer struck the bricks. Knee deep in snow the crowd roared encouragement and out on the street the people shouted too.

"Give it some, Bill!" they cried. "Good luck, Walter!"

Walter and Potty stood with Mr Bateman, their throats dry as the masonry crumbled under Bill's cautious blows. Mr. Jollie stood just a little further back with Jigger-Poo and Burt. Arthur and Mable hovered close by, though Jigger-Poo gave a tiny growl whenever the Mayor looked at him. Everybody held his breath. One by one the Dragon Knights arrived, joining Pongy and Lefty at Walter's side.

"Where are the twins?" asked little Nancy Dancer, looking around.

"Taking Edna to the church with Willie's friends," whispered Stephen Smallbody. "I saw Mr. Pinch in green wellies an' a red carnation. He did look funny!"

Bill straightened up and looked at Walter. He wiped his brow.

"Nearly done," he said. "Another go – there!" and he stepped back as the last few bricks tumbled down.

He bent down and began to throw them onto the jumbled pile outside the hovel.

"Only room for one, son," he said kindly as Walter rushed to help him. "Not long now pal. Step back a bit."

Potty smiled at the little ceramicist.

"Nearly there," he said but he had been unable to eat even the smallest sausage that morning.

"Right," said Bill at last, using his foot to scrape the last of the debris out of the hovel so that the footing was clean and safe. "Alright, Burt?"

Burt came forward and the crowd rippled with anticipation. This was it. One at a time, Burt passed out the rough saggars of the stockade to Bill's team who stacked them tidily in the little green shed. Walter and Potty craned their necks. Everyone did the same, even Jigger-Poo. Then, in the darkness of the interior, Walter saw a golden gleam.

"It's the wings!" he shouted wildly. "The wings are still there!"

"The wings," chorused the crowd. "The *wings* are still there!"

Walter's heart pounded in his chest. If only he were taller and the kiln not so dark! He strained his eyes – then another saggar came down.

"It's the head!" he shouted, almost beside himself. "The head's still there!"

"The head!" cried the crowd. "The *head's* still there!"

So his wonderful dragon hadn't gone up in smoke! Walter's legs began to tremble and Potty's knees began to shake too. Deep in his pockets his fingers were crossed again. Potty turned and saw Mr. Jollie, a picture of polite anxiety, and Arthur Shortlegg, looking at Walter oddly.

"A picture of rapacity, if ever I saw one," thought Potty, who had little liking for the man. "We mustn't let it get into *his* hands!"

"Look Potty! The pearl!" cried Walter, pointing to something pure and opalescent, gleaming against the dark interior.

"The pearl....the *pearl*...." the crowd intoned, their voices hushed, their hands clasped almost in prayer.

Then for a long time, Walter and Potty could see nothing, nothing but the burly backs of Bill's team as they bent and lifted, lifted and passed.

Finally, "Ok, Walter," said Burt, peering out over a broad back. "This is it, mate."

"Ooooosh!" went the soft intake of breath on the allotments.

"Good luck, Walter!" cried the Dragon Knights, surging forward with impatience.

Pongy and Lefty held their breaths. It was the greatest moment of their lives too.

Walter's head was throbbing. Burt passed out the last saggar and stepped back inside, out of sight.

Flash! Flash! Flash!

Alan Padder's camera caught the boy as he rushed into the oven and caught the great dragon in his arms.

"Oh!" he cried. "Oh! Oh! Oh!"

There beneath his hands was the huge dragon, its golden scales glinting, its vast tail perfectly encircling the sublime vase. There it was, solid, substantial, real. He stroked it tenderly.

"Thank you," he said quietly. "Thank you."

He half expected one of the great eyes to wink at him, to give some sign of complicity, but there was nothing. The dragon was slightly warm, that was all. A little needle of disappointment shot through him. It *had* been alive! His friend! His saviour! Walter ran his hand over one long leg. It was perfect. What had he expected? A *pet* dragon?

A sudden ray of sunlight entered the kiln, shining directly onto the boy and his vase.

"Oh!" he shouted. "The colours! The *colours* Potty!"

Potty came in, beaming with relief.

"Aah," he said, staring in disbelief. "Wonderful, Walter. Wonderful!"

"You'll see it better outside," said Burt, but the boy could not be parted from his dragon. Minutes passed as he gazed at it, remembering every moment of its creation.

"My dragon," he said softly. "My very own dragon. Cor!"

"The vase! The vase!" came the chant from outside as Pongy's eager face peered into the hovel.

"Cor!" he exclaimed. "Bring it out, mate! We can't wait!" he cried.

Slowly and carefully the dragon vase was lifted, slowly and carefully the team stepped out backwards, slowly and carefully they laid it onto the waiting board.

"Oh!" cried the crowd in amazement. "Oh! Oh! Oh!"

They surged forward but the Strong Man met them and with a mighty arm waved them back.

"Polite distance, please!" he said, frowning.

Potty knocked the side of the vase and again the bell-like note rang out around the yard and across the snowy allotments. It echoed down the little alleyway so that the trumpeters, hearing it, lifted up their golden instruments and blew as the drummers beat out a joyous tattoo.

"It's alright, son, see?" said Potty. "That crack was nothing. I thought so," he said happily as Walter knocked too, listening with a bursting heart to the ringing voice of his dragon vase.

The sun shone in the clear blue sky, its rays made more dazzling by the snowy roofs all around. The dragon vase sparkled. Light danced upon it like sunbeams upon the sea. The lustres were the brightest purest colours that Walter had ever seen. They shimmered, almost insubstantial, the dragon appearing like a mirage in that sooty, snowy yard; a visitor from some foreign clime perhaps, strange and exotic, like a bird of paradise glimpsed and then gone, too rare for human sight. Never had a creature been so fierce and yet so exquisite! No one who looked upon it could look away.

"How strange!" thought Walter. "That out of smoke and dirt comes such colour!"

He looked around at Mr. Jollie.

"Tremendous!" said Mr. Jollie. "Simply tremendous Walter. Tremendous!"

He wiped his eyes and Jigger-Poo jumped up.

"Woof!" he said. "Woof! Woof! Woof!"

Two figures appeared at the entrance to the little alleyway. They were tall and elegant but red faced and dishevelled.

"Isabella and Theodora!" cried Walter, running over to them. "I thought you weren't coming!"

"Had to walk most of the way!" gasped Isabella. "Car got stuck after a mile. Road's jammed up the whole way!"

Theodora was standing like one in a trance, speechless.

"It's come out just like you said," said Walter.

The glaze wizards circled the vase in silence, scrutinising the lustres closely.

"I've never seen anything like it!" said Theodora at last. "It's excelled our wildest expectations. What a result, Walter!"

Everyone thumped Walter and Potty on the back. Alf was surrounded by Bill's team who were shaking his hand and passing around a little flask. Alf smiled at Walter.

"Congratulations, son," he said. "Time for a speech now lad, I think!"

"Speech! Speech!" cried the crowd and Walter's heart sank. He would have preferred a trip to the dentist.

"Just a short one, son," said Potty.

Walter sucked in his cheeks and looked at his dragon vase. Alan Padder fitted a new flash bulb and drew a sharpened pencil from behind his ear. Walter put his hand on the dragon's tail.

Flash! Flash! Flash!

"I haven't done it by myself," Walter began. " Edna saved everything on Poodle Friday and The Dragon Knights were always there for me too. Then Billie and Willie saw off Old Ma with Dragon's help. And my aunties have been brilliant putting up with me since September!"

He paused for breath and looked around at the sea of smiling faces.

"Potty showed me how to do absolutely everything and Mr. Bateman is the best mould maker ever!" he went on. "Mr. Pinch bought me the clay and let me off lessons and stuff. He's the best Headmaster ever! Bill and his mates fixed the kiln and baited the fires and Burt had the idea about the saggars. I wouldn't even be here without Mr. Jollie! There was nowhere else to fire it and he bought me all the coal."

Walter smiled happily.

"Marvellous!" said Mr. Jollie warmly. Marvellous!"

" Isabella and Theodora gave me the wonderful glazes and my Auntie Louie showed me how to use them," said Walter, wishing Louie could be there instead of at home with Sally, trapped by the snowy day. "And I'd never have got it fired without Alf. Nobody else could have done it." He paused and looked around at everybody. "You've all helped me," he said, "and it belongs to everybody really. He isn't just my dragon. He belongs to all of you. We're taking him to live at The Grove so that everybody can see him. Thank you all, very much indeed."

A huge cheer went up from the crowd but Arthur Shortlegg adjusted his chain; shoving himself to the front he struck a pose with one hand on the dragon's foot. He looked mean-ingfully at Alan Padder who responded with a quick flash of his camera.

"Congratulations, Walter," he said, puffing out his chest and enjoying the large crowd. "This is a great day for our city. An 'istoric day," he added importantly but Mable looked at him with disgust.

She was bitterly cold and needed the ladies' room. Edging around her husband she leaned over and shook Walter's hand.

"Well done, dear," she said. "It's lovely!" Then leaning in she whispered, "Dunner trust 'im duck. 'e's up to something!"

Walter's eyebrows shot up.

"What...." he began but the Lady Mayoress had backed off and was looking somewhere else.

"Now then, Walter," said Arthur, shooting his wife an angry glance, "I've got a better idea. "What about the Town Hall, lad? Big place to display it permanently. Lots of people can see it and it'll be nice an 'safe. What about that, eh?"

"I don't know," said Walter slowly. "I never thought of that. What do you think, Potty?"

"Ah," said Potty, "an interesting proposition, Mr. Mayor. But the choice is entirely Walter's. It will be quite safe at The Grove, son. You know that. Perhaps the best place after all."

"Nonsense!" said Arthur. "Too good for an elementary school, a vase like that! Needs to be at the Town Hall, Walter. The Town Hall!"

Mr. Jollie's eyes were turning from blue to steely grey. He watched Jigger-Poo who was sniffing at the Mayor and emitting a constant low growl. He knew Jigger-Poo recognised a rat when he found one.

"Walter's decision, Shortlegg!" he said. "Safe at The Grove, Walter. Amongst all y' friends. Best place if y'ask me!"

Arthur sensed his prize slipping away from him and his ears flushed a deep shade of red. He knew of a collector in Chicago who would pay a fortune for something like this, no questions asked. He waved his hand at the circus people and gestured towards the elephant waiting patiently at the end of the little entry.

"Gone to a lot of trouble on your behalf, lad," he said a trifle too sharply, his nose turning a violent shade of puce. "The Town Hall is the very best place for something like this. I'd be failing in my civic duty if I allow you to do otherwise."

Theodora bristled with annoyance.

"Now look here," she said, stepping forward and towering over the little man. "This is Walter's vase and it's not up to you to *allow* anything, one way or the other."

"Certainly not! The cheek of it!" said Isabella, colouring angrily. "It's entirely up to Walter! What do you want to do, dear?" she said, turning away from the Mayor in contempt. "Shall we ask these kind people to take it to The Grove?"

"Don't interfere, my good woman!" began Arthur, his eyes bulging and spittle appearing on his lips. "This is a civic matter. It isn't any of *your* business...." but he was interrupted by the Strong Man who pushed forward and glowered at the mayor.

"Polite to ladies please!" he growled through his shiny teeth. "Ladies have good opinion! Walter do what he likes. What you like Walter?"

"The Grove!" said Walter decidedly. He didn't like Arthur Shortlegg at all. "It belongs at school," he said, "with everybody who's helped me." The crowd gave a roar of approval. "Can we get it back for the party, Potty?" he added hopefully.

Mable smiled broadly.

"Good decision, dear," she said. "Right, Arthur, time to get back and change. My feet are ruddy freezing!" and she hustled her furious husband up the alleyway to their waiting car.

The board was lifted and Bill's team trod slowly and heavily across the mats and down the little alleyway. Shouts of amazement greeted them as they emerged onto the pavement outside. With meticulous care the dragon vase was stowed safely in the big red sleigh, its lower fifth nestling securely inside the padded interior.

"Fits like a glove," said Bill with satisfaction as Walter hovered anxiously. "Nice 'an snug. Dunner worry, son. It won't budge an inch an' it'll 'ave a really smooth ride!"

"Cor!" gasped the crowd. "Cor! Just look at that!"

Nothing in the circus was as colourful as the vase, nothing glowed with the same shimmering iridescence, nothing, not even the elephant, could compare to the great shining dragon with his golden scales and his wonderful outspread wings. Walter checked and rechecked but Bill was right. It was a very good fit.

"Beg pardon," said a foreign voice. "You would like to ride up there?"

The dark-eyed mahout gestured up to the elephant's back. A huge smile split Walter's face in two.

"Really!" he exclaimed. "Can we really?"

"Oh yes," laughed the mahout. "And your friends too!"

"Cor! Yes!" cried Lefty, pushing Walter forward. "Go on, mate! Get up!"

"I think Walter is riding with me," said the Mayor, who had not yet relinquished his attempt to appropriate the dragon vase. "In you get, son."

But Walter was already wrapped in the elephant's trunk and being lifted, as light as a feather, to his seat behind its enormous ears.

"Oh no," he said. "I'm riding up here. Thanks anyway."

Mable snickered and climbed into the warm car. Arthur got in beside her, hitching his wet gown inside after him but as the door shut the crowd pointed and smiled. At least a yard of red velvet was shut outside, trailing sadly in the snowy gutter.

"Nice boy, that," said Mable, watching as Walter and his friends sat clutching each other high above the snowy street. She waved to them as the elephant set off, swaying majestically, drawing the heavy sleigh smoothly behind him.

"Cheer up, Arf," she said, passing him her little flask of gin. "There's no way you was knocking down any of my walls, if that was what you was thinking. Aah, thought as much!"

388

she added, glimpsing an expression of thwarted intent as the mayor thrust the flask back at her.

"Anyway, Arthur," she went on in a more serious tone, "that dragon'd only spell trouble for you. Get you into all sort of scrapes, that would. And you can't 'old onto something like that against its will anyway. It belongs with Walter until the time comes...." she paused and looked at her red-faced husband. "You've 'ad a lucky escape really, dear."

"Are you going mad, Mable?" Arthur snorted. "'ow much of that gin 'ave you 'ad?"

"Not enough to keep me warm," she said smiling. "Now get me 'ome! I shall look a right fright if I don't 'ave enough time to change!"

The car moved off, the big engine roaring as the chains sought for purchase on the snow. Ahead of them the procession made its way through the little streets past crowds of people who cheered and waved.

"Long way round, Walter?" asked the Mahout and they all cried, "Yes please!"

Nothing in Walter's dream had been as rich, as profoundly different as this real ride. The strong musty scent of the elephant filled his nose and mouth and he felt its thick hairy skin beneath his hands. Past little houses and shops they swayed, the boys looking down on their town with a new perspective; over little bridges and canals they rode, where the barges were roofed with white and the towpaths made narrow white ribbons against the inky black canals.

The elephant swayed on, past pot banks smokeless now for Christmas, but stacked full of precious wares soon to be consigned to the flames as Walter's dragon had been; soon to emerge shining and gilded from their rough saggars; soon to be shipped off across the world as fragile ambassadors for this magical city of coal and clay.

Past Christmas trees they went, winking and blinking their colourful lights in the windows of the little houses; past hordes of children who ran with the Dragon Knights alongside the sleigh, stumbling and laughing through the powdery white.

Then once more the circus turned a corner and approached the top of Walter's street.

"Boom! Boom! Rat-a-tat-tat!" shouted the drums as the trumpets blew and the bells on the sleigh tinkled aloud.

Sally opened the door.

"Oh my!" she cried. "Oh my! Oh my! Oh my!"

Louie appeared behind her, well wrapped up.

"Congratulations, dear!" she called, waving to her nephew perched high above her. "Are you satisfied with it, dear?"

"Yes Auntie," cried Walter. "It's brilliant! Look! Can you see....?"

And for ten minutes the patient elephant waited in the snow whilst the drums and trumpets went silent and the boy and his auntie pointed out first one part of the wonderful dragon vase and then another. It was all exactly as they had dreamed, the vivid colours fresh from Africa itself, as if no distance at all lay between the emerald forests and the city of coal and clay.

"I can almost hear the waterfall," sighed Louie at last. "It seems alive with hummingbirds' wings, its shimmers so. And your dragon, dear." She looked steadily at Walter. "Where ever he goes, he must be happy."

She looked meaningfully at her nephew and he nodded his head.

"I know," he said. "He'll be happy at The Grove, I think. For now, at least."

Snowballing had begun so the procession moved off again, drums booming, trumpets blowing. And there at the bottom of the hill were Edna and Mr. Pinch climbing into the open carriage as Minnie and Thelma showered them in confetti, the tiny pink and blue paper petals settling and dissolving on the snowy ground.

Willie and Freddie stood staring in astonishment by the patient Prince as Tom and his men shovelled away the snow, clearing a path for the great horse to pull the bride and groom the short distance to The Grove. They leaned on their shovels and stared in disbelief. Billie ran up to the elephant.

"Cor!" he cried. "A dragon *and* an elephant! Cor! Look at this everybody! Look at Walter's dragon! Its legendary mate!" he cried. "It's epic!"

Everyone clustered around the sleigh, looking up at the sparkling dragon.

"It's completely and utterly fabulous, dear!" cried Minnie. "It's like something out of "The Faerie Queen!""

Few brides have to compete with a dragon *and* an elephant at their wedding but Edna turned in her seat and waved.

"Congratulations, Walter!" she cried happily and "Congratulations, Mr. and Mrs. Pinch!" Walter shouted back from his warm and musty perch.

Edna stood and tossed her bouquet high into the air. It rose up above the lamp post with its little bonnet of snow and tumbled down – into Minnie's arms.

"Oh!" she said in surprise.

"Oooh Minnie!" laughed Thelma. "Something you haven't been telling me?"

She glanced over at Mr. Jollie, who had belatedly joined the wedding party with his friends from the kiln. His face had lit up, and for a moment he seemed no more than a youth again. But Minnie smiled at him affectionately and then looked away.

"Where's Rosie?" she said quietly. "These should be hers by rights."

Then Prince bent his head and the carriage moved off. The band began again, filling the air with sound as the church bells finished their clamorous peal and the elephant lumbered forward, trailing her precious cargo behind.

"Come on everybody!" cried Minnie, linking arms with Thelma and Mr. Jollie. "Off to The Grove!" and off they went, followed by the Dragon Knights and indeed all of the people who loved Walter and Edna and Mr. Pinch.

Alf was lifted up and carried shoulder high by the Strong Man as the crowds cheered. Harry Mudd ran along beside them. A feast lay ahead of him and he couldn't get there fast enough.

There was Rosie skipping through the snow clutching Edna's red bouquet and George striding close behind her with Isabella and Theodora tripping daintily in their smart little boots. There were Willie and Billie laughing and chatting with the canal folk, and Burt and Bill with his allotment team, handing Miss Lush and her colleagues through the snowy streets as they all made their way to The Grove, where Mr. Slope had the radiators roaring and the wedding breakfast was waiting for Mr. Pinch and his bride.

And there at the end of the hall stood the empty stage, its red velvet curtains drawn wide. All morning the empty room had waited, hushed and expectant. But through the sharp clear air came the sound of trumpets and bells and the Boom! Boom! Boom! of the drums. In a little while the stage would be empty no more. Soon the dragon vase would be carried in and lifted up and the dragon would spread his golden wings over the wedding party in a shimmering benediction. It was Christmas Eve, and across the snowy playground Walter's Dragon was coming home!

"clutching each other high above the snowy street..."

Epilogue
November 1941

The kettle whistled loudly and Edna reached across for the knitted pot holder. She poured the hot water into two waiting thermos flasks and screwed them up tightly. Into her basket they went, along with two packets of sandwiches tightly wrapped in greaseproof paper.

"No cheese again!" she thought sadly, but then smiled as she lifted down a jar of Mr. Jollie's plum jam. She spread a little on two scones and wrapped them carefully too. Then she popped an unopened jar into her basket and buttoned up her coat.

"Soap! Water!" she called, opening the kitchen door. The old dogs ran in happily, though Soap was a little stiff.

"Come on!" she said. "Dinner!"

The poodles rapidly cleared their plates and Edna fastened on their leads.

"Off we go!" she said brightly, then paused, as always, to stand by the dresser with its silver framed photograph.

"Ten years next week!" she thought in amazement. "How they have flown!"

Her own lovely face stared back at her amid a shower of lace and roses and Mr. Pinch stood beaming, arm in arm with his enchanting bride.

"Come on!" she said to the patient poodles. "Let's keep him company!"

The streets were glistening after the recent rain but there was still some light left as Edna closed the front door and made her way past the shadowy park, its leafless trees dripping, its lost leaves slippery beneath Edna's feet. Soap and Water sniffed noisily, always glad to be out in the smoky air.

"Yes!" said Edna. "You'll see Blackie soon!"

"Woof!" they barked. "Woof! Woof! Woof!"

The little house at the top of the hill was as dark as all the others. No lights shone upon the wet cobbles, no lamp posts shed their comforting yellow glow.

Minnie answered the door.

"Come in Edna," she said. "Hello Soap, good *dog* Water!"

"How's Sally?" asked Edna. "How's she coping?"

"Bearing up," answered Minnie. "As we must."

Edna gave her friend a hug.

"Look, I've brought you some of Mr. Jollie's plum jam," she said, rooting in her bag and holding the glowing jar up to the light. "Lovely colour!" she said.

"Oh Edna, what a treat!" cried Minnie. "How is he these days?"

"Not too bad for an old 'un, like me!" laughed Edna. "Rosie's still with him of course. She looks after him well."

"I know she does!" said Minnie. "She's got her hands full these days and no mistake! Sally!" she called, "Come and see what Edna's bought us!"

Sally appeared and Blackie burst through after her, romping happily with his brother and sister around the little front room.

"He misses Walter," said Sally as she embraced Edna. "Two years now and he still waits for him at tea-time."

She bent stiffly and patted the black dog.

"We all miss him, Blackie," she said.

"But we've had a letter from him," cried Minnie, rushing into the kitchen. "Here," she said, passing it to Edna. Minnie looked around cautiously, as if the little house might be harbouring alien intelligences, "We have our own idea where he is, though we can't *say* of course!"

"What's it ....?" Edna flushed and broke off. She remembered such letters sent to her, full of light hearted prattle and jokes. And then the silence, and nothing, only the telegram.

Minnie kissed her.

"It's not too bad, we think," she said softly. "Will you have a cup of tea with us, dear, and some of this lovely jam?"

"I have to get on," said Edna, shaking her head. "I'd better get down to the school before I lose all the light. Don't want another fall!"

"How is your hip, dear?" asked Sally. "Should you be fire-watching again?"

"Oh, I don't mind, I'm fine!" said Edna cheerfully. "And I like to keep John company. Well, I'm so glad you've heard from him, so glad."

But tears had sprung to her eyes and Sally and Minnie hugged her close before she left, stepping out into the nearly black street, Soap and Water wagging their tails as they licked Blackie goodbye.

"You know Pongy's ship went down," said Edna as she stood outside. "But he was lucky. He was pulled out of the water quickly enough."

"Yes, we heard," said Minnie. "I wish Lefty had had more luck."

They stood silently, remembering the late summer of 1940.

The whole neighbourhood had turned out for Lefty Knype. His headstone, of North Staffordshire sandstone, read simply:

RICHARD "LEFTY" KNYPE
1919-1940
"ONE OF THE FEW"

And there could be no greater tribute than that, the reverend Cupp had told the hushed congregation, sitting stunned in the hot church as the sun beat through the sooty glass and flies buzzed drunkenly on the dusty windowsills.

Walter and Pongy, on special leave from their training grounds, had stood under a blackened maple as Lefty's family gathered around the grave. They were joined by Billie and Willie, smart and lean in their khaki uniforms.

"He was an ace!" said Pongy vehemently.

"He was!" said Walter.

"Come on mates," said Pongy. "We've got an hour or so before our trains. Let's 'ave a pint for Lefty in the Potter's Daughter!"

"Last chance for God knows how long," agreed Billie. "I'm off next week, I think."

"Oh bruv!" said Willie.

"Right!" said Walter. "Let's drink to Lefty and...."

"The Company of the Dragon Knights!" cried Willie. "Together wherever they may be!"

Minnie closed the door and switched on the light again. She stood quietly with Sally looking around the little front room, now empty and cold.

"Come on dear," she said to Sally. "Let's feed Blackie. I got some lovely scraps for him today. And then we'll put the kettle on and listen to the wireless. With any luck it won't be bad tonight. We're lucky here, you know."

Edna walked downhill to the school, treading carefully in the near dark. Mr. Pinch was standing in Walter's empty classroom when she found him. It was his habit to stand there at the end of each day, silently surveying the empty desks and thinking of the children who had peopled them, year after year.

As Edna came in, he was looking sadly at a desk, third from the left on the back row.

"Hello Edna," he said quietly, leaning forward to kiss her. "As lovely as ever, my dear. Hello Soap, hello Water," he added, rubbing the two curly heads which were shoved into his hands. "Been fed, I suppose?"

"Oh, yes!" said Edna. "Eating better than us these days, dear."

She handed him the sandwiches apologetically.

"Not much," she said, "but the scones will be nice."

They ate and sat together in a companionable silence though Mr. Pinch was withdrawn and as Edna watched him a tear appeared in the corner of his eye, growing steadily bigger until it spilled out onto his cheek. Another followed it, and another and another.

"Oh John," cried Edna softly. "Who dear? Who?"

"Tobruk," Mr. Pinch managed before he broke down and wept openly. "Captain Billie Grunter, Eighth Army, outstanding bravery...." he said at last, wiping away his tears.

"Oh no!" cried Edna. "Not Billie. Not Billie!"

They sat in the dark classroom, each with an arm around a comforting warm poodle.

"Do you remember all the gardening he did for us?" said Edna after a little while. "He and Willie together. How they helped us, John, that summer of '35? When we got out all those old rhododendrons? What a job that was! How they dug and dug!"

"They were fine young men," said Mr. Pinch, smiling. "And they always wanted to make it up to you, Edna. They thought the world of you. As do I," he said, squeezing her hand gently.

Edna sighed.

"I wonder where Willie is now?" she said. "Did you think, John, when you came home from the last one, that you would live to see another?"

"No one did, Edna," said Mr. Pinch sadly. "But I do believe we have to fight this one. I never thought I'd ever say that," he added sombrely. "I saw so much. But here we are and we must make a stand, though it grieves me unutterably to say so, Edna."

Edna nodded dumbly but she had lost too much to agree.

At ten o' clock they heard the sound of airplanes, high overhead. Mr. Pinch made another careful round of the school and looked outside. All was completely dark: no light or flames showed anywhere.

"Manchester," he suggested. "Or Liverpool perhaps."

The night wore on. The school and the little streets around it remained unmolested. The bottle ovens snoozed, the ware safe in their warm bellies.

"And what about Walter?" Mr. Pinch asked as the sky began to lighten and they made their way home for a few hours' sleep. "Have they heard from him lately?"

"Oh yes!" said Edna. "I should have said. Safe and well as far as they know. I must write to him again. He loves to hear about the dogs, and all the old crowd, you know."

They reached their front door and went inside.

"I'm so lucky to have you, John," she whispered. "Whatever did you want to go and marry me for? Nearly a decade older and you so handsome too."

"Ah, Edna," he said, gathering her in his arms and burying his face in her silvery hair. "You make this world worthwhile. Just you alone, Edna. You do that."

Edna smiled.

"And Soap and Water too," she laughed. "Don't forget them, John!"

§

Italy 1944

It was October and the night was bitterly cold. The Northern Apennine air was sharp and clear, the stars radiating a fierce white light which lit up the mountainside, glinting on the gun barrels and on the jagged stumps of trees jerking up out of the ruined ground.

Months of bombardment from the German fortifications had rendered the terrain a deep and hopeless mire in which men and machines floundered as the unseasonable rains poured down, soaking through the inadequate second issue greatcoats and seeping miserably into the sodden boots of the entrenched Eighth Army.

Walter was huddled inside a hen coop for warmth.

"Get in there, Walt!" his corporal had said at ten o'clock. "You're small enough!"

The wooden boards cut the biting wind but no sleep came. Walter's mind was crowded by terrible visions and his ears throbbed with dull explosions. The day had been horrendous – yet a source of wonder too.

For weeks, the fighting had been ferocious and Walter and his mates had manned their guns incessantly, sending shell after shell flying off to pound the German line.

Whoompff! Whoompf! Whoompf! The incoming fire had burst all around them, cratering the ground and sending huge earthfalls into the air so that the gunners had the mountain in their eyes and ears: they breathed it and ate it too, a constant gritty companion in every mouthful of food and water. Their faces were black and exhausted.

Hour after hour they had loaded and fired, loaded and fired in the drenching rain, struggling and slipping through the squelching mud, deaf to the boom of their guns and their sharp racketing recoil.

Then in the late afternoon came a lull, a moment of pure calm. The rain ceased and the clouds drew away northwards, towards Bologna. At last the company was able to straighten their backs and take stock. Walter looked up. The smoke was clearing and high above him the sky was turning to a heavenly blue, the fresh celestial blue of an Italian Ascension. He drew a crumpled packet of cigarettes from his top pocket and turning, offered one to Joe.

Whoompf! All went dark and he fell to the ground, crushed by a huge weight.

"Am I dead?" he wondered, his mouth full of earth, unable to move, pinned so that he could hardly breath. Just a little air entered one nostril from the cavity of his displaced helmet. Earth showered down on the gun emplacement. Whoompf! Whoompf! Whoompf!

Walter lay crushed, stunned, unable to think. Five minutes passed, then something stirred. The weight moved and slid off sideways. Someone groped for his hand.

"Walter!" came a familiar voice. "Walter!"

He was pulled to his feet by a huge man in a soil covered greatcoat. He smelt strongly of horses.

"Willie!" cried Walter in disbelief. "Willie Grunter!"

"Sorry mate," said Willie, "but you would have been a gonner...." He hung his head and Walter saw something terrible out of the corner of his eye.

"Don't look, mate," said Willie kindly. "Direct hit. Gun's buggered too. Nothing for you here. Come on."

Walter allowed Willie to lead him back behind the line a little way. The guns were still again now. The sun broke through with real autumnal warmth and the land began to steam as fresh men marched up to replace the weary gunners now trailing back to camp in exhausted little groups.

Willie sat Walter down on a broken wall and gave him a flask. A robin, stunned by the bombardment, perhaps, alighted on Walter's knee and perched there silently.

"Been following your lot for weeks," said Willie. "Heard you were here. Been trying to catch up with you."

He took back the flask and administered it to himself.

"Better," he said, re-screwing the top and returning it to his pocket. "Grappa. Not bad when you need it!"

Walter looked at him dazedly.

"You?" he said. "Here?"

The robin still perched, oblivious to everything, even the sound of birdsong returning to the silent evening air, beautiful and alien.

"Wherever are they?" thought Walter, looking around. "Why aren't they all dead?"

"Can you eat anything, Walter?" asked Willie.

Walter shook his head.

"Can you?" he said.

"I could!" said Willie. "Come on! Let's get to camp, Walter!"

Gently, Walter lifted the stricken robin on his index finger.

"I don't like to leave him," he said.

"Bring him then," said Willie.

Later, as they sat by the fire, Walter fed the robin with scraps from Willie's plate.

"I've known Joe for years," he said at last. "All through basic training, Palestine, everything. He was always there."

Then his face dropped.

"*You* lost your brother," he said, looking up at Willie sadly.

"Tobruk," agreed Willie heavily. "1941. Seems years ago now." They sat in silence, thinking what time had done. "But he loved his tank Walter! He was a wizard! He captured three Panzers, him and his men. Got them to surrender and took them prisoner! The German tank commander thought he was bloody marvellous!"

Walter managed a little laugh.

"Billie!" he said, and thought what a good man he would have been to have by his side, as he had been once before.

"How are your Mum and Dad?" he asked.

"Coping," said Willie. "Dad's better than I thought he'd be. Mum's a bit done in."

Walter nodded sadly.

"I'm so sorry," he said. "He was a great mate to me. The places we went on that bike of his!"

"I was sorry to hear about Louie," said Willie, accepting another mug of strong tea.

"She did well," Walter said, smiling. "Another six years! We never imagined that!" he looked at Willie. "What *are* you doing here, Willie?" he asked.

"I'm your mule man!" laughed Willie. "The Germans have left hundreds of horses all over the place. Hundreds of them! I've been promoted!" and he pointed to his sleeve. "I'm the lieutenant in charge of shifting your guns - when you move on, mate. It's a lot easier with mules in this mud. We can go north together, Walter!"

Walter looked into the distance, over towards the German line from whence death and destruction visited him every day.

"Do you remember that evening in Mr. Beany's yard?" he asked quietly. "When you said you'd be the best mate I ever have?"

Willie nodded, his face sombre.

Walter reached over and took his big dirty hand.

"Well," he said, squeezing it hard. "I can't argue with that now. You've been the best of mates, Willie!"

But Walter lay awake that night, unable to shake off the fearful visions of the day before. There wasn't even room to toss and turn although the cramped shelter was better than none at all. Willie had gone off at six to see to his mules and Walter lay alone, only the little robin perching outside on the roof of the coop, silent, its feathers fluffed up against the mountain cold.

"I must think of something else," he told himself, rubbing his eyes as if that would wipe clean his mind.

He tried to think back over the campaign, to see again the steep river valleys he had fought through, with their precipitous hill towns perched high above and higher still the lonely monasteries reaching up to God. He screwed up his eyes to recapture the almond groves which had swathed the lower slopes in cloudy white but always the same pictures returned and would not be blotted out.

Then, strangely, at two o' clock, the robin began to sing, all alone in the darkness, its throat pulsating as the song poured out into the silent camp. Walter listened, and as he listened his mind grew stiller, softer, opening up to happier thoughts.

He remembered old Mr. Bateman, knocking out his pipe against the wall of his house and Mr. Jollie offering him a pipeful of his own tobacco, rich and perfumed, falling in tiny flakes as Mr. Bateman's stiff fingers stuffed it down into the bowl. He smelt the fragrant smoke and with it the tarry scent of Sally's fire leaping and crackling in the kitchen grate as the clock ticked on through the night and Walter wasn't sure whether he was awake or asleep.

And through all his thoughts and dreams roved the happy thought of his great dragon, the joy of making it and the exultation of seeing it made. He dreamed of waterfalls and hippopotami and of canal boats legging it under dark tunnels - and when the tunnel ended it was day.

When Walter awoke, the robin had gone. He tumbled out of the hen coop stiff in his body but refreshed in his mind.

"Flew off, Walt," said another gunner, passing Walter a bowl of porridge. "A few minutes ago. Seemed alright to me!"

Walter ate the porridge, the gunner watching him closely.

"Had a really funny dream about you last night, Walt," he

said. "Dreamt I woke up and saw a bloody great green dragon sitting on top of your hen coop!"

He laughed, but Walter could see something in the man's eyes.

"You'll have to take more water with it, Douggie!" he said, scraping his bowl and smiling. "Thanks for the porridge though."

But his heart had skipped a beat and he turned away to hide his astonishment. Thirteen busy years had passed since the green smoke dragon had rescued him from Old Ma Grunter, during which time Walter had grown up, thinking less and less about it all until he hardly believed in the magic anymore.

If you had asked him about the strange events at Mr. Jollie's yard on the night of Rosie's sixteenth birthday party, he would have smiled and shaken his head.

"It was a long time ago," he might have said, "and I was only a little boy."

And yet here was Douggie from Gravesend, sober as a judge and clearly telling the truth. His dragon! Here! Walter sorted through his kit and made ready for another day's assault on the German line. But his hands were shaking and he could hardly believe what he had just heard. Willie Grunter and his dragon *here*, just when he had needed them!

He looked around at the vast Appennines, peak after peak disappearing into the blue distance as the sun rose higher over the Adriatic and his mates fell into line to begin the trek back to their guns. But his mood was solemn and he thought of Joe and others like him who had been lost along the way, the lovely valleys filled with English dead.

"You're with Plum," said his Captain, waving Walter over to a new emplacement. "And give them hell today son, because you're sure to get it back!"

Within minutes the cannonade had begun again. The air filled with smoke and the earth showered down like heavy rain.

"But we'll get through it," thought Walter at the end of the day, as he shared a packet of cigarettes with his pals. "And it'd be nice to go north with Willie."

He asked around, but the mule-man had been sent off elsewhere and he could get no news of him. The war had another year to go and the mountains kept the two men well apart. It would be years and years before they saw each other again.

§

Milton 1960

Every Saturday morning Walter walked down into the village to do the family shopping. Behind him the road wound up to a steep edge, where little fields and low stone walls looked down on the pleasant row of semi-detached houses below. Long green gardens stretched out behind, where his children played at house in the apple trees and held a hopeful ghost club in the dilapidated shed.

Ahead of him, the road descended to the village crossroads, bank on the left, grocer's on the right, bookmaker's straight ahead over the zebra crossing. Unless Walter's family needed shoes or clothes, the village shops could supply them with almost everything they needed. But a Saturday morning shop was a lengthy affair. The butcher's, the greengrocer's, the grocery store, the paper-shop, the chemist – all had to be visited and queued for, then greetings exchanged along with heavy half-crowns or brown ten-shilling notes. Sometimes there was the post office too, or the tiny wool shop with its ceiling-high shelves stuffed with coloured yarns, or the hardware shop or the oatcake shop, smelling deliciously as the thin batter was poured onto the sizzling hotplates.

But one Saturday in the spring of 1960 Walter left his bags with his friends at the chemist's shop and walked down to the canal in the warm daffodil-scented air. It had seemed a long winter.

On the opposite bank stood the grim edifice of the aluminium works; on the other side ran the narrow River Trent, here no more than a sluggish stream, which trickled via a short concrete channel into a little overflow basin by the canal, where his girls caught tadpoles and sticklebacks in the weedy water. Walter stood watching their tiny shapes flicker underneath the water-boatmen, whose long legs dimpled the surface of the pond but never broke it.

An ice-cream van chimed from the road above, heralding warmer weather and longer days. Walter looked up. The sky was blue and the sun had real comfort in it.

He set off along the tow path, folding his heavy tweed jacket over his arm and taking off his cap to let the sun shine on his head. The dark canal began to sparkle and blackbirds sang in the hawthorn trees. On a bend up ahead, he saw a barge moored, its roof cluttered with ropes and cans and all the other detritus of life lived on the water in a confined space.

He rearranged his jacket and minded his footing as he walked past. The ground was a little muddy and slippery still.

"How do, Walter!" came a familiar voice.

Walter spun around.

"Willie!" he cried, full of unexpected delight.

He leapt over a puddle and shook his old friend's hand.

"Willie! How are you?"

"All right, Walter!" said Willie, beaming broadly. "Long time no see, mate!"

"I've been wondering how you got on, Willie," said Walter. "You're still on the canals, then?"

"What's left of them, I am," said Willie, shaking his head sadly. "That winter of '47 finished off a lot of us. Never the same after that!"

"I know," said Walter. "That was a bad one. How are your Mum and Dad, Willie?"

"Lost them both," said Willie. "A few years ago. Come on board Walter, and have a cup of tea."

Walter stepped onto the barge and sat next to Willie outside the little cabin.

"Looks cosy," he said, peeking inside.

"Oh aye," said Willie. "I wouldn't be anywhere else, Walter."

Walter looked around. A large black dog licked his hand and a cat basked on the cabin roof. But there was no horse grazing on the towpath.

"No horse?" he asked.

"No go these days, Walter," Willie said with a sigh. "Too expensive and not enough work to keep us going. Miss my horses a lot, I really do."

"Shame," said Walter. "How long did you have Dragon, Willie?"

"Oh, a good many years," replied Willie, smiling. He was a big ruddy-faced man, rather grubby but with blue twinkling eyes and a ready laugh. "I worked him for Mr. Jollie before the war and then for a bit after it, like."

He looked off in to the distance.

"We were down Bristol way when that bad weather set in, in '47. There were barges everywhere frozen into the ice. Nothing could move. Not for months. But I walked him back, all that way, back to his stable at Mr. Beany's!"

"Cor!" said Walter. "That took some doing! How old was he by then, Willie?"

"Twenty by then, Walter," said Willie proudly, "but strong as an ox he was! Wouldn't stop in his stable! We had some adventures, we did," he added softly and Walter could see them, the big man and his horse, together, come what may.

"Best time of my life!" said Willie, his eyes misting. "Just him and me, walking miles every day together, stopping at a farm every night. I slept in the straw, anything so long as we were undercover. He had plenty of hay and I had what I could get. Helped the farmers, like, to earn our keep. They were glad of a hand in that lot." He went silent, remembering. "Just him and me and the snow," he said. "Magical, Walter, magical."

"I bet it was," said Walter. "I bet it was."

"Marvellous!" said Willie laughing. "That's what he said when we got home. Marvellous, Willie! Marvellous!"

"He was a grand old chap," said Walter, laughing too. "What he did for me."

"Him and Mr. Pinch," said Willie. "They don't make them like that any more."

He offered Walter a cigarette and blew out a perfect circle of smoke.

"I lost touch," said Walter. "I shouldn't have done really. How old was he when...."

"About eighty-six, I think," said Willie. "Rosie and George lived with him. Children too, of course! He left everything to her. She was like a daughter to him in the end. Made up for a lot, I think."

"And what about Dragon?" asked Walter. "What happened to him?"

"Oh, he had a long life, he did!" said Willie. "We worked him until he was about twenty-three and then he retired out to Endon. Gwenny went there too, but years before, like. Bit of green grass for her at the end. Turned into a riding school now, that place."

They drank their tea and smoked their cigarettes. The cat came down from the roof and lay on Walter's lap.

"Can't be without animals, Walter," said Willie after a while. "What about you – you got a family? I heard you have."

"Two little girls," said Walter, smiling. "Six and eight."

"Also heard you married a Gwenny!" burst out Willie, roaring with laughter.

"I did!" laughed Walter. "From Goldenhill!"

"You've done alright, haven't you Walter," said Willie, smiling at his friend. "Doulton's? Designer? What you wanted?"

Walter nodded.

"But I didn't get to be a modeller," he said. "No places going for that. Not enough of those jobs about. But yes, a designer. A good job, Willie."

"Designs going off all over the world, then?"

Walter nodded again.

"Yes," he said modestly. "I've done alright, Willie."

"You deserved it, mate," said Willie warmly. "But we never thought your vase would end up *there*, did we!"

"We didn't!" said Walter. "That was the biggest surprise of all!"

"I suppose it's still there?" asked Willie curiously.

"I suppose so," said Walter. "I've never heard any different! But I don't tend to hear about it at all."

"Those were the days," he added, remembering the warmth of the little house and the kindly streets in which he had grown up. Then he thought that for Willie they were better left in the past, buried and forgotten about.

"Do you ever hear about Pongy?" he asked, the scent of the green jumper wafting back over the years.

"He's done well, has Pongy!" cried Willie. "Loves his boats! Phillip Slipp drinks in The Potter's Daughter. He told me Pongy's got a little boatyard down in Devon. Makes little sailing boats. Very nice, I believe."

"Fancy that!" said Walter. "Devon!"

"You've never wanted to move away then, Walter?" asked Willie.

"Oh no," said Walter. "This is home. What about you?"

"Go where I can," said Willie. "Do a bit here and there. Always come back, like. Not the same community as there was on the canals, though."

"Perhaps it'll change?" offered Walter hopefully. He stood up. "I shall have to get back. We're going to Gwen's family this afternoon. "

"I was sorry to hear about Minnie," said Willie. "And then Sally?"

"They did well," said Walter. "And they were wonderful. It's a shame the girls never knew them. We had Sally with us for a couple of years – before the little one arrived. Margaret might remember her."

"Times-past," said Willie, looking down into the dark canal. "But a lot of the old bunch are still around, you know. Harry Mudd's lad opened a fish an' chip shop in Cobridge. I hear he's never out of there!"

They both laughed.

"And Potty's still with us," said Walter cheerfully. "He lives on the village with Bob and his family. I often bump into them on a Saturday. They still go to The Vale!"

"Beggars for punishment, then!" laughed Willie. "What about you, Walter?"

"Oh, too busy these days," his friend said, a little sadly. "Still follow them though, Willie.

"Well, that's the way of things," said Willie, straightening up. "I was sorry I lost touch with you in Italy, Walter. They sent me off down south again to pick up more horses. I never got up to Bologna again. But you got through all that ok, anyway."

"Thanks to you I did!" said Walter. He hesitated. There was something he was longing to ask. "What did Billie tell you, that night?" he said, looking up at Willie quickly. "What did he say happened at the yard? You know, when ...."

"I can hardly remember," said Willie, screwing up his face in concentration. "Something very strange happened. Not like in the paper. But exactly what...."

Walter hung his head: he had hoped that someone else would remember the event clearly, someone who would say, "Yes! There was a green smoke dragon, Walter! There really was!"

"Oh well," he thought. "It was so long ago." But his heart had sunk a little, even so.

He shook Willie's hand.

"Take care of yourself, Willie," he said, clasping the big hand tightly. "Perhaps I'll see you before too long."

"Hope so, Walter," said Willie, smiling at his friend. But his star had a separate course mapped out for him and the two men never saw each other again. They parted a little sadly, conscious that the straight canal was in truth a crossroads which would take them off in different directions.

Walter had only gone a few yards when Willie called after him.

"Walter!" he shouted. "Your dragon vase was bloody *marvellous,* mate!"

Walter smiled and waved back.

"But we never thought it'd end up *there*!" shouted Willie as the dog wagged its tail in approval.

"No," thought Walter proudly, as he made his way back along the sunny towpath to the chemist's shop. "I never thought it would end up *there*!"

The End

"I never thought it would end up there..."

A Brief Explanation and Glossary

At one time, before the war, the Potteries had over two thousand working bottle ovens and no one would have needed a glossary to explain words like hovel, saggar or chimney-bag. If you didn't work on a pot bank you had a brother or a sister, or a mother or a father who did, and many of your friends would have worked in the industry too - or in one of the many allied trades which supplied the potters with their raw materials. But times have changed and although the City still produces a great deal the bottles ovens are long since gone and some people may be unfamiliar with words that were once common usage, or with the basic construction of a bottle oven. The glossary below offers a very brief explanation of such things.

BOTTLE OVEN: A bottle oven was a large bottle-shaped structure built of brick, which was used to bake or FIRE clay ware. It might be beer-bottle shape or very much more rotund and massive but it would always have a tall chimney going seventy or more feet up into the air. *Inside* this brick outer shell, or HOVEL, was another brick structure, the KILN or OVEN.

HOVEL: The hovel encloses the kiln/oven like one Russian doll enclosing another. A circular passage runs all around between the inside wall of the hovel and the outer wall of the kiln so that the firemen could access the FIREMOUTHS with the FUEL. The hovel also importantly helped to create the draught necessary to keep the firemouths burning.

FIREMOUTHS: A bottle kiln would have numerous fire-mouths, depending on its size. They were built into the wall of the kiln/oven at regular intervals, being fed or BAITED with coal by the firemen in the passage. Hot air from the firemouths then went up the CHIMNEY BAGS built onto the inner wall of the kiln/oven. The firemouths also sent hot air along FLUES built underneath the brick floor of the kiln. By this means the kiln could reach 1200C, the massive temperature needed to transform raw clay into ceramic. A single firing needed up to 14 tonnes of coal.

FIREMAN: This was the title given to the man who fed or BAITED the firemouths with coal. A team of firemen would be needed for this exhausting task, all overseen by one chief FIREMAN who needed all his skill and experience to achieve the correct temperature. If this was not achieved then the ware inside the kiln could be ruined.

KILN/OVEN: This is where the clay was baked or FIRED inside clay SAGGARS. As I have said, the oven nestles inside the hovel. You step into the kiln/oven via an iron-bound hole called the CLAMMINS. You can see this in the illustration to chapter 26. The floor of the oven/kiln is convex to allow hot air in the flues to spread up underneath it. The roof of the oven/kiln is domed and has a damper in its crown which could be opened and shut by pulling on chains, to control the temperature.

CLAMMINS: The clammins was the iron-bound hole in the kiln wall through which the ware was carried in and out. Once the kiln was full the clammins was bricked up to keep in the heat. A SPY HOLE would be left for the fireman to look through, so that he could assess the temperature inside the kiln/oven. A light mortar was used between the bricks because once the firing was completed, the clammins had to be knocked down so that the ware could be removed.

BULLER'S RINGS: These were pyrometric devices which were put into the kiln before the clammins was bricked up. At certain times the fireman would draw them out with a long metal hook through the spy hole. They would then be measured, the amount of shrinkage indicating the temperature that the kiln had reached.

SAGGARS: A saggar is a large rough container made of clay. Usually oval in shape they were filled with clay ware, carried on a PLACER's head and stacked in tall BUNGS inside the kiln/oven. Very tall ladders were used to build the bungs, which reached right up to the ceiling of the oven. The saggar protected the cups and saucers etc from the dirt and smoke inside the kiln and enabled thousands of pieces of clay ware to be fired at once.

BISCUIT WARE: Once a piece of clay ware has been fired once it is referred to as being in the biscuit stage. The raw clay has been transformed into ceramic but it is still porous and unfit to eat or drink from. A GLAZE is thus applied, either dipped or sprayed or painted on, after which the ceramic undergoes its second firing to chemically transform the glaze into a permanent unperishable hardness. Metal oxides are added to the glaze to create colour.

LUSTRE GLAZES: Lustres are particularly beautiful iridescent glazes with added shimmer and sheen!

SLIP: Slip is liquid clay, ie clay particles suspended in water. The consistency of double cream, it is used like glue to join two pieces of clay together. When the item is fired the water evaporates and the clay bonds together perfectly.

A pot bank would have a number of bottle ovens, all busy firing the factory's wares. The best place to see them now is the Gladstone Pottery Museum (Uttoxeter Road, Longton, Stoke on Trent ST3 1PQ) which is a wonderful day out. But, finally, this book is a story, not a technical exposition, and I am sure that any reader who is initially unfamiliar with the wonderful bottle oven will soon be at home with them and as he or she becomes immersed in the story of Walter and his friends.

Bottle Ovens

Acknowledgements

I was born in 1954 and grew up in Milton, a village bordering on the countryside whist still being within the City of Stoke on Trent. It was a lovely place in which to live and go to school, full of friendly people and exciting places to play. I am glad too, that I worked on the pot banks, boxing mugs and dinner services in my college holidays and then working as a figurine paintress for a few months at Royal Doulton. I always felt that the city was a special place, so full of creative energy and talent, and although work and marriage have taken me away, I feel that I will always belong to it and that like a stick of rock, I have Potteries stamped all the way through.

My story is partly a love poem to this great city, and although I was fortunate to benefit from the clean air act of 1956, I have always loved looking at photographs of the Potteries before the war when the skies were black and the horizons were crowded with the fabulous if unhealthy bottle ovens. What a unique place!

In 2005 my parents sent me a pocket sized book by Ian Lawley, simply entitled *The Potteries*. Full of engaging photographs of Potteries life before the war, it has been a huge stimulus to my imagination. When my parents' house had to be cleared after the death of my mother, Gwen, I found a volume which had belonged to my great Uncle Bert and his wife, my great Auntie Doris: *A Sociological History of Stoke on Trent,* by E.J.D. Warrilow, is another fund of wonderful old photographs, which, like Mr. Lawley's book, provided me with a window onto the past. But most of the landscapes in the book are generic, rather than actual, though the drawings of the exterior of the little house, the school and the park are closer to reality.

A visit to a local antique fair in Kinver provided me with *Cup and Saucer Land,* by the Reverend Malcom Graham, a lovely book produced by the Staffordshire and Stoke on Trent Archive Service which details the pre-WW1 production of clay ware from its raw materials through to the finished product, listing many of the terms unique to the pottery industry. At the same fair I also found *The Humber,* by Nick Georgano, a very lucky discovery since I had already decided that the Humber was the car the glaze wizards would drive.

1930's Britain, by Robert Pearce for Shire Living Histories, was again helpful for the feel of the era and *Stoke on Trent A Journey Through The Potteries,* published in association with Goodwin PLC, revived more memories for me. I also love *The Lost City Of Stoke On Trent,* by Matthew Price, whose drawings are so superior to my own.

When I came to the illustrations for the twins' canal adventures I looked at *Waterways of the West Midlands,* by Robert Davies, and *A Picture of a Moment in Time,* by Robert Birkbeck, whose photographs helped me to draw the canal barges. Again though, the views are imagined rather than actual.

Having said all this, I fully accept that there will be inaccuracies in my illustrations which are intended to enliven and entertain rather than to instruct.

Next I must mention the Gladstone Pottery Museum, a visit to which was an absolute delight. I believe I was there for over four hours, completely absorbed by the bottle ovens and offices, the workshops and storerooms, so all as I had imagined it to be. A helpful email from the museum also provided useful information about the firing of the city's bottle ovens and a phone call to the Potteries Museum and Art Gallery also helped me with this but I must stress that I take full responsibility for all the improbabilities involved in the production of Walter's dragon! It is, after all, a novel and not a biography, let alone a history.

This brings me to my father, whose imagined childhood is the substance of the book. He was a very kind father, much loved by his family and the aunts in the story and by other aunts and uncles too. He was a quiet and private man and if he is looking down upon me I hope he will understand the love that has gone into this book and forgive me for writing it. The Grunters are mere fiction, but a good story needs at least one villain and I have given it three! Thank you to both of my parents for my upbringing and my education.

I would also like to acknowledge the role that Royal Doulton played in the life of my family, providing a lifelong career for my father, employment for my mother who met him when she was working in the laboratories there after the war, holiday work for my sister in the offices and a short but enjoyable job as a paintress for me at their Paladin Works. I quit only because of ill health but have often wondered about an alternative life I might have had in the company. When I went to Leeds University in 1977, to study English and the History of Art, I received a very welcome endowment of about £250 from the Royal Doulton Education Fund for the children of employees. It was a great help with buying my art history books.

My story was written in longhand and when the time came to word process it all, I could not have dealt with the gremlins in the laptop without the help of my husband, David Gillibrand. David also worked hard on the computer graphics for the book cover so a very big thank you indeed to him for all his help and also for his constant support and encouragement. He was the first person to read the story and to urge me to produce and illustrate it in book form. Thank you also to my sister Margaret and the friends who read the story in manuscript and encouraged me to forge ahead.

Thank you to Bob Fowke at "YouCaxton Publications" in Bishops Castle for his advice and encouragement and to Adrian and Clive at A and G Printers in Stourport on Severn for their help in scanning my illustrations.

Last but not least, thank you to my lovely if rather unreliable horse Blackie, who was the inspiration for Mr. Jollie's Dragon! So many aspects of my life have gone into the writing of this book, so many influences both remembered or forgotten. It was written at a very particular time, after the death of my father when I felt I was living as much in the past as in the present. I know that I could not repeat it now, four years later. I wish my mum and dad could read the story, but since they cannot I hope it will be enjoyed by readers in the Potteries and perhaps by others a little further afield.

Jean E Hayward
February 2018